EMPIRE IN FLAMES

THE LEGEND OF THREE BROTHERS

THE THREE KINGDOMS
BOOK ONE

KELLIE VEIL

LUO GUANZHONG

This book is based on the ancient Chinese classic novel Romance of the Three Kingdoms (Sanguo Yanyi) by Luo Guanzhong, which itself draws from real historical events that occurred during China's tumultuous Three Kingdoms period (220-280 CE). While remaining faithful to the original storyline and character portrayals established by Luo Guanzhong's masterwork, this adaptation has been reimagined and dramatically retold for contemporary readers.

The core narrative follows the historical framework and legendary figures documented in Chinese historical records. Yet, this retelling employs creative interpretation, dialogue, dramatization, and character development to make these ancient stories accessible and engaging for modern audiences. Where historical records are sparse or conflicting, this adaptation draws upon the rich tradition of storytelling that has kept these tales alive for over six centuries.

The characters and events portrayed in this book represent a blend of historical fact, classical literature, and creative adaptation. While many of the central figures —including Liu Bei, Guan Yu, Zhang Fei, Cao Cao, and others—were real historical persons who lived during the Three Kingdoms era, their portrayal in this work follows the literary tradition established by Luo Guanzhong rather than strict historical documentation. The dialogue, internal thoughts, specific scenes, and dramatic interpretations are products of literary imagination designed to illuminate timeless themes and human truths.

Any similarity between the dramatized portrayals in this work and real persons, living or dead, beyond those historical figures deliberately featured in the classical source material, is coincidental and not intended by the author.

ISBN-13: 979-8-9985337-4-7
LCCN: 2025919576
Cover design by: Mentor NYC LLC

To Liam
and to all heroes and legends yet to rise—

May you find courage in every journey,
and light in every story.

"A journey of a thousand miles begins with a single step."

Laozi

CONTENTS

INTRODUCTION

~

The empire was crumbling. Across ancient China, villages burned while corrupt officials grew rich. The emperor sat powerless on his throne as greedy palace ministers pulled the strings of government. Common people suffered in silence, watching their world fall apart. Then came the rebellion.

But in this darkest hour, three men met by fate and discovered they shared the same dream. In a blooming peach garden, they knelt before Heaven and made a sacred vow to be sworn brothers.

A Classic Reimagined for the Modern World

This ancient story speaks powerfully to our contemporary world. In an age of endless digital distractions, the tale of three brothers offers something precious: the chance to think deeply, discover what truly matters, and learn to navigate life's complexities with wisdom and virtue.

Readers witness Liu Bei's compassion in action, Guan Yu's unwavering integrity under pressure, and Zhang Fei's fierce loyalty to those he loves. They also see the consequences when others choose differently—how pride leads to downfall, how betrayal destroys trust, and how selfishness ultimately brings ruin.

Through these vivid examples, young minds develop the ability to recognize virtue while gaining the strategic thinking skills needed for an increasingly complex world. They discover that real strength comes not from armies or wealth, but from the bonds we forge and the choices we make.

True to Classic Yet Fresh

Many authors have attempted to retell the legendary *Romance of the Three Kingdoms*, but this series offers something truly special. *The Three Kingdoms* remains faithful to Luo Guanzhong's original plot while dramatizing and reimagining the characters to resonate with today's English-speaking audience.

The original novel spans 120 chapters and nearly a million words—a daunting challenge even for dedicated adult readers. More challenging still, it assumes deep knowledge of ancient Chinese culture, political systems, and historical context.

This series follows Luo Guanzhong's vision while bringing characters to life through vivid dramatization that makes their motivations and struggles immediately understandable. Complex cultural concepts are woven naturally into thrilling narratives.

Ancient military strategies unfold through exciting action sequences. Historical figures become three-dimensional characters whose emotions and decisions feel authentic to modern readers.

Timeless Wisdom, Thrilling Adventures

A timeless masterpiece vividly reimagined and dramatically retold, this series transforms ancient wisdom into page-turning adventures that deliver enduring messages of courage, virtue, loyalty, and perseverance. Through dynamic storytelling and richly dramatized scenes, it explores human nature, motivation, and strategic thinking that remain as relevant today as they were centuries ago.

In East Asia, this beloved classic has captivated readers across generations—from young children discovering their first epic tales to adults finding new wisdom in familiar stories. Its universal themes have made it a cultural touchstone that transcends age boundaries.

Crafted for advanced preteen readers through adults, this adaptation offers exciting, fast-paced storytelling that keeps young readers completely engaged from beginning to end. Vivid battle scenes, compelling character dynamics, and dramatic plot twists ensure readers will never be bored, while strategic insights and profound observations about leadership, friendship, and honor speak directly to modern challenges.

Whether you're seeking timeless wisdom, thrilling

adventure, or a deeper understanding of human motivation, this dramatically reimagined classic offers an exhilarating reading experience that illuminates both historical wisdom and contemporary life— guaranteeing that young readers will be captivated from the very first page.

CHAPTER I

THE PALACE OF
SHADOWS

≈

The palace glittered with jade and gold, but beneath the shine was rot. Lanterns blazed on high pillars, shadows stretched across painted dragons on the walls, and the air swirled thick with incense.

Upon the Dragon Throne lounged Emperor Ling, his dragon-embroidered robe spilling like a river of silk over the steps. He toyed with a jeweled goblet, bored eyes half-closed, while servants fanned him with peacock feathers. The business of ruling held little interest for him—he had wine, music, and gardens filled with dancers.

But there were others in that chamber who cared deeply for the affairs of the empire. The Ten Eunuchs, slim and sharp-eyed, hovered about the throne like crows circling carrion. The most cunning among them, Zhang Rang, leaned close to whisper in the emperor's ear.

"Your Majesty, today a loyal subject comes with an offering."

The doors opened, and in came a merchant clad in embroidered robes brighter than a general's banners. Behind him, servants staggered under the weight of lacquered chests. They laid them out one by one before the throne: bolts of shimmering silk, carved boxes of fragrant tea, and—at last—heavy ingots of gold stacked high enough to catch the lamplight.

The merchant dropped to his knees, forehead pressed to the cold jade floor.

"Your Majesty," he said, voice trembling with rehearsed humility. "I bring tribute to the Son of Heaven, to aid in the burdens of governance."

Emperor Ling gave a languid nod but said nothing, sipping instead at his wine. It was Zhang Rang who stepped forward, folding his hands with a smooth motion.

"Most commendable," Zhang Rang purred. "It is customary for those seeking titles to contribute to the treasury. The required amount is well known—yet this humble servant has brought twice the offering."

The emperor stirred, his attention finally caught. "Twice?" He blinked at the gleaming ingots, his eyes lighting as though the sun had risen inside the hall.

"Twice, Your Majesty," Zhang Rang confirmed. "Surely such loyalty deserves reward." He cast a quick glance at his fellow eunuchs, who all nodded in unison.

Another eunuch added, "The empire needs men of wealth and resource. Why should such loyalty not be honored?"

Emperor Ling leaned forward, his face warming with

sudden enthusiasm. "Very well. He shall be granted a title. Something worthy..." He looked to Zhang Rang for guidance.

Zhang Rang bowed low, concealing a smile. "Might I suggest the office of Inspector of the Eastern Commanderies? A position of high influence, fitting for a man who shows such devotion."

The emperor laughed, raising his cup. "That is certainly a fitting role for such a dedicated man of loyalty. Rise, Inspector, and serve your emperor well."

The merchant prostrated himself again, forehead pressed hard against the jade floor, and cried out in a trembling voice that seemed both earnest and desperate:

"Your Majesty's grace is beyond measure!"

The words rang through the hall with practiced devotion, yet every man there knew their price.

With silk and gold, he had purchased not just favor, but power.

It was a triumph to both the merchant and the eunuchs —one exulting in his sudden rise, the other savoring the chime of gold coins and the tightening of their grip on the empire.

As the court applauded, the eunuchs exchanged subtle smiles. Each of them had already taken his share from the "tribute," and each knew more merchants would come, eager to buy rank and title with overflowing coffers.

While laughter echoed beneath the gilded ceilings of the palace, beyond its gates, the world groaned under the strain. Fields lay fallow beneath crushing taxes. Families starved while the court feasted. And in the countryside, whispers spread among the weary and the hopeless—whispers of men in yellow scarves who promised a new age, a new Heaven.

An empire does not collapse in a single night. It rots first from within, piece by piece, as gold weighs heavier than honor.

Thus began the final days of the Han.

CHAPTER 2

PAVILION ON THE MULBERRY TREE

∼

The year was 174 CE, the third year of *the Yanxi era, known as the "Prolonged Brightness" era.* But in the villages beyond the capital, brightness was hard to find. In a faraway land, there was a small village tucked between the hills of Zhuo County. The village was so tiny that travelers often passed by without even noticing it. It had no grand gates, no majestic temples, no vibrant market-places. Just about thirty simple houses were scattered across a dusty field, all with roofs made of straw and walls built from packed mud.

The village was called Lou Sang Village, and although most of the world had never heard of it, the people who called it home knew it was a very special place. At the very edge of the village stood an enormous mulberry tree that anyone had ever seen. The trunk was massive and twisted with age, telling stories in every groove and knot of its bark.

Thick roots curved up from the earth like the arms of some gentle giant, creating natural seats and hiding spots that had sheltered generations of dreamers.

When you looked at it from the hills above, the tree seemed to float like a sacred pavilion in the clouds, its canopy so gracefully curved and perfectly formed it looked like a temple where gods might come to rest. The way its branches swept outward in elegant arcs made it appear as though divine architects had crafted it as a meeting place between heaven and earth. Nobody could remember a time when the tree hadn't been there—even the oldest grandparents in the village would shake their heads and say, "That tree was already ancient when I was your age, and my grandmother said the same thing to me."

In summer, the tree's branches were covered with deep green leaves, so many that they made a roof all their own. The sun would shine through them in little patches, lighting the ground below in dancing shapes. On hot afternoons, children would run to the tree to escape the sun, and old grandmothers would sit in the shade and tell stories.

It also gave the place its name. Lou Sang Village meant "Pavilion on the Mulberry Tree," as if the tree were a royal palace floating in the sky. There were no riches in Lou Sang Village. The people worked hard, raising silkworms, planting in rocky soil, and patching their roofs every time it rained. But under that tree, life felt peaceful and abundant.

Behind the tree stood a humble house with a thatched roof—just like any other house in the village—where a boy lived with his mother. Beneath the giant tree, the boy often sat quietly, staring up into the green canopy overhead. His name was Liu Bei. A thirteen-year-old boy of a slim build, he had sun-darkened skin and wide, thoughtful eyes. His clothes were patched and worn, and his sandals looked as if they'd walked too many miles for someone so young. But there was something about him that made the villagers stop and watch.

"He is no ordinary child," the blacksmith would mutter, wiping sweat from his brow.

"Always thinking, that one," the silk weaver would say. "Sometimes I feel that a wise old man is sitting inside that small body."

But Liu Bei didn't mind what people said about him. The other children would race through the village, chasing chickens or throwing rocks at frogs, but he preferred sitting under the tree, sometimes reading a book, sometimes lost in thought. When the village was quiet and the sky began to darken, he would sit with his knees pulled up to his chest and imagine the tree telling him stories of ancient warriors and wise emperors.

One afternoon, as golden light stretched across the dusty road like honey poured from heaven, a neighbor boy came looking for Liu Bei beneath the great tree.

"There you are," he said, dropping to the ground with a satisfied grunt. "What are you doing all alone? Daydreaming again?"

Liu Bei sat in contemplative silence, his dark eyes following the ancient branches as they swayed in the evening breeze. The boy's silk shirt shimmered in the bright sunlight, its fine threads catching the golden glow of the sun. It was rare—almost unheard of—for anyone in their poor village to wear such a thing. But his family had started a silk harvesting business the year before, and prosperity, however modest, had begun to show.

His parents had once come pleading to Liu Bei's mother, humbly asking to use the leaves from the mulberry tree in front of her home. There were others in the village raising silkworms and weaving silk, but the tree that belonged to Liu Bei's family was different. Its leaves were larger, glossier, richer in color—and it turned out, they produced a finer silk, cloth smooth enough to be fit for a king.

With quiet generosity, she had granted permission, and from there, their enterprise had begun to bloom. But the boy never seemed to know—or care—where the opportunity had come from.

"My father says silk's going to make us rich," he went on, puffing his chest proudly.

"He and my uncles are selling bundles in the market now. My mother even traded some for roasted duck last week—imagine that, duck! And my sister Shao Mei got a red silk sash. She's going to fill that thing with coins soon, you wait! Haha!"

He glanced at Liu Bei, who still hadn't looked away from the horizon.

Liu Bei remembered Shao Mei, the boy's younger sister —a quiet girl with round, watchful eyes and a voice barely louder than a whisper. She was often seen trailing behind her brother, lingering at the edges of village games, curious but too shy to join. She would blend into the background, unnoticed. But around Liu Bei, she was different.

She would blush when she saw him, the color rising like warmth behind her cheeks, and cast quick glances in his direction before hiding behind her brother's shoulder. She never spoke to Liu Bei directly, not even once, but her smile —nervous, fleeting—seemed reserved only for him.

It wasn't just Shao Mei. Others in the village, especially the girls near their age, had started to take notice of Liu Bei. There was something in him—a gravity, a stillness, a strange maturity that set him apart. He didn't chase attention, but attention found him nonetheless. Some called it charm. Others said it was the way he listened when you spoke to him, and the way he made you feel like the only person in the world who mattered.

One afternoon, he'd heard a rustle outside his room and opened the door just as Shao Mei was placing something gently on the step. It was a small, carefully wrapped piece of taffy—her favorite kind, no doubt a treasure saved from the market. The moment the door creaked, she gasped and darted off, her braid bouncing behind her as she fled around the corner.

The boy broke the silence, "I don't get you sometimes. Always reading and thinking and weaving those mats that don't even make much money. My mom says you and your mom work too hard for too little."

"Do you ever wonder," Liu Bei said finally, his voice barely above a whisper, "what lies beyond those hills?"

The neighbor boy snorted and gave him a sideways look.

"Trees. Dirt. More villages just like ours. Life is the same for lowly villagers like us—wake up, work, eat, sleep, repeat until we die. I'm just happy when my belly is full and I have a warm spot to lie down at night." His eyes suddenly brightened with the kind of joy that comes from simple pleasures. "Oh! This weekend, when the street market opens in town, the traveling merchant with the wagon full of honey taffies is coming back! Maybe I'll have saved enough copper coins to buy one. I've been thinking about it all week."

The boy went on without even waiting for Liu Bei's reaction, "Oh, but do you know what I reeeeally want? It's Tanghulu—It's even better than taffies! My cousins have had them before and bragged about it. It is really shiny, just like my silk, haha... and super crunchy on the outside, with juicy fruit inside. Can you even imagine!?"

But Liu Bei's gaze had turned distant as he spoke.

"How can you believe life must be the same in every corner, or remain unchanged for all time? We have been taught that this empire is vast and grand." Then he paused, chewing over his own words. *If one could be content with a warm meal, with sweet taffies on rare occasions—that wouldn't be such a bad life.*

"You've been reading too many books," his friend groaned, half in jest. Whether to lighten the mood or because he could not carry the weight of Liu Bei's thoughts, even he didn't know. He tugged at a handful of grass and tossed it aside, as though trying to scatter the heaviness of the moment.

"Books are full of stories made to pass the time. Real life is... life. All villages are the same. We should be grateful we haven't been found by those tax men yet."

His voice dropped to a whisper. "When my uncle visited last month, he said merchants and farmers alike are being ruined. Some by corrupt officials, others by bandits disguised as collectors. They take what they want, and if you can't pay, they burn your house to the ground. I pray every night they never find our little corner of nowhere."

The boy's eyes grew weary, the resignation of one who already accepted hardship as fate.

"As long as we stay hidden and keep our heads down, we'll be fine. Just like our parents and grandparents." He shrugged and continued, "My folks used to work someone else's silk farm, but now we've got our own silkworms, our own setup. We mind our business and stay out of trouble. That's how we'll live."

He said it with the confidence of someone who believed keeping one's head down meant safety, never noticing the irony as he sat there in a silk shirt, its shimmer catching the afternoon light.

"I don't even know why my father makes me go to the village school. Reading and writing won't fill our baskets. Silk will." After a pause, the friend asked, "What about your mother? Doesn't she want you weaving mats, helping her sell more, instead of burying yourself in dusty books?"

Liu Bei did not answer. His gaze flicked once to the boy's silk shirt, then drifted past the mulberry groves, to the hills, to the horizon where the clouds glowed with the fading light of day.

That night, as the moon rose like a pearl above Lou Sang Village, silence fell. Families surrendered to sleep, but Liu Bei lay awake beneath the guardian mulberry tree. His hands rested behind his head, his mind burning like wildfire through dry grass.

What am I truly meant to do with this life?

He had no sword, no wealth, no men to call his own. Only questions. Yet even the asking began to shape him. The mulberry tree loomed above, its branches whispering in the night, bearing witness to the birth of a destiny the boy himself could not yet fathom.

CHAPTER 3

THE MYSTERIOUS MONK

~

The next day, just as the sky glowed gold with the setting sun, a traveling monk arrived at the edge of Lou Sang Village. His robes were dusty, his straw sandals falling apart, and his long staff worn smooth from the many miles he had wandered.

He paused at the foot of the village's great mulberry tree. The sunlight bathed the broad green leaves in a golden shimmer, and they sparkled in the light like the scales of a dragon flying through the sky.

The old monk leaned on his walking staff and whispered to himself, "What a magnificent tree. It looks as if the Emperor himself might ride in it."

Just then, Liu Bei stepped out from his house beneath the tree. The monk looked at him and froze. In all his seventy years of wandering, he had never seen a child like this. The boy's face—gentle yet dignified—seemed to outshine even the glorious tree. His large ears were shaped like crescent moons, and bright, shining eyes glowed with kindness and curiosity. Tucked under one arm was a book, and there was something noble in the way he walked.

"Is that mulberry tree yours?" the monk asked.

"Yes, it belongs to our family," the boy replied politely.

"Where have you come from, sir?" The boy's soft tone and gentle manners impressed the old monk even more.

"I am a wandering monk," he said. "Is this your home?"

"Yes, it is," the boy said.

"How long have you lived here?"

"My grandfather said we came here during his youth," the boy answered.

"What is your name?"

"My surname is Liu, my given name is Bei, and my courtesy name is Xuande."

The monk's eyes narrowed thoughtfully. "Liu... Bei..."

Then, almost in a whisper, he repeated the name to himself. A shiver ran through him, for something deep within insisted this child bore the blood of the imperial Liu clan—the lineage of the Han itself.

"Well then, Liu Bei," the monk said softly, "where are you going with that book?"

"I'm heading to the village school," Liu Bei replied.

"It's time for our evening study," Liu Bei continued. "It's getting dark, Sir. Do you have a place to stay tonight?"

The monk blinked, startled. In all his years of wandering, no one—especially not a child—had asked him that question.

"I usually sleep wherever I can," the monk said. "If

someone offers a place, I take it. If not, I sleep in a shed—or under the stars."

"You're an elder," Liu Bei said seriously. "It isn't right for someone your age to sleep in the open air."

The monk smiled. "Are you offering me a place to stay?"

"I would invite you to my home," Liu Bei said honestly, "but it's a bit humble. That building on the hill is the village school. It's clean and quiet. You may sleep there tonight. I'll show you the way."

The monk smiled warmly. "You're very kind. But I can find it. You should gather your classmates. I'll rest here a while first."

He sat down on a rock beneath the tree and stretched his tired legs.

Soon, Liu Bei ran through the village calling, "Come on, everyone! It's time to study!"

Children came out of their homes and gathered under the mulberry tree. Liu Bei greeted each one with kind words.

"You said your stomach hurt earlier. Is it feeling better?" he asked one boy.

And to another, "I heard your family ran out of rice. Were you able to eat dinner?"

Though he was the same age, Liu Bei spoke like an older brother—caring, calm, and full of quiet strength.

As Liu Bei stepped away for a moment, the children huddled together like sparrows, their voices dropping to conspiratorial whispers.

"Look at that old man," one boy said, pointing a grimy finger toward the figure hunched beneath the tree.

"What's he doing just sitting there?"

"Probably some beggar monk," another chimed in, wrinkling his nose.

"Those robes look like they haven't seen water in months. And smell that—"

"Shh!"

The eldest boy glanced around nervously, but their cruel observations tumbled out anyway, each child trying to outdo the others with increasingly cutting remarks about the stranger's weathered hands, his threadbare robes, his bent posture.

They weren't malicious children. They were simply young, their worlds small and unexamined, their tongues quick with the thoughtless cruelty that comes before wisdom. But their whispered mockery carried further than they imagined.

Liu Bei had heard every word. When he turned back to face them, the children fell silent. There was something different in his expression—not anger, but a gravity that made the air itself seem heavier. His voice, when it came, was soft as silk yet sharp as a blade.

"Tell me," he said, settling onto his haunches so he could meet their eyes.

"When you look at that man, what do you truly see?"

The boys shuffled their feet, suddenly fascinated by the dust beneath them.

"He's old," Liu Bei continued, his tone growing gentler but no less serious.

"Do you not understand? A monk travels, trains, and suffers to seek wisdom—not for comfort, nor for vanity."

He paused, letting the weight of his words settle. "You see only what serves your amusement."

One of the younger boys began to sniffle.

"Would you speak this way if your grandfather sat there? Your uncle? Or perhaps,"

Liu Bei's voice dropped to barely above a whisper, "If you knew that a stranger could hear every word you've spoken?"

The children's faces drained of color as understanding dawned upon them. They turned as one toward the monk, who sat motionless in the shadows, and suddenly wondered if the slight tilt of his head meant he had been listening all along.

"I'm sorry," the eldest boy whispered, the words cracking like his changing voice.

Liu Bei nodded slowly and said, "Everyone has struggles you can't see. Don't judge by looks."

The boys nodded solemnly, their shame transforming into something more profound—a dawning awareness that they had witnessed something profound. Liu Bei possessed a rare wisdom, the kind that could reshape hearts with gentle words rather than harsh commands.

Then, without another word, Liu Bei turned and asked the children to wait outside. He disappeared back into the house for a few quiet moments. When he returned, he was carrying a newly woven pair of straw sandals—modest but clean, the weaving tight and careful, still smelling faintly of dried grass and sun.

He walked up to the old monk and knelt, presenting the sandals with both hands.

"These are for you, honored sir," he said, his voice steady but warm.

"We had misunderstood an order and ended up making

an extra pair. They've been sitting unused, waiting for someone who needed them. I noticed your soles were worn through... and their size—it almost feels like they were made for you."

The monk looked at the sandals, then at Liu Bei, and smiled—a smile that seemed to reach into another lifetime. He accepted the gift graciously, nodding in silent thanks.

If he had heard the children's earlier mockery—about his tattered robes, his dust-covered feet, or how he resembled a ghost from some forgotten shrine—he showed no sign of it. His eyes remained clear and kind, as though he could see past the surface ridicule but felt neither bothered by it nor surprised, perhaps simply accustomed to such treatment.

The boys watched in silence, occasionally stealing glances at one another. In Liu Bei, they began to recognize something beyond a mere peer—a figure who embodied both humility and grace, someone worthy of emulation.

As the children slowly dispersed, the monk remained motionless beneath the ancient tree. His weary eyes tracked Liu Bei's departing figure with quiet, penetrating interest.

"That boy," the monk whispered, "has the face of a dragon... the face of a future emperor."

He stood and began walking toward the school, his staff tapping lightly on the stones. When he arrived, he heard the children reciting from their books. An old caretaker stepped out to greet him.

"Welcome, Venerable Monk," the man said with a respectful bow.

"I'm only a wandering beggar," the monk replied, surprised by the warm welcome.

"Even so," the man smiled warmly, "young Liu Bei told me you were coming. He asked me to serve you dinner and prepare a clean place for you to rest."

The monk was speechless. He had only just met Liu Bei, and already the boy had arranged everything for his comfort.

"Thank you so much for your hospitality," he said, his voice thick with gratitude.

"I don't even remember the last time I slept in such a safe and welcoming place."

The man led him to a small guest room, clearly converted from storage space but kept spotlessly clean and made comfortable with thoughtful touches. There, the monk savored a simple yet tasty meal—freshly steamed rice accompanied by carefully seasoned vegetables.

Later, as he settled into his makeshift bed within the schoolhouse, warmth spread through the monk's chest at the unexpected kindness these strangers had shown him. The gentle murmur of children's voices drifted through the walls as they practiced their evening recitations, weaving a peaceful backdrop that promised the restful sleep he so desperately needed.

But despite his exhaustion from the day's travels, he could not fall asleep. His mind kept returning to that desolate country road where he had been left stranded earlier that day.

The afternoon sun had been merciless, beating down on the dusty path that stretched endlessly through the barren countryside. The monk's sandaled feet moved slowly as he made his pilgrimage from village to village. It was silent, the distant cry of a hawk circling overhead.

Then came the sound that shattered everything—the desperate thunder of bare feet pounding against packed earth.

A man burst from behind a cluster of scraggly trees, his clothes torn and soaked with sweat, his eyes wild with terror. He stumbled, caught himself, and ran straight toward the monk. Blood trickled from a gash above his left eye, and his chest heaved like a bellows.

"Master!"

The word tore from his throat in a ragged gasp. He desperately grabbed the monk's hand, pressing his palms together. "Please help... A bandit hunts me like an animal. He'll gut me where he finds me. I have little children at home waiting for me to bring food..."

The man's whole body shook as he spoke, his voice breaking.

"If he comes asking, if you see him..." His eyes darted frantically to the towering cornfield that stretched along the right side of the road, its green stalks swaying in the hot breeze.

"Please tell him I went the other way. I beg you!"

Before the monk could even open his mouth, the man had vanished into the maze of corn, the stalks swallowing him completely.

The monk stood frozen in the sudden silence, his heart racing.

Then he saw the chaser. The bandit came out of the heat haze like a ghost. He was an older man, maybe forty, with a stern face marked by years of violent life. Gray streaked his messy hair, and deep lines around his eyes showed he'd done terrible things. But his eyes were what scared the

20

monk most—cold and cruel. He held a curved sword loosely in his scarred hand, its blade dark with old stains. His clothes were covered in blood—some wet, some dried brown.

"Old man!"

The bandit's voice cut through the air like a whip crack, rough and commanding from decades of intimidation. He strode forward with sharp, aggressive steps.

The monk's mouth went dry. His hands, usually steady from years of meditation, began to tremble.

The bandit's eyes swept the road, the fields, the monk—cataloging everything with predatory efficiency.

"You must have seen a man pass," he snarled, his blade jerking impatiently in the harsh sunlight.

"Tell me where he went. Now."

The monk's eyes darted to the cornfield, then back to the bandit's scarred face. Those pitiless eyes missed nothing. He froze where he stood, terror rooting him in place. His lips trembled, but no words came.

Suddenly, the bandit lunged and seized his robe, dragging him close. The monk gagged as the stench of blood and sweat flooded his breath.

"Listen, now!" He hissed, his voice dropping to a deadly whisper.

"I'm tired, and my patience died somewhere back on the road with the last fool who tried to lie to me."

The blade pressed against the monk's throat, its edge cold and sharp.

"You have exactly five seconds to tell me which way my prey ran, or I'll open your throat and find him myself."

"Five," he began counting, his voice deadly calm.

"Four."

The monk's heart hammered violently. Sweat poured down his face despite the blade at his throat. His eyes swept desperately across the landscape—the cornfield to the right, where the man had vanished, the open grassland to the left with its sparse cover.

If I tell the truth, that man dies, his mind screamed. He has little children at home, waiting for him. But if I lie, even if this monster believes me at first and runs into the wrong field, he will quickly find out that I lied and chase me down. And I'll die instead.

"Three... Two."

The blade pressed deeper. A warm trickle ran down the monk's neck.

There's no choice, the monk realized with crushing despair—no clever third path.

"One."

Feeling paralyzed and unable to move his lips, the monk agonizingly raised his hand and pointed toward the corn-field with his trembling fingers.

"There you go."

The bandit released the monk with a shove that sent the old man stumbling backward.

Without another word, he melted into the cornfield, leaving the monk alone on the empty road with the weight of his betrayal.

After a few minutes, somewhere in that green labyrinth, came a brief commotion—shouts, the sound of bodies colliding, a strangled cry for mercy.

Then the scream.

It was a sound the monk would carry with him until his

dying day—high and sharp and utterly human. The silence that came afterwards felt so cruel and merciless.

The monk sank to his knees in the dust, his whole body convulsing with silent sobs. He remained on his knees for a long while as his lips moved in endless, whispered prayers —for the dead man's peace, for his children who would grieve this loss, for forgiveness he knew he could never earn.

Now, in the safety of the schoolhouse, surrounded by innocent voices reciting ancient wisdom, the monk pressed his face into his hands. *I could have lied,* he told himself for the thousandth time. But even as the thought formed, he knew the terrible truth: when faced with that blade at his throat, when confronted with his own mortality, he had chosen his life over another's. He had chosen survival over honor.

Then he noticed the classroom had fallen quiet. The children were already packing their books, ready to go home. From outside the guest room, he heard Liu Bei's gentle voice.

"Sleep well, Sir. We must return home now."

"Wait," the monk said, rising from his mat. He slid open the door that led into the courtyard of the schoolhouse.

"Before you go, may I tell you something?"

Though Liu Bei was only a child, something—whether desperation or a deep respect for this extraordinary boy— compelled the monk to seek his counsel.

The children turned back, curious.

The monk sat up slowly.

"Something terrible happened to me today..." After a brief pause, the monk confessed, "I killed a man."

There were gasps and confused faces.

"You... what?" one of the boys whispered.

"I didn't strike him down myself," the monk said.

"But I may as well have. A man was running from a bandit. He begged me to protect his secret. But when the bandit threatened me with a sword, I became afraid. I told him where the man was hiding... and the man died."

The children sat frozen, eyes wide.

"I couldn't think of another way," the monk said. "I chose to protect my own life... but I can't stop thinking—was there something else I could have done?"

One of the boys spoke up. "Sir, you had no choice. The bandit would've killed you!"

"Yeah," said another. "Anyone would've done the same."

The monk nodded, but his eyes turned to Liu Bei, who had remained quiet.

"You," the monk said softly. "You haven't spoken. What do you think?"

Liu Bei stepped forward, his expression serious.

"You made a mistake," he said, not unkindly. "The man trusted you. He begged for your help. It wasn't right to betray him."

"But... I would've died," the monk said.

"There was another way."

"What do you mean?" the monk asked, leaning forward.

"You had your staff with you, right?"

"Yes."

"Then you should have closed your eyes and pretended to be blind. Even a bandit wouldn't ask directions from a blind man."

The monk sat back in shock.

"Pretend to be blind... of course!" He slapped his knee. "Why didn't I think of that?"

Liu Bei said gently, "Everyone feels fear, and even good men may falter in its grip. But—being clever can sometimes protect more lives than telling the plain truth."

The monk looked down, tears stinging his eyes.

"You're just a boy," he said softly, "but your mind is clearer than mine. You have the wisdom of the sages."

Liu Bei bowed. "You honor me, Master. I may be calm now, but anyone would have trembled in your place. Please —do not blame yourself."

The monk suddenly fell to his knees and bowed deeply.

"You... you are the one who will bring peace to this broken world. You are the young emperor this age has been waiting for."

Liu Bei blinked, startled.

"Sir, please rise."

The boy stepped forward and gently helped the monk to his feet.

"Please don't blame yourself forever," Liu Bei said kindly.

"Even the greatest people stumble. If you learn from it, then that man's death will not have been in vain."

The monk's eyes shone with gratitude and hope. He had come to this village expecting only a place to rest. Instead, he had found a boy with the wisdom of a sage and the heart of a ruler.

That night, the moon hung low over Lou Sang Village. It was late. Crickets chirped softly beneath the mulberry trees.

At the small wooden gate of Liu Bei's humble home, the mother stood, wrapped in a thin shawl. Her figure, though slightly bent with age, held a quiet dignity. Her eyes searched the darkened road with unwavering patience.

At last, hurried footsteps broke the silence.

"Xuande," addressing her son by courtesy name, said, "you're finally home!"

Liu Bei came into view, slightly startled to see her still outside.

"Mother, you're waiting *again*?" he said, stepping quickly to her side.

"The night air is cold and damp—it's not good for your health. You should have waited inside."

He took her arm gently, guiding her back into the house.

His mother smiled, brushing off his concern with a maternal warmth that transcended years.

"When my son goes out to study, how could his mother rest comfortably beneath a roof, knowing her heart is out there on the road?"

She patted his hand affectionately.

She was nearly sixty, with her lines on her face deepening, but there was a light in her eyes—an ageless fire, shaped by wisdom and resolve.

Liu Bei helped her sit. "Mother, you speak strangely," he said with a soft smile.

"What son wouldn't want his mother to stay safe inside? When you stand outside like this, I worry for *you*."

She gazed at him for a long moment, as if weighing something heavier than mere words.

Then she said, "No, Xuande. You have to always remember. You are not a mere child. You carry the blood of emperors. How can I treat your return like any common event?

Since your father passed, our lives have been humble. But your path is not a common one."

Liu Bei had heard these words before—spoken many times, always with that same mixture of pride and burden. Yet tonight, they resonated differently.

"Mother," he said slowly, "today something unusual happened. A monk bowed deeply before me and called me... a 'young emperor.'"

The old woman's back straightened, her expression sharpened.

"A monk said that to you? Why? Tell me *exactly* what happened."

Liu Bei recounted the events at the school—the bandit, the monk's strange behavior, and his words. His mother listened with keen attention, her hands resting quietly on her knees. When he finished, she nodded solemnly.

"That was no ordinary man."

"But Mother, he was just a monk—an odd one at that. He fled in fear, and his actions led to another man's death. How could such a man be considered remarkable?"

His mother shook her head slowly.

"Even wise men make mistakes before finding clarity. The divine doesn't always come in shining form—sometimes it speaks through flawed messengers. Is he still there?"

"He should be in the schoolhouse. Likely asleep by now."

"Then we must go. *Now.*"

She rose without hesitation, already untying her outer robe.

"Mother—it's the middle of the night!" Liu Bei said, alarmed.

"Can't we wait until morning?"

"No," she said firmly.

"If that monk departs at dawn, the window to receive the message of fate will close. We must not miss it."

Reluctantly, Liu Bei obeyed. They returned to the school in silence. But when they arrived, the monk had vanished— no bedding, no footprints, not even a trace.

His mother stared at the empty space for a long while, then whispered, "This was what I was fearing... but Xuande, I hope you will recognize him when you encounter him next time... although we don't know when it'll be."

CHAPTER 4
THE FAMILY HEIRLOOM

~

Back home, Liu Bei's mother sat with solemn grace before her son. The candlelight flickered gently between them.

"Xuande," she said, her voice calm but weighty, "do you know what it means to be an emperor?"

Liu Bei knelt, as if before a teacher. "An emperor... rules the nation."

"Correct. Then tell me—what is the best method to rule?"

He paused, thinking, "Some use power. Others have cunning tricks and strategies. Some depend on law and order."

"And you?"

"I... would choose to rule with virtue."

She smiled, as if she had waited years to hear this answer.

"That is the highest path. Power breeds fear. Cunning tricks, mistrust. Law, though necessary, cannot reach the heart and move people from deep inside. But virtue... virtue unites people in spirit. Only through virtue can an emperor earn lasting loyalty—not through force, but through reverence."

She paused, then her eyes grew serious. "Xuande, do you know who you truly are?"

"I believe I do."

"Then say it."

Liu Bei straightened his shoulders, his voice carrying the weight of generations.

"I am Liu Bei, courtesy name Xuande. My father was Liu Hong, a man of humble means but noble heart, who served faithfully until his early death left our family in poverty."

He paused, allowing the weight of his lineage to settle before continuing.

"My grandfather was Liu Xiong, who upheld our family's honor through times of hardship. And my great-grandfather was Liu Xuande, from whom I take my courtesy name, a scholar who served the court with distinction during the reign of Emperor An."

After a brief pause, Liu Bei continued, "I ultimately descend from Liu Sheng, the Prince of Zhongshan and son of Emperor Jing of Han. I am of the Imperial Liu clan, a descendant of the dragon throne, though fate has seen fit to humble our circumstances."

He clasped his hands before him in a gesture both respectful and regal.

Liu Bei's mother nodded slowly, satisfied. Then, with solemn grace and deliberate motion, she approached the old wooden cabinet set into the wall—its hinges creaked softly, like the murmur of forgotten years. She opened it with care, as one might lift the veil from a relic long sealed away from mortal eyes.

Inside, resting alone upon a faded silk cloth, lay a sword.

Its sheath was darkened with age, the lacquer cracked in places, yet the intricate patterns etched along its surface still gleamed faintly under the lamplight—dragons coiled in silence, phoenix feathers curling like rising smoke. Time had not dulled its dignity; if anything, the years had deepened its presence. It was not merely a weapon. It was history made solid, the breath of generations captured in iron and wood.

As she reached in and drew it out with both hands, her movements slowed. It carried the weight of not just metal, but a legacy.

Its guard was cast in the shape of twin *qilin*—Chinese unicorn—heads, their eyes wide with eternal vigilance. The hilt was wrapped in faded red silk, worn smooth by the hands of ancestors. And though the blade remained hidden, a strange tension hung in the air, as if it remembered battles fought and dynasties upheld.

When she turned and offered it to Liu Bei, her arms trembled with the gravity of what she was entrusting.

"This," she said, voice hushed yet unwavering, "is the blade passed down through our family line. It is a symbol, a reminder that leadership must never fall to tyranny or pride. You must be as frost against injustice, but as gentle as spring when sheltering the innocent."

She offered it to him.

Liu Bei received it with both hands, bowing his head low.

"I will engrave your words into my heart, and live by them always."

His voice was soft, but behind it was a steel resolve. His eyes, still youthful, gleamed with rekindled purpose. The candle's light caught the edge of the sword, and just like that, the ancestral flame of the Han flared again.

CHAPTER 5

THE GOLDEN EMPIRE CRUMBLES

~

In the days before ruin came to the Han Dynasty, China had known peace. The great Emperor Liu Bang had crushed his rivals and forged a unified realm from the chaos of war. For centuries thereafter, the people had prospered under Han rule, their fields fertile, and their roads safe. Farmers worked rich soil and grew more food than they needed. Markets were full of silk, spices, and lively chatter of haggling. Scholars read books under the shade of trees. The emperor ruled from the shining capital of Luoyang, where wide roads and beautiful palaces sparkled like jewels.

It was truly a golden age.

But even the most peaceful times are only brief rests between the storms of history. As time passed, the rulers grew increasingly lazy. Officials took bribes. The rich got richer, and the poor suffered more and more.

The grand palaces of Luoyang still shimmered under the

sun, their tiled roofs catching golden light like relics of a glorious past. But behind the jade walls and silk drapes of the Han Imperial court, rot had already set in. The dynasty that once unified a continent now trembled from the insidious poison within.

At its center sat Emperor Ling, a monarch in name but a puppet in truth. Though he wore the dragon robe and sat upon the golden throne, his heart belonged not to his people, but to pleasure. Women in perfumed robes, banquet halls echoing with music, and ceaseless games of indulgence dulled his senses. Ministers came and went like shadows, forgotten between sips of rare wine and the laughter of dancing girls.

But even as the emperor reveled, a cold war raged within the palace walls—a war fought with whispers, bribes, and assassinations. On one side stood the eunuchs, the infamous *Ten Attendants*, men without lineage but with unmatched cunning and toxic influence.

Eunuchs were originally servants—men who had been neutered and rendered unable to father children so they could serve in the Imperial palace without threatening the emperor's bloodline. But now, these once-humble attendants had become the empire's puppet masters. They slithered through the palace corridors like serpents, their silk robes rustling as they whispered poison into the emperor's ears.

Their names were feared more than generals, their power unchecked. They did not wield blades—they wielded seals, which represented power and influence, and that was far deadlier. These scheming courtiers would fabricate reports of rebellions to justify seizing lands from innocent nobles, forge Imperial edicts to redirect tax revenues into their personal coffers, and sell government positions to the highest bidders.

They murdered rivals with poisoned wine served at seemingly friendly banquets, blackmailed ministers with manufactured scandals, and even went so far as to hide news of natural disasters from the emperor while they profited from selling emergency grain stores. Their painted faces and perfumed bodies masked hearts as dark as winter's grave, and their soft voices carried the power to topple dynasties.

Ten of them who became especially powerful called themselves the Ten Attendants, and their leader, Zhang Rang, even compelled the emperor to address him as "Father."

The true ruler of China had become a puppet.

Opposing them were the Imperial in-laws—siblings and family members of the empresses and concubines. They too thirsted for influence, claiming it their birthright to rule behind the throne. The palace became a battleground of rival households, each clawing for power over an emperor who cared more for indulgence than for empire.

While they quarreled, the emperor himself sank deeper into ruin. Addicted to women, wine, and revelry, he bled the treasury dry to keep his nights blazing with music and gold. And when the coffers could no longer sustain his hunger, he issued a decree that sounded the death knell of order:

"Let those who bring forth eighty catties of gold be granted an official rank."

Thus, in 178 CE—the first year of the *Guang He* era, which ironically meant *'Radiant Harmony'*—Emperor Ling decreed the infamous Eighty Ranks for Gold system. From that moment, government posts were no longer granted for merit or service, but openly sold at fixed prices to those with wealth enough to buy them. Corruption no longer crept in the shadows—it strutted boldly through court in embroidered robes, clutching Imperial decrees. The empire's heart, once proud, now beat with the hollow sound of coins.

Thus, the once-mighty Han administration became a theater of purchased loyalties and paper virtues—men with no merit ruled provinces. Bandits became magistrates. True scholars were cast aside while greedy fools were welcomed into the court. Justice and reason were nowhere to be found.

While the empire was rotting from within, and its decay reached every corner of the realm, a movement was erupting to resist the corrupt government. In the distant province of Julu, far from the poisoned halls of the capital, a man named Zhang Jiao witnessed this suffering. He was an educated man, skilled in both the healing arts and the wisdom of ancient texts. But what he saw across the countryside broke his spirit—starving children, burned-out villages, and people who had lost all hope.

Zhang Jiao decided to fight back—at first, not with sword and spear, but with something more dangerous to tyrants: ideas. He gathered hundreds of followers, teaching them to read and write, to think, and to prepare for war. He gave them yellow headbands to wear as symbols of their cause, and they became known as the Yellow Turbans.

To the desperate masses, they proclaimed a coming transformation—a new world where peace and justice would bloom again from blood-soaked soil. The people listened with ears long deafened by suffering. They were bone-weary from pain and hunger, and in Zhang Jiao's words, they heard the promise of salvation.

He called himself the "Great Teacher" and gave his two brothers powerful titles as well—Zhang Bao, the General of Earth, who was said to wield sorcery in battle, conjuring illusions and casting spells to terrify imperial troops and embolden his followers; and Zhang Liang, the General of Humanity, cunning and resourceful, whose clever stratagems and sudden ambushes kept the rebellion alive long after its first defeats. Together, the three brothers commanded a swelling host of peasants, farmers, and dreamers, who believed Heaven itself was on their side.

To give people hope, they spread a mysterious song:

The Azure Heaven is already dead,
The Yellow Heaven shall rise instead.
When the year of the Blue Rat arrives,
Good fortune will fill all lives!

Everywhere in the countryside, people sang the song, dreaming of the day the Yellow Turbans would bring change.

Zhang Jiao had already built a massive army of desperate peasants, but he knew something crucial: you can't defeat an empire from the outside alone. He needed someone on the inside—someone with access to the emperor himself.

His target was Feng Xu, one of the infamous Ten Attendants. These palace eunuchs were corrupt, power-hungry, and always looking for ways to eliminate their rivals. If Zhang Jiao could convince Feng Xu that helping the rebellion would benefit him, they could destroy the Han Dynasty from both inside and out.

Zhang Jiao chose Ma Yuanyi, one of his most trusted followers, to broker the deal. Ma Yuanyi, in turn, selected a man named Tang Zhou to carry the secret letters to the capital.

Even though he was hand-picked by his superior, Tang Zhou was far from happy. He knew it was a suicide mission disguised as an honor. As he traveled toward Luoyang, every step felt like walking toward his own grave.

If the Imperial Guards find these documents, they'll torture me until I beg for death, he thought, sweat dripping down his face despite the cool morning air. *They'll make an example of me in the public square.*

As the golden roofs of the capital came into view, a different thought crept into his mind: *But what if... what if I disobey the order? I may become a traitor to one, but a hero to another...!*

Standing outside the palace gates, Tang Zhou's hands shook as he touched the hidden scrolls one last time. He could still complete his mission. He could still be loyal to Zhang Jiao and the cause of the oppressed peasants. Instead, fear and greed whispered louder than honor. These letters could be worth more than gold—if delivered to the right person. And he would not only escape death but be richly rewarded.

Tang Zhou approached an Imperial Guard, his voice barely above a whisper: "I have urgent information about a plot against His Majesty's life."

The guard's eyes widened as Tang Zhou produced the damning evidence. Within minutes, the letters were racing through the palace corridors, passed from hand to trembling hand.

When the court officials finished reading Zhang Jiao's detailed plans, the palace exploded into panic.

"THE YELLOW TURBANS ARE COMING!"

Ministers and servants burst into the throne room where Emperor Ling was, as usual, being entertained by women and wine.

"Your Majesty!" they screamed, falling to their knees.

"The rebels plan to strike during the Spring Festival! They have accomplices within these very walls!"

Emperor Ling's face drained of all color. For the first time in years, he was facing an immediate and direct threat to the throne. The Spring Festival was only days away—the perfect time for an attack when everyone would be distracted by celebrations.

"General He Jin!" the emperor shouted, his voice cracking with panic.

"Deploy every soldier in the capital! Search every house! Find these traitors before they destroy us all!"

But Zhang Jiao had learned long ago never to trust just one messenger. His spy network stretched across the empire like a giant spider web, and word of Tang Zhou's betrayal reached him almost instantly.

A breathless messenger stumbled into Zhang Jiao's hidden temple, falling to his knees in the dust.

"Great Teacher," he gasped, "Tang Zhou has betrayed us to the Imperial dogs. They know everything—the timing, the inside man, all of it."

The room fell silent. Zhang Jiao's followers watched their leader, waiting to see if their cause was lost before it had even begun. Then Zhang Jiao's eyes blazed with the fury of a man who had spent years watching his people suffer under Imperial oppression.

"Then we no longer have the luxury of patience," he declared. "Send a word to every province, every village, every hidden camp—the time for hiding is over!"

He turned to face his assembled generals, his voice rising to a roar that seemed to shake the very walls: "Let the yellow scarves rise like the dawn! If they want a rebellion, we'll give them one they will never forget!"

It was no longer about perfect timing or careful strategy. Tang Zhou's betrayal had forced their hand, but perhaps that was for the best.

Across the empire, hidden camps received the message. Peasants picked up their farming tools and prepared to use them as weapons. The yellow headbands that had been sewn by the village women in secret were finally tied around determined heads.

The rebellion that was meant to spread quietly had now exploded into the open, and neither the empire nor the rebels would ever be the same again.

The Yellow Turban Rebellion had begun.

Across the land, yellow banners fluttered like autumn leaves in a dying wind. Zhang Jiao's followers swept through provinces like wildfire, their war cries echoing from mountain passes to river valleys.

"The blue sky is dead! The yellow sky shall rise!"

They chanted as they stormed government offices and freed prisoners from Imperial dungeons.

The Imperial army, bloated with corruption and weakened by years of neglect, crumbled before the peasant uprising. Soldiers deserted in droves, some joining the rebels, others simply fleeing home to protect their own families.

Cities fell within days—their gates thrown open by starving citizens who greeted the Yellow Turbans as liberators.

General He Jin's armies stumbled from defeat to defeat. At Changshe, twenty thousand Imperial troops scattered before half their number of farmers wielding scythes and makeshift spears. The capital itself shook as refugees poured through its gates, bringing stories of prefectures swallowed whole by rebellion.

For months, the yellow tide seemed unstoppable. Zhang Jiao styled himself the *General of Heaven*, while his brothers carved up provinces like a banquet. Officials abandoned their posts, clutching whatever gold they could carry.

The empire groaned beneath the weight of chaos. What had begun as ragged peasants with scraps for banners now surged like a flood, drowning city after city. The Han court— once the pillar of all under Heaven—stood hollow: its armies broken, its ministers faithless, its emperor a shadow behind silk screens. And above it all, the Yellow Turban banners climbed ever higher, their cry echoing across the land: the Mandate of Heaven had shifted.

CHAPTER 6
HEAVEN'S COMMAND

~

Yet amid this nationwide catastrophe, Liu Bei, once called the "boy emperor," continued his quiet existence in Lou Sang Village, his calloused hands weaving bamboo mats and sandals by flickering candlelight while his mind devoured ancient scrolls deep into the night. Ten years had flowed past like the Yellow River in flood, and Liu Bei had transformed from a thoughtful youth into a magnificent man of twenty-four. His shoulders had broadened from years of labor, his hands grown strong and steady, and his dark eyes now held the sharp gleam of intelligence tempered by compassion.

One spring morning, when cherry blossoms drifted like snow through the village lanes, Liu Bei sat cross-legged at his work, fingers dancing across the bamboo strips in practiced rhythm. But something felt wrong—the familiar sounds of his mother's morning routine were absent. No gentle humming from the kitchen, no soft footsteps padding across wooden floors.

"Mother, are you feeling unwell today?" he called, setting aside his half-woven mat.

"Xuande, please come inside," came her voice, but it carried an unusual weight that made him feel nervous.

Expecting to find her still tucked beneath quilts, Liu Bei was startled to discover her sitting in formal dress upon the heated floor. Her silver hair was arranged in perfect coils, her best silk robe, albeit worn and fainting in color, draped around her frail shoulders, and her weathered hands folded with the solemnity of one preparing for a ceremony. The morning light streaming through the paper windows seemed to make her glow like an ancient spirit.

"Mother, why do you remain inside so late this morning? The sun is already climbing high."

"Xuande, sit down." Her voice was gentle as falling leaves, but beneath it lay bedrock determination. "I have a request—will you grant your mother's final wish?"

The word 'final' hit him like a physical blow, but he kept his expression steady.

"Mother, whatever your desire, I would climb mountains or drain seas to fulfill it. Please tell me what your heart seeks."

His mother's eyes, still bright despite her seventy-plus years, gazed at him with the accumulated love of decades. When she spoke, each word dropped into the silence like stones into still water: "I am already past seventy winters and will not see many more springs. Before the ancestors call me home, there is something I long to taste—just once before I leave this earthly realm."

"What is it, Mother? Name it, and it shall be yours."

"I wish to drink the finest tea from Luoyang's Imperial gardens—Gong Cha, the tribute tea that graces the emperor's table. Can you obtain it for your old mother?"

The request struck him like lightning. The premium tea from Luoyang was legendary—leaves so precious they were weighed against silver, so rare that even wealthy merchants could barely afford a single cup. For someone as poor as Liu Bei, it might as well have been liquid starlight. Yet he had long known of his mother's love for tea, had watched her eyes close in bliss over even their coarse village brew, had secretly hoarded copper coins for years, hoping someday to surprise her with something finer. What little he had was nowhere near enough.

Still, filial devotion burned in his chest like forge fire. To refuse his mother's dying wish was unthinkable.

"Mother, do not trouble your heart with worry. By whatever means necessary—if I must walk to the capital on bare feet—I will obtain Gong Cha for you."

A smile ghosted across her lips. "Thank you, my beloved son. Then depart today, while the roads are still safe for travel."

Startled at the suggestion to leave immediately, but Liu Bei obeyed, "Yes, I will leave after the morning meal."

His mother studied his face in profound silence, as if memorizing every line and shadow. Then her voice carried a strange formality:

"Xuande, bring me the mat you were weaving."

Puzzled but obedient, Liu Bei retrieved the half-finished bamboo creation from its wooden frame. His mother rose with surprising grace and moved to the wall cabinet where their most sacred treasure rested—the ancestral sword that had been passed down through generations of Liu blood, its lacquered scabbard gleaming like dark water.

Drawing the ancient blade from its sheath, she calmly sliced through the mat with a single, decisive stroke. The bamboo strips scattered like fallen dreams across the floor.

"Mother! Why do you destroy my work?"

But his mother sheathed the sword with ceremonial precision and presented it to him with both hands, as if offering incense to the gods.

"This blade has been yours for a while now, but the time has finally come. Take it with you on your journey. Never forget the sacred spirit of our ancestors that dwells within this steel. Their courage, their honor, their Imperial blood— all of it lives in this sword, and now it passes to you."

"I remember well the sword's meaning, Mother. But why did you cut the mat?" Liu Bei bowed deeply as he asked, accepting the weapon with trembling hands.

His mother's eyes blazed with sudden fierce pride.

"You are twenty-four years old now, my son. You must no longer remain hidden in this forgotten corner of the world, weaving mats like a common craftsman. The realm writhes in chaos—while you seek the tea I have requested, explore the kingdom, witness the suffering of the people, see what lies beyond our peaceful borders."

Her voice rose like a battle cry. "From this day forward, banish all thoughts of mat-weaving from your mind forever. You were born for greater things than this!"

Liu Bei suddenly understood. His mother wasn't simply requesting tea—she was setting him free, pushing him toward a destiny she had always seen but never dared voice.

He bowed again and said, "I comprehend your wishes, Mother. Your wisdom guides me, as it always has."

"Then depart quickly, before courage abandons us both."

"If I leave now, I may wander far and long before returning. How will you manage alone in this remote place?"

"Do not worry about this old woman—just go, and may the ancestors light your path."

Though his heart ached to leave her, Liu Bei arranged for their neighbor, Zhu Lan from a few houses over, to care for his mother during his absence. But even as he made these preparations, a deeper truth gnawed at his understanding.

Liu Bei's mother possessed an unshakeable faith that her son was destined to wear the dragon robes of empire. The realm writhed beneath the Yellow Turban plague like a wounded dragon, and though she had yearned for years to send him forth, maternal love had chained her resolution—until now.

In fact, the previous night had brought her a vision so vivid that it seared her soul. In the dream, she had walked beside her son through misty mountain paths when suddenly, the distant clash of weapons and cries of the dying echoed from the plains below like thunder.

"Mother," Liu Bei had called in the vision, his young face blazing with righteous fury, "let me descend and stop that slaughter!"

But she had grabbed his wrist tight and scolded him: "Foolish boy, do you really think you can fight against them all by yourself? And would you leave your old mother to go live with strangers?"

Then the sky had cracked open with thunder, and

through the clouds came their ancestor Emperor Jing himself, dressed in bright golden robes, wearing the Imperial crown. His voice boomed loud and powerful:

"Liu Bei's mother, listen to Heaven's command! Why do you hold back that boy and stop him from doing what he must do? The world is in chaos, people are dying everywhere, and it's time for him to step forward! Send him out now, without fear or delay, or Heaven will punish you for getting in his way!"

She had awakened with her heart hammering against her ribs like a caged bird, cold sweat dampening her nightclothes. The vision had blazed with such supernatural intensity that she knew beyond doubt it was no mere dream, but a direct command from the ancestors to send Liu Bei to the bigger world.

By midday, Liu Bei had shouldered his simple pack and strapped the ancestral sword to his side. The weight of the ancient blade felt heavy, yet somehow comforting. His mother stood in the doorway, her small frame silhouetted against the warm interior, watching him with eyes that held both pride and barely contained sorrow.

"The road to Luoyang stretches long before you," she said, pressing small cloth bundles into his hands. "I have packed what little coins and food we have for you. May it sustain you on your journey."

Liu Bei felt the meager weight of the package—perhaps a few coins and two days' worth of rice cakes. It was all she had to give, and he knew it.

"Mother, what will you eat while I am gone?"

"Zhu Lan will bring me what I need. Do not concern yourself with an old woman's meals." Her voice carried the firmness of a general dismissing a soldier, but Liu Bei caught the slight tremor beneath her words.

He knelt before her one final time, pressing his forehead to the worn wooden threshold.

"I will return with the finest tea in all the empire, Mother. This I swear by our ancestors' spirits."

"Rise, my son. Emperors do not kneel."

Liu Bei looked up to ask what she meant, but she had already turned away, disappearing into the dark corners of their small home. Only the branches of the majestic mulberry tree swayed softly in the breeze, as if to say farewell.

Liu Bei walked through Lou Sang Village as the afternoon sun slanted golden through the trees, casting long shadows across the dirt paths he had known since childhood. At the village edge, he paused to look back one final time. Smoke rose peacefully from cooking fires, and the distant sound of his mother's neighbor chopping wood echoed across the valley. It was a scene of perfect tranquility —the kind of peace he had known all his life, but somehow understood he might never see again.

The road wound through rolling hills bright with spring flowers. Liu Bei had never traveled beyond the next village, and now the world's vastness filled him with equal parts terror and excitement. Yet as the ancient saying taught: a journey of a thousand miles begins with a single step. Each step carried him further from everything familiar and deeper into the unknown realm his mother had spoken of— a world of chaos and suffering he could barely imagine.

As the sun began to sink toward the western mountains, painting the sky in shades of gold and crimson, Liu Bei's legs grew heavy and his stomach hollow. The village sounds had long since faded behind him, replaced by the whisper of wind through grain fields and the distant lowing of cattle. He had passed a few travelers—a merchant's cart heading back toward Lou Sang Village, a group of young men who eyed his sword with suspicious glances before hurrying past.

Ahead, smoke rose from a farmstead nestled in a grove of pear trees. Liu Bei approached the modest dwelling with careful respect, noting the patches in the thatched roof and the worn wooden tools leaning against the wall. A man emerged from the fields, his clothes stained with honest earth, his face weathered by countless seasons under the open sky.

That evening, Liu Bei found lodging with this farming family. The kind-hearted peasant welcomed him warmly but apologized profusely for his poverty.

"We have an honored guest, but nothing proper to offer!"

"Please do not concern yourself. But how did your family's circumstances become so difficult?" asked Liu Bei.

"A few years ago, we lived quite comfortably. However, recently, the Yellow Turbans have raided us almost monthly, stealing everything of value. Now we're practically destitute."

"Are they truly causing such severe damage?"

"Beyond description! They came just a month ago, and we never know when they'll return. Until the Yellow Turbans are eliminated, ordinary people cannot sleep peacefully for even a single night."

"Cannot the Imperial armies protect you?"

"The government forces are weaker than the bandits themselves! Mark my words—whoever defeats the Yellow Turbans will become the next emperor!"

Whoever defeats the Yellow Turbans will become emperor.

These words struck Liu Bei like lightning, rekindling the great hope that had been buried deep in his heart since his childhood, when the monk had called him "young emperor."

That very night, Liu Bei could not easily fall asleep. Countless thoughts churned through his mind, and just as he began to drift into slumber, a violent commotion shattered the silence outside. Through a gap in the wooden door, he glimpsed more than ten fierce men brandishing torches as they poured into the courtyard, each bearing the dreaded yellow headband of the rebels.

For the first time in his life, Liu Bei was witnessing the Yellow Turban terror firsthand—and the sight filled him with terrible resolve.

The Yellow Turban bandits burst into the courtyard, their torches casting hellish shadows that danced across the walls. Without mercy, they seized the farmer and his wife, who appeared meek as lambs, and dragged them into the center of the yard like wolves hauling their prey.

Those damnable fiends, Liu Bei seethed through clenched teeth as he peered through the crack in the door, his fists trembling with barely contained rage. *How dare they terrorize such innocent people!*

The bandits showed no trace of human compassion. One of them began beating the farmer's back with a spear shaft while roaring like a rabid beast:

"You know who we are, old man! Hand over all your valuables—NOW!"

The farmer bowed his head submissively and replied with heartbreaking humility: "Sirs... I would gladly give you our valuables if we possessed any. There are only a few ears of corn in the kitchen. If you need them, please take them."

"WHAT did you say?"

A particularly vicious-looking bandit with a face twisted by cruelty backhanded the farmer across the face, the sound cracking through the night air like a whip. Then he wheeled around to address his subordinates with cold, merciless authority: "Search every corner of this hovel! The grain storehouse, the main room, the kitchen—tear it all apart! If there's anything of value, FIND IT!"

More than ten Yellow Turbans scattered like vultures at the command. Four or five charged toward the granary while others stomped into the main quarters without even removing their muddy boots, tracking filth across the family's modest home.

Hidden in the upper room, Liu Bei pressed himself against the wall, his heart hammering against his ribs as he watched the systematic destruction of innocent lives. Every fiber of his being screamed for action.

Liu Bei's mind raced. *If those demons discover me, how should I respond?*

At his waist, the ancestral sword seemed to beat in time with his racing heart, each throb reminding him of the choice he had to make. For a moment, he saw himself charging out, cutting down every bandit in a whirlwind of steel. But suddenly, his mother's sacred words echoed through his mind with crystalline clarity:

"This sword is stern as winter frost against injustice, yet gentle as a loving parent in protecting the innocent."

Those words should have compelled him to charge into battle immediately, to strike down these agents of evil without hesitation. Yet Liu Bei forced himself to master his burning fury and think with the cold calculation of a future emperor.

The Yellow Turban plague extends far beyond these few wretches before me, he reasoned, his tactical mind overriding his emotional impulse.

They swarm across the land like locusts, bringing devastation wherever they march. What purpose would killing these handful serve? If destroying this small band could bring peace to the realm, I would gladly sacrifice my life in battle this very instant. But slaughtering the bandits in this courtyard cannot save the empire.

His hand unconsciously found the sword hilt as he whispered to himself with iron resolve:

I need to think about saving everyone, not just getting revenge on a few bandits. If those demons discover me and force a confrontation, then I will have no choice but to fight, he acknowledged grimly. *But until that moment comes, I must exercise restraint and wisdom.*

From below came the sounds of systematic pillaging— chests being overturned, wall cabinets ransacked, accompanied by the increasingly frustrated curses of the bandits:

"Damn this miserable hovel! They don't even have a single decent piece of clothing!"

"Why did we even bother raiding this pathetic place?"

The bandits who had searched the granary emerged and shouted to their leader: "Boss! There's nothing in the storehouse but a few ears of corn. Should we take even that?"

Liu Bei strained his ears, desperate to hear the leader's response. Surely even bandits possessed some shred of conscience—surely they wouldn't steal the last few ears of corn from a destitute family?

But the chief's answer shattered any illusion of mercy: "What kind of idiotic question is that? Did we come here to show charity to this household?" His voice dripped with contempt and rage, causing his subordinates to shrink back in apparent fear of their leader's wrath.

Even the final scraps of food... Liu Bei's jaw clenched tightly. These weren't merely bandits—they were monsters wearing human faces, demons who would steal the very air from a drowning man's lungs if they could profit from it.

A bitter irony twisted in his chest. The Yellow Turbans had once risen with noble purpose, fighting against the corrupt officials who bled the people dry. Zhang Jiao had preached of justice, of a new world where the hungry would be fed and the oppressed would find peace. But with their Great Teacher dead and their original leaders scattered to the winds, what had they become? The very parasites they had once sworn to destroy.

The true horror wasn't just their cruelty—it was their complete absence of any spark of humanity. They would leave this gentle family with absolutely nothing, condemning them to starvation without the slightest flicker of remorse. The revolution that had promised to save the ordinary people now preyed upon them like wolves among sheep.

"Ah," Liu Bei thought to himself, "Heaven must have

brought me to this house tonight so I could see these heartless bandits with my own eyes and save the people from their terror!"

"Well," continued the bandit chief, "take those corns, and look one more time if there's really nothing valuable in the main room! Did you also check the upper room? Do not leave a single stone unturned!"

CRASH!

The door to Liu Bei's hiding place burst open! A blazing torch suddenly lit up the small room. Liu Bei flattened himself against the wall, not daring to breathe. His hand gripped his sword tightly. If the bandit spotted him, he would have no choice but to fight for his life.

But fortune smiled upon him. The lazy bandit didn't even poke his head into the room. He just waved his torch around once, muttered something under his breath, and trudged back to the courtyard.

"Empty as everything else," he grumbled.

Liu Bei let out a sigh of relief and finally loosened his grip on the sword.

Soon, all the bandits gathered in the courtyard like a pack of wild dogs. Their chief kicked at the dirt in frustration and snarled at the trembling homeowner.

"Listen here, old man! If you're going to live this poor, you might as well become a bandit like us! What's the point of suffering like this when you could be living like a king?"

The poor man bowed deeply, his body shaking like a leaf in the wind. As the bandit chief lifted his head, moonlight caught the jagged scar above his right eyebrow, and recognition struck him like a physical blow. His breath caught in his throat—he knew that face, that distinctive mark.

Wang the Wine Seller, the old man thought, memories flooding back. This man had once worked at the nearby night market, peddling cheap liquor from a rickety wooden stall. The old farmer remembered the scandal well—Wang had been caught selling millet wine so heavily diluted with water it was practically colored river water, yet charging full price to unsuspecting customers. When a drunken guest discovered the fraud and confronted him, a vicious fight erupted. Pottery had shattered, sending sharp fragments flying, one of which had sliced deep into Wang's eyebrow, leaving that unmistakable scar.

So this was what had become of the dishonest wine merchant. When the world fell into chaos and the Yellow Turbans rose, Wang had traded his watered wine for a yellow headband, finding new ways to cheat and steal from honest people.

"I'm sorry, sir, but I don't have the guts for such a life. I'm just a coward," the old man whispered, his voice barely audible.

The bandit chief—the former wine seller—spat on the ground. "Ha! A weakling like you wouldn't even qualify to be one of my men anyway!" He turned to his gang and shouted, "Alright, boys! We struck out here, so let's move on to the next village. Since we're already out in the night, we might as well make our sleepless hours worth something!"

Just like that, the Yellow Turban bandits vanished into the night.

The moment the bandits were gone, Liu Bei sprang from his hiding place and hurried to the aid of the shaken family.

"Master of the house!" he called out, breathless with

concern. "You must have been terrified—please, come inside and rest!"

The old man staggered into the room and collapsed to the floor like a sack of rice. But to Liu Bei's surprise, his expression was calm, almost serene.

"You know," the man said, offering a weary smile, "I've lived through this sort of thing so many times, I've grown used to it. When you've got nothing left worth stealing, thieves lose their power to frighten you." He paused, then added quietly, "And besides... those Yellow Turbans—they were once just common folk like me and my neighbors. No matter how monstrous they've become, part of me still pities them."

Liu Bei looked at the old man, poor in possessions but rich in dignity, and felt a fire kindle deep within him. How long had decent people like this endured the cruelty of bandits and the neglect of those in power? Someone had to rise and defend them.

And in that moment, Liu Bei knew—it had to be him.

He didn't yet know how.

CHAPTER 7
THE MIGHTY YELLOW RIVER

～

As the first light of dawn spilled through the windows, Liu Bei gathered his few belongings and stepped outside. The old farmer and his wife were already waiting for him beneath the soft morning sky.

Liu Bei bowed low, his young face solemn with purpose.

The old man looked at him with regret. "I can tell you're meant for something greater—on a mission far beyond these fields. I'm sorry, we have no warm breakfast to offer. Even our last ears of corn are gone. It shames me to send you off like this."

Without a word, Liu Bei reached into his pouch and pulled out a few of the coins he had been saving to buy his mother's favorite tea.

"Please, take this," he said, pressing the money into the farmer's calloused hands. "It should be enough to buy food for a few days."

The old man's eyes welled with tears as he tried to return it. "No... I can't accept this. You're the one on a journey. I should be the one helping you."

But Liu Bei gently folded the man's fingers over the coins. "I insist," he said softly. "Helping each other—especially when it's hard—that's what makes us human."

With a final bow, Liu Bei turned and began his long journey toward the Yellow River.

The road stretched ahead across the empty plains. The land was wide and bare, and the sun moved slowly overhead as he walked on.

Step by step, mile after mile, his mind replayed the farmer's words—about his mission to do something great for the country. Perhaps this journey wasn't only about a gift of tea for his mother. It became even clearer to him that it was the beginning of something far greater.

The land around the Yellow River stretched out before Liu Bei like a vast ocean of golden grass. No matter how far he walked, the plains seemed to go on forever and ever. The sun rose from one edge of the world in the morning and slowly traveled across the sky to set on the opposite horizon at night.

"Oh my," Liu Bei whispered in amazement, "the world is so much bigger than I ever imagined!"

Having grown up in a small mountainside village, Liu Bei had never seen such endless flat lands. As he walked across the boundless plains, he felt his heart expanding with wonder and excitement. The cramped feeling he'd carried in his chest for so long seemed to melt away like snow in spring sunshine.

From dawn until dusk, Liu Bei walked with determined

steps. Finally, just as the evening stars began to twinkle, he reached the banks of the magnificent Yellow River. Liu Bei had never seen a real river before in his entire life! He stood on the riverbank, staring in absolute amazement at the water that seemed to flow on forever.

The gentle spring breeze cooled his sweaty face as he watched the most beautiful sight he had ever seen. Elegant merchant ships floated gracefully on the water like swans, their white sails billowing in the wind.

"I never knew," Liu Bei said softly, his voice filled with wonder, "that a river could be so magnificent and beautiful!" As Liu Bei gazed at the glorious river in the golden evening light, he remembered something he had read in an ancient book: *"The wise man is like water."* This meant that truly wise people understood the mysterious nature of life and flew around obstacles, just like water flew around rocks.

"Yes," Liu Bei murmured to himself, his eyes alight with newfound clarity. A drizzle touched his face—first a drop, then another, then more. He glanced down at his sleeve, where one bead of water clung, round and unbroken.

Water seemed so small, so simple: a droplet falling with spring rain, or morning dew glimmering like jewels on flower petals. Yet gathered together, those droplets became streams, rivers, and mighty oceans.

"And look what water can do!" Liu Bei exclaimed. "It bears great ships with ease, it nourishes every living thing, it sustains life itself. Yes... I must become like water—humble yet powerful, gentle yet unstoppable."

Just then, an elderly man with a long white beard walked by, carrying a walking stick.

"Excuse me, honored elder," Liu Bei called out politely,

bowing respectfully. "I've heard that ships carrying tea from the capital city of Luoyang stop near here. Is that true? Do you happen to know when the next ship might arrive?"

The old man smiled kindly, his face lined with the years of a hard life, and raised a gnarled finger toward a bend in the river. "You're in luck, young man," he said. "Just beyond those willow trees—see there? A merchant ship from Luoyang is anchored at the bank. "You'd best hurry," the old man said. "The ships will close early if the rain starts pouring."

Liu Bei followed the man's gesture and spotted the vessel: a large river junk, its sail emblazoned with the mark *"Luoyang Trading House"*. The ship gleamed with lacquered wood, its hull high and proud above the water. Around it bustled a growing crowd of villagers, traders, and peddlers —men in coarse hemp robes, women with baskets slung across their backs, barefoot children chasing each other between the legs of donkeys and oxen.

The scent of sandalwood and dried orange peel drifted on the breeze, mingled with the louder smells of river mud and livestock.

Liu Bei's heart leapt. The special chrysanthemum tea his mother loved—cultivated only in the hills outside Luoyang —might be aboard that very ship. He could almost taste its delicate bitterness on his tongue.

Clutching the small pouch of coins at his side, he broke into a run, weaving along the narrow footpath between reeds and willows. Raindrops speckled his straw sandals as he splashed through the damp earth, hurrying toward the crowd.

The riverside was a whirlwind of noise and motion.

Farmers bartered noisily for medicinal herbs, merchants shouted the virtues of their lacquerware, and eager buyers waved copper coins and strings of cash.

Liu Bei pushed through the crowd and approached a tough-looking boat captain with weather-beaten hands and a permanent scowl. Taking a deep breath, he bowed respectfully.

"Excuse me, Sir," Liu Bei said, stepping forward through the crowd. "I've come to buy tea. Do you have any fine tea on board that you could sell me?"

The captain, a leathery old man with sharp eyes and a beard that rustled like old rope, turned to face him. He gave Liu Bei a once-over, from his travel-worn sandals to the faint calluses on his palms.

"Tea?" he repeated, incredulous. "You want to buy tea? From *this* ship?" He barked a laugh, half disbelief, half mockery. "Boy, we don't sell dried weeds to common folk. This vessel carries *Gong Cha*—tribute tea, grown on mist-covered slopes, picked by girls with jade fingers, sent directly to Luoyang for the Emperor's cup. Do you even know what that means?"

Liu Bei's back straightened. He nodded once. "Yes, sir. *Gong Cha*—tribute tea—is no ordinary drink. It is the finest leaf from Imperial gardens, meant for Heaven's Son. It bears not only fragrance, but favor."

The captain blinked. He studied the young man again—more carefully this time. Something in the way Liu Bei stood, how he carried his words, struck him as unusual. Calm. Dignified. A rural accent, yes, but softened by education.

"What is your name?"

"My name is Liu Bei. I am from Zhuo County."

The captain's breath caught. "Liu... Bei?" He muttered it as though testing the weight of the words. "Zhuo County... the Liu clan... That line traces back to the Imperial house of Han."

"Yes, you are right. My family descended from Prince Jing of Zhongshan," replied Liu Bei.

The captain narrowed his eyes. The boy did have that long, noble face—brows like lying silk, eyes like a quiet well. And the way he spoke—there was restraint and purpose that could not be faked.

The captain had traveled most of his life, sourcing and selling goods in every corner of the empire. He had learned to read men as sharply as he sized up the worth of jade or silk. One look at Liu Bei told him this was not an ordinary man.

"Well, well..." he muttered, scratching his beard. "Tell me, young master Liu—what would a descendant of emperors want with *Gong Cha* from a merchant's ship?"

Liu Bei looked down at the worn pouch of coins in his hand, then back up with quiet conviction. "It's for my mother. She is old and ill, and the taste of true tea has not touched her lips in years. I've walked three hundred miles to bring her something worthy of her, even if I must offer everything I have."

The captain went still. For a long moment, the only sound was the faint patter of drizzle on the deck. Then the drops grew heavier, thickening into a steady rain that speckled the sails and darkened the planks underfoot. He looked out at the river, the shifting water rippling under the gray sky. When he turned back, the hardness in his face had softened.

"Wait right here," he said at last. His voice had lost its edge.

He disappeared below deck and returned carrying a small lacquered container—red wood, gold trim, bound with silk cord. Even in the dim light, it gleamed like treasure.

"This," Zhang Shun said, running a rough thumb along the cord, "is the finest chrysanthemum tea—picked from the cliffs near Mount Song, harvested the first morning after the solstice. I had hoped to sell it to the highest bidder. But these days..." He shook his head. "Merchants scrape by, and there are not many who can afford luxuries like these, whether for sale or for consumption. If it would not sell, I thought of sending it to the palace as tribute."

He paused, eyes narrowing at the thought. "Yet the court is rotten to the core, I'm sure you heard too. To place this tea in the hands of those parasites would only dishonor the leaf itself. No—I would sooner let it spoil."

He looked back at Liu Bei, studying him as if weighing scales only he could see. At last, he pressed the container into the young man's hands. "This tea belongs with you. Take it to your mother."

Liu Bei's eyes widened in disbelief. "Sir, I... I cannot accept such a gift."

Zhang Shun gave a low chuckle and lifted a finger. "Not free. Just... remember my name if you ever find yourself in a palace. Zhang Shun—the merchant who deals the finest tea in this country."

Liu Bei bowed low and received the tea with both hands. "Captain Zhang, I cannot promise what Heaven holds for me. But I will remember your name with gratitude as long as I live."

The old merchant studied him for a moment more, then gave a slow, satisfied nod. He had traveled half a lifetime trading silks, herbs, and teas from one end of the empire to the other, and in that time he had learned to read men as sharply as ledgers. This man did not boast, did not bargain —yet his humility and graciousness rang truer than gold.

As Liu Bei vanished into the misting rain, red tea tin clutched to his chest, Zhang Shun stood at the riverside watching his figure fade into the crowd.

The old captain smiled to himself. "The tea," he murmured, "has found its rightful owner."

CHAPTER 8
DANGER EVERYWHERE

~

Clutching the precious tea container and imagining his mother's smile, Liu Bei made his way to a small roadside inn, kindly recommended by one of the merchants from the ship. His cloak was damp and heavy from the rain, but the downpour had already begun to ease. By the time he reached the door, the storm had slowed to a soft drizzle, the clouds breaking just enough to let a sliver of moonlight through.

Everything seems to be going smoothly today, he thought, his cloak wet but his heart light with contentment.

The innkeeper, moved by the young traveler's sincerity, offered him a spot in the barn for just a couple of coins. Grateful and weary, Liu Bei settled onto the straw and soon drifted into sleep, the faint scent of tea lingering at his side.

But sometime around midnight, he was jolted awake by the innkeeper shaking him frantically.

"Wake up! Wake up!" the man whispered urgently.

Liu Bei sat up, confused and alarmed. Through the slightly parted barn doors, he could see flickering lights dancing outside like ghostly flames.

"Is there a fire next door?" he asked.

"No, it's much worse!" the innkeeper hissed. "The Yellow Turban bandits have attacked! They learned merchants from the capital were lodging nearby—and now they've come to take everything they can get their hands on!"

Liu Bei's blood ran cold. These bandits were everywhere, like a plague that never ended.

"If they catch you, it'll be terrible!" the innkeeper continued. "You need to escape through the back door right now, before they find you!"

Liu Bei grabbed his precious tea container and prepared to run. Would he make it to safety? Would his mother ever get to taste the tea he'd traveled so far to find?

If the bandits discovered him now, they would surely tear it from his hands without mercy, leaving him with nothing to show for his perilous journey except the bitter taste of failure.

His heart pounding like war drums, Liu Bei rose stealthily and crept toward the back door, every fiber of his being focused on escape. Through the darkness, he could see the neighboring courtyard ablaze with torchlight—dozens of Yellow Turban bandits raising their hellish clamor as they pillaged another innocent family's home.

How can ordinary people survive when these devils descend upon them every evening like ravenous wolves? Liu Bei thought as he slipped into the shadows. The injustice of it all clawed at his heart like a living thing. *By whatever means necessary, I must destroy the Yellow Turban plague and restore justice to this suffering land.*

After narrowly escaping the night's attack, Liu Bei came to a sobering realization: obtaining the precious tea had not been the end of his journey—it was only the beginning. The road home would be even more perilous, weaving through war-torn lands, avoiding bandit patrols, and sleeping in hidden valleys. He could no longer count on the kindness of a village headman or a sympathetic innkeeper. From here on, the path would be even longer, lonelier, and full of unexpected dangers.

After many grueling days on foot, Liu Bei's soles were blistered, his robes threadbare, and his body aching from the burdens he carried. Still, he pressed on—driven by a son's devotion and the promise he had made.

Weary and searching for any sign of shelter or life, he pushed through the last stretch of a pine grove when he suddenly stopped in his tracks. Through the morning mist, a temple complex emerged on a nearby hill. Its golden roofs gleamed in the early light, eaves curving toward the sky.

It was unmistakably a shrine to the Great Sage—Master Confucius himself—one of those sacred places that graced each county of the empire, a lighthouse of learning and virtue amid the age's chaos.

Liu Bei's heart leapt with hope.

Since boyhood, he had admired Confucius not just as a scholar, but as a savior of order in a broken world. To think his weary steps had brought him to that very threshold filled him with new purpose.

With measured, respectful steps befitting a pilgrim, Liu

Bei began to climb the winding path toward the temple. The morning air was crisp and clean, filled with birdsong that seemed to herald a moment of life-changing experience.

As he ascended, he bowed his head in silent reflection.

Master Confucius, Liu Bei reflected as he climbed, *seven hundred years ago, you emerged to bring order to a chaotic world. You were a saint whose brilliance illuminated the darkness of your age.*

Reaching the main courtyard, Liu Bei approached the towering statue of the sage with deep reverence. The stone figure seemed to radiate an aura of timeless wisdom, its serene expression offering comfort to all who sought guidance in troubled times.

Liu Bei prostrated himself before the statue, pressing his forehead to the cold stone as he poured out his heart in desperate prayer:

"Venerable Master Confucius, though the world was troubled in your time seven hundred years past, today's chaos far exceeds even those dark days! The people suffer under the heel of brigands who know neither mercy nor justice. You sought to heal the world through the gentle arts of benevolence and culture, but I—your unworthy disciple —must pursue peace through the way of the righteous sword!"

Liu Bei believed himself alone in this sacred place, his words echoing only among the ancient stones and morning mist. But his fervent declaration was shattered by an explosion of coarse laughter that rang out from the temple's main hall like thunder splitting a clear sky.

"HAHAHA! Did you hear that, brother? This fool thinks he's going to bring peace to the world!"

Liu Bei's blood turned to ice as he spun around, only to see a fearsome warrior with the build of a tiger charging toward him from the shadows. Before he could even think to draw his sword, iron hands seized his neck with crushing force.

"You miserable wretch!" the giant roared, his voice thundering through the courtyard, breath thick with the stench of wine and bloodlust. "Peace to the world? Have you lost your mind?!"

Before Liu Bei could reply, the brute seized him by the collar and yanked him forward like a sack of grain. His feet scraped uselessly against the stone as he was dragged toward the temple hall, powerless against the man's overwhelming strength.

When Liu Bei looked up in fear, he found himself face to face with another menacing figure. This second man was better dressed than his captor, his robes indicating that he was of rank among the rebels. But his eyes held the same cruelty that had destroyed so many before.

The moment the leader saw Liu Bei, he burst into mocking laughter that rang through the temple.

"So this pathetic wretch is the one who thinks he can eliminate all bandits and bring peace to the world?" His voice dripped with contempt.

"Yes, Commander," replied the giant who had captured Liu Bei. "What shall we do with him?"

The leader waved dismissively, his expression one of supreme arrogance. "Let him go. Where could such a pitiful creature possibly run? "If he dares to fly, he's no more than a moth to the flame. If he dares to leap, he's only a flea."

His words carried the casual cruelty of a man who had

grown accustomed to wielding life and death with impunity.

This was Ma Yuanyi, one of Zhang Jiao's most trusted lieutenants and commander of the Yellow Turban forces in this region. The giant who had seized Liu Bei was his subordinate, Gao Hong, a man whose reputation for brutality was whispered in fearful tones throughout the countryside.

Though it was Liu Bei's first time encountering them, the yellow headbands marked their allegiance to the Yellow Turbans. His jaw tightened—he had walked straight into the lair of the very evil he had sworn to destroy.

"Tell me, you wimpy little dog," Ma Yuanyi sneered, his voice like poisoned honey, "where exactly do you crawl from to dare show your face in our presence?"

"I am from Zhuo County, where I make my humble living weaving mats," Liu Bei replied, his voice steady despite the danger that surrounded him like hungry wolves circling a lone traveler.

"A mat-weaver from the mud dares to tell warriors and lords how to save the world?" Ma Yuanyi's loud laughter rang across the temple. "What gives a miserable peasant the right to speak so arrogantly in the presence of your superiors?"

Liu Bei stood defiantly, surrounded by a sea of hostile eyes—knowing that his next words could very well be his last.

"Surely he's not a lunatic... is he? Why won't he answer?" Ma Yuan-yi narrowed his eyes, then scoffed. "Look at him—fine enough face, but babbling like some fool lost in a dream."

After a pause, Ma Yuan-yi turned to one of his men.

"Killing him outright would be a waste. Gan Hong, put him with the baggage train. If we're taking him along, he might as well earn his keep."

"Yes, Chief. I'll assign him to the pack team," Gan Hong replied.

Liu Bei, still in shock, could hardly believe what had happened. He had risked everything to escape the Yellow Turbans under the cover of night, running with nothing but fear and determination—and now, somehow, he had ended up as their servant, forced to carry their loads like a pack animal.

What cursed luck is this? he thought bitterly. *From fugitive to pack mule in a single night.*

Powerless to resist, Liu Bei was forced to shoulder the rebels' loads and march alongside them into the dawn.

As the bandits marched through the pale darkness just before dawn, Liu Bei trudged at the rear, burdened with sacks and bundles slung across his aching back. Every step felt heavier than the last. His arms burned, and his legs threatened to give out beneath him—but he pressed on in silence.

The group rounded a bend in the road and came upon a hunched figure sitting by an old temple—a ragged monk wrapped in threadbare robes and sandals, his face weathered like cracked bark.

One of the bandits snorted. "What's that ghost doing here? Nearly made my heart jump," sneered Gan Hong, flicking a pebble at the monk. "Get lost, you worthless beggar... nothing but bad luck."

Ma Yuan-yi chuckled. "Probably hasn't had a meal in days. Maybe he's meditating his hunger away."

The bandits passed without a glance.

Liu Bei did not look up at first, trudging on with his head bowed. But then his eyes fell upon the monk's worn-out sandals—their weaving, their faded color, the fraying material. Something about them stirred him. Slowly, he raised his gaze to the monk.

The old man's eyes shifted from the jeering bandits to the youth bent under his burden. When their eyes met, Liu Bei froze as if struck by lightning. The monk, too, went rigid, as though he had just seen a ghost.

It was him.

The same wandering monk who had spent a single night at the village schoolhouse in Lou Sang Village ten years ago, wearing the same pair of sandals Liu Bei had gifted him. He was the one who had looked into Liu Bei's young face and murmured with quiet certainty: *"This boy carries the bearing of an emperor."*

Liu Bei stepped closer, heart pounding. "Venerable one... do you recognize me?"

The monk slowly rose to his feet, joints creaking, and pressed his palms together in a solemn bow. His voice was quiet and hoarse, but full of warmth.

"Though these eyes have dimmed with age, how could I forget the boy-emperor?"

Liu Bei's throat tightened. He glanced back at the bandits, then turned to show the ropes digging into his shoulders and the load strapped to his back.

The old monk's expression fell. "Ah..." he whispered, sorrow thick in his voice. "So this is what fate has given you. You walk among wolves, but your heart remains your own. Please... restrain yourself and endure."

"I didn't choose this path," Liu Bei said quietly. "But I will endure it."

The monk nodded, as if no explanation was needed. "Go carefully. For both the earth and the heavens are witnesses to the road you walk."

Just then, Gan Hong's voice came slicing through the air. "Hey, you! What are you whispering about back there? Move your legs before I move them for you!"

Liu Bei turned back to the monk and gave a low, silent bow. The monk returned it with a gentle smile, one that hid both grief and hope. And then Liu Bei turned and hurried away, back into the shadow of his captor.

Liu Bei had felt a flicker of hope upon seeing the monk again, a familiar face in a world turned upside down. But that hope quickly soured into helplessness, seeping through his chest like ink in water.

How laughable, he thought bitterly. *A boy emperor—they once called me that. And now look at me. A beast of burden, dragging sacks through the mountains for common bandits. What emperor crawls like this?*

Shoulders slumped, his eyes fixed on the ground, Liu Bei followed the Yellow Turbans with reluctant steps—disillusionment thick in his heart, and shame riding on his back heavier than any load.

Then Ma Yuan-yi turned suddenly to Gan Hong and said, "By now, they should've returned."

"You mean the men who went to raid Luoyang Pass last night?"

"Yes. Li Zhufan's unit. We were to meet them this morning at the mountain fortress."

"They're likely waiting there for you now, Chief. Let's hurry and head up."

They climbed the rugged mountain trail for some time until they reached the ruins of an old fortress, half-collapsed in the depths of the forest. Yellow Turban soldiers were everywhere, crowding the ruined stronghold. It seemed this was the gathering point for those who had attacked Luoyang the night before.

As Ma Yuan-yi and his party entered, a man named Li Zhufan came out to meet them.

"Chief! You're here!"

"Hmm. So, how was last night? Any good haul?"

"Nothing major, but not disappointing either. Though... there's one regret—we let a young fellow slip away."

"A young man?" Ma Yuan-yi raised an eyebrow. "What about him? Was he carrying treasure?"

"No treasure, as far as I could tell," Li Zhufan replied, "but word is, he had a canister of top-grade Gong Cha from Luoyang. And you know how our Grand Leader, Elder Master Zhang Jiao himself, is helpless before fine Luoyang tea. If we'd brought that young man in, it would've made a fine tribute for the Master... but we lost him. A pity."

Liu Bei felt a chill race through his chest. Instinctively, his hand went to the tea canister hidden beneath his robes.

Ma Yuan-yi noticed and glanced sharply at Liu Bei.

"This young man—how old did you say he was?"

"I didn't see him myself," said Li Zhufan, "but the men say he looked to be in his twenties... and had unusually large ears."

Ma Yuan-yi narrowed his eyes. "Then... that one over there—isn't it him??"

Li Zhufan looked at Liu Bei and froze, his face suddenly stiff.

"Then it *must* be him! Wait—let's confirm with Zheng Gong. He saw the buyer with his own eyes."

"Zheng Gong! Where are you?"

"Yes, here I am," a wiry man called out, hurrying forward.

"Yesterday, down at the port, you saw a young man buying tea. Was it this one here?"

Zheng Gong stared at Liu Bei, eyes narrowing, scrutinizing every feature. Then he said firmly: "Yes. Without a doubt—it's him."

In truth, Zheng Gong had been watching the merchant vessel for days, waiting for the right moment. Word had reached him through his web of contacts that a Luoyang trader was transporting Imperial-grade teas—tribute blends once reserved for the emperor's court. He had planned to raid the ship that very night.

Liu Bei's heart sank like a stone.

Li Zhufan suddenly seized his arm and twisted it behind his back. "If you don't hand over the tea right now, you'll regret it."

Liu Bei's vision blurred; too shocked to respond. All he could think of was his mother's face. No matter what, he was determined to bring the tea to her.

"Just cut his neck off if he keeps being stubborn!" shouted Ma Yuan-yi from nearby.

With that, Li Zhufan drove his iron-booted foot into Liu Bei's waist. Liu Bei stumbled back several steps before collapsing onto the ground.

"That bastard...!"

A surge of rage flared in him. Beneath his cloak, he had carried his ancestral sword the whole time, hidden from prying eyes. If he drew it now, he could cut down more than a few of these rebels.

But just as his hand brushed the hilt, his mother's face rose in his mind. She must be waiting anxiously for him to return home alive. He couldn't throw his life away here.

Then another memory surfaced—the words of the old monk from that morning: *"Restrain yourself and endure."*

Yes. He must not act rashly, not lose everything over a moment of pride or anger, especially not against these bandits.

Yet he also couldn't bear to give up the tea. Swallowing his pride, Liu Bei bowed respectfully to Li Zhufan and untied the sword from under his cloak.

"I will give you this sword. Just please—don't take the tea."

Ma Yuan-yi stepped forward and snatched the weapon, examining its sheen.

"Hah! This is indeed a fine blade. I'll keep this for myself."

"I've had my eye on that since earlier. You were foolish to think you could keep it hidden underneath," he added with a smirk. "As for the tea—I couldn't care less."

It was the mindset of thieves to the core.

But Li Zhufan was not finished. He was determined to take the tea no matter what. His eyes burned with greed as his voice rose in pitch. "You insolent brat! Are you testing my patience? Hand over the tea—*now!*"

Left with no choice, Liu Bei took the tea caddy from inside his clothes and handed it over.

In the end, not only did he fail to protect the tea, but also lost his sword.

Once the matter of the tea was resolved, the group prepared to resume their journey. But just then, a scout came running in from a distance.

"Sir! If you leave now, it will be disastrous. About two or three miles north of here, there's a detachment of about five hundred imperial troops camped by the river. It's best to stay here for the night."

Upon hearing this, the Yellow Turban bandits decided to spend the night in the mountain fortress.

Liu Bei silently rejoiced. The imperial army was less than three miles away, and now that the rebels were camping here for the night, it was the perfect chance to escape.

Yes. I'll escape tonight. He repeated the vow in his heart over and over.

He deeply regretted losing the tea and the sword. But he knew that once something fell into the hands of thieves, there was no getting it back. It was pointless to linger on it. Liu Bei firmed his resolve and waited for nightfall.

The bandits fell into a heavy, early sleep—wearied from their exploits and preparing for another night of mischief. Having robbed the village under the cover of darkness just the night before, exhaustion weighed heavily upon them. After a quick, meager supper, they sprawled in the cool grass outside the hall, their breathing deep and steady, punctuated by loud snores that echoed into the night.

Inside the dimly lit hall, however, only two men remained awake—Ma Yuan-yi and Li Zhufan. Their cups clinked softly between stories and low murmurs, the sharp tang of alcohol loosening their tongues.

Ma Yuan-yi's gaze remained sharp and alert, scanning the room as if waiting for unseen threats or opportunities. Beside him, Li Zhufan leaned back, savoring the burn of the liquor, his fingers drumming impatient rhythms on the wooden table. Though their bodies relaxed, their minds remained far from rest—plotting, waiting, and watching the night unfold beyond the walls.

Liu Bei pretended to sleep in the grass, but he couldn't even think of sleeping. He kept his ears tuned and eyes barely open, waiting for the right moment.

Close to midnight, the whole gang was snoring so loudly they wouldn't notice if someone carried them away.

This is it, Liu Bei thought. *This is the time to escape.* He cautiously lifted his head and looked around. Everyone was fast asleep, except for the two leaders, who were still drinking.

Finally, Liu Bei rose fully and crept toward the fortress gate, minimizing his footsteps. With every step, his heart pounded and his body trembled.

Once he made it past the gate, he finally breathed a sigh of relief. He turned to head north, but suddenly, two black shadows sprang out from the grass like lightning. They blocked his path with spears and shouted menacingly:

"Where do you think you're going!?"

Liu Bei's heart sank.

Of course—guards. He had tried to slip out, unaware that a few had been posted right outside the gate. Liu Bei thought briefly of fighting through, but cold spearpoints were already pressed against his chest and back.

His only choice was to feign innocence. "I'm not going anywhere—I only stepped out to relieve myself."

The guards sneered. "Ha! What a joke. Tie him up and take him to the chiefs."

Dragged back inside, Liu Bei was thrown before Ma Yuan-yi and Li Zhufan. Both looked up from their wine.

"What is this?" Ma Yuan-yi demanded.

"We caught him trying to escape," a guard replied.

Ma Yuan-yi's eyes narrowed. "You wretch. We spared your life, and this is how you repay us?"

"He must be a spy!" Li Zhufan barked. "Kill him now—leaving him alive was a mistake!"

Liu Bei lowered his head. *So this is how it ends.*

"Shall we execute him?" one guard asked.

"Do it!" Li Zhufan growled. "He's ruining the mood."

But Ma Yuan-yi lifted a hand. "Wait. If he's a spy, we might get information out of him. Bind him and throw him into the pit. We'll interrogate him in the morning—then kill him."

"Yes, sir." The guards dragged Liu Bei to the rear of the fortress and hurled him, bound, into a deep pit—nearly six meters down. The impact knocked him out.

When he woke, the world was black. A few stars flickered high above, but no light reached the well-like shaft.

This is it. At dawn, they'll question me—then kill me. Bound hand and foot, escape was impossible.

A sigh escaped him. *So be it. Death no longer frightens me.*

What pained him most was not his fate, but that he would die without fulfilling his duty to his aging mother.

Liu Bei sat down on the dirt floor with his eyes closed, sinking into despair. Suddenly, something lightly tapped his head from above.

What could that be? He opened his eyes in alarm, but it

was pitch black—he couldn't see a thing. However, just from the sensation, he could tell it was a rope.

Ah, someone must be trying to rescue me by lowering a rope from above!

Liu Bei stood up quickly. Sure enough, what was brushing against him was indeed a rope. *Who could it be...?* He looked up at the ceiling, but still, he could see nothing.

Just then, as if urging him to hurry, the rope gave two or three urgent tugs. Of course, Liu Bei understood what it meant. But no matter how much he tried to grab the rope, his arms and body were so tightly bound that he couldn't do anything.

So he shouted a single word toward the ceiling: "Knife! Knife!"

The rope above gave another tug. Feeling along it, Liu Bei realized a knife had been tied to its end. He clenched the hilt awkwardly in his bound hands and twisted, trying to bring the blade against the cords at his wrists.

It was clumsy work. The knife scraped and slipped, biting shallowly at first. Each movement strained his shoulders and sent jolts of pain through his arms. But he kept at it, sawing and twisting, until at last the fibers began to fray.

With one final tug, the rope snapped. Liu Bei gasped in relief as his arms came free.

Wasting no time, he looped the rope around his body, gripped it firmly with both hands, and began to climb. Slowly, painfully, he pulled himself upward out of the pit.

As he hauled himself over the rim of the pit, Liu Bei's eyes fell on a familiar figure waiting before him. It was the old monk—the very same man he had met that morning at the temple.

For a heartbeat he froze, stunned. Could fate be so cruel, yet so strange? The one who had offered him quiet hope at dawn was now the very presence pulling him back from the jaws of death. Shock and gratitude surged together, setting every nerve alight.

This was no mere coincidence—it was a sign that his path was entwined with something far greater than he had ever imagined.

"Sir! How did you know I was imprisoned here?"

Liu Bei asked, overcome with gratitude, grabbing the monk's hands tightly.

"This is no time for useless questions," the monk said sternly. "Don't say a word. Just follow me."

He tugged Liu Bei's sleeve and hurried ahead, leading him to a hidden shed behind an old temple. Liu Bei recognized that he had passed the temple with the bandits the day before.

"Sir, how did you know I was caught in a trap and imprisoned?" Liu Bei repeated his earlier question, still overwhelmed by gratitude.

Waving his hands, the monk replied, "There's no time for idle chatter. We must flee immediately. But... before that, I have one request."

"You saved my life, a life as good as dead. I will do whatever you ask, even at the cost of my life," Liu Bei replied.

"You're too kind. But you must know, you are someone sent by the heavens. No matter how ferocious the Yellow Turbans may be, how could they possibly harm the future emperor? The heavens would never allow it."

"Your words are too generous. But please, tell me what it is you want me to do."

Instead of replying, the monk walked to a door and opened it. He brought out a white horse and called into the room, "Dear Lady, please come out."

As Liu Bei watched in curiosity, a young woman stepped out from the room. She was breathtaking—truly a beauty beyond compare. Perhaps around eighteen years of age, dressed entirely in white, graceful and elegant. With her head slightly bowed, she walked softly, modestly—like a fairy from the tales.

The monk, leading both the lady and the white horse, turned to Liu Bei and said,

"This young lady is the daughter of the lord of this town. When the Yellow Turbans attacked, the city burned, and her father died a tragic death at their hands. I have been protecting her ever since. But now I can no longer provide for her, so I must send her away. A little over two miles north of here, the government army is stationed by the river. The lord of the town was a man of great virtue, respected and beloved by many. Though danger now forced his loyal followers into hiding across the countryside, their devotion has not wavered. Should fortune favor you and you encounter one of these steadfast souls, know that they will stop at nothing to aid you—and to rescue the lady in peril. If you escort her there, they will surely help her with care and respect. It's a lot to ask, but since you are already fleeing, I beg you to accompany her there."

Liu Bei felt a sudden pounding in his chest as he looked at Lady Lotus's beautiful face. Without hesitation, he agreed.

"Of course. I'll take her there."

"Thank you so much. Now I can send her off in peace.

Hurry, before dawn breaks—who knows when the enemies might return."

The monk turned to the girl. "Dear Lady, trust this man and mount the horse."

Lady Lotus walked silently and held the reins. Liu Bei gently lifted her slender waist and placed her on the horse, then turned to the monk.

"When will I see you again, Sir?"

"Meetings and partings are bound by fate. Now go—your path is urgent."

Liu Bei swung into the saddle. When he saw Lady Lotus in tears, the monk's tone grew firm, almost commanding. "This is no time for tears, my lady. Every moment lost brings greater peril. Go swiftly!"

Liu Bei straightened, bowing low from horseback. "Then I ride as Heaven wills it. Until we meet again."

He cracked the reins, and the horse galloped into the breaking dawn.

CHAPTER 9

THE FIERCE MAN OF YAN

~

United as one, Liu Bei and Lady Lotus raced northward through the cool morning air, swift as a gale. Lady Lotus, braving her shyness, wrapped her arms tightly around Liu Bei's waist. Driven by the fear that they might again encounter Yellow Turbans, Liu Bei pushed the horse to its limits.

Halfway through the two and a half mile journey, a noise suddenly arose behind them. Liu Bei glanced back—and saw five riders charging toward them at breakneck speed. They wore yellow scarves around their heads.

There was no mistake—Yellow Turbans were on their trail.

"They're chasing us!" screamed Lady Lotus in a terrified voice.

Liu Bei drove the horse hard, but with two riders its

speed faltered. No matter how fiercely he lashed the reins, the pursuers gained with every stride.

If we can just reach the government troops ahead... he told himself, pushing the horse onward. But the gap kept shrinking.

Behind him, Lady Lotus clutched his waist, her trembling hands betraying her fear. Liu Bei forced his voice steady. "Don't be afraid. Once we reach the government troops, it won't matter how fast they come."

He said it to calm her, though in his heart he knew the truth—they might not make it in time.

"They're getting closer! What do we do?" she cried.

"Hold on tight," Liu Bei shouted, "and don't let go!"

He had driven the horse so hard that the fresh branch he used as a whip was already stripped bare and splintered. But he knew they were almost there—beyond the small hill ahead, and at the far edge of the plain, there would be a river and the camp of the government troops next to it.

As they galloped across the field, the glint of the river appeared in the distance.

"There's the river! Lady Lotus, we're almost there!"

But alas, the Yellow Turbans were only a few dozen paces behind and shouting loudly. "You there! If you want to live, stop right now!"

Liu Bei pushed the horse with every last ounce of strength toward the river.

At last, after relentlessly racing the horse, they reached the riverbank, hearts pounding with hope and anticipation. The early morning mist curled lazily over the water's surface, but the place where the army was meant to stand was eerily silent—no banners fluttered, no sentries paced, no soldiers waited in formation.

Liu Bei's face paled as the weight of their absence sank in. "No! This can't be!" he cried, the words ripping from his throat like a desperate plea.

The Yellow Turbans soon caught up, closing in on both sides like lightning. An iron rod came crashing down, felling the horse instantly. Liu Bei and Lady Lotus were thrown to the ground.

She lay unconscious, but Liu Bei leapt to his feet and roared, his voice shaking the air:

"You bastards! Why torment innocent people?"

The sheer force of it made the rebels hesitate, faces blanching as they staggered back. But in the next heartbeat, they surged forward again.

"You filthy dog! How dare you speak so boldly here?"

Liu Bei set his jaw. If death was certain, he would not meet it quietly—he would drag at least one of them down with him.

He burned with regret over his empty hands—his sword, his only defense, had been stripped from him by Ma Yuan-yi, leaving him utterly powerless in the face of danger. But like the old saying goes, if he had no teeth, he would fight with his gums.

Liu Bei snatched up a rock at his feet and hurled it at an oncoming enemy's head.

"Agh!" the Yellow Turban screamed and collapsed. Seizing the chance, Liu Bei grabbed the fallen man's spear and shouted:

"You villainous thieves who bring chaos to the world— Liu Bei will not let you live!"

Watching from atop a horse, Li Zhufan sneered. "Ha! This peasant thinks he's something special. Want to taste my spear?"

Li Zhufan leaped down like a flash and charged with his weapon.

Liu Bei was not famed for his swordplay, but the force of his conviction—the roar of a man fighting for more than himself—drove Li Zhufan back a step.

Their weapons clashed, steel ringing and sparks leaping with every blow. At first the duel seemed evenly matched, neither man giving ground. But as the minutes dragged on, Liu Bei's strength began to ebb—his breath coming heavy, his movements slowing.

Li Zhufan's men had stood back at first, smirking in confidence that their leader would end it swiftly and unwilling to wound his pride. Yet as they watched Liu Bei endure, their amusement turned to unease. Realizing he would not fall so easily, they began to press forward, their hesitation hardening into menace as they closed in from all sides.

Outnumbered and utterly exhausted, Liu Bei dropped his weapon. Li Zhufan lunged in like a thunderbolt. Barely dodging the attack and stumbling backward, Liu Bei fell onto the sandy ground. Li Zhufan's spear came thrusting toward his chest—just as a cloud of dust exploded in the distance.

It was then that a man charged in on horseback, whip flying in the air. In the blink of an eye, the rider was upon them. A thunderous voice boomed: "Enough!"

The Yellow Turbans turned toward the voice in shock.

"Who is that?!"

It wasn't Ma Yuan-yi. The man on the horse was tall and broad and had a thick black beard.

"Zhang Fei?! What are you doing here?!" they shouted in disbelief.

The man who had roared while galloping forward was none other than Zhang Fei, who had entered the Yellow Turban stronghold just a few days ago.

Li Zhufan's men tried to stop him, but Zhang Fei ignored them. He fixed his glare on Li Zhufan, who had Liu Bei pinned.

"Hand that man over to me," Zhang Fei said coldly.

"Are you mad?! Do you know where you are? How dare you bark orders?" Li Zhufan shouted in rage.

But Zhang Fei answered firmly, "That was an order. What are you going to do about it?"

"You bastard!" Li Zhufan, now fuming, raised his spear to attack—but in the exact moment, Zhang Fei swatted the spear aside, hoisted him into the air, and slammed him to the ground.

"Agh!" Li Zhufan cried out, writhing in pain.

His subordinates, stunned by the sight, charged at Zhang Fei all at once. "So you're betraying us?! We never forgive traitors!"

Zhang Fei grabbed one attacker by the ankle and swung him like a club.

"Agh! No! Help!" One by one, the Yellow Turbans were knocked down like leaves in the wind.

Zhang Fei's strength was the stuff of battlefield legends —raw, explosive, and terrifying. When he roared, it sounded like thunder, freezing men in place. His arms were thick as pillars, veins bulging with power. He could swing his heavy sword one-handed, though most men couldn't lift it with both. A single blow could cut through shield, armor, and bone. When he charged, he was like a boulder rolling down-hill—unstoppable. Men who dared stand before him were either scattered or sent flying like rag dolls.

Finally catching his breath, Liu Bei brushed the dust off himself and stood up, gazing carefully at Zhang Fei's face. He was a towering man, nearly seven feet tall, with a fierce black beard and piercing eyes. His face was stern and rugged.

"May I ask who you are, sir, that you've come to my aid?" Liu Bei asked respectfully, bowing before Zhang Fei.

Zhang Fei didn't answer the question. Instead, he first walked over to the unconscious Lady Lotus, gently helped her to her feet, and greeted her with utmost courtesy.

"Lady Lotus, you must have been terribly frightened. I am Zhang Fei, once a loyal retainer of your late father. I heard that you were being pursued by the Yellow Turbans and came at once to rescue you."

Upon hearing this, Liu Bei shouted in surprise: "You're a Yellow Turban, and you say you came to rescue Lady Lotus?!"

"You misunderstand," Zhang Fei replied. "You may have mistaken me for one of them, but I am not. I once served the lord of this city. When the Yellow Turbans attacked, they burned the city and killed our lord in cold blood. I only pretended to surrender to them to avenge him. I had to disguise myself as one of them to infiltrate their ranks."

Liu Bei's heart stirred. In a land where allegiance shifted with the winds, here was a man whose loyalty endured even beyond death.

"Hearing your story, I can only say—you're a man of rare honor. Allow me to introduce myself." Liu Bei met Zhang Fei's gaze firmly. "I am Liu Bei Xuande, of Zhuo County in You Province."

Recognition flickered in Zhang Fei's eyes. "Xuande, your reputation precedes you. My name is Zhang Fei, courtesy name Yide, a man from Yan. I owe you thanks for bringing Lady Lotus here safely."

Liu Bei shook his head. "No, Sir Zhang. If not for you, we wouldn't have survived at all. I have to thank *you*. May I ask, how did you know we were in danger and follow us here?"

"Last night, I was among the Yellow Turbans when you were ambushed at the mountain fortress and had your sword and tea case taken. I only learned this morning that you were captured while trying to escape and thrown into a cave. I went there myself to rescue you, but you had already disappeared. I figured the only one who could have saved you was Master Shanhai, so I went to him."

"Master Shanhai? Who is that?"

"The old monk who rescued you last night—his Dharma name is Master Shanhai."

"Ah, so that was his name." A pang of shame struck Liu Bei for not knowing it sooner. Yet now, hearing it, the monk seemed to truly stand apart from ordinary men—just as his mother had once said it. His presence felt more real, and somehow more mysterious at the same time, as though his very name carried the weight of fate.

"*Shanhai... Mountain and Sea...*" Liu Bei murmured, turning the name over in his mind. It was a name fit for someone who had walked endless roads across the world's vastness, seeking sacred wisdom.

"When I found him, he said you were on the run with Lady Lotus but would likely be in danger, so he urged me to go after you right away. I followed—and it seems I arrived just in time. Had I not come, things would have gone badly for you both."

"Indeed... We owe our safety entirely to Master Shanhai and to you, Sir Zhang. I cannot thank you enough." Liu Bei bowed once again.

"I simply did my duty to our late lord," Zhang Fei said, glancing at Lady Lotus.

As if recalling something, Zhang Fei reached into his robes and produced a tea case.

"Here—this belonged to you. I took it back from the Yellow Turbans."

Liu Bei gasped, his heart surging. "Did you really... recover it? This is truly unexpected. Heaven itself could not have shown me greater mercy."

Zhang Fei then unfastened the sword at his waist and offered it as well. "And this—your sword. A blade like this should never rest in their hands."

Ashamed yet grateful, Liu Bei received both treasures with both hands. "We've only just met, yet you've saved my life and returned what I'd thought lost for good. How can I ever repay you?"

"Please, don't speak of debts," Zhang Fei said gruffly. "Master Shanhai spoke often of your virtue. If anything, I should apologize—you suffered greatly today while protecting our Lady Lotus."

Liu Bei nodded. "Then let us speak no more of thanks. If this world is to be righted, the Yellow Turbans must be destroyed. Let us join forces—not only in battle, but in purpose. We share the same vision for the nation, and under one banner we will bring justice to the land."

Zhang Fei firmly nodded and said, "For me, it is also a duty to my fallen lord."

Zhang Fei's words were brusque, but they overflowed with sincerity and earnestness. Not only was his martial prowess remarkable, but his extraordinary loyalty to his lord was deeply inspiring.

If a man is this loyal and sincere, then he's someone I could share life and death with, thought Liu Bei. With this realization, Liu Bei held out the sword he had just received back toward Zhang Fei and said:

"Master Zhang, in gratitude for today's kindness, I would like to offer you this sword as a token. Please accept it. I believe this blade is far more fitting in the hands of a hero like you."

Startled by the offer, Zhang Fei asked, "You would give this sword to me?"

"Yes. It is a token of my sincerity—please, don't refuse it."

Zhang Fei frowned. "At a glance I knew this was no common blade. Surely it is an heirloom. Why would you give it to me?"

"It is a treasure, yes," Liu Bei said, "but what possession is too precious for the man who saved my life? More than that—I feel I have found a true friend in you. That alone is worth the gift."

Zhang Fei hesitated, then accepted the sword with both hands. Strapping it to his waist, he smiled broadly. "Then I will strive to live worthy of this blade."

"Thank you," Liu Bei replied. "Let us work together to bring order to this troubled world."

Zhang Fei's eyes gleamed. "Since we are kindred spirits, fate will surely bring us together again. For now, return home safely. I'll see Lady Lotus to safety, and when the time is right, we'll meet once more."

Liu Bei nodded. "Yes—fate will reunite us. Remember, my home is in Lou Sang Village, Zhuo County."

With a hand pressed to his chest in solemn promise, Zhang Fei turned to Lady Lotus, who had been listening quietly, a faint smile softening her face. "My lady, you've waited long enough. Allow me to escort you now."

He helped her onto the saddle, then swung up behind her. Liu Bei, heavy with regret at parting, mounted the horse Li Zhufan had left behind.

"Until that day, I'll look forward to our reunion," Liu Bei said. "May you and Lady Lotus ride safely."

"Thank you. Farewell—for now."

They waved their hands and rode off in opposite directions. Lady Lotus glanced back over her shoulder, her gaze lingering on Liu Bei—long and wistful—until the road carried them apart. This was the man who had shared danger and life with her, even if briefly. Though custom forbade men and women from close exchanges, and she could not even say a proper farewell, her eyes brimmed with sorrow at their parting. Liu Bei, catching her gaze, felt a deep, indescribable emotion and a stirring pain in his heart.

Never before had he interacted so closely with a woman. He had shared life and death with her for a time. *Would I ever see her again?* he wondered.

A feeling of loss tugged at Liu Bei's heart.

CHAPTER 10

A HERO'S RESOLVE

~

The journey home was brutal. Liu Bei hid in forests and valleys, avoiding bandits and sleeping under tree roots or in hollow logs. His feet were raw with blisters, his clothes torn, and his body ached from exhaustion. He was hungry and afraid. Yet he pressed on, driven by the image of his mother waiting. When he finally caught sight of the pavilion-shaped mulberry branches reaching skyward and the familiar rooftops of Lou Sang Village glowing beneath the setting sun, Liu Bei's knees gave way beneath him. A wave of exhaustion, relief, and disbelief washed over him—he was home at last.

"Mother! Mother! I've returned!"

He stepped through the gate, calling out loudly. But there was no reply from inside. Even Zhu Lan, who was supposed to be attending to his mother, was nowhere to be seen. Liu Bei quickly opened the door to the room, but it too was empty.

Where could they have gone?

He ran outside again, heading toward the back garden. And it was right there, in the small peach orchard, where his mother had built a Seven-Star Altar. She was seated before it, offering purified water and praying for her son's safety.

Seeing her frail back, devoted in prayer, Liu Bei's eyes stung with tears. He stood silently, waiting for her prayer to finish. Then he spoke softly.

"Mother, I've come home."

Startled, the elderly woman turned around. "Oh! My son has finally returned!" She embraced him, her voice trembling with emotion.

"Mother... where is Zhu Lan? Why are you alone?"

"Zhu Lan was taken away...," said Liu Bei's mother in a solemn voice.

She continued her tale of that horrific day. "Zhu Lan had gone to fetch water that morning. The soldiers came without warning—rough men in dusty armor, demanding helpers for the war effort. She screamed and resisted, but they dragged her away before anyone could protest. I begged and pleaded, but... it was no use. Since then, no one has heard a word of her fate. And she was not the only one —many other young women in the village were taken too, vanishing without a trace."

Liu Bei's face darkened. "Oh no... That is horrible! I can't believe that happened to poor Zhu Lan... and to so many others. You must have suffered terribly while I was away. I'm so sorry for returning so late, knowing nothing of this."

"Do not say such a thing. Let's go inside now. Tell me, how was life out on the road?"

"I'm still young—what hardship could truly trouble me? But I'm sorry for the difficulty you endured alone."

Mother and son sat together, warmly reunited. She gazed deeply into his face.

"You've grown so gaunt. Did you at least see the world?"

"Yes, I've learned a lot in many ways. Has anything happened in the village other than...?"

With a deep sigh, the mother continued, "Right after you left, the Yellow Turban rebels came raiding four or five times. They stormed every home, taking whatever valuables they could find. Our village is in ruins now." She frowned and sighed deeply.

"That's just horrible... I never imagined they would reach this remote village..."

Just hearing the name filled Liu Bei with rage and shivers.

"If the world is ever to return to peace, those rebels must be destroyed."

Determined, Liu Bei pulled out a box from his coat. "Mother, I brought you the tea you wanted to try."

"Is this really the tea from Luoyang I told you about?"

"Yes. It's the finest Gong Cha from Luoyang." Liu Bei said proudly.

"Gong Cha? Oh, my dear son. You went out and brought back such a rare gift for me. I am overwhelmed." Overjoyed, she took the tea box with both hands, unsure what to do in her delight.

"Mother, please try it right away."

"How could I taste something so precious without first

offering it to our ancestors?" She took the tea box to the ancestral shrine, placed it on the altar, and conducted a simple offering. Then she returned to the main room.

"Now that our ancestors have been honored, I shall enjoy the taste of this tea." She set a kettle on the brazier.

"If this tea can restore your health, I will ask for nothing more," said Liu Bei, standing to change his clothes.

Her face glowed with pride and joy—then, as if a shadow passed over her, her expression darkened.

"Why... where is the sword you wore when you left?"

"Mother..." Liu Bei said carefully, almost stumbling over his words. "I... I gave it away, to repay a great debt—to a man named Zhang Fei."

"You *gave away* our precious heirloom!?" Her face was flushed with anger.

"Please don't be upset. It's not that I didn't understand its worth. Zhang Fei saved my life. He is a man of great loyalty and righteousness, someone I could walk the same path with for the rest of my life. Someone I will surely meet again. That's why I gave it to him."

Liu Bei earnestly tried to explain, regretful for upsetting his mother. But her ears no longer heard his words. Lips trembling with fury, she suddenly sprang to her feet and grabbed her son's wrist.

"Come outside with me," Liu Bei's mother said sternly.

"Where are we going?"

"Wherever it may be—just follow your mother."

With firm resolve, his mother grabbed Liu Bei's wrist with one hand and picked up the tea container with the other, then marched outside. They walked for a while until they reached the large well at the edge of the village. There, she stopped and turned to him.

"My son," she said, her voice trembling between sorrow and anger, "how could you prize tea above your ancestral sword? Do you not see where your true duty lies? This tea, however fine, is worthless beside the honor of our family."

With that, she hurled the treasured tea container—the very prize Liu Bei had risked his life to bring home—into the well.

Startled, Liu Bei cried out, "Mother! Why are you so angry?" He rushed forward, seizing her hand in alarm.

Still seething, she continued her scolding:

"When I raised you, it wasn't so you could weave straw mats and scrape by in some remote corner of the countryside. As I've told you before, you are a descendant of the imperial family of Han. I, a widowed mother, raised you in hiding in this rural place not just to survive, but because I hoped you would one day revive the fading House of Han.

"And yet you gave away our ancestral sword—a symbol of duty to both family and nation—to a stranger, without even a flicker of shame!"

Tears welled up in Liu Bei's eyes. He bowed his head and begged for forgiveness. "Mother, I was wrong. I'll never do something like that again. Please scold me as harshly as I deserve—punish me if you must."

"I don't want to hear it. What good would punishment do now?" she shouted, her voice unexpectedly powerful for her frail form.

Liu Bei stood in silence, head bowed in shame. After a long pause, he finally spoke in a quiet, steady voice:

"Mother, may I ask just one thing?" After a pause, he

continued, "The sword handed down from our ancestors is indeed precious. But I believe the spirit that the sword represents can only be fully realized when one finds a true comrade who shares their cause. I met such a man, and so, in the desire to share my purpose with him, I gave him the sword as a token of our bond. Was that truly so wrong?"

Liu Bei's mother sat in silence for a time, then spoke at last, her voice low and weighted with thought: "To give away a sword, yet gain a comrade—what meaning do you place in such a trade?"

Liu Bei then explained in detail how he had met Zhang Fei, how the man had saved his life, and the background that led him to offer the sword.

"Mother, just as you've always wished, I have long held the great ambition to bring order to this chaotic world. By chance, I met a man named Zhang Fei who helped me in a moment of great danger. After getting to know him, I strongly felt that he was someone I wanted as a lifelong comrade. That is why I did not hesitate to gift him the ancestral sword, passed down through our family."

Upon hearing his words, the anger that had clouded his mother's face began to soften, slowly giving way to gentleness. The disappointment in her eyes faded, replaced by warmth and understanding. She reached for his hand, clasping it tightly as her voice trembled.

"My son," she whispered, "even I know—it is rarer to find a man of true virtue than to win a thousand battles. If such a person crossed your path and moved you so deeply that you gave away your most precious possession, then surely you did what was right. I should not have scolded you. With your heart, you have already brought honor to our family. It was rash of me to react in anger."

As her hand rested on his shoulder and her words sank in, Liu Bei's breath caught. Overwhelmed, he bowed his head, and silent tears fell—tears of tension, worry, disappointment, and the relief of being finally understood—all of it sweeping through him at once like a whirlwind.

Liu Bei gazed into the well, where the once-prized tea container lay shattered, its scattered leaves drifting like lost memories. For a long moment he said nothing—still burdened with frustration of being misunderstood, yet at the same time lighter, as though a great weight had finally lifted. All the tangled emotions within him whirled together, then slowly dissolved, leaving behind some clarity.

The journey, the hardship, the loneliness he had endured—it had never truly been about tea. His mother had not sent him away for the taste of a rare tribute. She had wanted her son to step beyond the borders of a quiet village, to walk through chaos and cruelty, and to return with vision. She had not sought treasure for herself, but awakening for her son.

As the sun dipped low behind the rooftop of his childhood home, Liu Bei stood in silence, the wind brushing past like a gentle hand, as if to comfort him. He was no longer just a boy from Lou Sang Village dreaming of a greater world. He had walked its roads, endured its cruelties, and witnessed its fleeting kindness—the suffering, greed, and betrayal, but also the warmth, loyalty, and hope. The village was too small to hold him now; beyond it stretched a world that would test, shape, and remember his name.

CHAPTER II
A FLICKER OF HOPE

~

Years passed as the empire slid deeper into decline. The Yellow Turbans, once scattered and desperate, now plundered villages in broad daylight, unopposed.

In Luoyang's Forbidden Palace, corruption festered like cancer in the empire's marrow. The Ten Eunuchs—castrated courtiers who had clawed to the Emperor's ear—clutched the realm's throat in perfumed, jeweled fingers. Zhang Rang, their leader, sat like a spider in a web of silk and gold, his soft hands counting tribute that should have fed the starving. "Ten thousand gold for a prefecture," he whispered to men crawling at his door. "Twenty thousand for a commandery. Pay well, and even the barbarian lands beyond the Wall can be yours to plunder."

Incense thickened the palace air, masking the stench of decay. Eunuchs drifted like ghosts in stolen silk, their shrill laughter echoing down halls where emperors once issued noble decrees.

What rotted at the empire's heart spread through every province. Men who purchased office descended like vultures, seeking only to recoup their "investment." Mansions rose on land meant for orphaned children, built with stolen relief funds.

"Tax collection" became the empire's cruelest joke. Grain was demanded in silver; salt taxes collected on imaginary salt; "administrative fees" multiplied endlessly. Collectors were thugs in bureaucrat's garb—clubs speaking louder than the forged seals they carried.

Scattered like stars in a storm-dark sky, a few honest officials remained, but their reports vanished into palace archives. They watched in anguish as corruption smothered the realm.

From palace to village, the Han devoured itself like a serpent swallowing its tail. Each stolen coin weakened the army. Each purchased rank placed a fool where a wise man should stand. Each forgery hollowed the law. Four centuries of strength bled away through ten thousand small cuts, while barbarians gathered at the borders and disasters struck the land.

The virtuous sighed in despair as the great Han slid toward ruin.

Liu Bei's hometown was no exception. Returning from the market and preparing for yet another journey, he noticed a figure beneath the old mulberry tree. There, under its gnarled trunk, sat a teenage girl in a torn hemp dress, her face streaked with tears.

"Pardon me, what troubles you?" Liu Bei asked gently as he stepped closer.

The girl lifted her head, eyes red and swollen. "Master Liu... they took everything," she said, her voice breaking.

Liu Bei knelt beside her, heart heavy. "Who did? Tell me."

"The tax collectors," she whispered, clutching a torn piece of silk. "They said we sold without permits. Called us thieves. They smashed the looms, seized the silkworms, and..." Her words dissolved into sobs.

Recognition lit Liu Bei's face. "You're Shao Mei, from the silk farm, aren't you?"

She nodded through tears, but her eyes shone with admiration as she looked up at him. In truth, she had hoped he might appear beneath the mulberry tree that day. Softly she asked, "Do you remember me?"

"How could I forget?" Liu Bei replied with warmth. "Your parents tended this tree..."

Liu Bei's thoughts drifted back to that hopeful spring day.

"Honored Lady Liu," the weathered man from the neighborhood had said, bowing deeply to Liu Bei's mother.

"We've heard of your family's kindness. Our children are hungry, and we've learned the art of silk cultivation. Might we tend to your mulberry trees and raise silkworms? We would share the profits fairly."

His mother had paused, and said. "This tree has stood here for three generations. Do you see how its roots run deep and its branches spread wide?"

"Yes, honored lady."

"This tree belongs not just to us, but to our entire village. Every spring, children climb its branches. Every summer, its shade shelters the elderly. In autumn, its fruit feeds whoever is hungry. It has given endlessly, asking nothing in return." She smiled warmly. *"If you wish to use its leaves for your silkworms, I ask only this—be thankful for its generosity, treat it gently, and ensure it continues to thrive so future generations may also benefit from its gifts."*

The man's eyes had filled with tears of gratitude. "Lady Liu, I swear on my ancestors' graves—we will care for this tree as if it were our own family. We will take only what we need, never more than it can spare."

"And you will teach your children the same?"

"They will learn to bow to this tree each morning, to thank it for its sacrifice, and to tend its soil as lovingly as they tend their own gardens."

"Your family kept that promise," Liu Bei said softly. "I remember your brother collecting only the fallen leaves, and your mother whispering prayers before each harvest."

"We were happy then," Shao Mei sobbed. "For a few years we ate well. The tree grew greener, stronger. My parents worked so hard..."

"What exactly did these tax collectors say?"

Her voice turned bitter. "They claimed we needed a permit from the prefecture—fifty silver for the license, twenty more in 'back taxes.' When Father reminded them we cared for your family's tree with permission, they laughed."

Her voice wavered, but she swallowed her sob. "I came here because I didn't know where else to go. I thought I might find peace under this tree. And..." she whispered, "I hoped I might see you here."

Liu Bei studied her more closely. Her eyes lingered on him, as if he were a beacon in the chaos—someone who might be able to steady her world. His face softened despite the anger boiling inside. He lifted his gaze to the mulberry branches, where late light filtered through like blessings from the past.

"This tree has stood here longer than us all. It gives shade, leaves, and strength, asking for nothing but care in return. And it still stands. As long as you breathe, you can begin again. Never give up. No matter what they take, they cannot take your will."

Then, almost like a blessing, he added: "Be grateful for what remains. The roots are still here. So start again."

Shao Mei wiped her cheeks and sat a little straighter. A faint smile touched her lips, and when she looked at Liu Bei, it was with quiet longing, a flicker of hope in her eyes. His few kind words had planted that seed within her—proof of the rare power he carried, to move hearts and kindle hope in desperate times. To her, he seemed larger than life, someone she could both admire and quietly long for, though she knew those feelings were hers alone.

CHAPTER 12

THE IMMORTAL OF HEDONG

~

One warm spring day, a tall man with a long beard sat alone on the sunlit veranda, white-feather fan in hand. The hills beyond were painted with peach and apricot blossoms, yet the world had not changed. Only the night before, Yellow Turban bandits had raided a nearby village, leaving it in ruin.

Spring had come to the land, but not to the hearts of the people. While nature bloomed, the common folk sank deeper into fear and misery.

The man sat in silence, slowly waving his fan, his thoughts churning. To be born a man, to study the wisdom of sages and master the art of war, only to sit idle while the realm collapsed? He could not endure it.

"If only there were allies who shared my heart for this troubled land," he muttered.

For years, he had resolved to act. Yet alone, what could

106

he achieve? He had long hoped to find a kindred spirit, but none had appeared. With a deep sigh he murmured, "The world is full of people... and yet, how rare to find the right one."

Still, he knew—in times of great crisis, heroes arise. Suddenly, he slapped his knee and stood. "Of course! One cannot wait for destiny to arrive."

"Boy! Where are you?" he called.

His young servant came running. "Yes, sir?"

"I'm riding out. Ready my horse—and bring the Green Dragon Crescent Blade."

The boy dashed off and quickly returned with the massive weapon, eight feet long and weighing forty pounds, a blade fit for a general. The man strapped it to his side, his bearing transformed. He looked every inch the warrior of legend.

He set out for Zhuo County, only a few miles from home, yet far enough to glimpse a world beyond his own. Perhaps there he would find something different—perhaps even the companion his heart longed for.

His horse waited. In one fluid motion, he mounted. A crack of the whip—and the steed leapt forward like lightning. Dust rose in clouds behind them, and in an instant, horse and rider vanished from sight.

Bold as thunder, the charge was unstoppable. Three miles passed in a blink. Cresting a hill overlooking Zhuo County, he pulled the reins. The dust settled, revealing the man's commanding figure atop his horse, green battle robe fluttering, eyes fixed on the horizon.

"...Who are those people?" he murmured, narrowing his gaze.

To most, the land seemed empty. But the man's hawk-like eyes caught faint movement in the distance—and, drifting on the wind, the echo of shouts and clashing steel.

He spurred his horse forward, branches whipping past as he tore through a forest path. The trees opened onto a wide field—where battle raged.

One man stood alone.

A towering warrior, black-bearded and broad-shoul-dered, fought against a swarm of Yellow Turban rebels. They circled him like wolves, but he was no prey. He was a storm.

The earth was littered with corpses—two dozen men already slain—yet he fought on, fierce and unyielding. With each swing he crushed bones, hurled men into the air, and scattered foes like straw. Terror spread through the rebels. One by one, they faltered—then broke, fleeing in a panic.

"Cowards! You think you can run?"

His roar split the sky. He charged, seized two men by the collar, and slammed them to the ground like sacks of grain.

From a distance, the man watched, heart pounding—not with fear, but with joy. *At last... a man worthy of being called a warrior.*

When the last Yellow Turbans had fled, the black-bearded giant stood tall, scarcely winded. Dusting off his sleeves, he turned to leave.

He dismounted and approached, his voice warm yet dignified.

"I don't know who you are, good sir, but that was the finest battle I've seen in years. No doubt those Yellow Turban dogs will think twice before returning."

The warrior gave him a long, measuring look. Then, in a gruff voice, asked, "And who are you?"

"My name is Guan Yu," the man said proudly. "From Heliang Village in Hedong—courtesy name, Yunchang. Like you, I seek to rid the land of these rebels and restore peace. If we share that goal, then let us at least know each other's names."

At the sound of his name, the broad-shouldered warrior's stern face broke into a grin. He bowed slightly. "So you are Guan Yunchang! I have heard your name many times. I meant to seek you out myself. Fortune has brought us together. I am Zhang Fei—style name, Yide."

Guan Yu's brows rose. "You were coming to find me? How so?"

Zhang Fei laughed, his booming voice carrying across the field. "I've searched everywhere for men of valor. They told me in Hedong lived a man of might and virtue—Guan Yunchang. I resolved to find you. Now, seeing you in person, I know they spoke true. You have the bearing of a hero."

Guan Yu smiled, his heart stirred. "Your words are as welcome as rain after drought. I too have been seeking worthy companions. And you, Zhang Fei—you are such a man. Let us join forces."

"Agreed!" Zhang Fei clapped his hands. "Then what say we head into town and seal our bond over a jug of wine?"

Rough around the edges though he seemed, Zhang Fei was a man of unshakable loyalty and disarming honesty. Guan Yu could sense it instantly.

"Nothing would please me more," he said. "How could I refuse wine shared with a brother-in-arms?"

The two men sat together on a worn wooden bench in the tavern. One was broad-shouldered and fierce, his face flushed, still carrying the fire of battle in his eyes. The other sat tall and composed, noble in bearing, his long black beard flowing like a dark river stirred by the breeze. Side by side, Zhang Fei's raw might and Guan Yu's grave dignity made them appear less like ordinary men than legends from battlefields.

Guan Yu raised his cup with a smile.

"Thanks to you, Brother Zhang, I've had the pleasure of witnessing a truly satisfying sight. It's been a long time since something stirred my heart like that."

Zhang Fei emptied the cup in one gulp and let out a booming laugh, his face flushed with warmth and wine.

"And I've never felt more alive! Watching those Yellow Turban dogs scatter like rats—it cleared the gloom from my chest. But more than that... meeting you, Brother Guan— that's the real blessing."

Guan Yu turned, brow arched, voice laced with amusement.

"Zhang Fei," he said, sipping slowly from his wine cup, "I knew you were fierce with a spear, but who knew you drank like a whale? Now tell me—how did you end up brawling with the Yellow Turbans today?"

Zhang Fei let out a low laugh, "Let me tell you some-thing, brother." He wiped his mouth with the back of his hand and leaned in, eyes gleaming.

"I'm a butcher now—but I wasn't always chasing pigs in these hills. I was once a commander, leading brave men, serving a worthy lord. Then the Yellow Turban rats stormed the county. They cut down our noble magistrate like he was nothing, and I barely escaped with my life."

He looked away, jaw tight, the firelight dancing in his dark eyes.

"Tried to rally the old troops. Cowards, all of them. Vanished like ghosts. I was alone. Furious. Powerless."

His voice cracked slightly, eyes clouding with old anger. "So one day... I gave up. Just like that. Wandered into the forest, bottle in hand. Nothing left in me. No hope. Not even rage... I didn't care if I came back. Didn't want to."

He drew a long breath, his tone hollow. "I stumbled for hours, drunk and empty. I lay down on the ground and let the bottle slip from my hand. I remember thinking—this is it. No one will even know. I will be forgotten..."

He paused. A strange light flickered in his eyes.

"And at that moment," Zhang Fei said, eyes gleaming with the memory, "wouldn't you know it—a wild boar the size of a damn horse burst out of the brush."

He paused, letting the image settle.

"I just stood there and thought, *So this is how I go.* But something happened—right there, heart pounding, death charging straight at me—I *roared*. Not in fear, but something primal."

He tapped his chest with a fist. "Maybe it was the wine. Or the madness. Or maybe... I realized I wanted to live. Desperately. I *had* to live. Even through the haze of drink, instinct took over. My body moved before thought could form."

He paused, poured another cup, and downed it in a single gulp. "I grabbed the sword," he went on. "Not just any sword—the old blade I've carried every day since it was entrusted to me. My hand found it on its own, as if it had been waiting for that very moment."

He mimed the motion—drawing it from his side, fast and fluid.

"And I charged back at that beast like I'd been *reborn*—*blade* slashing. Bones cracking. I don't remember all of it—just flashes. Blood. Screaming. Rage."

His voice swelled with awe.

"When I woke, the forest *reeked* of death. A dozen boars, all slaughtered. And me, lying in the middle like some demon out of a fireside tale."

Guan Yu blinked, stunned, unsure whether to speak or not. Zhang Fei smiled faintly, his tone softening into something almost reverent.

"And in that moment, lying in that blood-soaked earth, I knew why I was still breathing. I remembered the starving faces in the village. Hollow eyes. Children too weak to cry. So I dragged the carcasses back. Built a fire. Roasted every last one. Handed out meat till the sun came up."

His eyes burned with renewed life.

"They came back the next day. And the next. So I set up a stall—roasted boar, hot and cheap! Soon the air was thick with smoke and laughter. Coins poured in faster than I could count, but that wasn't the real reward. I shared food with those willing to lend a hand, gave work to the jobless, and helped the most desperate start over. People filled their bellies, found purpose again—and in giving them life, I found my own."

He sighed, leaning back with a satisfied groan.

"But of course, word spread. And where there's silver, the tax men came sniffing first. Bogus officials, all of them—I tossed them a share just to keep the stall running. But the real trouble was the Yellow Turban scum. They came next, sniffing around like rats. Thought I was just some fat merchant to push around. Ha! I showed them what happens when you corner a drunken butcher who knew how to swing a general's sword."

He slammed his empty cup down and looked Guan Yu dead in the eye.

"I didn't just fight them. I tore through them like fire through dry grass. They'll think twice before touching another coin of mine."

Guan Yu smiled slowly, impressed. "So," he said, "you turned pig fights and boar roasts into a war campaign. Remind me never to underestimate your... strategy again."

Zhang Fei let out a booming laugh at Guan Yu's remark, then wiped his mouth and set the cup down with a heavy thud. "Strategy? No, brother. That's just survival—with a little wine and fire in the belly."

His grin lingered for a moment... then slowly faded. His voice dropped, quieter now. "But you're right."

He looked out toward the darkened hills, where smoke from the village fires curled into the darkening sky. "I never forgot what I was meant to do."

He clenched his calloused fist on his knee. His gaze met Guan Yu's, sharp and unshakable.

"I didn't survive to sell meat and die fat and comfortable. That was never the plan. I played the fool. Now, I remind them who Zhang Fei really is."

As the sun dipped low and the sky turned gold, they drank deeply, their voices rising and falling with talk of war, justice, and a world buckling under corruption.

Then, without a sound, a figure emerged—slowly, almost ghostlike—from the shadowed room beyond. The firelight caught her just enough to reveal the edge of a faded sleeve, the glint of a clay jug cradled in her arms.

She moved with the silence of someone long practiced in not drawing attention. Her steps were light, but not graceful—more like someone trying not to wake a sleeping beast.

She reached their table and lowered the jug with careful, practiced hands, followed by a chipped plate of dried fish scraps. Her threadbare clothes clung to a frame worn thin by labor, her fingers rough and reddened from years of scalding water and splintered wood.

"Thank you, ma'am," Guan Yu said, inclining his head respectfully. Then he glanced behind her—and paused.

In the far corner of the room, three skinny children huddled around a single wooden bowl of rice, taking turns with careful fingers. They did not speak. One of them glanced up at Guan Yu, then quickly looked away.

"Are they yours?" Guan Yu asked gently.

The woman hesitated, then gave a slight nod.

He studied her face—a face weathered by hardship—and his voice softened further.

"Where is their father?"

She did not answer at first. Her gaze fell to the floor, and when she finally spoke, her voice was scarcely louder than a breath.

"He left months ago," she said quietly.

"May I ask why?" asked Guan Yu in a gentle voice.

"We could hardly make ends meet, just scraping by selling millet wine. One night, a few drunkards accused him of watering it down. A terrible fight broke out."

At first her words were flat, almost routine. Then she faltered, her voice tightening. "But I—I didn't do it... I mean, people said everyone else was watering theirs, but... that's not the point." Her tone had grown sharp, defensive, as though she suddenly regretted revealing too much.

She looked away, lowering her voice again. "Anyway, he was badly hurt and humiliated. One morning, he stood up and said he would join the rebellion—to punish the bad guys, and bring back silver and grain..."

Her mouth twisted, and she blinked rapidly. "He promised he'd return before the first frost. But the snow came and went. We've heard nothing since."

For a moment, there was only silence. Zhang Fei stared into his cup, and Guan Yu lowered his eyes. At last, Guan Yu spoke, not to her, but almost to the air:

"This is what becomes of a broken land. Men vanish into flames, and families are left with ash."

The woman bowed once and quickly returned to the backroom where the children were. Guan Yu leaned back, his gaze fixed on the horizon where the last threads of sunlight tangled in the trees. His voice was calm, deliberate.

"Zhang Fei... you are strong. Raw, untamed strength. A storm in the shape of a man. When your heart is aflame, no gate can hold, no army can stand."

Zhang Fei grunted, but there was a flicker of pride in his eyes.

"And I," Guan Yu continued, tapping his chest, "I am patient. Discipline. I strike only when the time is right. Between the two of us, we are force and precision."

Zhang Fei raised a brow, unsure where this was going.

"But force and precision... they are not enough." Guan Yu's voice dropped a tone. "We lack vision."

Zhang Fei frowned. "Vision? Speak plainly, brother."

Guan Yu turned to him now, eyes steady.

"We fight well. We hold to honor. But we do not ignite the fire in people. We may not truly inspire people to follow, not in the way we think a leader should. They fear your rage. They respect my blade. But they do not dream and believe *they* can do something when they look at us."

He paused, letting the weight of that truth settle.

"We need someone who can light the fire in others. Someone who sees what lies beyond battlefields. Who can gather men not just through strength, but belief."

Zhang Fei's jaw tightened. He poured another cup, but didn't drink.

"We swore to restore this land," Guan Yu went on. "To tear the rot from its roots. That will take more than two blades. It will take a banner. A voice people can rally behind."

He looked into Zhang Fei's eyes. "We need a third. Not just a fighter. A leader."

There was a long silence—only the crackle of fire and the distant hoot of an owl. Then Zhang Fei leaned in.

"There's one man I met—just once, by chance. But I remember him. Name of Liu Bei. Style name Xuande. Wore the bearing of someone born to lead. Wove straw mats and sandals for a living, believe it or not."

Guan Yu's interest sharpened. "And where is he from?"

"They say he's of imperial blood. He lives in Zhuo County now," Zhang Fei paused, as if searching for the right words.

"There was something about him... the way he stood, the way he spoke—calm, but unshakable. You could tell he was someone destined to lead, someone with *purpose* and what you would call... *vision.*"

Zhang Fei leaned forward even closer, tapping his cup with a callused finger.

"When I met him, he had nothing. No title, no land, not even decent shoes on his feet."

He straightened again, eyes fixed on Guan Yu. Guan Yu said nothing at first, but his heart stirred. A man of royal lineage who lived among the people and burned with righteous purpose—such a figure could rally hearts, draw followers, give their cause a name. Still, Guan Yu spoke with care.

"Brother Zhang, if he impressed you so... seek him out again. Find this Liu Bei. Speak with him."

Zhang Fei nodded. "I only know that he lives nearby. But if he's still weaving mats, I'll find him."

Guan Yu refilled their cups one last time. "To Liu Bei, then. May fate guide our steps."

The two men drank, their minds already leaning toward the unknown future. And then suddenly, Zhang Fei paused mid-sip, smacked his lips, and frowned.

"Wait a minute," he muttered, peering into his cup. "This wine *is* watered down!"

Guan Yu glanced at him and gave a subtle shake of the head, a quiet gesture that said, *Let it be. We have bigger battles to fight.*

Zhang Fei grumbled, but said no more. Outside, the sun hung low on the horizon, casting long shadows over the tiled rooftops and weathered wooden eaves.

Guan Yu said, "It's getting late. Let us part here for today, but I hope we'll meet again very soon. I'm always at home—you'd honor me if you came by tomorrow."

Zhang Fei's smile faded. His eyes narrowed with sudden frustration.

"What's this now?" he barked. "You spoke of joining forces to accomplish great things—now you're saying we should *part* like casual drinking companions?"

"Brother Zhang, your temper flares quickly, doesn't it?" Guan Yu chuckled softly.

"Let's just go find out Liu Bei's home right now!" Zhang Fei continued to grumble.

Guan Yu laughed and strode toward his steed, who stood waiting just beyond the gate, his tall frame silhouetted in the amber light. The horse shifted his weight but did not stir, his breath rising in quiet plumes into the evening air. His coat, still flecked with dust from the road, shimmered like lacquered flame.

Guan Yu ran a hand along the animal's strong neck and said with a half-smile, "This fellow's worn out. I'll need to find him a good place to stretch those legs."

The horse flicked his ears, as if in agreement, and remained still—patient and loyal.

"We've got work ahead," Guan Yu murmured. "Tomorrow, we ride with purpose. Tonight—we rest."

CHAPTER 13

THE THREE BROTHERS

~

Zhang Fei stood frozen, his boots rooted to the earth as he watched the figure of Guan Yu on the horse gallop into the distance, his cloak snapping like a banner in the wind. For a long while, Zhang Fei stood still— his eyes fixed on the retreating silhouette.

And then, almost under his breath, he muttered, "At last... a man worth calling brother. Just by his bearing... I could follow a man like that into the flames. He's no ordinary fighter. He's someone a kingdom could be built beside."

Still caught in thought, Zhang Fei ambled toward the town. The wine still clung to him—slowing his steps, adding a swagger to his walk. As he entered the heart of the market square, the last traces of sunlight bled from the sky, leaving a bruised purple haze overhead. Lanterns flickered to life along shuttered stalls, their glow casting long, uneasy shadows across the cobblestones.

A curious sound—a hush, broken by the occasional murmur—drew his attention. A dozen or so townspeople stood gathered near the old shrine wall, their faces turned upward, bathed in the soft orange light of swaying lanterns. Eyes were fixed on something posted high above.

"Huh? What's got everyone standing around like statues?" Zhang Fei lumbered forward, the weight of his boots echoing faintly on the stone, and gently shouldered his way through the cluster of villagers.

Nailed to the wind-worn plaster beneath the shadow of the tiled eaves, a great proclamation scroll shivered in the evening breeze. The parchment caught the lamplight with a dull sheen, while its bold black strokes—slashed across the page like blades—seemed to scream at him, fierce and unyielding.

The townsfolk whispered, their voices hushed as if in the presence of something sacred—or dangerous. Zhang Fei's eyes locked on the scroll. He squinted against the dimming light, his lips moving slowly as he began to read.

To THE PEOPLE of the Realm:

It is a truth known throughout the land that the Yellow Turban rebels have grown ever more brazen in their depredations. Even our peaceful Zhuo County, once a haven of tranquility, now suffers daily under its mounting outrages, while the common folk struggle deeper into misery with each passing day.

Therefore, I hereby issue this call for righteous volunteers to join our cause—to eradicate these Yellow Turban bandits utterly, *restore the proper order of our nation, and relieve the people from their present torment. Let all patriots hidden away in field and forest take my words to heart and answer this summons to arms!*

P.S. Write down your name to volunteer.

— *Liu Yan, Governor of Youzhou*

Seeking soldiers to fight the Yellow Turban rebellion

"Liu... Yan...? Hmm... at last, someone's finally coming to their senses," Zhang Fei muttered to himself as he read the proclamation from afar.

But as the curious onlookers finished reading, they merely clicked their tongues, shook their heads, and drifted away one by one. Though everyone knew well enough that the Yellow Turbans had to be destroyed before peace could return, when it came to their own precious lives, none seemed willing to answer the call to arms.

Zhang Fei crouched behind a low wall, hoping someone would step forward to enlist.

The crowd receded, and finally, only a single man remained, standing motionless before the notice, gazing up at it as if he was frozen in time.

Zhang Fei found himself quietly impressed. *This fellow... he's got some guts,* he thought. But that flicker of admiration quickly turned to irritation. The man remained motionless at the gate, staring at the notice. Zhang Fei lost patience.

"That damned fool! If you're going to volunteer, then write down your name and volunteer already! Why dawdle like some lost child?"

He stood there, trembling with rage. And then... the man finally turned—and began to walk away. That was it.

Zhang Fei's anger exploded.

"YOU CURSED COWARD!" he roared, his voice booming like thunder rolling down a mountainside. "You looked at that posting for so long, and still turned away?!"

Before the man could take another step, Zhang Fei shot forward like lightning, grabbed him by the scruff of the neck, and hurled him through the air as if he weighed nothing at all. An ordinary man would have died on impact, but he floated down and landed upright, calm and composed. Straightening his robe, he looked back at Zhang Fei and spoke, his voice calm and almost disarmingly gentle.

"Who are you to lay violent hands on a man who has done you no wrong?"

That unshaken poise struck Zhang Fei like a slap. His rage flickered for a moment—but pride flared right back up. No one dared to challenge *him*, especially not with such self-assured calm. He took a threatening step forward.

"You dare talk back to *me*? Do you even know who I am?!"

"If I have offended you," the man replied, still unshaken, "then I ask your forgiveness. But you will have to explain to me first why you're angry."

His humble tone, so devoid of fear or mockery, left Zhang Fei momentarily at a loss. Still, he was too furious to calm down,

"You were *right there*, reading that notice! I saw you with my own eyes! You're the only one here!"

The man answered, unbothered: "Yes. I read it."

Zhang Fei burst out again, voice raw with disbelief.

"And after reading that call for volunteers, you just

turned away, like it meant *nothing* to you?! What kind of man does that?!"

The man blinked slowly, unfazed.

"Explain plainly what you're trying to say." The man offered nothing, all the while staring intently at Zhang Fei's face—as if studying it for a clue.

Zhang Fei, however, remained utterly indifferent to the scrutiny. His tone still sharp, he barked:

"The empire is falling apart because of those damned Yellow Turbans, and you—young, able-bodied—just read the call for volunteers and *walk away*? Who do you think is going to save this country if cowards like you keep turning tail?!"

The man's gaze sharpened, his eyes narrowing as he squinted into the flickering lamplight, struggling to see clearly through the growing darkness. And yet—oddly—as Zhang Fei raged louder, the stranger's expression grew more focused and intense.

"Why are you just *staring* at me like that? Have I got shit on my face or something?!" Zhang Fei flared up again, fists clenched and voice thundering.

But then, the man's face lit up bright as the first full moon of the new year. His eyes widened, and without warning, he opened his arms and stepped forward.

"By the heavens... it *is* you! You are Lord Zhang Fei, are you not? I am Liu Bei—Xuande—whose life you once saved. I've often wondered what became of you... and to finally meet again like this...!"

Zhang Fei froze. His eyebrows shot up in surprise.

"Wait... You're... Liu Bei?!"

He squinted hard at the man's face. It *had* been nearly

four or five years since they last met—and much had changed. The features had matured. The clothes were modest. But those thick, noble earlobes... that dignified, benevolent nose...

It was him.

"Ah... Liu Bei... Forgive me! I didn't recognize you and acted shamefully."

"No need to apologize," Liu Bei replied, smiling warmly. "We've both changed over the years. It's no wonder we didn't recognize each other at once. Tell me—how have you been?"

Zhang Fei looked away slightly, as if ashamed of his own answer.

"As you see... I've been the same. Just... living and breathing."

"And the plan?" Liu Bei leaned forward. "You once spoke of leading Lady Lotus into safety and crushing the Yellow Turbans. What became of that?"

Zhang Fei gave a weary, half-hearted chuckle.

"My resolve hasn't wavered an inch," he said, his voice rough with dust and memory. "But I've come to under-stand... this fight can't be won by one man alone." His words were edged with disappointment and lost hopes.

Liu Bei hesitated. He wanted to ask—*How about Lady Lotus? Where is she now?*—but before the words could form, Zhang Fei quickly shifted the focus to Liu Bei, as if he'd already heard the question and wanted to avoid it.

"And you, Lord Liu Bei—how have you been?"

"I am the same as well. Still living in Lou Sang Village with my aged mother," Liu Bei answered quietly. "Making ends meet, weaving straw mats, same as before."

Liu Bei was no longer merely the man of Lou Sang Village. He had already begun planning a long journey beyond its borders. But for now, he kept those thoughts to himself.

But even as he spoke, his thoughts lingered on Lady Lotus—her name hanging unspoken between them like mist on a mountain path, her fate unanswered, hidden just out of reach. Then, Zhang Fei said with sudden excitement, "Come. Let's go to the tavern and catch up over some wine!"

Soon, they were back at the tavern—where barely an hour ago Zhang Fei and Guan Yu had shared drinks and resolutions. But now, night had settled in. The stars blinked faintly above, half-veiled by drifting smoke from cooking fires, and the tavern's lanterns cast a soft, amber glow over the worn wooden tables outside.

A pair of loud merchants sat at one of them, already deep into their cups, their loud but tired voices echoing down the otherwise quiet street. The door to the back room was shut tight; there was no sign of the children. But the woman was still there—moving silently between tables like her day's work was far from over.

She looked up as they approached, brushing a loose strand of hair behind her ear. Her eyes widened with recognition.

"Masters—please, come sit," she said quickly, gesturing toward a freshly wiped table near the lantern's edge. "This one's clean, I made sure of it." Her voice carried the practiced brightness of someone used to pushing through exhaustion.

"I'll bring some millet wine... yes, sir?" she added, eyes

flicking toward Zhang Fei with a hint of a smile, seeking his approval.

Zhang Fei nodded towards the woman and broke the silence, "Lord Liu, you saw the proclamation today, didn't you? What feelings did it stir in you when you saw it?"

Liu Bei continued to play innocent. "It was a proclamation recruiting volunteers to suppress the Yellow Turban rebels."

"We all know what it was about, but Lord Liu, I am asking what you were really thinking when you were standing there for so long?"

"I merely kept thinking... how chaotic this world has become," Liu Bei said quietly, his eyes lowered.

At those words, a flicker of disappointment crossed Zhang Fei's face. Without caring who might be watching, he let out a long, frustrated sigh.

"Heaven's mercy! Did this fool mistake a cricket for a dragon?" he lamented. His voice cut through the tavern's low murmur. The two merchants at the other table turned sharply, startled by the outburst.

"Lord Zhang," Liu Bei said, frowning, "what do you mean by that? Why are you raising your voice?" Liu Bei glanced around quickly, scanning the room. Then he turned to Zhang Fei and spoke in a low, firm voice, his expression suddenly grave.

"Zhang Fei," he said, warning in his tone.

Only then did Zhang Fei seem to register the attention they had drawn.

"Lord Liu..." he said earnestly, "why do you try to hide your heart from me? I am not a man who betrays trust. Now that I think on it... the reason you lingered at that proclamation earlier, the reason it weighed so heavily on you—was because you finally decided that it was time to make a move, wasn't it?" He leaned in, voice low and sincere.

Just then, Liu Bei noticed the woman at the tavern standing nearby—half hidden in the shadows, wine tray in hand. She was half frozen in place, quietly listening... her eyes locked on Liu Bei. Noticing this, Liu Bei let out an exaggerated laugh.

"Haha... Come," Liu Bei said quietly, pushing back from the table, "Let's forget about drinking and go outside and get some fresh night air."

He had realized—Zhang Fei was already drunk when he ran into him at the square. A flicker of caution passed through him. Nearby, the woman still stood in the shadows, watching them with narrowed, unreadable eyes.

Zhang Fei protested, "But we just ordered a whole jug," gesturing to the table. "Can we at least finish—"

Before Zhang Fei could finish the sentence, Liu Bei placed several coins on the wood with a soft clink and stood, already turning to leave. Zhang Fei hesitated, then reluctantly followed without further protest.

The two men walked in silence, slipping past the tavern's lamplight and into the quiet night. They climbed a narrow path that led to a low hill overlooking the town. From there, they could see the twinkling lights of the market fading into darkness, the sounds of revelry below now muffled and distant. Liu Bei paused, scanning the area, then turned to face Zhang Fei beneath the open sky.

"Lord Zhang," he said softly, "you are far too impatient by nature. Tell me—what wrong have I done, that you would speak so recklessly in a public tavern?"

Zhang Fei let out a long breath. He remembered Guan Yu offering a similar rebuke not long ago. But he waved it off, shrugging with an easy grin.

"What does it matter who hears? The world is in ruin. When wine flows, how can a man not cry out in frustration?"

Liu Bei's tone was soft, but his gaze remained firm.

"I know well your upright heart, Lord Zhang. Your words come from righteousness, not malice. But even the purest intentions can invite disaster when spoken too freely or too prematurely."

Liu Bei's voice lowered, steady as the night wind.

"A true warrior does not cast his grief to the winds, where spies and petty men may catch it. Important plans must be whispered in private, not shouted in a tavern. In times like these, malicious forces do not always wear armor or bear swords. They hide in plain sight. And a single careless word... can undo the work of years."

He glanced back toward the distant tavern, now a small, glowing square of light in the valley below. He looked Zhang Fei in the eye.

"I apologize if I've been too stern. But I've placed my trust in you for some time now. I've been waiting for the day we would meet again like this."

Zhang Fei's expression shifted. The haze of drink seemed to lift, if only for a moment.

"You mean... you've been waiting for *me* all this time?"

"I have," Liu Bei said simply.

Emotion stirred in Zhang Fei's chest. He reached out and grasped Liu Bei's hand with sudden force. Liu Bei returned the gesture, gripping his hand with equal strength.

"What would I hide from you, Lord Zhang?" he said. "I am a descendant of Liu Sheng, Prince Jing of Zhongshan. The blood of Emperor Jing flows in my veins. How could someone like me not burn with the desire to set this world right?"

Zhang Fei's eyes widened in delight.

"I knew it! You are of the Imperial Liu family!" he exclaimed, his voice brimming with renewed conviction. "Of course—you've been waiting for the right moment... and the right people—to set this broken world right."

Then suddenly, he remembered something.

That sword!

The sword he had carried all these years. The sword that was crucial in saving his own life from the wild boar attack that fateful night, and changed the entire course of his life when he had thought he had nothing more left in life. A memory surged up like lightning—years ago, a chance meeting, a short but unforgettable encounter, and a gift: an extraordinary sword that Liu Bei had once placed in his hands.

Zhang Fei had never spoken of it to anyone. But from the moment Liu Bei gave it to him, he knew it wasn't just a weapon—it was something greater, something imperial in make and spirit. From the day he received it, Zhang Fei had told himself one thing:

If I ever see Liu Bei again, this sword must go back to him. And today... was that day.

Without a word, Zhang Fei turned and sprinted down the hill, his footsteps echoing against the quiet night.

Startled, Liu Bei called after him:

"Zhang Fei? What is it?"

"I'll be back!" came the answer, quickly swallowed by the wind.

Moments later, Zhang Fei returned, breathless but purposeful. In his hands, wrapped in worn silk, was a long bundle. He stopped before Liu Bei and slowly unwrapped it. Inside was the sword—the Imperial Liu family heirloom.

Liu Bei's eyes widened the moment he saw it.

"You... protected this sword this entire time!"

Zhang Fei nodded, his voice softer than usual.

"Yes. Even then, I could tell it was no common blade. And I knew you were no ordinary man. I told myself: *If I ever meet Liu Bei again, I'll return this sword to its rightful owner.*"

He held the sword out with both hands, offering it like an oath.

"Lord Liu, the time has come. This sword never belonged to me. It always awaited your return. Just as I did."

Liu Bei stared at the weapon, emotion rising within him. The blade gleamed under the moonlight, untouched by time —just as the memory had remained in Zhang Fei's heart.

"I gave this to you freely, Brother Zhang," Liu Bei said gently.

"And I return it freely," Zhang Fei replied, unwavering. "All things of true importance carry a soul of their own—a purpose woven into them from the start. In time, each finds its way back to where it truly belongs. The sword has waited long enough. It is time... to return to its rightful owner."

Liu Bei hesitated. But then his mother's words echoed in his mind:

"You will know the men who are meant to walk beside you. Destiny will place the right weapons, the right people, into your hands."

With a solemn nod, Liu Bei accepted the sword and buckled it once more at his side.

Zhang Fei smiled, visibly moved.

"And now, the sword is home."

The two men clasped hands firmly—it was a silent pact that went deeper than words.

Then Zhang Fei spoke again, his eyes bright with purpose:

"There's one more person you must meet. A warrior I hold in the highest regard. His name is Guan Yu."

Liu Bei's brow lifted in recognition.

"Guan Yu?" he repeated. "I've heard of him. A man renowned for both the brush and the blade—master of literature and war alike. To possess such harmony between the pen and the sword... that is rare indeed."

Zhang Fei thumped his chest with pride.

"Then let's strike while the iron is hot and bring him into our fold at once!"

But Liu Bei raised a hand, ever the voice of measured reason.

"If you eat your rice ball too hurriedly," he said with a faint smile, "you'll only choke on it. Let us move deliberately and with care. Such men of virtue are not gathered by haste, but by sincerity."

Zhang Fei let out a half-grumble, half-laugh.

"Lord Liu, I suppose you are right. I won't argue this time!"

Liu Bei turned toward the horizon, where the stars shimmered faintly over distant rooftops.

"Three men, if bound by trust, can turn the tide of a nation. But the foundation must be firm—like the stone that anchors a temple. So yes, let us proceed... but let us do so wisely."

And with that, the two men descended the hill. They were standing on the road now, when Liu Bei reached out his hand to say good night.

"My aged mother at home will worry if I linger too long. So for tonight, I'll take my leave. Let's reconvene first thing tomorrow morning."

This time, Zhang Fei agreed without protest.

"Remember, I live in Lou Sang Village. You can ask anybody where the giant mulberry tree is. That's where I live. It's hard to miss."

Zhang Fei clasped his hands in farewell, but no sooner had he said "Good night" than he was already sprinting off into the dark.

CHAPTER 14
THE OATH OF THE PEACH GARDEN

~

Z hang Fei's footsteps thundered along the dusty country road in darkness as he ran three miles without rest—straight toward the modest home of Guan Yu.

Inside, the house was quiet. A single candle flickered gently on a wooden desk, casting long shadows across the walls. There sat Guan Yu, broad-shouldered and calm, engrossed in a volume of *Spring and Autumn Annals*, the light dancing softly across his long, flowing beard.

The door burst open.

"Brother Guan!" Zhang Fei called out, barely pausing for breath.

Guan Yu looked up slowly, unstartled, his expression as steady as ever.

"What brings such urgency at this hour, Brother Zhang?"

"Aha! I knew it! I knew you'd be hunched over some dusty scroll like a scholarly owl!"

Zhang Fei bounced on his toes, unable to contain his excitement at seeing Guan Yu again.

"Careful there—lean any closer to that candle and your magnificent beard might catch fire! Haha!"

Guan Yu let out a low chuckle, as if bemused yet faintly amused by his companion's boyish antics, and waited for his next word.

"But listen! You'll never believe it—I bumped into Liu Bei right after we left the tavern! Can you imagine? There I was, minding my own business in the market square, when who should appear but the very person we were talking about! We got to talking and—oh, all the great things we talked about to save this country!"

Guan Yu was quietly listening to Zhang Fei and gently closed his book and rose to his feet, his movements deliberate and thoughtful.

"Hmm," he said, stroking his beard.

"Are you certain it was him? It seems rather convenient that he should materialize from thin air just after we spoke of him. Yet if your eyes did not deceive you, then surely the hand of fate is at work."

Zhang Fei slapped his knee emphatically.

"It was *him*, I tell you! *He* recognized me first—when I was getting all worked up and talking nonsense to him, thinking he was a random stranger! I nearly dropped to my knees in shock. We spoke of our last parting, of how we've each been wandering this turbulent world like scattered leaves."

Guan Yu nodded slowly, a knowing gleam in his eyes.

"The three of us were never meant to walk separate paths. This is Heaven's doing—we are bound by destiny to reunite."

"Exactly! Let's go right now! Who knows where Liu Bei might wander by morning?"

Guan Yu raised a calming hand. "Brother Zhang, where does Liu Bei reside now?"

"In Lou Sang Village, where there's a gigantic ancient mulberry tree. But enough talk—let's go! Now!"

Zhang Fei was already moving toward the door, his massive frame vibrating with barely contained energy.

"He even knew of your reputation without ever meeting you! I'm certain he'll leap at the chance to join us!"

"Brother Zhang," Guan Yu's voice cut through the urgency like a blade through silk—quiet, but impossible to ignore.

"The hour grows late, and wisdom counsels patience. The roads beyond town are treacherous in darkness, prowled by wild beasts and bandits who prey upon travelers."

Zhang Fei whirled around, his eyes blazing with frustration.

"Beasts? Bandits? Brother, I've once crushed a dozen boars all by myself! I fear nothing that walks or crawls!" He resumed his restless pacing.

"Don't you understand? We've only just found him! What if the Yellow Turbans attack his village tonight? What if he has to flee before dawn? What if—"

"Zhang Fei," Guan Yu spoke with quiet authority that made the larger man stop mid-stride.

"Tell me—would you have Liu Bei's first impression of

us be two desperate men hammering on his door in the dead of night, reeking of wine and wild with haste?"

Zhang Fei opened his mouth to protest, then closed it, his brow furrowing.

Guan Yu continued, his voice gentle but inexorable as flowing water.

"If Heaven has truly ordained this reunion, then one night will not undo what destiny has woven. Stay here, brother. Let us approach him at first light—refreshed, respectful, and worthy of the alliance we seek."

Meanwhile, by the time Liu Bei returned home, the night was deep and still. A faint mist clung to the ground, and the stars shimmered above like quiet witnesses to what had just unfolded.

He stepped softly into the house, careful not to wake his mother, but to his surprise, she was already seated in the lamplight, her needlework forgotten on her lap. She looked up as he entered and smiled gently.

"You're back."

Liu Bei bowed his head respectfully and approached, his voice warm.

"Yes, Mother. I would like to tell you something... Something extraordinary happened tonight."

He carefully unfastened the sword from his waist and laid it across her lap. Her eyes widened.

"This... isn't this the sword you gave away long ago?"

Liu Bei nodded, his voice touched with emotion.

"To Zhang Fei. I gave it to him many years ago, trusting that fate would one day reunite us. And tonight, by chance —or perhaps by fate—we met again. He returned it to me."

He told her everything: the unexpected encounter, the

hilltop conversation, the returned sword, and the mention of another warrior named Guan Yu. As he spoke, his mother listened in thoughtful silence.

When he finished, she looked down at the sword, running her fingers lightly along the worn, elegant scabbard.

"You say you met this man by chance," she said, her voice low and full of wonder. "But I no longer believe in chance."

She set the sword gently aside and looked up at him, her expression now glowing with quiet certainty.

"I must tell you what I saw in a dream last night."

Liu Bei straightened, listening intently.

"In the dream, you were riding on the back of a great dragon—its scales shone like jade and gold. And beside you flew two other men, one on each side. One bore the aura of strength, the other of wisdom and fire. The three of you soared high into the heavens, leaving streaks of colored light across the sky."

She paused, her voice softening.

"Below, people filled the earth, looking up at you all. They were cheering, crying with joy, calling your names. The sky blazed with color. It was a vision unlike any I've had before."

Liu Bei's eyes were wide with astonishment.

"A dragon... with two beside me..."

He whispered the names aloud: "Zhang Fei... and Guan Yu..."

Liu Bei bowed deeply before her; his heart moved by the sense that what had seemed like a coincidence was, in truth, a carefully laid path. He rose with new resolve.

"At dawn, I will meet them again. And together, we shall forge the path the heavens have shown us."

The next morning, even before the rooster had stirred, Liu Bei was already awake and dressed. The sword rested at his waist, and the sky outside had just begun to soften with the colors of approaching dawn.

He stepped outside, the morning air crisp and still. As he looked toward the eastern road that led toward Heliang, he stopped in his tracks. There—framed against the first golden rays of the rising sun—stood two tall silhouettes: one stocky and bold in stance, the other upright and composed, with a calm presence that seemed to still the air around him. They stood side by side, motionless, almost glowing in the halo of morning light.

Liu Bei blinked, awestruck.

"Zhang Fei... and... that must be..."

The taller man stepped forward and gave a respectful bow. His eyes were steady, his voice clear.

"I am Guan Yu. I've long heard of Lord Liu Bei's virtue. Last night, Zhang Fei spoke of your heart and your vision. I could not rest until I saw you myself."

Zhang Fei grinned and clapped a hand on the taller man's shoulder.

"I told you we'd be here before the rooster crows!"

Liu Bei took a breath, the morning wind stirring his robes. The dream his mother had spoken of now shimmered before his very eyes—three men, standing as one, beneath the heavens. He stepped forward and offered both men his hand, voice steady with purpose.

"Then let us walk this path together. Please, come on inside. We have a lot to talk about."

The three clasped hands beneath the dawning sky. As the first light spilled over the earth, the tide of history began to turn.

Inside Liu Bei's humble home, modest and sparsely furnished, Liu Bei, Guan Yu, and Zhang Fei sat cross-legged on the floor, shoulder to shoulder. Their voices filled the quiet space with talk of the broken empire, the suffering people, and the corrupt officials who preyed upon the weak. All day, they spoke of justice, of loyalty, of war, and peace. With each word, their hearts drew closer.

At last, Guan Yu looked between the two and spoke in a low, steady voice.

"Brothers... the world is adrift, and men of virtue are scattered like fallen leaves. I say this plainly—let us bind ourselves to one another in brotherhood. Let us vow to face life and death together, to share both hardship and glory as one."

Zhang Fei rose at once, eyes shining.

"Say no more! I've wanted to call you both brothers from the start! Let us swear it now, and never look back."

Liu Bei smiled—but after a moment, his expression grew thoughtful.

"This bond we are about to form is no small thing. Before I make such an oath, I must seek my mother's blessing."

Without delay, Liu Bei rose and stepped into the adjoining room where his mother sat quietly folding old cloth. He knelt before her.

"Mother," he began, "I have met two men— extraordinary in heart and spirit. One is as fierce as thunder, the other as steady as a mountain. I believe Heaven brought us together. We wish to become sworn brothers. I ask your permission... to take this step."

His mother set down the cloth. Her eyes, soft with age, searched his face. For a long moment, she said nothing. Then, quietly, tears began to fall.

"My son..." she said, her voice trembling. "From the day you were born, I knew you were meant for something grand."

She took his hands in hers, her fingers thin but firm.

"The burden of our family name has always rested on your shoulders. And now, to hear that you have met true men of valor—men who would share your path—I have no greater joy. You have my blessing, my son. Even if I were to die tonight, I would have no regrets."

Liu Bei bowed low, tears stinging his own eyes.

"Let's prepare an offering," she said. "Today, we honor our ancestors. This is not just a vow among sworn brothers —it is a calling sealed by Heaven and Earth."

That afternoon, they gathered in the sacred grove behind Liu Bei's humble home, where ancient peach trees stood in eternal bloom.

Liu Bei's mother had hurried to the local butcher and then to a stable hand. With quiet urgency and reverence, she procured the sacred offerings: a black ox head, representing *yin*, as an offering to the earthly world, and a white horse's mane, representing *yang*, as tribute to the divine world.

Before the altar, the three men bowed in unison. The air was thick with the sacred smoke of incense, curling toward the sky. Their words rose in unison, voices firm and unwavering.

. . .

"THOUGH BORN OF DIFFERENT FAMILIES, *we now swear ourselves as brothers.*

With one heart, one will, we shall face all hardship as one—
to lift each other in times of peril,
To stand firm through storm and fire.
Above, we shall serve and repay the nation;
Below, we shall bring peace to the people.
We ask not to be born together,
But we vow to die together—on the same day, the same month, the same year.
May the Heavens above and the Earth below bear witness to this oath.
And should any of us break this sacred bond,
May Heaven and Man alike strike us down in righteous wrath."

THIS SOLEMN PLEDGE had been penned by Guan Yu himself, each word steeped in blood-bound honor.

After announcing the vow, each man bowed three times in profound silence, their foreheads touching the earth in submission to forces greater than themselves.

There, beneath the canopy of pearl-white blossoms that drifted like snow in the gentle breeze, they knelt as equals before Heaven and Earth. The afternoon sun filtered through the branches, casting shifting patterns of light and shadow across their upturned faces.

Then they rose, three figures silhouetted against the golden afternoon, and joined their hands beneath the blessing of the peach blossoms.

In that moment, a brotherhood emerged that would

shake empires, challenge tyrants, and inspire poets for a thousand generations. They had become something greater than the sum of their selves.

The Peach Garden Oath was sealed. The world would never be the same.

CHAPTER 15
THREE PILLARS OF WAR

∼

The incense had long since burned out. Only the faint trails of smoke lingered above the altar as the three sworn brothers sat in the peach garden, their faces lit by the amber glow of a setting sun.

They had sealed their oath. Now came the harder task—leadership.

Zhang Fei was the first to break the silence, pounding his fist into his palm.

"We've sworn ourselves as one, but even among brothers, someone must take the lead! Let's not waste time—who among us shall command?"

Guan Yu stroked his long beard, his voice calm and deliberate.

"This bond is one of equals. But in any endeavor, unity requires a pillar. We must choose a leader—not for pride, but for guidance."

Their eyes turned to Liu Bei, who sat quietly, gaze lowered in thought. Zhang Fei stood and pointed to him.

"It should be you, Brother Liu. You may not be the oldest, but more than that, you descend from the royal house of Han. Your bearing, your gift for stirring hearts—none among us surpasses you in virtue."

Guan Yu nodded.

"Bloodlines may fade, but yours has not. The Empire's flame still glows in your veins. You carry the legacy of the Han Dynasty. It would be against Heaven's will to place anyone else above you."

Liu Bei raised his hand slowly, shaking his head.

"My brothers... You speak with honor, but I am no emperor, nor a prince. I have tilled the soil, woven mats, and sandals with my own hands. The Han blood in me is little more than ink on a genealogy scroll. What matters is *heart*, not heritage."

But Zhang Fei pressed on, his voice firm.

"Exactly. And it is your heart and vision for the country that proves you worthy. Not the lineage alone, but the way you carry it—with humility and honor. Let the world call you our elder brother. Let us follow you—not because you demand it, but because we believe in you."

Liu Bei fell silent for a long moment, eyes clouded with emotion. Finally, he stood, hands clasped before him.

"If so," he said softly. "If Heaven wills it, and if my brothers truly see fit... then I shall lead—not as a ruler, but as your guide. Let us rise and fall together, with one spirit."

Zhang Fei, still riding high on a wave of emotion, could hardly contain his excitement. He threw his arms wide and roared with laughter.

"With the three of us united and under Brother Liu Bei's leadership, it's as good as over! Victory is ours before the first battle's even begun!"

But Guan Yu, ever the voice of reason, spoke calmly, his tone like tempered steel.

"Let's think with reason—and keep our feet on the ground. There are three pillars to any campaign: leadership, troops, and provisions. We have leadership, but without all three, no cause can stand. We need concrete steps."

Liu Bei nodded gravely, the weight of leadership already settling on his shoulders.

"We need troops. Men must be gathered. I was born and raised in this very town. I studied with its children, taught in its village school, and guided many of its youths as they grew. They know my heart. If I call upon them, they will come—not out of fear, but out of trust."

True to his word, he began to recruit. And as Liu Bei stirred the hearts of the people, Guan Yu—renowned not only for his valor but for the power of his pen—took up his brush with quiet purpose. With bold strokes, he penned a rallying proclamation—a call to all brave young men of the region who dreamed of glory, who longed to serve a just cause under honorable leaders. Once finished, they entrusted the local children to paste the broadsides on walls, doors, trees—anywhere eyes might fall.

And soon, they came.

In droves, the youth of the surrounding villages flooded in—farmhands, blacksmiths' sons, scholars' apprentices—all with fire in their eyes and purpose in their step. What began as a trio of brothers was quickly becoming the spark of something far greater.

By week's end, nearly five hundred had answered their call. The dusty yard behind the village temple had become a training ground.

And it fell to Zhang Fei to shape the army. Though hot-tempered and larger than life, Zhang Fei took his new role seriously. One morning, he climbed onto an overturned barrel and addressed the assembled men. His arms were crossed, his voice thunderous.

"Listen up! You came here as farmers, sons, and workers. But from today, you are soldiers. And soldiers live by *rules*."

He held up four fingers, each one like a thick, gnarled branch.

"Rule One: Obey your superior's orders without question. Even if you don't like them, this isn't a family picnic—we move as one, or we fall."

"Rule Two: The nation comes before yourself. You don't fight for gold, or pride, or revenge. You fight to protect the people. You put the land and its future ahead of your own life."

"Rule Three: Anyone who steals from others or harms the people, we execute them. No excuses, no second chances. If you terrorize those we swore to protect, you are no better than the bandits we fight."

A heavy silence fell over the crowd. He let it settle before delivering the final rule.

"Rule Four: Disrupt the discipline of the army, and you die. Laugh during orders, fight with your comrades, sneak off during duty—anyone who breaks the military code weakens us all. And weakness kills."

He swept his gaze over the men. His eyes were sharp, and there was no trace of a grin.

"If you cannot follow these rules, *now* is the time to leave. No shame. No blame. Just go home with your head held high, before you get someone else killed."

For a moment, no one moved.

Then a boy—barely sixteen, with dirt still caked under his fingernails from the morning's fieldwork—took a deep breath and bowed low. His shoulders trembling slightly, he stepped back from the ranks with deliberate, measured steps.

Zhang Fei's weathered face softened, and he nodded.

"That takes courage. Go home in peace."

The boy's act rippled through the assembled crowd like a stone dropped into still water. Eyes darted nervously from face to face, searching for judgment, for permission, for solidarity. A middle-aged merchant with calloused hands slowly raised his trembling arm. Then a young father who said his wife waited at home with their newborn. One by one, a handful more found their courage in the boy's example, raising their hands with sheepish expressions before shuffling away with hurried, grateful steps.

The rest stayed rooted in place, their jaws set with grim determination.

Meanwhile, Guan Yu was quieter, methodical. He had taken a group of older recruits aside and was demonstrating footwork on the packed dirt, his calm voice steady like the flow of a river.

"Discipline, not strength, wins battles. Know where your feet are. Know where your blade will land *before* you swing."

And Liu Bei—though neither the loudest nor the strongest—was everywhere. He moved through the training grounds not like a commander, but like an older brother among kin. He called the boys by name, recalling who had once studied beside him in the village schoolhouse, who had lost a father to bandits, who still bore the fading bruises of violence past. His memory was sharp, but it was his heart they remembered most.

He asked after their mothers, their siblings, their aching limbs. He noticed every improvement, however small, and praised it without reserve. He offered a steady hand to the nervous, a reassuring nod to the uncertain, and never once gave an order without a kind word first. In him, they saw not merely a leader, but a man who bore their pain as his own. And in return, they stood taller, fought fiercer, and pledged to give their all for the army he led.

But soldiers could not fight with empty hands—or empty stomachs. One night, seated under an oil lamp in their modest war-room in the back of the temple, the three brothers laid out the next part of their plan.

"Weapons," said Guan Yu, tapping a finger against a crudely drawn map.

"We can train with sticks, but we'll need real steel before we face any army."

"And grain," added Liu Bei. "Food is as important as swords. Armies march on their stomachs. Without grain, even the strongest army collapses."

Zhang Fei leaned back, cracking his knuckles.

"There's an old weaponsmith two valleys over. I met him once during a festival. Tough old man, but fair. Some said his ancestors used to build swords for the imperial generals. I'll ride out at first light. If he won't help, I'll drink him under the table until he agrees!"

Liu Bei laughed. "Let's hope persuasion works before the wine runs out."

As for food, they decided to visit the village elders the next morning. Liu Bei would speak on behalf of the people —not as a noble, but as one of them. He would ask for grain, scraps of meat, wagons, and moral support.

"We're not robbing from the innocent people," he said firmly. "We're building a force to protect them. Against chaos, against greed, against the warlords who tear this land apart."

The following day, the three brothers went their separate ways: Zhang Fei set out to procure weapons, Guan Yu departed to scout routes and gather intelligence, while Liu Bei ventured forth to rally support among the villagers in the surrounding countryside.

Later that evening, the brothers met again in their war-room, lit by flickering lamps and smelling of old scrolls and damp stone. The talk now turned to another crucial element that was still missing.

"Food is coming," Liu Bei reported. "The elders have agreed to donate grain, beans, and whatever unwanted parts of the meat, if any, from the village stores. It won't last forever, but it will keep us alive while we train."

"I've spoken with a few smiths," Zhang Fei said. "Most are uneasy, but one—whose family has worked the forge for generations in service to the Han—swore to provide swords and spearheads in return for labor and protection. I promised him both. They'll melt down whatever scraps they can find into weapons. It won't be enough, but we'll find a way to secure the rest."

Guan Yu was standing by the doorway, arms crossed, thinking.

"Good then, but we are missing one crucial thing," he said quietly. "Horses. Foot soldiers can defend, but they cannot chase. They cannot strike swiftly or retreat when needed. If we are to move with strength, we need cavalry. At least a few dozen to begin with."

Liu Bei nodded.

"I have been thinking about that too. I'll send word to some friends in the north—they used to breed horses. Maybe they still do."

Zhang Fei smirked, a glint of mischief in his eyes.

"Breeders? They've been squeezed dry. Either the corrupt officials have taken their cut, or the Yellow Turbans have stolen the rest. Horses are vanishing like honesty in government. Maybe it's time we find them ourselves. Wouldn't mind a good ride—and if fate's feeling generous, maybe a good fight too."

The brothers laughed, but they all knew the truth: the road ahead was no game.

Just then, shouting broke the quiet. A young trainee came sprinting across the courtyard, dusty and breathless. He ran straight, looking for Zhang Fei, just as he was getting up.

"Captain Zhang! I saw something—on the far ridge. A man, leading a herd—*at least fifty horses!* Just slowly walking and grazing out there!"

Zhang Fei dropped his whetstone.

"Fifty?"

"Yes, sir! He was alone—no guards, no flag, nothing. Just one man and all those horses." The trainee lowered his voice and looked around. "We could take them. One quick strike, in and out. Fifty horses... enough to form our first cavalry."

Zhang Fei's eyes lit up. His grip tightened on the spear.

"Fifty horses..." he muttered. "With that many, we could move like thunder..."

The temptation was real—and heavy. After all, the horses were just there. No banners were flying, and there was no clear sign of ownership other than the one man who was idly riding on one of the horses with no care in the world.

Zhang Fei stood slowly, muscles tense, eyes gleaming with possibility.

"Tell the fastest ten men to get ready," he growled. "If we strike now—"

"No." The voice was quiet but firm.

Zhang Fei turned. Liu Bei stood up and walked towards him with a stern look on his face.

"Brother, don't do this," Liu Bei said.

"But think about it, Brother Liu!" Zhang Fei argued. "Horses—*fifty of them!* Just standing there. We need them. You said so yourself!"

Liu Bei didn't raise his voice. He looked him in the eye.

"And I said we fight to protect, not to take. If we steal now, even from one man, what happens tomorrow? Will our army become just another band of thieves?"

Zhang Fei hesitated. The wind shifted. The moment teetered. Then Guan Yu stepped out from the shadows, arms folded.

"A man who forgets his rules when tempted will drop them in fear," he said quietly. "And you *wrote* those rules, Brother."

Zhang Fei looked from one to the other, jaw clenched. For a long second, it looked like he might argue. Then—he laughed. Loud and rough, like thunder clearing from the sky.

"Fine, fine! You two win. I was only testing you anyway!"

The young trainee looked confused. "So... we're not taking the horses?"

Guan Yu answered instead. "No, not with weapons. However, we can try to use the power of words to *earn* them."

Zhang Fei raised an eyebrow. "Words? We're not buying rice at the market, Brother."

"And yet words can move hearts where swords create enemies." Liu Bei gave a slight nod. "If anyone can do it, it's you."

Guan Yu didn't respond. He simply turned and motioned to a few of the trainees to follow him.

The fields stretched out beyond the village like a sea of gold and dust. In the distance, a lone man led a trail of some fifty horses, their hooves kicking up clouds as they moved slowly down a sunlit ridge.

Guan Yu approached at a measured pace, not too fast— so as not to alarm—and not too slow—to show he had purpose. As they neared, Guan Yu noticed something odd. The man wasn't alone.

Trailing far behind, stumbling and out of breath, was a boy no older than eleven or twelve. The man would pause every few steps, turning to wait for the child to catch up. This was no merchant's caravan. This was a father and a son. When they finally met on the path, the man stopped the horses and watched Guan Yu with wary eyes. The man seemed to scan Guan Yu for a minute or so and appeared to feel relieved.

"I'm not looking for trouble," the man said in a tired voice. "We're just passing through."

Guan Yu bowed his head respectfully. "And I am not here to bring it. I only wish to speak."

The man glanced at the boy, who was now nervously climbing back on one of the horses, possibly trying to be ready to flee if needed.

"These horses... they belong to you?" Guan Yu asked.

"They do," the man replied.

Guan Yu's gaze swept over the herd; many staggered, sides heaving, tongues lolling in thirst.

"Or... what's left of them," the man continued. "We used to have hundreds in our farm, but what I have here is perhaps only fifty—maybe fewer, for some have already fallen along the road. Those who could not endure this cruel journey were left behind. And most of the hundreds we originally had were either stolen, or lost to the flames when the Yellow Turbans burned our village."

There was no bitterness in his voice—just exhaustion.

"May I ask where you are headed?" Guan Yu asked softly.

"We're headed to the barn by the street market," he added. "Hoping to sell them when the gates open again. We have no home to return to, but we know the owners of the barn and may be able to stay there for some time."

"Do you have a wife?" Guan Yu asked gently.

The man's lips pressed into a hard line.

"Gone. And my daughter. About a month ago. The Yellow Turbans took them." He paused, his voice rough with memory. "We stayed behind in the rubble—waiting, hoping they might escape and find their way back to us. But... we've lost hope now. All we have left is each other."

He looked at his son, then out at the horizon as if searching for something that no longer existed. Behind him, the horses shifted quietly, their breath steaming in the cool air. One let out a low snort, tossing its head.

Guan Yu stepped closer. His voice, deep and deliberate, carried the weight of both sorrow and purpose.

"Then perhaps, good sir, we are not strangers after all. For we, too, have lost much. But we stand now, not to escape—but to fight back. To protect others from the same fate."

"Are you soldiers?" the man asked.

"No," Guan Yu said. "We are allies and volunteers, but we *are* building an army. One born of oath and honor." He paused. "I ask you—would you consider giving some of the horses to our cause? And if so, tell me what we can offer in return."

The man studied him more carefully this time. There was no aggression in Guan Yu's stance, no threat. Just stillness—and something fierce behind the calm. Then the man gave a tired smile, the first in days.

"You don't owe me anything," he said. "If your army is real... if it truly fights the Yellow Turbans and protects the innocent people... then I'll give you every last horse."

Guan Yu blinked, surprised. "Are you sure?"

The man looked at his son.

"Before we set out on this road, I knew the odds. My family has been merchants for generations, and we know our math. We've heard the stories—raiders, warbands, soldiers who take what they want, not just those Yellow Turbans. I knew the chances were high we'd lose the horses, the silver, the steel... *everything*. And these horses are tired and hungry. It is a small miracle that we made it this far unharmed."

A stillness settled over them.

He looked past Guan Yu, eyes distant and unblinking.

"My son and I—we'll manage," the man said quietly. "We can scrape by doing whatever odd work comes our way. But we are exhausted and can't care for these horses the way they deserve anymore. All our workers are gone, scattered like dust. These poor animals have become more burden than blessing."

He gave a slight, weary shrug. "That's why we were heading to the next town—hoping to sell them, maybe start over. But the road is long, and the future's a fog. Too many uncertainties."

His eyes lifted to Guan Yu's, steady now.

Guan Yu, wordless, solemnly pressed his right hand to his heart in a gesture of profound appreciation. No words could capture the depth of gratitude that filled him in that moment.

The man stepped aside, gesturing toward the train of horses.

"The saddlebags are packed with silver coins, steel, animal hides, and a few humble possessions."

This was his family's entire life, bound tight for flight.

"Take them," the man said quietly, looking directly into Guan Yu's eyes. "We'll carry only what my son and I need to reach the next village—if such a place still exists where life can be rebuilt. We do not want to be targeted by the thugs by carrying any more than the very minimal amount needed for survival."

Guan Yu bowed low.

"Then please allow me to leave at least two horses with you and your son and provide an escort from our force to accompany you until you and your son reach safety."

Guan Yu gestured at two of the trainees who came along, who in return nodded in agreement. The man nodded slowly. Their eyes met. There was a shared understanding born of mutual respect and flickering hope.

By dusk, the last of the horses finally arrived at the training grounds. The journey—though only a few miles—had been anything but easy. The herd was a restless mix of stallions and mares, colts still learning their pace, and older beasts wearied by travel and age. Guiding dozens of untrained horses across uneven roads and through unfamiliar terrain tested the patience and strength of even the hardiest recruits. The animals snorted and skittered, tugging at reins, stamping at shadows.

But at last, beneath the deepening orange sky, they stood gathered—dusty, sweating, but whole.

Zhang Fei whistled as they came over the ridge, hooves pounding, saddlebags glinting with unexpected bounty.

"Well, he did it. With words."

Liu Bei stood at the edge of the grounds, his arms folded loosely as the sun dipped low behind the hills. A soft smile tugged at his lips as he watched Guan Yu and the young trainees lead the horses through the gates. They moved like an army returning home after a hard-won victory, exhausted, but with a big, proud smile on their faces.

Liu Bei exhaled, almost to himself.

"Guan Yu must have truly earned his trust. When people give freely, they give all they can, and their hearts are at peace. But when they are forced, they give only what they must, and their hearts fill with resentment."

The impact of securing the horses was immediate. The three brothers were convinced that it was a quiet affirmation that they had chosen the right path. To lead with hearts and words before weapons, to show restraint instead of wrath—this was the strength that would set them apart from the chaos sweeping the land.

Liu Bei looked out over the herd and said, "Heaven has entrusted us with these tools. Now we must prove ourselves worthy to wield them."

Among the herd, one horse stood apart—its coat pure white with an otherworldly luminescence. As if responding to Liu Bei's words, the magnificent creature galloped forward and approached him with regal bearing. Liu Bei gently stroked its mane, a silent acceptance passing between man and steed.

With this divine affirmation, Liu Bei wasted no time. He rallied the villagers' support to strengthen the growing army in whatever way they could. The steel carried by the horses—nearly a thousand catties—was immediately loaded onto carts and sent directly to the forge.

Soon, the village smithy roared to life. Bellows heaved with rhythmic force, and sparks flew like fireflies in a storm. Bladesmiths, their faces streaked with sweat and soot, worked alongside young apprentices with calloused hands. Hammers rang like war drums against the anvil, shaping steel into something far greater than its weight—swords, spears, halberds, and pikes destined to write history.

The three sworn brothers stood before the head blade-smith, a wiry man with ash in his beard and fire in his eyes. Despite his soot-streaked face and threadbare tunic, he stood with the confidence of a man who had known great-ness—and forged it with his own hands.

"You bring a thousand catties of steel," the old smith said, his voice low and deliberate, "but steel alone does not make a weapon worthy of your cause."

Liu Bei glanced toward the flickering forge. "We only wish to arm our men. The army must be ready."

"And they will be," the bladesmith said, wiping his hands on a scorched rag. "Each soldier will carry a blade fit for war. But some blades... are born for greatness." He stepped forward and continued, "Not all swords are the same. Just as not all men are the same."

The brothers said nothing, but their eyes remained fixed on him.

"I may be a humble blacksmith, but my family has forged blades for the royal house of Han," he continued. "For generations. I was trained not just to shape metal—but to read the man who wields it. And I see before me not just three warriors... but three pillars of something greater."

He turned first to Liu Bei.

"You—your leadership springs not from ambition, but from destiny... perhaps even burden. You will carry the weight of others' hopes, their lives, even a nation's fate. Your weapon must be swift, yet measured. Not one blade, but two. Balanced—like yin and yang, like female and male, like phoenix and dragon. The arms of an emperor, sheltering his people."

Liu Bei said nothing, though surprise flickered across his features.

The smith then turned to Guan Yu. "You," he said, nodding slowly.

"Your name already travels on the wind. The villagers speak of you like a legend passed down by firelight. You don't need a sword. You need a declaration. Something only you can lift yet will never break beneath your grip. A great crescent blade—heavy as justice, elegant as the moon's arc."

Guan Yu raised an eyebrow, a faint smirk curving his lips, but offered no protest.

Finally, the smith looked to Zhang Fei. "And you," he said, now grinning.

"You are a tempest barely contained. You need a weapon that speaks before you do. Long, fierce, impossible to ignore. A spear with reach—and wrath."

Zhang Fei laughed aloud. "Now you're speaking my language."

The blacksmith stepped back. "Let me forge for each of you not merely a weapon—but an extension of your very souls. Let your enemies know the legend you are before you even strike."

The theatrical flourish in his delivery brought hearty smiles to all three brothers' faces.

The forge hissed as the bellows surged anew. Outside, night had fallen completely. But inside the smithy, the light burned brighter than ever. And as the hammer rang out once more, it was not merely steel being shaped—but destiny itself.

The next day, Liu Bei, dignified and precise, was gifted a pair of exquisitely balanced Phoenix and Dragon Twin

Swords—one for defense, one for swift retaliation—symbolizing authority, harmony, and renewal.

Guan Yu, ever calm and formidable, received a weapon unlike any other: the Green Dragon Crescent Blade, forged from the finest portion of the steel and weighing a formidable 90 pounds. Its blade curved like a crescent moon and shimmered green in the sunlight, as though carved from jade and tempered in dragon's fire. It was a weapon befitting a warrior-sage—graceful, yet devastating.

Zhang Fei, fierce and relentless, claimed the Fourteen Feet Serpent Spear, a long, iron-shafted staff with a blade like a serpent's tongue and a rear spike like a war hammer. Heavy and merciless, it suited him perfectly—crafted not for elegance, but for shattering enemy formations.

With weapons in hand, horses saddled, and silver secured for provisions, the brothers stood at the threshold of something greater than mere rebellion. They were no longer simply dreamers with noble ideals—they had become the beating heart of a rising army, forged in grief, fire, and unbreakable brotherhood.

CHAPTER 16

THE FIRST BATTLE

~

The mist-shrouded peaks of the Daxing Mountains had become the heart of a spreading contagion. Like a plague of locusts, more than fifty thousand Yellow Turban rebels poured from the heights, flooding the valleys and overrunning Zhuo County. Their ragged banners snapped in the mountain winds like the wings of carrion birds, and their war cries rolled through the night, echoing from village to village. Wherever they passed, they left only smoldering ruins—and the cries of the innocent carried on the smoke.

They had evolved into something more than bandits— they moved with the terrible purpose of an army. From their mountain fortress, they watched and waited like wolves circling wounded prey, biding their time for the perfect moment to descend in overwhelming force. They had one main goal: to wipe out all the government troops and make Zhuo County their own violent kingdom.

It was against this tide of chaos that Governor Liu Yan had issued his desperate proclamation—a final, defiant call echoing through the realm for any brave soul willing to stand between civilization and the abyss. And it was right before this very proclamation, not long ago, that Liu Bei stood, his mind forging the blueprint of an army while Zhang Fei watched him restlessly from a distance. The fate of an entire county hung in the balance, and one misstep could plunge it into irreversible chaos.

Emboldened by the warhorses and the gleam of freshly forged steel, Liu Bei felt a tide rising within him—an urgency he could no longer suppress. He turned to his sworn brother, his voice steady yet charged with purpose:

"Guan Yu, ride out and seek Liu Yan, the author of the proclamation. It is said he is a distant cousin of mine, though we have never met. My mother once spoke of him— how he rose to become a Governor of Youzhou. When I saw his name written in the proclamation at the market square, something within me stirred. I lingered and stood there for a long while, wondering if fate was pointing the way. But it was not yet time. I had no army, no allies—only ambition untested. That was right before I met you and Zhang Fei. Before our swords found purpose. Now... the moment has come. If Liu Yan is a man of virtue, if he truly seeks to restore peace to this fractured realm, then he will recognize the strength of our cause."

Without a word, Guan Yu bowed, turned, and mounted his steed. The crimson plume of his helmet fluttered like a banner of justice in the wind as he galloped westward through dust and dusk.

He reached Liu Yan's gates and slid from the saddle with effortless poise. Broad-shouldered and unyielding, he carried the silent weight of a man armed not only with steel but with principle, and the guards ushered him toward the governor.

There, before the weary but sharp-eyed Liu Yan, Guan Yu bowed deeply, then raised his gaze.

"I am Guan Yu of Hedong. Governor Liu, I thank you for granting me the honor of speaking before you." His voice was firm and measured, carrying both respect and resolve. "The land is bleeding, and the people cry out beneath the weight of chaos. Yet there is still hope—if we stand together. With your permission and support, we will not merely resist the Yellow Turbans—we will break them."

Governor Liu fixed his gaze on Guan Yu, his face unreadable, betraying no reaction at all.

Guan Yu continued, "I speak for Liu Bei of Zhuo Commandery. A man of your blood, though you may not yet know him. A man of virtue, not ambition. He does not seek power, but peace. He leads with justice, not fear. He commands not with pride, but with compassion."

He spoke, too, of Zhang Fei—bold and unshakable, a thunderclap on the battlefield whose fury scattered foes. And of the army, though young, whose spirits burned brighter than banners in the wind.

"We are few," Guan Yu admitted, "but our unity is our weapon. Our hearts are stronger than their swords."

Governor Liu Yan studied Guan Yu in silence, weighing

each word like a jade porcelain tested for authenticity. After a long moment of silence, he leaned forward and said, with a voice low but resonant:

"Liu Bei... yes. That name is not unknown to me." His voice carried both curiosity and weight. "If he truly bears the spirit of our house, and the virtue of our forebears, then perhaps the heavens have not turned from us after all."

Guan Yu met his gaze with unwavering steadiness. His words, though few, struck with precision and purpose. He spoke not in the flowery phrases of court speech, but with the weight of a man who believed deeply in the cause he carried. His voice held strength, but also restraint—an iron hand wrapped in silk.

Liu Yan's brow furrowed, then softened. Suspicion faded from his mouth, replaced by the faintest trace of agreement, and his stance loosened as if drawn toward the promise of a better future.

Sensing a shift in Liu Yan's stance, Guan Yu seized the moment to press his proposal further.

"We've received intelligence that the Yellow Turbans are running rampant on Mount Daxing," he said. "I respectfully request permission to lead our forces and eliminate them."

Liu Yan narrowed his eyes. "They have fifty thousand men. How many do you have?"

Guan Yu stepped forward, his voice calm but ringing with conviction.

"Yes, they number fifty thousand—but they are a horde driven by greed, not discipline. A mob hungry for spoils, not bound by loyalty or purpose. They follow the loudest voice, not the wisest mind."

He continued, "We are five hundred—young,

unshaken, and forged in the fire of hardship. Every one of us has chosen this path not for gold, but for justice. And above all, we move not in chaos, but under the command of Liu Bei—a leader of unmatched vision, whose mind is sharper than any sword. This is not a war of numbers. It's a battle of resolve, unity, and strategy. And if you grant us this chance, we will show the world that five hundred men with purpose can cut through fifty thousand lost souls."

After a brief pause, Guan Yu said with resolution, "Let this battle be our proof."

Liu Yan seemed satisfied by the answer, a faint nod betraying his approval. He turned to his attending general and gave a firm command.

"Assemble the government forces at once. They will stand ready to support Liu Bei's army. Liu Bei will lead the march to Mount Daxing without delay."

Then, rising to his full height, his voice solemn and resolute, Liu Yan declared before all present:

"From this moment forward, Liu Bei shall serve as Commanding General for this campaign. All ranks will answer to his command."

Dawn broke in a blaze of gold, spilling across the slopes of Mount Daxing. The chill of night still clung to the air as Liu Bei's army of five hundred began their climb. Their boots struck the earth in a steady rhythm, armor whispering and spears glinting with each step.

Above them, fifty thousand Yellow Turbans sprawled across the mountain's crown—men scattered like leaves, some still wrapped in sleep, others yawning, stretching, or idly tossing dice. A few early risers lounged along the ridge, squinting into the pale morning light. Then one of them sat upright, pointing down the slope.

"What the heck is that?" he shouted.

Heads turned. There, far below, a speck of steel glimmered in the dawn—Liu Bei's force, neat and bristling in sharp formation. For a heartbeat the men blinked in disbelief. Then came the laughter, harsh and booming, rolling down the mountain like an avalanche.

"Wait—so the rumors were true!" one of them bellowed, clutching his sides with laughter. "This must be that army of drunkards and castoffs! My own wife heard it at my tavern—some fool who stumbles in multiple times on a single night, babbling about leading men to glory. Ha! And here he is!"

But the five hundred did not falter. At the center rode Liu Bei, poised with regal authority atop his luminescent white steed. He was a calm axis amid the gathering storm, his unwavering gaze fixed on the distant summit.

Guan Yu shadowed his left, tall and unshakable, his Green Dragon Crescent Blade resting with lethal patience. On the right, Zhang Fei's eyes burned like coals beneath his helmet, his grip tightening on the shaft of his Serpent Spear. They climbed as one—undaunted, unbroken, as if their destiny lay not ahead but already in their grasp.

On the ridge, the Yellow Turban leader Zheng Yuan-zhi appeared, his yellow-clad troops spilling behind him like a flood. The newborn sun struck his armor, setting it ablaze like sheets of fire. He strode to the very edge, boots grinding against the stone, and gazed down upon the five hundred below. A booming laugh burst from his chest—scornful, echoing across the mountain.

"Ha! So this is the so-called mighty army defying us?"

The laughter had scarcely faded when Liu Bei's voice split the air like a thunderclap.

"Zheng Yuan-zhi! Lay down your arms—and surrender at once!"

The Yellow Turbans roared with fresh jeers. Zheng Yuan-zhi's grin widened, and with a flick of his hand, he gave his order without even looking at his lieutenant.

"Bring me the head of that arrogant wretch in the center," Zheng Yuan-zhi snarled, his voice laced with disdain.

The man spurred his horse, tearing down the slope in a storm of pounding hooves and whipping dust. Steel flashed in his grip as he lowered his blade for the kill. The world seemed to narrow—the sound of the horse's breath, the glint of the sun on metal, the ground trembling under its charge.

And then—a roar. Deep, primal, and savage. Zhang Fei exploded from the formation like a thunderbolt given flesh. His Fourteen Feet Serpent Spear swept up, the blade catching the morning sun in a blinding arc—one motion—swift and fatal.

The strike found its mark. The lieutenant's head flew free, spinning once before vanishing into the dust. His body slumped in the saddle, lifeless, before collapsing to the earth with a dull, final thud. Silence swallowed the ridge.

Zheng Yuan-zhi's face twisted with rage, the veins in his neck bulging as his laughter died in an instant. With a roar that shook the ridge, he spurred his warhorse forward, charging straight at Zhang Fei without a breath of hesitation. The ground trembled under the pounding hooves, dust swirling in his wake like the herald of a storm.

Zhang Fei braced himself, his Serpent Spear lowering for another killing strike. But before the blow could fall, a flash of emerald steel cut across his line of sight.

Guan Yu had moved. With the grace of a master and the precision of a headsman, he stepped forward, his Green Dragon Crescent Blade sweeping in a single, fluid arc. The blade sang through the air, and Zheng Yuan-zhi's head was severed cleanly from his shoulders. His body, still astride the galloping horse, swayed for a heartbeat before toppling lifeless to the ground.

The battlefield froze. With their leaders gone in a matter of a few minutes, the jeers of the Yellow Turbans died into a stunned, suffocating silence. Eyes widened, weapons trembled. Then, as if struck by the same thought all at once, they broke. Dropping shields, spears, and anything that weighed them down, the fifty thousand turned into a flood of fleeing men, desperate to escape the slaughter.

But Liu Bei's army gave them no such mercy. With a unified roar, the five hundred surged forward, cutting through the panicked mob like fire through dry grass. Steel flashed, hooves thundered, and the cries of the fallen echoed across Mount Daxing as justice carved its way through the ranks of the faithless.

When the dust settled, Mount Daxing was a redstreaked panorama—bodies lay out across the slopes, armor dented, banners drooped. Thousands of Yellow Turbans, stunned and broken, were bound and herded like a tide of captured shadows.

Liu Bei's five hundred moved through the aftermath like

a slow, inexorable tide: tending the wounded, securing the prisoners, and standing watch over the spoils of a day won against impossible odds. The mountain itself seemed to breathe again, the wind carrying the metallic tang of blood and the low, ragged moans of the fallen.

At the head of the column, Zhang Fei rode with chest thrust forward, eyes bright with grim pride. He slammed his fist against his breastplate so the sound echoed down the line.

"This is only the first," he bellowed, voice ringing against the ridges. "Give me three more days like this and I will tear the Yellow Turbans from the land!"

Guan Yu's expression never wavered. He sheathed his Green Dragon Crescent Blade and stepped close, his voice low and grave.

"Do not raise the banners of celebration yet," he warned. "We have won one battle, but the war has only begun. They did not know who we were before—now they do. Let that knowledge be the spark that lights our caution as well as our blade."

They marched triumphant back to Youzhou beneath a sky bruised by the day's violence, the prisoners trailing in ironed lines. Word of the rout raced faster than their banners; Governor Liu Yan had already been told.

Tension hung in the governor's hall like a held breath—and when the column finally entered the city, the gates opened to fanfare prepared in haste. Musicians tuned drums and pipes; cooks and servants hurried to lay out steaming trays of meat and stacked bowls of rice. Lanterns were strung, and servants arranged cushions for honored guests.

Yet beneath the glitter of celebration, there was the

sober echo of Guan Yu's warning. Victory had been won on the slopes of Daxing, but the shape of the war had only just revealed itself.

In halls of silk and shadow, feasts were held and praises sung, while at the map's edge, enemies gathered with renewed resolve—hungry for those bold enough to face them.

CHAPTER 17

BLAZE OF FIRE

~

The last echoes of laughter faded into the night. Empty wine cups lay scattered among the dying embers of cooking fires, and the air still held the sweet scent of roasted meat and celebration.

Liu Bei pulled his cloak tighter against the cool night air, watching as his weary soldiers sought their rest. Some had already collapsed where they sat, heads pillowed on their arms. Others stumbled toward the makeshift shelters they had built, their voices reduced to drowsy murmurs. It had been too long since his men had reason to celebrate—he was glad to see them in such spirits.

The camp was settling into peaceful quiet when hoof-beats shattered the stillness.

A rider broke through the perimeter, his horse dripping with sweat and foam. He jumped down quickly, almost stumbling. His clothes were torn and muddy, and his face showed the strain of a man who had ridden hard to deliver urgent news.

"My lord!" the messenger called out, his voice cutting through the night. "My lord Liu Wan!"

The few soldiers still awake scrambled to their feet, hands moving instinctively to their weapons. Liu Bei stepped forward, his heart already sinking as he recognized the look in the messenger's desperate eyes.

"Here!" came a voice from across the camp.

Governor Liu Wan's guards hurried over. Behind him was Liu Wan, calmly approaching the scene, his official robes hastily thrown over his sleeping clothes, clearly roused from rest by the commotion.

"What brings you at this desperate hour?"

The messenger dropped to one knee before Liu Wan, gasping for breath.

"From Qingzhou, my lord. Governor Gong Jing sends word." He paused, struggling to catch his breath. "The situation is desperate. He begs for your immediate aid."

Liu Wan's face drained of color as he broke the seal and unrolled the scroll. By torchlight, he scanned the words, then turned sharply toward Liu Bei, who stood nearby, his eyes clouded with worry.

"General Liu," Liu Wan said, his voice low but edged with urgency, cutting through the smoke of the command tent. "I must seek your counsel—the enemy advances faster than we feared."

Liu Bei met the governor's gaze. The torchlight flickered across his features, etching the wear of countless burdens. He answered with only a slow, deliberate nod. There was no choice. Duty called once more—and he would answer, once again.

The celebration fires still crackled beyond the tent walls, where a handful of soldiers shared the last drops of wine, their voices subdued by the knowledge that within hours, they would march right back into battle.

In the pre-dawn darkness, the three sworn brothers stood side by side. Liu Bei placed his hands on the shoulders of his brothers, feeling the familiar weight of shared destiny.

"Once more, my brothers," he said quietly, his breath visible in the cold morning air.

As the sun crested the horizon, painting the sky in shades of amber and crimson, they mounted their war horses with practiced ease. Behind them, their army stirred to life—soldiers who had barely tasted rest now shouldering their weapons with grim determination. The thunder of hooves and the rhythmic march of feet began once more.

When they crested the hills overlooking Qingzhou, the sight before them was both familiar and daunting. Another fifty thousand Yellow Turbans filled the valley like a golden sea, their banners snapping in the wind. News of the clash at Daxing Mountain had already spread, and the rebels were waiting for Liu Bei's army.

Though Qingzhou was the seat of the government forces, the city lay encircled and paralyzed—its strength strangled by the Yellow Turbans' grip. Liu Bei weighed his options carefully, knowing no aid could be expected from the trapped government army. Yet before his thoughts could settle into a plan, Zhang Fei—still flushed with the intoxicating triumph of their last victory and wine hot in his veins

—spurred his horse forward. His serpent spear gleamed in his grip, a wild grin splitting his bearded face.

"Let's race and see who can kill them all first!" he roared, his voice carrying across the battlefield like thunder.

Without waiting for orders or strategy, he spurred his horse forward, charging straight toward the nearest cluster of Yellow Turbans with the reckless abandon that had served him so well before.

But this time felt different. The rebels didn't scatter like startled birds. They held their ground, their formations tightening like a trap about to spring. Last time, they had won because the enemy commanders—drunk on their own power and eager for glory—had foolishly positioned themselves at the front lines, making themselves easy targets for skilled warriors.

But now, Liu Bei's sharp eyes scanned the enemy ranks and found no silk robes or ornate banners marking commanders. The leaders had learned their lesson, strategically positioning themselves deep behind layers upon layers of expendable troops.

Will a direct confrontation work again this time? Liu Bei wondered, his heart sinking as he watched his sworn brother disappear into the enemy's human wave tactic— endless ranks of bodies designed to exhaust and overwhelm through sheer, grinding attrition.

The enemy generals commanded from the safety of the rear, orchestrating their forces like puppet masters pulling invisible strings. Wave after wave of foot soldiers swarmed forward like angry hornets, their sheer numbers seemingly endless. No matter how many Liu Bei's vastly outnumbered army cut down—slashing through ranks with desperate efficiency—the tide of yellow-clad warriors kept surging forward, as relentless as flood waters.

Liu Bei's soldiers, their arms heavy with exhaustion and their formations buckling under the crushing weight of numbers, began to falter. Step by agonizing step, they found themselves retreating, their earlier confidence crumbling like sand castles before a tsunami.

At that critical moment, Liu Bei's voice rang out above the cacophony of battle, reaching his sworn brothers through the chaos.

"This time we need different tactics!"

Guan Yu, his magnificent beard now streaked with sweat and dust, nodded grimly as he parried another desperate thrust.

"You're right. We're hopelessly outnumbered. We should request a reserve unit of two thousand soldiers as reinforcements."

But even as the words were spoken, Liu Bei realized the futility of the situation. With Qingzhou encircled and the government forces cut off, no reinforcements would come any time soon.

"Everyone retreat immediately!" Liu Bei commanded. They could not risk bleeding out their small army.

Without delay, Liu Bei dispatched his swiftest messenger, the man's horse thundering across the battlefield toward the provincial capital—instead of the nearby Qingzhou—to request a reserve army. As their forces regrouped behind hastily erected defenses, the three brothers huddled in urgent conference, their heads bent over a crude map drawn in the dirt.

"Tonight, around midnight, I'll lead our five hundred

men in a frontal assault on their main camp," Liu Bei declared, his finger tracing attack routes in the dust.

"You two will each take a thousand soldiers from rein-forcements and lie in ambush—Guan Yu on the left flank, Zhang Fei on the right. When I retreat and sound the bronze gongs in apparent defeat, strike simultaneously from both sides. We'll crush them in a pincer movement they won't see coming."

As the midnight descended like a shroud over the battle-field, Liu Bei's army struck the war drum with thunderous resonance. Its battle cry pierced the darkness as Liu Bei led five hundred warriors in a desperate charge toward the enemy encampment. The enemy soldiers emerged with contemptuous snorts and jeering laughter, utterly dismis-sive of this seemingly foolhardy assault.

The clash erupted in savage fury—steel rang against steel, spears thrust and parried, and the night air filled with the grunts and shouts of mortal combat. Then, as suddenly as it had begun, Liu Bei's force appeared to falter. With what seemed like defeat etched across his features, he wheeled his horse around and began a frantic retreat. His men appeared to panic and scatter behind, following their leader in retreat.

The enemy erupted in triumphant roars, their blood singing with the thrill of easy victory. They surged forward in pursuit, like hunting wolves, their formation dissolving into an eager, chaotic mass as they chased what they believed were broken remnants fleeing in terror.

But as the pursuit crested the mountain ridge, Liu Bei's retreating army suddenly rang out with the sharp, piercing notes of bronze gongs—the pre-arranged signal that would turn the tide of battle.

From the left flank, Guan Yu's war cry split the night like thunder as he charged forth with his legendary might. From the right, Zhang Fei's serpent spear gleamed wickedly in the moonlight as he burst from concealment with a roar that seemed to shake the very mountains. The enemy, caught completely off-guard by this devastating pincer attack, found themselves trapped in a killing ground of Liu Bei's design.

In that moment of perfect coordination, Liu Bei himself wheeled about, his "retreat" revealed as masterful deception. Now the hunters became the hunted as the three sworn brothers launched their combined assault with devastating precision.

The enemy ranks, stretched thin from chasing too far, gave way at once and fell into chaos. What had moments before been confident pursuers now became desperate survivors, their formations shattered and their courage evaporating into the night air. The three generals, now commanding twenty-five hundred soldiers, swept through their opponents with the unstoppable force of a mountain torrent.

The rout became a massacre as they pursued the fleeing remnants all the way to the walls of Qingzhou city itself. There, Governor Gong Jing, who had been trapped within the besieged walls, burst forth from the gates with his remaining forces. Hemmed in on all sides, the thousands of enemy soldiers were utterly destroyed.

In the aftermath, as dawn broke over the liberated city, Governor Gong Jing emerged to offer his profound gratitude to the three heroes who had saved his domain from destruction. The siege of Qingzhou was broken, and Liu Bei's renown as a master tactician was forged that night.

The victory banquet resumed with even greater fervor the following day. Wine flowed like rivers, and the air rang with songs of triumph as the heroes were celebrated throughout the liberated city.

Yet amidst the revelry, Liu Bei learned something that would change the course of their campaign.

Governor Gong Jing, his face grave despite the festive atmosphere, leaned close to Liu Bei during the feast.

"There is something you should know," he said, his voice dropping to a confidential whisper. "You might know Master Lu Zhi. He has risen to the rank of General of the Household. Even now, he leads the imperial forces against the Yellow Turban chieftain Zhang Jiao himself—the very architect of this rebellion."

Liu Bei's wine cup froze halfway to his lips. Master Lu Zhi—the scholarly gentleman who had taught him the classics, who had instilled in him the virtues of loyalty and righteousness—was now locked in mortal combat with the self-proclaimed prophet who had plunged the empire into chaos.

Without hesitation, Liu Bei set down his cup and rose from his seat. His voice carried clearly over the celebration:

"My honored teacher, Lu Zhi, fights for the empire while we feast. How can we sit idle when our master needs us?"

His eyes burned with determination as he looked to his sworn brothers.

"We must go to his aid immediately."

Zhang Fei slammed his cup down, then angrily tore into

the meat before him as if it were his last chance to eat. Grease glistened on his beard, and between mouthfuls, he cursed the summons that had disrupted his festive mood. Guan Yu, in contrast, rose with measured calm, one hand already resting on the hilt of his great blade, his steady gaze fixed toward the coming battle.

As dawn broke the next morning, their army was already in motion, leaving behind the grateful citizens of Qingzhou. The road ahead would lead them to Zhang Jiao himself—the mastermind whose twisted teachings had ignited the Yellow Turban rebellion across the empire. His forces would be seasoned veterans, elite troops hardened by months of successful campaigns. Against such opponents, even the brilliant Master Lu Zhi would surely be fighting for his very survival.

The thought drove Liu Bei's forces forward with renewed urgency, their banners streaming in the morning wind as they marched toward their greatest challenge yet.

Days later, when the familiar figure of Lu Zhi appeared on the horizon—older now, his scholarly robes replaced by military armor, but still carrying himself with that same dignified bearing—his weathered face broke into a smile of genuine joy and relief.

"My student," he called out, his voice carrying both warmth and weary gratitude, "you have come at our darkest hour."

Liu Bei approached his revered teacher with solemn reverence. Three times he bowed in the ancient ritual of respect, his forehead touching the earth as he honored the man who had shaped his understanding of virtue and duty.

Lu Zhi raised his weathered hand, his eyes soft with paternal affection yet sharp with military urgency.

"Rise, my faithful student. Though my heart swells to see you, there is no time for long reunions."

His voice carried the authority of command mingled with genuine concern.

"Here, we face Zhang Jiao's forces across the field—a stalemate that benefits no one. But at Yingchuan, the battle rages with desperate fury."

The old scholar-general's expression darkened as he continued.

"Generals Huangfu Song and Zhu Jun fight for their very lives against two of the Yellow Turban leaders, Zhang Jiao's brothers—Zhang Bao and Zhang Liang. These are cunning commanders leading seasoned troops. Our imperial forces falter, their spirits flagging under relentless assault."

His eyes locked with Liu Bei's, conveying both trust and urgency.

"Go to them. I will provide you with one thousand reinforcements. Lend your strength when they need it most."

Liu Bei bowed once more, accepting the mission along with the one thousand reinforcements. The combined force of fifteen hundred men set out immediately on the grueling forced march to Yingchuan, their banners snapping in the wind as they raced toward the distant sounds of battle.

But when they finally arrived at the city and Liu Bei introduced himself to General Zhu Jun, the general's response was curt and unyielding. The general lounged arrogantly in his command tent, his silk robes untouched by battle despite the carnage raging beyond the camp's walls. His eyes swept over Liu Bei with undisguised contempt, noting the dust of hard travel and the simple armor of a man who fought alongside his troops.

"And from where do you claim to come?"

Zhu Jun's voice dripped with disdain, as if addressing a lowly servant.

"We are volunteer forces, General," Liu Bei replied with quiet dignity, "who have taken up arms of our own accord to serve the empire in its hour of need."

At these words, Zhu Jun sneered, the sound of a harsh laugh breaking from his throat. "Ah, so you are mercenaries," he sneered, his tone dripping with scorn.

He muttered with open disdain, yet loud enough for all to hear: "Nothing but rabble—peasants in rags, pretending to be soldiers."

The insult hung in the air like a drawn blade, reducing Liu Bei's hard-won victories and the sacrifice of his men to mere banditry. The contrast between the noble Lu Zhi and the arrogant Zhu Jun could not have been more stark.

Yet Liu Bei showed no flicker of emotion. He rose steadily from his bow, lamplight glinting in his eyes.

"Ragged though we may be, General," he said evenly, "your army needs our support."

The words landed with quiet weight. A ripple went through the tent; a few officers shifted, caught between unease and respect. For the first time that night, Zhu Jun's scorn faltered—giving way to calculation.

Zhu Jun studied Liu Bei's composure in silence. At last, he gave a clipped reply: "You may take the eastern field."

He waved a hand to dismiss them, then, without meeting Liu Bei's eyes, added: "Hold it as you see fit."

Dismissed without ceremony, Liu Bei's force marched

out of camp under the glaring summer sun. The eastern field lay ahead—an open stretch choked with waist-high grass, the stalks swaying lazily in the heat.

This was Yellow Turban country, and their strategy was as cruel as it was simple: vanish in the sea of overgrowth, then erupt without warning, cutting men down before they could raise a shield.

Zhang Fei's jaw tightened as he surveyed the ground. His fury simmered just beneath the surface, like a storm cloud swollen with lightning. Finally, he spat into the dirt.

"So that arrogant bastard hands us this empty grass field to bleed upon and die?" he growled, his voice thick with bitter scorn. "We're nothing but shields for their own hides —meant to be shattered and thrown aside."

He forced a slow breath through his nose, the taste of anger still hot on his tongue.

Liu Bei reined in his horse and scanned the field. The plain stretched wide before him, a sea of tall, dry grass swaying in the restless wind. His men were few, their armor dented and dulled from battle after battle. To *hold the ground* here was not defense but an invitation to slaughter. Face the rebels head-on, and they would be swallowed whole.

For a long moment, he was silent, his eyes narrowing against the glare of the sun. Then he noticed how the grass bent and shivered, each stalk brittle, starved for the rain that would not come. The wind tugged at cloaks and banners, eager, hungry, feeding on every spark.

A thought caught fire within him.

"Tonight," Liu Bei said at last, his voice low and resolute, "we are going to attack. The wind will fight for us."

That night, beneath a moon veiled in gathering clouds,

his command spread through the camp: each soldier was to bind a bundle of withered grass, brittle as bone. Hours crept by, the world hushed beneath the weight of night, until at last Guan Yu and Zhang Fei led their men through shadowed paths toward the enemy's slumbering camp.

The enemy lay tangled in dreams, unaware of the doom creeping near.

A thousand soldiers crept close, their hearts hammering as they neared the shadowed tents of the enemy. Then, with a single spark, the night exploded into flame—a roaring blaze that turned shadow to blazing daylight. The sky itself seemed to crack as a deafening war cry tore through the inferno, and they surged forward like a tidal wave of fire and steel.

The startled foe awoke in a tempest of terror—blind, disoriented, they hacked at shadows, attacking members of their own troop in frantic confusion. Torches soared like flaming arrows, setting their own camps aflame, while flames devoured cloth and flesh alike, swallowing the night in an all-consuming blaze. The battlefield became a hellscape of crackling fire and blood-curdling screams.

The battle was almost over—shouts fading to cries, the clash of steel giving way to silence. Victory felt within reach. Then, beyond the smoke and heat, the earth began to tremble. At first, it was a low rumble, then it grew until the ground shook like an earthquake.

Through the haze, a tide of horsemen emerged, red banners unfurling like rivers of blood. Their charge cut through the chaos like a blade, scattering Yellow Turbans and Liu Bei's troops alike. Friend or foe, no one could tell.

Liu Bei's eyes narrowed. These were no Yellow Turbans

—their ranks held firm, armor gleaming, steeds moving with trained power.

He straightened in the saddle.

"Hold the line. Do not provoke them," he commanded. Then, looking to his brothers, "We go forward."

Zhang Fei scowled but followed, spear in hand. Guan Yu rode silent and steady. Together, they advanced into the firelit haze.

Liu Bei lowered his spear and raised his hand in a gesture of parley.

"Halt! Declare yourselves!"

The lead rider reined in smoothly, his crimson plume swaying. Sharp eyes swept over the brothers, missing nothing.

"We are five thousand troops from Luoyang," he said, voice calm and commanding. "And you? I see that you are no Yellow Turbans."

"I am Liu Bei, styled Xuande, of Lou Sang Village in Zhuo County," Liu Bei replied. "I lead a militia against the rebels. And who are you?"

The man inclined his head, a subtle, knowing curve to his lips as though he had recognized something. Firelight glazed his pale, porcelain features; his eyes were sharp, calculating, and his expression polite yet carefully measured.

"I am Cao Cao of Peiguo, styled Mengde, Commander of the Imperial Guards in Luoyang. We march against Zhang Bao and Zhang Liang. Your fire attack tonight broke their strength, leaving me only the fleeing remnants."

He let the silence stretch for a heartbeat, his gaze steady.

Then, with a faint curl to his lips, he added, "Perhaps, from here on, we might fight as one."

The name hung in the air. Liu Bei met his gaze, and in that moment both men understood: here was no common foe, but an equal—one to respect, to ally with when fate demanded, and to rival when destiny left no other path. History itself would not keep them apart for long.

Cao Cao's gaze flicked over Zhang Fei's scowl and Guan Yu's watchful stillness before returning to Liu Bei. His eyes were sharp, though his mouth curved in a faint smile.

"You've held well. Few militias could endure in open grassland."

"I thank you for the praise, Lord Cao," Liu Bei said evenly. "But these men are not mere militia. They fight because they must, and because the people's cause is worth more than numbers or terrain. That is why we endure."

Cao Cao's smile curled faintly.

"Nobility often dies before the man who carries it."

"Or it lives on in those who refuse to let it die," Liu Bei answered.

For a moment longer, they studied one another, each weighing the other's mettle.

Then, with the mutual grace of warriors who recognized both an ally and a rival, they exchanged a final nod.

CHAPTER 18
THE MAKING OF A WARLORD

∾

Cao Cao, whose courtesy name was Mengde, was born in 155 CE in Qiao County, Pei State. His family was not of Imperial blood, but they carried enough prestige to move in powerful circles. His father, Cao Song, had risen to the position of Grand Commandant—one of the highest offices in the Han court —not through noble heritage but through adoption: he was adopted into the Cao clan from the powerful Xiahou family.

This meant that young Cao Cao had ties to both the Cao clan and the martial Xiahou clan, a network that would later form the backbone of his military career. His cousins, Xiahou Dun and Xiahou Yuan, would be his lifelong allies, bound not just by loyalty but also by bloodlines that criss-crossed through adoption and marriage.

From an early age, Cao Cao's household was one of

subtle ambition, surrounded by whispers of court intrigue. Servants spoke in cautious tones, and visitors came bearing news from the capital. The boy grew up watching adults navigate a world where a smile could hide a knife.

When he was young, he was known for a cunning mind and a streak of mischief that unsettled his elders. Rumors soon followed. In Luoyang lived a famed face reader, He Shou, whose judgments were said to never miss. After studying Cao Cao's features, he gave a verdict that would cling to Cao Cao all his life:

"This young man will be a capable minister in times of peace—yet in times of chaos, a treacherous hero."

Some repeated it in awe. Others, in dread.

One sweltering afternoon, Cao Song—his father and Grand Commandant of the Han Empire—sat in the shaded hall with a cup of cooled tea. Across from him, a middle-aged cousin leaned forward, voice lowered, as he shared the latest whispers from his inner circle at the palace.

Then, catching sight of young Cao Cao darting through the garden with a bow in hand, chasing some unseen quarry, the cousin's voice faltered. He shifted in his seat, his report on palace matters giving way to a sharper, more personal tone.

"Your son, Mengde, is clever," the cousin began, his tone edged with disdain, "but far too clever for his own good. Always scheming, always turning some petty trick. He idles in the streets, shirks his studies. A boy like that—" he paused, letting the bitterness sharpen his words, "—is as likely to shame your name as to honor it."

Cao Song's brow tightened. The warning planted itself

like a bitter seed. Outside the hall, a slim figure crouched under the eaves, listening. Young Cao Cao smiled to himself.

The next morning, as the cousin arrived for another visit, a commotion broke out in the front courtyard. Servants whispered of calamity.

"Young Master Mengde has collapsed! He's unable to move his legs!"

The cousin hurried in to find Cao Cao lying on a bamboo mat, pale and motionless, eyes half-closed.

"He's gravely ill!" the man exclaimed, his voice cracking with alarm. "Brother, you must fetch the physician at once—"

But before the words were finished, Cao Cao sprang to his feet with the speed of a startled cat. He dusted his sleeves, grinning.

"Well," he sneered, "if you're simple enough to think I'd die from such pathetic playacting... then perhaps my father is a fool to trust your judgment of me. What do you think?"

The cousin's face went red with fury. Cao Song froze for a moment—and then, to the cousin's shock, let out a reluctant laugh.

From that day, Cao Song looked at his son with new eyes. This boy was not merely mischievous; he was a quick-thinking manipulator who could turn a rebuke into an advantage.

The cousin's warning and its reversal became a small legend inside the Cao household, told in whispers over tea. But Cao Cao himself seemed unmoved by it, as if fooling an elder was no different from playing a boring game of elephant chess. If anything, it only sharpened his appetite for new games.

Not long after, he began taking short walks into the town's busy market, trailed by a single servant carrying a parasol. The market was a living maze of voices: hawkers shouting over the smell of fried dough, merchants swearing their silk was from Shu, beggars clanging bowls for coin.

Out of the sudden, he spotted a minor official—fat, pompous, with a jeweled belt—shoving a cloth merchant away from his stall. Cao Cao paused, watching. Then he stepped forward, his voice loud enough for the crowd.

"Ah, how fortunate Qiao County is to have an official so honest and upright! Why, even the Emperor himself would be glad to have you guard his gates."

The official froze, startled and embarrassed by the sudden praise. Heads turned; eyes stared. No man liked to be seen bullying under the gaze of a crowd now expecting virtue. With an awkward cough, the official let the merchant go and straightened his robe as though it was part of a routine inspection.

As Cao Cao strolled away, his servant whispered, "Young master, why flatter a man like that?"

Cao Cao smiled without looking back. "Because when people believe they are being watched, they behave better—whether or not it's true."

There was another time, when a group of older neighborhood boys tried to corner him in an alley, seeking revenge for some insult. Cao Cao reached into his sleeve and produced a small wooden crossbow, its string drawn back with a pellet.

"You'd better run," he said. "If I loosen this, you'll regret it."

They hesitated, glancing at each other. Then Cao Cao shouted toward the far end of the alley, "Cousin Dun! Now!"

The bullies scattered like sparrows before a hawk, not waiting to see whether Xiahou Dun was really there. Cao Cao lowered the crossbow, chuckling to himself. No one appeared at the alley's end.

Later, he would tell his real cousin, Xiahou Dun, "You don't need arrows to win a fight—only the fear that you have them."

By the time he reached fifteen, Cao Cao had drawn his cousins Xiahou Dun and Xiahou Yuan into his orbit. The three trained with spears in the courtyard, plotted imaginary campaigns, and swore that one day they would ride together in real battles.

Although he was in his teens, Cao Cao's mind was already shaping the future. He listened closely to gossip from the capital—about the Emperor's favorites, about the power of eunuchs and the pride of generals—and stored every detail like a miser counting coins.

Once, when Xiahou Dun asked why he paid so much attention to such talk, Cao Cao replied, "Because someday, the Empire's fate will rest in the hands of men who understand *people* better than they understand swords."

The summer he turned seventeen, Cao Cao began walking at night. Qiao County was quiet after dark; only the guards at the watchtowers and the occasional drunk stumbled through the lamplit streets.

One evening, one of his cousins, Xiahou Yuan, hurried into his study, cheeks flushed.

"The county magistrate has a son," he said, "who

harasses every merchant and their daughters. No one dares complain, because his father controls the law."

Cao Cao tilted his head. "Then the law must be made to see him differently."

Two nights later, the young men waited outside the magistrate's compound. The target appeared, laughing with his friends, half drunk. Cao Cao stepped forward, holding a tall walking staff painted bright red.

"Stop," he commanded, his voice steady. "By order of the Commandant's house, you are under watch for suspicious conduct."

The magistrate's son blinked in confusion.

"What? I've done nothing."

Cao Cao twirled the staff, allowing the red paint to catch the moonlight.

"This is the mark of those suspected by the capital. When I see someone unfit to walk freely, I make it a point to carry this and let it be known. Every guard who sees you now will think you're being watched."

The boy's friends shifted uneasily. The red gleam looked almost like fresh blood in the lamplight. By the next day, rumors had spread: the magistrate's son was under investigation. The official, embarrassed and frightened, quietly reined in his son's behavior.

Xiahou Dun laughed when he heard the story.

"You made the whole thing up! What if the magistrate had confronted you?"

Cao Cao set the staff against the wall.

"Then I'd have said it was a simple walking stick. But the *fear* would have already done its work."

Since that incident, whispers spread through the hushed

corridors of Qiao County's gentry halls. They spoke of young Mengde as a man who could sway people without lifting a hand—who could wield a symbol like a blade sharper than steel.

Some admired him for it. Others, in silence, began to fear.

CHAPTER 19
REIGN OF TERROR

~

T he story of the painted staff traveled farther than Cao Cao expected. Within months, it reached the ears of an official in Luoyang, who was seeking sharp young men to keep order in the capital. The court was choking on corruption; the Emperor's eunuchs ruled the palace, generals bickered over commands, and in the city's narrow streets, thieves and drunkards prowled without fear of the law.

So, at barely twenty years old, Cao Cao was summoned to serve as a Captain of the Northern District.

The capital was unlike Qiao—its walls thick and high, its gates guarded by men who barely glanced at passes if the bribe was heavy enough. Bronze lamps lit the main streets at night, but beyond them, shadows pressed close like an unseen crowd.

The first week, Cao Cao walked his district in plain

clothes. He learned where the gamblers hid their dice, which alleyways the knife-men preferred, and which taverns the guards themselves used to drink away their patrol hours.

His conclusion was simple: fear had to return to the streets—and it had to return fast.

He ordered his men to patrol at night carrying nothing but short clubs... and whistles. If they found anyone on the streets past curfew without a valid reason, they were to strike them with the club on the spot, with *no exceptions*.

Then, on his first night leading the patrol, Cao Cao himself took the whistle. The sound cut through the darkness—high, sharp, and cold. Dogs barked, shutters slammed, and footsteps scattered into silence.

"Remember," he told his men, "the law means nothing unless people *fear* that it can come for them. The whistle is the voice of the law tonight."

Only days later, the most dangerous test came. A young man, richly dressed, swaggered down the street long after curfew, flanked by attendants. Someone whispered to Cao Cao that this was the Emperor's own uncle's son.

Cao Cao didn't hesitate. He stepped forward, struck the youth with the cudgel, and ordered his men to bind him.

By dawn, the entire city buzzed with the news: the new captain had beaten the Emperor's nephew for breaking curfew.

Some officials were outraged—how dare a mere captain touch Imperial kin? But the ordinary people whispered with praise, and even certain members of the court privately smiled. A man who dared such things might be dangerous... but also very, very useful.

From then on, the whistle in the dark became a sound

both feared and respected in Luoyang. And Cao Cao—no longer just the mischievous youth of Qiao County—was now a figure to watch.

One freezing night, Cao Cao was patrolling the streets with his lieutenants as usual. When they were near the north gate, they heard the shouting—guttural, urgent. Cao Cao signaled for silence and moved toward the source of the noise.

In a narrow alley, lit only by a swaying oil lamp, three men stood over a fallen merchant. One gripped a short sword slick with blood; another was rummaging through the dead man's satchel. The third turned and froze as he saw the patrol, his hand halfway to the dagger in his belt.

"Drop it," Cao Cao ordered.

The man didn't move. The sword-bearer smiled, thin and cruel.

"We're friends of Captain Zhang. Do you really want trouble with him?"

Cao Cao stepped closer, voice even.

"The only trouble I have is with those who think a *name* will shield them."

The sword-bearer lunged.

It happened in an instant—Cao Cao's cudgel cracked the man's wrist, sending the blade spinning into the shadows. His other hand shot to his belt, drawing a short knife, which he drove into the man's chest with a sharp twist. The killer gasped once and collapsed onto the wet stones.

The other two tried to flee, but Cao Cao's men caught them before they reached the mouth of the alley. The patrol stood in the chill air of the barracks yard, the corpse lying at their feet like a shadow that had lost its owner. Cao Cao studied it in silence, his gaze traveling from the glazed eyes to the blood-matted tunic.

"Take him to the market square," he said at last, his voice level but carrying the weight of iron. "Hang a sign around his neck: *Murderer, slain in the act.*"

A lieutenant hesitated. "Captain, in the open street?"

"In the busiest place you can find," Cao Cao replied coldly. "Let them see what breaking the law buys. Let mothers point to him when their sons grow restless. Let merchants remember him when their hands itch for another's coin."

By midmorning, the body swayed on its rope before the grain stalls, the signboard clacking in the wind. People gathered in wary silence. Some cheered openly; others crossed the street to avoid passing too close to the horrific scene. A few officers muttered that killing a man on the spot without trial was excessive—but no one challenged Cao Cao to his face.

When a fellow captain later asked if he'd feared punishment, Cao Cao replied with an easy smile, "When you kill the right man, the law thanks you for it—even if it's too proud to admit it."

From that night onward, Luoyang's thieves whispered a new warning: *If Cao Mengde catches you with blood on your hands, you'll leave the street in a shroud.*

Cao Cao himself, washing the blade by lamplight, felt no tremor in his hands.

It was the first time he had killed—and he knew, without question, it would not be the last.

By the spring of 184 AD, the capital was choking on more than politics. The Yellow Turban Rebellion had begun.

The Emperor's court lurched into motion. Orders were scribbled in haste; messengers galloped until their horses collapsed. Every captain with a pulse and a sword arm was summoned to take the field.

For Cao Cao, it was the first true summons to war. His record in Luoyang—quick justice, unflinching strikes—had caught the eye of the General-in-Chief. He was granted a thousand men and told, *"Break the rebels wherever you find them."*

Cao Cao moved with speed, breaking small rebel bands before they could merge with the main force. His scouts spoke of a cluster of loyalist troops farther south, led by a man named Liu Bei—a name Cao Cao had never heard. They were locked in a drawn-out fight with a Yellow Turban detachment near a riverside hamlet.

By the time Cao Cao's vanguard reached the ridgeline, the battle below was already a blur of red and black. The rebels' camp had erupted into chaos—fire roaring through rows of tents, sparks leaping into the night like fleeing spirits.

And there, at the heart of the inferno, astride a magnificent white steed, sat a man serene in the storm. Cao Cao needed no introduction — he knew at once he was looking at Liu Bei.

CHAPTER 20
UNSUNG HEROES

~

T hough the fire attack at Yingchuan had ended in a blaze of triumph, no laurels awaited Liu Bei. In the command tent, Zhu Jun's words dripped with reproach.

"Because of you," Zhu Jun snapped, "the bandits have scattered in all directions, throwing the region into greater chaos. They will flee to Guangzong and trouble General Lu Zhi. Take your men there at once and aid him."

No commendation. No gratitude. Only cold dismissal.

Zhang Fei's temper flared like oil on a flame. "I'll kill him where he stands!" he roared, hand already tightening on his spear.

Inside, Liu Bei's chest tightened at the sting of Zhu Jun's words. Praise had never been his aim, yet the bitterness of being scorned in victory was hard to swallow. Still, he forced his breath steady, refusing to let his face betray him.

He stepped forward, voice controlled but resolute. "General Lu Zhi is my benefactor. We will go to Guangzong and give him our aid."

Just like that, the troops began marching again the next morning, even without a proper rest. The road ahead was long, and their bodies ached with exhaustion. Yet as they marched, Zhang Fei's grumbling never ceased.

"Hmph. Liu Bei lets himself be pushed around from place to place. Did we choose the wrong leader...? What the heck is he really thinking?" he muttered, loud enough for the night air to carry.

The road to Guangzong wound through dusty hills and sparse villages. The men marched in weary silence—until they heard a rhythmic clatter of hooves. From behind a bend came a prisoner's carriage, flanked by guards and drawn by official war horses. Liu Bei's gaze swept over it—and his heart jolted. Inside the barred compartment sat none other than General Lu Zhi.

Without thinking, Liu Bei broke into a run.

"Teacher!" he called.

The guards stiffened, hands instinctively drifting toward their weapons. But Zhang Fei and Guan Yu moved in without a flicker of threat, their towering frames sliding into the narrow space between the soldiers and the carriage.

With disarming grins, they peppered the escorts with harmless chatter, their words spilling like an easy stream. Zhang Fei produced a gourd and tipped it toward a guard's cup.

"Come, have a drink. We've all been marching for days —dust in the mouth is worse than an enemy's blade."

The guards glanced at one another, half-wary, half-tempted. In the end, they accepted the sips, the bite of the wine loosening their shoulders.

"It seems our brother has stumbled upon his long-lost teacher," Guan Yu said mildly.

"Nothing dangerous in that. A few words of comfort, that's all. We've no appetite for trouble—not after battle upon battle. Just let the moment pass."

The soldiers' grip on their weapons eased, their attention drifting to the warmth in their cups rather than the quiet conversation in the carriage.

Liu Bei reached the bars. Lu Zhi's face was gaunt, but his eyes burned with controlled fury.

"I've been framed, Liu Bei," he said in a low, quick voice. "I refused to send bribes to the court. A corrupt official spread lies—that I avoid battle, that I spend my days feasting and idling. They believed him. And now here I am. They have already assigned Dong Zhuo as Commander of the Imperial Guard to the post in Guangzong."

Liu Bei's grip tightened on the bars. "This is an outrage—"

"Quiet," Lu Zhi warned.

"There is nothing you can do here. But the Yellow Turbans must still be stopped. Go on. Do not waste your blade on my chains."

Behind them, Zhang Fei's laughter boomed as he traded wild tales with the Yellow Turbans, keeping the mood loose just long enough for Liu Bei to slip away before suspicion could take root.

The carriage rolled away in the dust. Liu Bei watched it disappear, anger rising at the injustice he had just seen.

With Lu Zhi's arrest, the road to Guangzong felt

suddenly hollow. The fire in their mission had gone out, replaced by a heavy, sour taste. Liu Bei kept his eyes on the road, but his thoughts churned. He was committed to fighting the Yellow Turbans—that much was unshakable —yet the truth gnawed at him: they were spilling their blood for the country, aiding the government army without coin, reward, or even a word of thanks. Meanwhile, the court's officials still dined in comfort, spinning lies and manipulating the truth to their own advantage, their corruption untouched by the chaos that consumed the land.

Quietly, Liu Bei repeated the name Dong Zhuo in his mind. He had heard it before—rumors of a ruthless commander from the northwest, a man as cunning as he was ambitious. Now it was he who replaced Lu Zhi. But Liu Bei could not shake the thought that such a post was not given by chance. No, Dong Zhuo must have had a hand in the intrigue that toppled his benefactor. The name itself left a bitter taste, a warning of darker days to come.

Liu Bei rode in silence for a few more hours before he finally said, "There is no point in aiding Dong Zhuo in Guangzong now. We turn north to Zhuo County. Perhaps there, in our home ground, we can make ourselves of use."

Guan Yu agreed, his face unreadable. But Zhang Fei's scowl deepened with every step of his horse.

"So that's it? We fought like madmen, risked our lives, and for what? Our leader's teacher gets thrown in chains, and no one cares." He spat into the dust. "We'd have been better off staying home. I could have kept hunting wild boar —selling the meat, the tusks—I'd be rich! Instead of marching in circles for scraps of thanks."

His voice carried across the column, sharp enough to draw uneasy glances from the men behind them.

Liu Bei didn't answer. His gaze was fixed on the northern horizon, where the road bent toward Zhuo County. Somewhere out there, he told himself, their efforts would count for something.

For now, only the clatter of hooves remained—broken by Zhang Fei's muttered curses and the bitterness of disappointment.

CHAPTER 21
THE SORCERER GENERAL

～

or three days, they pressed on, the road unrolling in a haze of dust and heat. Around a sharp bend, the air ahead rippled with noise—shouting, the metallic clash of arms, the frantic pounding of hooves.

Zhang Fei's eyes lit up. "Stay here!" he barked and charged ahead.

Moments later, he came pounding back, chest heaving, dust streaking his face.

"The government troops from Guangzong!" he gasped. "They're in full retreat — the Yellow Turbans are right behind them!"

His voice dropped, thick with urgency. "It's the Yellow Turbans' mastermind, Zhang Jiao, himself leading the chase. I saw his banner—*Great Teacher of Righteousness*. If we leave them be, they'll be crushed to the last man."

Liu Bei's eyes narrowed. "Ha... the moment Lu Zhi is

taken, the Yellow Turbans strike. Zhang Jiao kept that stalemate for a reason—waiting for a new commander who knew neither the men nor the land. This was the chance they wanted."

Zhang Fei slammed a fist into his palm. "I knew it! Let's smash them now! Those Guangzong cowards will never outrun Zhang Jiao's horde."

Guan Yu cut him off. "Charging blind is the quickest way into their trap. We don't know their numbers—or the ground."

Thunder rolled closer—shouts, steel, the pounding of hooves. A dust cloud swelled over the ridge. Liu Bei sat tall in the saddle, gaze steady. He could almost see the desperate faces in flight.

"If we turn away, we leave them to slaughter." He raised his hand. "Form up. We ride."

He pointed to the rocky slope looming over the valley. "Up there. I want the field in sight before we move."

The column scrambled up the winding path, boots and hooves kicking loose stones down the hillside. At the crest, the valley spread before them—a battlefield in motion.

Below, the Imperial Army staggered backward under relentless pressure, fighting and retreating simultaneously. Yellow Turban warriors swarmed around them like ants on a wounded beast. Yet among the chaos, one banner stood out above the others—the bold black characters for *General of Heaven's Might* rippling in the wind.

Liu Bei commanded, "We ride—now!"

The three brothers spurred their mounts, thundering down the slope like an avalanche.

Liu Bei's twin swords flashed first, carving clean arcs of

silver through the sunlit dust. He moved with swift precision, his strikes measured and certain, every cut opening a
path for the men behind him.

Guan Yu's green-dragon blade swept wide in great,
lethal crescents. Each swing tore through multiple foes at
once, the steel gleaming with the cold light of inevitability.
His enemies fell in silence, their cries cut off before they
could leave their throats.

Zhang Fei roared as his serpent-spear lashed forward
and back, but at his side hung a heavy cleaver-like blade—
and when he drew it, the weapon cleaved shields, helmets,
and men as though they were reeds before the storm.

They carved a wedge through the Yellow Turban ranks,
the three blades striking in perfect harmony—one precise,
one sweeping, one brutal—and in their wake, the official
army surged forward with renewed fury.

After a while, the Yellow Turbans' momentum broke.
The *General of Heaven's Might* banner dipped and wavered as
its bearer fell. Shouts of retreat echoed across the field, and
the rebels began to scatter, leaving the ground strewn with
their dead.

On the bloodied earth, the brothers stood shoulder to
shoulder, their blades slick with the proof of victory. The
valley was quiet again, save for the ragged breath of men
who had lived to fight another day.

The dust was still settling when the man who appeared
to be the Commander of the Imperial Guard rode forward,
flanked by armored retainers. His armor, lacquered black
and gold, strained against his swollen girth, the plates clattering with each movement.

A broad, greasy face loomed above it, cheeks sagging like

overripe fruit, a drooping beard matted with oil. His small, sharp eyes glittered with conceit, sweeping over the three brothers and their men as though appraising livestock.

This was Dong Zhuo.

"Summon the one who leads you," he barked, his voice thick, rolling with arrogance and self-indulgence.

Liu Bei stepped forward, swords sheathed, and bowed deeply from the saddle.

"I am Liu Bei of Zhuo County," he said with measured respect. "These are my sworn brothers, Guan Yu and Zhang Fei. We saw your army in peril and came to render aid."

Dong Zhuo's gaze lingered on them for a moment, weighing their bearing, their weapons, their calm amid the chaos.

"And what post do you hold in the Imperial forces?"

Liu Bei straightened slightly. "We hold no official commission, my lord. We fight for the Han because it is our duty."

The arrogance in Dong Zhuo's eyes curdled into contempt. His gaze hardened.

"No commission?" he echoed, his tone cold and dismissive. "Then you are mere wanderers with swords."

His horse shifted under him, and he turned away with the faintest curl of his lip. "The field is secure. You may take your leave."

Zhang Fei's jaw clenched until the muscles twitched, his hand drifting toward his spear. Guan Yu's face stayed composed, though the slight narrowing of his eyes betrayed the anger he held back. Liu Bei inclined his head in calm, though the insult cut deep within him. They had saved his men from slaughter, yet they were nothing in the eyes of the Han court.

Dong Zhuo—style name Zhongying—hailed from Lintao in Longxi. Once the Administrator of Hedong, his reputation for arrogance had preceded him to every post. But arrogance after being saved from inevitable defeat was more than Liu Bei could stomach.

Liu Bei kept his composure as he turned his horse, leading the brothers and their men away from the government camp. His face was calm, but shadowed.

"A man may hold high office," he said quietly, "yet that does not excuse him from gratitude."

Zhang Fei spat into the dirt. "Gratitude? That pig from Longxi looked at us like beggars! You know who knows how to deal with a pig? Me. I'll make him squeal louder than any hog I ever butchered! I'll gut him here and now for the insult."

With a violent tug on the reins, he wheeled his horse toward Dong Zhuo's command tent. Guan Yu's hand shot out, seizing Zhang Fei's bridle.

"Think, brother. He's a commander of the Han. Strike him down, and we'll be branded traitors—our faces nailed in every marketplace, hunted as fugitives forever."

Liu Bei moved his own mount alongside, his voice firm.

"Our cause is the restoration of the Han, not our pride. Leave him to his arrogance. His own character will bring him to ruin. A man who cannot master his own conduct will one day be mastered by the consequences."

Zhang Fei's nostrils flared, but after a long, tense moment, he yanked his reins back toward the road.

"Hmph. One day, I'll make him choke on that smug face of his."

Without another word, the three brothers turned northward, the clamor of Dong Zhuo's camp fading behind them. The insult burned in their chests, but the road ahead called them onward.

The brothers rode in silence, but the same thought gnawed at each of them. No matter how hard they fought, no matter how clean and brave the victory, the court would never see it—and if they were unlucky, it would twist their deeds into blame or slander.

Liu Bei's gaze never left the road, yet within he vowed: *I will endure for now—but in the end, Heaven will see the truth, and I will act upon it."*

Defeated in spirit yet unwilling to stop, they marched on. Days later, they crossed the Yellow River at last.

The water stretched vast and endless beneath the open sky, just as it had long ago when Liu Bei had come here in search of gong cha for his ailing mother. The river and the mountains were unchanged, as if time itself had been standing guard over them—but he was not the same man who had crossed here before. Battles fought, victories soured, insults endured; his life had twisted into shapes he had never imagined.

As he looked at the river, memories stirred, and a wave of nostalgia came over him. A thought slipped into his mind: *Should I go home and tend to Mother instead...?* But the sight of the water reminded him of his vow—to become a man like the water itself, steady and unyielding, always moving forward. With that, the hesitation passed.

Crossing through Yingchuan, they chose to pass by Zhu

Jun's base before taking the road north. After the sting of Dong Zhuo's arrogance, they could not help but recall that, at the very least, Zhu Jun had entrusted Liu Bei's army with a post.

The Zhu Jun they met again was not the same man who had once dismissed Liu Bei with cold indifference. Now, the commander was locked in a desperate fight against *General of Earth's Justice*, Zhang Bao, one of Zhang Jiao's two brothers. The clash had ground into a stalemate, and the strain was plain in his eyes.

When word came that Liu Bei and his brothers had arrived with their troops, Zhu Jun strode out himself to greet them. His face broke into a smile so wide it was almost unrecognizable.

"Mengde—no—General Liu! You've come at the perfect moment. Your valor will turn the tide!"

Liu Bei dismounted and returned the bow with courtesy, though inwardly he smirked at the irony—so, his army was worth notice only when the enemy's blade pressed against Zhu Jun's throat.

Just like that, the plan to ride home was gone. The three brothers found themselves once more tightening their armor, sharpening their blades, and marching into the din of another battle—this one fiercer still, where Zhang Bao's war cries rolled over the field like thunder and the Yellow Turban banners blotted the horizon.

The morning sky over Yingchuan was already dark with storm clouds when the scouts returned, faces pale.

"Zhang Bao's host is on the move," they reported. "One hundred thousand strong."

From the high ridge, the enemy army looked like a living

tide—ranks of yellow headscarves stretching to the horizon, banners snapping in the wind, war drums pounding like the heartbeat of some colossal beast. At their center, Zhang Bao himself rode beneath the *General of Earth's Justice* banner, his voice carrying over the din as he chanted the Yellow Turban war oaths.

In Zhu Jun's command tent, the map lay covered in weighted stones, each marking a battle line. He traced the likely point of the enemy's heaviest assault and then looked up at Liu Bei.

"This is the breaking point," Zhu Jun said.

"The fiercest fighting will be here. Hold it, and the line holds. Lose it, and the whole field will collapse."

Zhang Fei slammed his fist into his palm, his voice booming without a trace of restraint. "Why is it always us who get the hardest spot?"

Once, such a challenge might have drawn a cold rebuke, but now Zhu Jun gave a small, almost sheepish smile, as if choosing to smooth the ruffled mane of a valuable warhorse.

"Because," he said, pausing to phrase it better to make it sound like a compliment, "you can handle it—and not just handle it. Your army fights as fiercely as the finest of the Imperial Guard. I trust you with the toughest ground because you can hold it, as well as any man in the Emperor's service."

It was the highest praise they had ever received from someone of authority—a recognition that, for the first time, placed them on equal footing with the government's own troops. In such dire moments, even a few words carried the weight of steel, steadying the heart and stiffening resolve.

The tension eased; Zhang Fei's temper flickered into a grunt of satisfaction. Liu Bei met Zhu Jun's gaze and gave a single, measured nod.

"We'll hold."

The battle began, with the sound of the enemy's approach like a rolling earthquake. Dust rose in choking clouds, and the glint of spears formed a wall of steel.

They knew they were outnumbered. Again and again, Yellow Turbans surged, their sheer numbers threatening to drown the defenders. But the brothers stood like boulders in a raging river, each swing of their weapons cutting back the tide.

Liu Bei's twin swords cut swift, clean arcs, turning aside the first wave with precise, decisive strikes. Guan Yu's green-dragon blade swept in broad, lethal strokes, felling foes by the handful. Zhang Fei roared into the melee, spear flashing, cleaver hacking through shield and armor alike.

From a distance, Zhu Jun watched their line hold against impossible odds, the fiercest battle on the field contained by three men whose names the court still barely knew.

The clash raged for hours, steel and shouting blending into a single, ceaseless roar. At the height of the melee, Zhang Fei burst through the Yellow Turban front like a thunderbolt. His spear snapped a shield aside, and with a single, vicious slash of his heavy blade, he cleaved down the enemy's fierce deputy, Gao Sheng. The man fell without a cry, and the rebels' left flank wavered.

Liu Bei's forces pressed forward, momentum building like a flood. Every step drove the Yellow Turbans back toward their commander's banner. Victory felt close enough to taste.

Then Zhang Bao rose in his saddle.

With a sharp motion, he pulled the knot from his hair, letting the long black and silver strands whip loose in the wind. He gripped the hilt of a curved knife between his teeth, and his arms began to twist in strange, fluid motions —gestures that made even his own men shiver.

The sky darkened.

A sudden whirlwind tore through the battlefield, whipping dust and banners into the air. Sheets of rain slammed down without warning, drenching men and horses alike. Lightning cracked overhead, and the ground shook under the blast of rolling thunder. Hail and ice pellets began to rattle down from the darkening sky.

Caught completely off guard, blinded by the storm, Liu Bei's lines faltered. The Yellow Turbans surged back with renewed fury, their chants rising in the gale. One by one, pockets of the official forces began to break and fall away.

"Retreat!!!"

Liu Bei shouted the order. His voice fought against the roaring storm. Reluctantly, the brothers pulled back, the roar of the storm chasing them from the field.

That day, they were defeated by Zhang Bao's storm—a strange force of nature that fought against them.

The rain didn't stop until after they completely withdrew from the field. By then, Liu Bei's army was soaked to the bone, their banners plastered against their poles, the campfires sputtering in the damp wind.

Zhang Fei hurled his helmet into the mud. "We had them! One more push and Zhang Bao would be headless— but no, Heaven decides to spit on us!"

Guan Yu sat quietly, sharpening his blade with a whet-stone—the scraping sound cut through the night air.

Liu Bei said nothing. His mind replayed the moment—Zhang Bao's loose hair, the knife in his mouth, the twisting gestures, the way the sky itself seemed to answer him. It hadn't been mere weather. Something darker was at work.

It was then that Zhu Jun came to their tent. His expression was grave.

"I've heard of this before. Zhang Bao is not just a rebel—he practices sorcery. If you meet him again unprepared, he will summon the storm once more and scatter you."

Liu Bei rose to his feet. "Then tell us how to break his spell."

"Another commander had faced Zhang Bao before," Zhu Jun said. "I thought it was just a one-time trick that could be easily broken, but apparently I was wrong."

Zhu Jun continued to explain that when that commander faced Zhang Bao's magic, he desperately searched for help. He found a witch—a former ally of Zhang Bao who had turned against him. She knew Zhang Bao's weaknesses, but her knowledge came at a steep price. The commander had to pay heavily for this information.

He continued grimly: "Get blood from three distinct animals—a boar, a sheep, and a dog was recommended. Mix them together. Hide your troops in the hills. When Zhang Bao's army passes below, scatter the blood into the wind. His magic will falter, and then you strike."

Zhang Fei's scowl twisted into something closer to a grin. "Good. My old hunting skills will come in handy. Let's see how his storms fare when we paint the hills red for him."

Liu Bei exchanged a glance with Guan Yu. They had been

humbled once, but the next time they met Zhang Bao, it would be on their own terms.

The next day, the valley trembled with the sound of drums. Zhang Bao's army poured in from the east, yellow banners rippling in the morning wind. At the front rode Zhang Bao himself, his hair tied high again, making him look like a silver fox, his curved blade glinting in the sun. His face carried the smug ease of a man who thought the battle was already won.

From the hills above, Liu Bei's army lay hidden, crouched behind rocks and thickets. In the shadows, jars of blood—taken from boar, sheep, and dog—waited in the hands of the soldiers.

"Not yet," Guan Yu said quietly, positioning himself with a small group of soldiers on the hillside, figuring out how to position himself closest to where Zhang Bao's forces would pass.

"We'll attack first, fight for a while, then pretend to retreat to the hillside," Liu Bei told Guan Yu. "While we're fighting, study the wind direction and Zhang Bao's position. Find the perfect spot to spread the blood."

The moment Liu Bei finished speaking, Zhang Fei charged forward with a wild battle cry, and the battle erupted in full fury. Liu Bei joined the assault alongside his sworn brother, their troops clashing with the Yellow Turban forces in the valley below. Steel rang against steel as the two armies collided with devastating force.

As the fierce fighting continued, Liu Bei began a carefully measured retreat back toward the hillside, drawing Zhang Bao's forces deeper into Guan Yu's range. Step by calculated step, he pulled his men upward along the slope, making it appear as though the Yellow Turbans were gaining ground.

When Liu Bei reached the perfect position, he suddenly halted the retreat. His army turned and fought back with renewed ferocity, creating a fierce standoff that frustrated Zhang Bao's advance.

Sensing this unexpected resistance, Zhang Bao grew angry. Once again, he released his hair, letting it flow wild in the wind. He placed the knife between his teeth and began repeating those same strange gestures, his hands twisting through the air in mystical patterns.

The sky darkened ominously. Thunder rumbled overhead, and storm clouds began gathering with unnatural speed.

It was then that Guan Yu reached the perfect position on the hillside where the wind was blowing directly toward Zhang Bao's troops. Guan Yu signaled his men to uncork the jars and fling the thick, dark blood mixture into the air. The wind carried it down diagonally toward the enemy ranks below.

Slowly, the thunder died away with an almost apologetic rumble. The storm clouds began to dissolve like sugar in rain, and Zhang Bao's voice cracked mid-incantation. He reined in his horse so abruptly that the animal stumbled, his eyes darting frantically to the sky as if personally betrayed by the heavens.

His hands flailed through the same mystical gestures— once, twice, then with increasing desperation, like a man trying to start a fire with wet kindling. He even shook his fists at the sky and repeated the ritual with exaggerated movements, his face reddening as nothing happened. The knife fell from his mouth as he gaped upward in disbelief.

The sky remained stubbornly clear and cheerful, the morning sun burning away any hint of cloud with what seemed like deliberate mockery.

From the ridge, Liu Bei's voice rang out.

"Now!"

The brothers thundered down the slope, weapons blazing like falling stars. Zhang Fei hit the front ranks with a roar, his spear smashing men aside like kindling. Beside him, Guan Yu carved sweeping arcs with the Green Dragon Blade, every stroke tearing gaps in the press for their soldiers to surge through.

Without his storm to protect him, Zhang Bao's army wavered. Their chants turned to shouts, then screams, and the tight formations dissolved into a panicked rout.

Seeing his army in shambles, Zhang Bao let out a furious cry and spurred his horse straight toward Liu Bei, knife raised high. But before he could close the gap, Guan Yu's green-dragon blade swept in a single, unstoppable arc. Steel met flesh, and Zhang Bao toppled from the saddle, his banner falling with him. The moment he hit the ground, the last of the Yellow Turbans broke and fled.

Liu Bei stood over Zhang Bao's fallen body, his voice ringing with finality.

"Dark magic steals its power from shadows—but Heaven's light burns it away!"

CHAPTER 22
FALL OF THE YELLOW TURBANS

~

I n the meantime, far from Yingchuan, Dong Zhuo's campaigns unraveled. Battle after battle slipped through his fingers, his forces scattering under the relentless pressure of the Imperial armies.

But one name rose again and again in the war reports—Huangfu Song. Victory seemed to follow him like a shadow. At Yangcheng in 184 CE, he struck down Zhang Liang, shattering the rebel stronghold there. Soon after, at Quyang, he crushed the Yellow Turban host and Zhang Jue, the self-styled General of Heaven, succumbed to illness and died before the battle was even done. Not long after, Zhang Bao fell in combat against imperial troops.

Within a single year, the three leaders of the Yellow Turbans who had set the empire aflame were gone. The rebellion that had thundered across China in the name of the Yellow Heaven lay broken.

Yet their deaths did not end it. History would remember that for more than two decades after the banners fell, remnants of the Yellow Turbans—tens of thousands strong —still roamed the provinces. Some were absorbed into new armies, others became the infamous White Wave Bandits, all continuing to plague the countryside and defy the court.

While the imperial armies cheered their victory, Liu Bei felt no triumph. He looked to the horizon. Perhaps the rebellion's end was not an ending at all, but the opening move of something far worse.

He thought of the villages they had passed—homes burned to ash, fields left barren, children with hollow eyes who no longer remembered peace. He thought of Lu Zhi, his master in chains; of Dong Zhuo's arrogance; of court officials already twisting the victory into their own glory, while the men who had bled for it went unnamed.

Even with the Yellow Turban leaders dead, the empire was far from peace. Across the provinces, rebel bands still roamed by the thousands, pillaging towns and defying the court.

The palace issued new orders: Zhu Jun was to sweep the land clean of the remaining Yellow Turbans. When he put the mission before Liu Bei, Guan Yu, and Zhang Fei, the three brothers agreed without hesitation once again.

Their first target was Han Zhong, the rebel who had seized Wancheng. With sixty thousand imperial troops, Zhu Jun encircled the city, sealing every road so that not a soul could escape.

After days of siege, a lone rider emerged from inside the gates waving a white flag. The man dismounted before Zhu Jun's command tent and fell to his knees.

"My lord," he pleaded, "Han Zhong and all within the walls beg for mercy. We will lay down our arms. Spare our lives, and Wancheng will be yours without another drop of blood."

The camp fell silent. Then Zhu Jun's eyes hardened.

"Begging for mercy—after slaughtering imperial soldiers, seizing the city, and terrorizing its people? Insolence."

Before anyone could speak, his sword flashed. The messenger's head rolled into the dust.

Liu Bei stared in shock. *We came here to restore order,* he thought, *not to slaughter those ready to yield.*

Zhu Jun turned away as if the execution were nothing more than brushing a fly from his sleeve.

"Prepare the assault. The city will learn what it means to defy the Han."

A wave of disbelief passed over him, sharpened by anger. Liu Bei stepped forward, voice steady but edged, unable to keep silent any longer.

"General Zhu, the rebellion is broken. Many among these men are not zealots, but farmers and laborers driven by hunger and despair. If we cut them down to the last, we waste lives that might yet serve the realm."

He paused, then invoked a name no Han loyalist could ignore.

"When Emperor Gaozu, Liu Bang, won the empire, he taught: *'When the people yield, accept them. Make them your own.'* It was through mercy, not slaughter, that he bound the realm together. Should we not follow the example of the founder of our dynasty?"

His gaze swept the assembled officers. "Kill them, and

the fields stay empty. Spare them, and they become soldiers, farmers, loyal subjects once more. This is how the Han will endure."

Zhu Jun paused, turning his gaze on Liu Bei. His voice was calm, but it carried the weight of command.

"History may offer its lessons, but each age must carve its own. Gaozu rose when the land longed to be united; we stand in an age that rips itself apart. Mercy built an empire back then, but mercy now will be seen as weakness, and every brigand left alive will seize upon it."

He stepped closer, lowering his voice so that only Liu Bei and his sworn brothers could hear.

"In chaos, you must first make the people trust that your rule is unshakable. Accept any who surrender today, and they will rise against you tomorrow—only to kneel again when cornered. That is not loyalty, that is opportunism. If you want stability, you must set a foundation that cannot be tested, and that means showing there is a price for rebellion."

Liu Bei stood silent, the words sinking in. Harsh though they were, they carried a stark truth—one the court would praise, and one the chaos of the times seemed to demand.

He wanted to reject them, to cling to the ideal that mercy could heal the land—but the sight of burned villages, starving children, and endless uprisings weighed heavily on him. The times were not kind to virtue.

At last, his shoulders eased, and he inclined his head. "I understand."

Zhu Jun studied him for a heartbeat, then turned back toward the city.

"Watch closely. This is how you hold a country together when it's falling apart."

That night, as the siege lines tightened, Liu Bei stepped into Zhu Jun's command tent. The map of Wancheng lay stretched across the table, lit by the flicker of oil lamps.

"General," Liu Bei began, "if we keep all four gates sealed, the rebels will know there's no escape. Men with nothing to lose will fight like devils, and the cost will be our own army's blood."

Zhu Jun raised an eyebrow. "And your answer?"

"Open the east and south gates. Keep the north and west sealed. When they realize the fight is hopeless, they will flee through those two open paths. We can strike them as they pour out. That way, they'll just run and scatter instead of cutting down our men in a final stand."

Zhu Jun's mouth curved into a rare smile.

"A serpent will always seek a hole when the stick comes down. Leave it just enough of an opening, and it will rush for it—and that's when you strike, killing it in the act of escape."

Liu Bei inclined his head. "Exactly. Let their fear lead them where we want them to go."

Zhu Jun tapped the map, marking the east and south gates with his brush.

"Very well. We'll do it your way. Let's see if Han Zhong's men are wise enough to spot the trap."

As planned, they pulled the troops from the east and south gates. The rebels poured out in a desperate stream— only to be caught between Zhu Jun's forces, closing in from both flanks.

Through the chaos, Zhu Jun's eyes locked on a single

figure—Han Zhong, spurring his horse hard, trying to cut a path through the crush.

"Han Zhong is mine!"

Zhu Jun bellowed. He seized a bow from his retainer, drew in one smooth motion, and let the arrow fly. It struck true, knocking Han Zhong from his saddle.

Zhu Jun leapt from his horse and strode to the fallen commander. With one swift stroke he took his head, then raised it high for all to see. The soldiers erupted in thunderous cheers at their victory.

"*I, General Pacifier of Rebellion, Zhu Jun, have slain Han Zhong!*" he roared for all to hear. "If any among you still dare to fight me—step forward!"

The challenge rang out across the field, and for a moment, the rebels faltered. Then, out of the blue, from the north, two banners surged into view—it was the marks of leaders Zhou Xing and Sun Zhong.

Their forces wheeled and charged, the ground trembling under their advance as they came straight for Zhu Jun, intent on avenging their fallen comrade.

What began as a confident pursuit had twisted into a desperate flight. In a cruel turn of fate, Zhu Jun's men— scattered, winded, and bleeding—were being driven hard across the open plain, Yellow Turban banners closing from every side. Dust swirled thick in the air, mingling with the roar of enemy voices, tightening around them like a noose.

Zhu Jun vaulted back into his saddle, gripping the reins as he fought to steady his mount. Spears glinted all around him, the deadly ring drawing ever tighter. Moments ago, he had been lifting Han Zhong's head in triumph; now, he was a heartbeat away from being cut down himself.

Through the chaos, a lone rider burst forth—armor dust-streaked, eyes fixed on Zhou Xing. His blade flashed in a single arc, and the rebel's head toppled into the mud.

The Yellow Turbans staggered at the sight. Sun Zhong, the last of the rebel commanders, broke from the fighting, spurring his horse in a desperate dash to escape. He had barely taken a dozen strides when an arrow split the air and struck him clean through the skull.

From atop a low ridge, bow still in hand, stood Liu Bei, slowly lowering the string.

The battlefield fell into a sudden stillness. With their leaders lying dead in the dirt, the rebel ranks dissolved, scattering in every direction.

Zhu Jun, bloodied and shaken, looked toward the ridge where Liu Bei stood—there was no trace of arrogance in his eyes, only admiration.

Liu Bei spurred his horse to Sun Zhong's fallen body and struck him down. Rising tall in the saddle, he raised the rebel's head high for all to see.

"The Yellow Turbans have been defeated!" he shouted, his voice ringing across the field. The cry rippled through the ranks—weary soldiers straightened, weapons lifted, and a ragged cheer rose in answer.

Still mounted, Liu Bei turned, scanning the field. The battle's chaos had left him little time to think, but now one question pressed forward in his mind: *Who was the general who cut down Zhou Xing so suddenly and saved General Zhu Jun?*

His gaze swept over the battered ranks—and then he saw a man.

A man on horseback, surrounded by a small entourage,

rode with unhurried poise through the aftermath. His fore-head was broad, his lips a vivid red against his tanned skin, and his eyebrows arched like crescent moons. There was something majestic in his bearing, like a tiger prowling the edges of the fight—yet in the same breath, there was a gentleness in his eyes that softened the fierce impression.

Is this the man? Liu Bei nudged his horse forward, weaving past the last knots of retreating rebels until he drew close enough to call out.

"General, may I have the honor of your name?"

The man reined in his horse, turning toward him. Up close, that balance of strength and refinement was even more striking. His voice carried easily over the trampled field.

"I am Sun Jian of Fuchun."

He dipped his head in greeting. "A descendant of Sun Tzu, the Master of War. I've gathered my own small force to aid the imperial armies against this rebellion."

Liu Bei straightened in the saddle, a smile breaking through the grime on his face.

"Then we fight for the same cause. Your arrival was most timely—without you, Zhu Jun might not have lived to see another battle."

Sun Jian's lips curved in the faintest smile.

"And without your arrow, Sun Zhong would still be breathing. It seems the rebels have a new reason to fear the Han."

The two men held each other's gaze—each knowing they stood before someone rare and extraordinary, a figure who would leave an indelible mark on the troubled age.

Soon, Zhu Jun himself rode up, his armor dented and

spattered from the fight, but his expression alight with relief.

"General Sun Jian," Zhu Jun called, dismounting with surprising energy for a man who had nearly been cut down moments ago. "I've heard your name whispered in the capital, but I had not expected to meet you here, in the thick of battle."

Sun Jian inclined his head. "I came of my own will. The rebellion threatens us all, and I could not stand idle while the Empire bled."

Zhu Jun's booming laugh rolled across the muddy field.

"Then the Han owes you much! And you, Liu Bei— today, Heaven itself seemed to place you both where I needed you most."

He gestured toward the camp. "Come! The victory is ours, and we shall celebrate it tonight. There will be wine enough to wash the dust from our throats and meat enough to quiet even Zhang Fei's appetite."

Liu Bei met Sun Jian's eyes, and the two shared a brief, knowing smile—pride in the win, and hope for the future.

That night, in the glow of the campfires, they would share the first cups of wine as comrades-in-arms.

CHAPTER 23
BEHIND SILK CURTAINS

~

The wine loosened tongues, and as the fire crackled low, Liu Bei asked, "Tell us, General Sun—where did your path as a warrior truly begin?"

Sun Jian's lips curved faintly.

"I remember... when I was seventeen," he began, "I was out with my father on a simple outing. We passed along the river and saw a band of pirates on the far bank. They had just robbed some merchants and were dividing the loot there on the hill."

He set down his cup and mimed the slope with his hand.

"I told my father, 'I'll give them a lesson.' Then I ran straight up the hill, shouting orders like I commanded a hundred soldiers. The pirates froze—thought the government troops were on them—and bolted. I chased them, caught one before he could reach the river, and put him down myself."

Zhang Fei let out a booming laugh. "A cub playing at being a tiger—and finding out he had the teeth for it!"

Sun Jian's eyes glimmered with the memory.

"The local officials thought the same. They gave me the rank of Colonel—a midlevel post, serious for someone so young, and it was the first step on the road that brought me here."

Liu Bei lifted his cup toward him. "From chasing pirates to cutting down rebel generals—it seems your road is one that runs toward danger. Hahaha..."

"And yours as well," Sun Jian replied with a laugh, their cups meeting with a quiet chime.

Zhang Fei gnawed on a strip of mutton, washing it down with a loud gulp of wine.

"Sun Jian!" he called over the spit. "We've heard of you chasing pirates as a boy—but surely you've done more than scare thieves and kill the odd rebel."

Sun Jian chuckled and leaned back, the firelight glinting on his armor.

"There was one other matter, years after the pirate business. In Kuaiji, there was a bandit named Xu Chang who gathered tens of thousands of followers. Bold man for he crowned himself the *'Emperor of Yangming.'*"

Zhang Fei's eyebrows shot up. "Tens of thousands?"

"I had scarcely a thousand under me," Sun Jian continued, "but we struck before he expected it. We cut through his camp like a blade through bamboo. By dusk, Xu Chang and his son Xu Shao had lost their heads."

Guan Yu gave a slight nod of respect. "And the court must have rewarded you well for such a deed."

Sun Jian's smile thinned. "The Administrator of Kuaiji

was eager to recommend me. The court, however, looked at my age and saw only inexperience. They gave me a petty administrative job in the Commandant's Office. Later, I became a Magistrate."

Liu Bei shook his head with a wry smile. "So there appears to be a pattern. The court undervalues its best men."

Sun Jian lifted his cup in silent agreement. "In times like these, recognition is rare. But a man's worth is proven on the field, not in the palace halls."

After a brief silence, he went on, "The Yellow Turban leaders are finished, but the fight is not over."

Liu Bei inclined his head. "That is especially true now, when those in the palace care for nothing but their own gain. So long as they chase their own interests above the empire's, the rot will spread, and the people will suffer."

After a sip of wine, Liu Bei said softly, "When the source of the water is tainted, every stream that runs from it is poisoned. The government's rot runs deep. If the court remains corrupt, another rebellion will rise, sooner or later."

Guan Yu's voice was quiet but firm. "If you cut the weeds without pulling the roots, they grow back in the spring."

Sun Jian met Liu Bei's eyes. "Then it falls to men like us to face more than rebels. Mark my words—one day, the bloodiest battles will be fought not in the fields, but within the palace walls.

Zhang Fei snorted, draining his cup. "Good—there are more to bring to justice. The fight is not over. I've still got plenty of strength left in me."

The fire popped, sending up a shower of sparks that vanished into the night. The battle was won, but under the starlit sky, they all felt the same truth—the war for the heart of the empire had only just begun.

It became clear soon enough that the three brothers' fight was far from over. The ministers in Luoyang had wasted no time reshuffling titles and offices, promoting some and demoting others, all according to convenience and faction, which served themselves first and foremost. Merit was secondary; politics ultimately determined the outcome.

Luckily, Zhu Jun was elevated to the honorable rank of *General of Chariots and Cavalry* and appointed Governor of Henan. Sun Jian was appointed Commandant of the *Separate Forces*. However, for the brothers? Not a word from the palace.

Liu Bei's army remained branded as "volunteers"—a private force, not worthy of imperial recognition. They were barred from even stepping inside the walls of Luoyang, left instead to stand guard outside the gates like common sentries.

The seasons turned, and winter crept in with its biting wind. Liu Bei's five hundred men shivered in thin, worn tunics, their breath rising in white clouds. Snow dusted the ground, and each gust cut to the bone.

Behind the imperial walls, the court indulged in endless banquets, their gilded halls alive with warmth and revelry. Not a single bundle of winter clothes was sent to Liu Bei's men, who had bled for the empire.

For weeks, Liu Bei had sent petition after petition through the palace bureaucracy, each one disappearing into the void of indifferent clerks and sneering eunuchs. Guards turned him away at the gates where he had once passed through, receiving a warm welcome. Liu Bei, dust-covered and battle-scarred, stood out like a wolf among lapdogs.

When word reached him that Zhu Jun—now *General of Chariots and Cavalry*—was visiting the court, Liu Bei seized the chance. Even then, it took hours of waiting before he could secure an audience.

At last, Liu Bei stood before his former comrade in a chamber lined with jade tapestries. The contrast was stark —Zhu Jun wore silk robes embroidered with golden dragons, while Liu Bei's simple armor bore the honest stains of campaign life.

Liu Bei saluted with rigid formality and explained his soldiers' plight—men who had bled for the empire now left without even warm winter clothes, not to mention proper pay.

Zhu Jun listened, his weathered face growing troubled. His eyes flickered toward the ornate doors, weighing his words against listening ears.

"I will speak to the palace," he promised, his voice carrying both sincerity and weariness. "They will hear of this."

But both men understood the bitter truth—in a court where eunuchs whispered poison and gold spoke louder than honor, the suffering of soldiers was just another inconvenience to be buried beneath ceremony and indifference.

On his way out after meeting Zhu Jun, Liu Bei spotted a familiar figure riding toward him—Langzhong Zhang Jun. Sliding from the saddle, Liu Bei bowed deeply in greeting.

Months earlier, Zhang Jun had visited the front lines, rallying the men with fiery words and commending Liu Bei's strategies in battle. He reined in his horse now, recognition brightening his face.

"General Liu! I had heard of your role in breaking the Yellow Turbans, but not seen you since. Tell me—how fare your troops?"

Liu Bei hesitated, then spoke plainly of their situation: barred from Luoyang's gates, given no recognition, and now left to face winter without proper clothing.

Zhang Jun's expression darkened.

"After all you've done for the empire? This is how they treat you?" He shook his head in disbelief. "No. This cannot stand."

Straightening in the saddle, he said with resolve, "I will speak to His Majesty myself. The court must hear the truth of your service."

For the first time in weeks, Liu Bei felt the faint stir of hope.

Zhang Jun was, in fact, on his way to the palace when they met, his mind already on a graver matter. He had come to discuss with the Emperor how to rid the court of the Ten Attendants—the corrupt eunuch faction that strangled every honest voice in the capital.

As he passed through the bronze gates of the palace, the scent of incense thick in the air, he requested an audience at once.

"I beg to see His Majesty, Emperor Ling," he told the guards.

In the outer hall, the Ten Attendants gathered together, their long sleeves sweeping the floor, their smiles polite but pretentious.

Zhang Jun's voice was calm but firm. "Gentlemen, this

matter concerns the empire's survival. I must speak to His Majesty alone. Leave us."

The eunuchs exchanged glances, their eyes narrowing, but Zhang Jun stood unmoving, a soldier's steel in his bearing. Reluctantly, they withdrew from the hall, the sound of their sly whispers and soft-soled slippers fading into the corridors.

Zhang Jun was well aware of the risk involved in what he was about to say. Emperor Ling preferred words that pleased him, and clung to the belief that the Ten Attendants were his loyal servants. To speak otherwise was to court his displeasure—or worse.

But Zhang Jun had not come to flatter.

He bowed deeply, then raised his head, voice steady.

"Your Majesty, I must speak plainly. The embers of the Yellow Turban rebellion are stirring again. This unrest is not born from the people's hunger alone—it is being fanned by rot within the court itself."

The Emperor's brows knit. "What rot?"

"The Ten Attendants," Zhang Jun said without hesitation. "They have been selling the empire's highest offices to any man with silver enough to buy them. Power now rests in the hands of the greedy and the unfit. This corruption festers at the heart of the state, and the people are aware of it. That is why rebellion stirs anew."

He straightened, meeting the Emperor's gaze without flinching.

"Your Majesty must act. Cut off the heads of the Ten Attendants, and hang them at the South Bridge for the people of this country to see. Let the empire know that the court's honor is restored."

The hall fell silent, and the air grew heavy. For a long moment, Emperor Ling said nothing. His eyes, once calm, hardened into a cold glint.

"Zhang Jun," he said slowly, "you dare speak boldly. The Ten Attendants have served me faithfully for years. To accuse them so is to accuse my judgment."

Zhang Jun did not lower his gaze. "Your Majesty, I accuse no one without cause. But a ruler who refuses to see the truth endangers the realm more than any rebel."

The Emperor's jaw tightened. His hand closed over the armrest of the throne.

"Enough!"

Before Zhang Jun could speak again, movement stirred behind the silk curtains of the imperial platform. From the shadows emerged several armed servants—the personal men of the Ten Attendants, hidden there all along.

Zhang Jun's eyes flicked toward them just as the first blade flashed. He drew back, but another attacker closed in, stabbing deep. A shout echoed through the hall, but the guards at the doors did not move.

Steel struck again and again. Zhang Jun fell to his knees, his voice still fierce even as it failed.

"The court will choke on its own rot... remember my words!"

One final blow silenced him. His body collapsed on the polished tiles before the throne.

Emperor Ling sat motionless, his face unreadable. The Ten Attendants slipped back into the chamber, their expressions serene, as though nothing had happened.

The Ten Attendants' brazen strike in the Emperor's own chamber said it all. Titles and seals were mere ornaments.

True power sat in these eunuchs' hands, and the wise stepped lightly in their shadow.

Now the Ten Attendants faced a different challenge—justifying Zhang Jun's death in the eyes of the court. With practiced tongues, they painted him as a traitor plotting against the throne, twisting his final words into proof of disloyalty.

Then, in the same breath, they called for proper rewards for those who had aided in the destruction of the Yellow Turbans—a clever stroke, for it would be seen as righteous, proof that the court listened and valued the voices of the people.

Among the names put forth was Liu Bei. The court granted him the position of *County Magistrate of Anxi in Zhongshan Commandery*—a role akin to a local constable or police chief. By the capital's standards, it was a modest station—but for Liu Bei, it was the first time his army's sacrifice had been recognized by the palace. He accepted it with heartfelt gratitude, holding fast to his respect for the Han. In his heart, he believed this was Heaven's sign, the first step that would lead him onto a greater stage, just as his mother had always wished.

The five hundred men who had fought under Liu Bei were compensated and sent back to their homes. Of them, barely twenty close and loyal comrades chose to follow Liu Bei and his sworn brothers to Anxi.

So, the three brothers rode for Anxi. After months of war and the sting of neglect, even a small command felt like a foothold—a place from which to begin anew.

CHAPTER 24

THE HAND THAT OFFERS, THE HAND THAT BINDS

~

Since moving to Anxi, Liu Bei devoted himself wholeheartedly to serving the small county. Within months, the change started to show. The roads felt safe again, thieves vanished into the hills, and the markets rang with the sound of laughter. Fields yielded their harvests without fear of raiders, and children played in the streets until sunset.

During this time of quiet prosperity, a government inspector named Du Wu arrived from the commandery. He came with a small escort, chin held high, speaking little to the townsfolk. From the moment he dismounted, he carried himself as if the town existed only to serve him.

Because Anxi lay deep in the countryside, Du Wu demanded that a clean, spacious, and well-furnished residence be prepared for his stay—a demand he repeated often, with an edge that made clear he considered refusal an insult to the government itself.

Du Wu was led through Anxi's main street, escorted by Liu Bei himself. He had ordered a clean and secure residence to be prepared inside an inn run by a trusted local family. Yet the man's mouth twisted as he crossed the threshold.

"Hmph. This is the best you can do? In Luoyang, even a servant's quarters are better than this."

His voice dripped with disdain, each word a little dagger thrown into the air. Liu Bei kept his composure, walking at the man's side. Du Wu gave him a sidelong glance, his eyes sweeping Liu Bei from head to toe as though measuring the worth of a servant.

"And you are? Remind me—who exactly are you?"

"I am Liu Bei, Magistrate of Anxi, Sir," came the even reply.

Du Wu's lips curled faintly. "Where are you from? And your father—what was his trade?"

"Zhuo County. My family descends from the Liu family of the Han Dynasty. I grew up under my mother, as my father passed away when I was young."

Liu Bei answered, his voice steady, without the slightest boast or bowing of the head.

Du Wu stopped mid-step. His gaze sharpened, the pretense of politeness gone.

"The imperial family? You?" His voice cut through the courtyard like a blade, sharp enough to make heads turn. "Do not mock the Emperor with such lies! A common servant dressing himself in noble robes—shameless."

The words landed like stones, but Liu Bei's expression did not flicker. He clasped his hands in formality and inclined his head. Behind Du Wu, his retinue smirked, their confidence swelling at their master's scorn.

Liu Bei stayed silent, while beside him Zhang Fei muttered under his breath, struggling to keep his temper in check.

When the formalities were finally done and Liu Bei turned to leave, Du Wu's assistant lingered at the doorway. He leaned close, glancing around as if to be sure no one important was listening, and murmured, "Did you... prepare anything for him?"

He made a subtle but unmistakable gesture with his hands—thumb rubbing against fingers—the universal sign for silver.

In that instant, Liu Bei understood. The sneer, the insults, the feigned outrage—all of it was nothing but the prelude to extortion. His stomach churned with cold anger.

"Tell your master," Liu Bei said evenly, "that I am here to govern the people, not to line pockets."

He walked away without looking back.

The next morning, just after sunrise, Du Wu's assistant arrived at Liu Bei's modest quarters, wearing a smile that was sly and insincere.

"My lord Du Wu wonders," the man said with mock courtesy, "if you have reconsidered your position regarding... proper appreciation for his guidance?"

Liu Bei's jaw tightened as he faced the man. "Tell your master this," he said, his voice firm and steady. "Do not expect tribute from Anxi. Our people work hard and bleed honest sweat to build a life, and I am here to help them make it happen—*not* to fill the bellies of corrupt officials."

His eyes burned with fury. "And tell Du Wu he is threatening the wrong man."

The assistant's mask of civility cracked, lip line tightened, and he departed with quick, angry steps.

By afternoon, the trap was sprung. Du Wu summoned Liu Bei's staff—loyal men who experienced Liu Bei's virtues firsthand for the past few months—into his temporary residence.

"I have grave concerns," Du Wu announced, his voice dripping false sorrow, "about your master's conduct."

He began weaving his web of lies with the skill of a master craftsman: Liu Bei had imposed crushing taxes on the ordinary people, he claimed. The young magistrate had fabricated his noble lineage for personal gain. He had enriched himself while the people he governed went hungry.

"You will draft an official complaint," Du Wu commanded, his words falling like stones into still water. "Detail these irregularities. The imperial court must know of such corruption in their ranks."

The staff exchanged glances heavy with dread. They knew the truth—Liu Bei was loved here. In just a few months, he had restored peace, brought thieves to heel, and given people a reason to laugh again. Now the townsfolk and his own men whispered in alarm, fearing the worst.

In a local tavern, a group of anxious locals approached Zhang Fei.

"General Zhang," one said, voice low, "anyone who refuses the inspector's orders is being locked up. They're beating people for speaking against him."

Zhang Fei slammed his cup down, wine sloshing over

the rim. His face was already flushed, his breath sharp with drink.

"Beating our people? Framing my brother?"

Before anyone could stop him, he stormed out into the street.

When Zhang Fei reached Du Wu's quarters, he heard the silky tones of flattery, women's lilting laughter, and the clink of wine cups. With a roar, he stormed up the steps and kicked the door open, the wood crashing against the wall with a splintering crack. At once, the laughter and chatter fell silent.

In the sudden silence, Du Wu turned, his face flushed from drink, an awkward half-smile frozen as the women pulled back and the attendants scrambled to the sides.

Du Wu, red-faced from drink, blinked in shock. "What —?" was all he managed before Zhang Fei crossed the room in two strides, grabbed him by the front of his robe, and hoisted him clear off the ground.

Moments later, Zhang Fei had the man hanging from a willow branch in the courtyard, his legs kicking helplessly. Snatching a whip from a guard, he struck him hard across the back. Each lash landed with a wet snap, the sound echoing down the winter street.

Zhang Fei's breath came heavy with each strike, the whip cracking like thunder. Du Wu's screams rose higher as his clothes split open, dark with blood. The onlookers gasped in horror, some turning away, others frozen where they stood—but not one dared step in to stop it, nor raise a hand to help.

Dangling from the willow branch, Du Wu writhed in pain, his fine robes in tatters, his voice breaking into high, panicked screams. At first Du Wu spat curses at Zhang Fei, shouting threats between screams. But as the lashes fell, his fury broke into pleas—begging, promising anything.

"Spare me! Spare me! I'll speak for you at the court! I'll have you promoted—higher than you've ever dreamed! Just let me live!"

The words tumbled from his mouth in gasps between the blows, the promises as desperate as they were hollow.

Liu Bei arrived to find the crowd gathered, eyes wide, mouths half-hidden behind sleeves. And though a deep part of him felt a grim satisfaction at the sight, he knew the danger of harming a government inspector all too well, no matter what the reason.

In one swift motion, he stepped forward and slapped Zhang Fei across the face—hard enough to halt the next strike.

"Enough!" he barked.

"Do you forget he is still a government officer from the capital? If you kill or hurt him, we are no better than the rebels we fought."

Zhang Fei's eyes burned with defiance.

"Brother, this man deserves—"

"I said enough!" Liu Bei's voice cut through the winter air like steel.

"We are bound by law, even when those in power are not. Lower him."

The whip trembled in Zhang Fei's hands, the urge to strike again still strong, but at last, he stepped back.

Guan Yu had heard the news from halfway across town and came at a run, his tall frame cutting through the crowd. By the time he reached the inn, the whip had already fallen silent, Du Wu hung limply from the willow branch, and Liu Bei stood before Zhang Fei, his voice sharp with rebuke.

"You forget yourself, Zhang Fei! He is still an officer of the Han—"

Guan Yu stepped forward, his deep voice breaking through the tension.

"Brother."

Both men turned toward Guan Yu. He looked from the hanging man to Liu Bei's face, his gaze steady and unhurried.

"The phoenix," Guan Yu said, his tone low as a whisper but resonant, "does not dwell in thornbushes."

He gestured toward Liu Bei's chest, where he always carried his magistrate's seal.

"This post... and your title, does not befit you. We are in the wrong place."

His eyes locked on Liu Bei's.

"If we mean to see our vision realized, we must leave this briar patch behind. We need a new place, a new plan—and we will not find it here. Our hands will always be tied by corrupt officials demanding bribes. Even if we survive this, there will be another, and another. Tell me, brother... is this truly where we can carry out our plans for the realm?"

The crowd was silent, the winter wind tugging at their sleeves. Even Zhang Fei, still breathing hard, dropped his whip.

Liu Bei stood still for a long moment, Guan Yu's words echoing in his mind. The wrong place... the truth of it was undeniable.

Slowly, he reached inside his robe and drew out the polished bronze seal of office—the symbol of his official title and authority in Anxi. He held it in his palm, feeling the weight one last time.

Then he strode to the willow where the battered inspector hung. With a flick of his wrist, he tossed the seal so it landed in the snow at the man's feet.

"You deserve to die," Liu Bei said, his voice low but carrying through the hushed crowd.

"People suffer because of corrupt officials like you. I still value human life—so if you wish to keep what dignity you have left, return to the court and deliver my message."

Du Wu blinked, trembling.

"Wh–what, what message... Sir?"

"That I will not serve in a system that feeds on the blood of its own people."

He turned away without another glance.

And so, less than four months after receiving the post they once believed would secure their future, Liu Bei, Guan Yu, and Zhang Fei left Anxi behind. The government's seal had promised legitimacy, yet it had guaranteed nothing. Their boots crunched over the frozen road as they moved on —somber, but more resolute than before, knowing they would have to carve their own path rather than cling to titles bestowed by a corrupt court.

The moment Liu Bei and his brothers disappeared down the road, Du Wu, still dangling from the willow, began to stir. Realizing he would be saved, his groans gave way to muttered curses.

"What are you doing, you idiots!! Lower me and untie me immediately!!"

Once freed, still trembling and bleeding, he screamed with a voice hoarse with rage.

"Call the doctor immediately! I will not die until justice is served!" he barked.

He raged on, voice breaking, words tumbling in gasping bursts:

"Send word to the Prefect of Zhengzhou! Troops—dispatch them at once! Hunt them down! Liu Xuande—yes, that wretch of a magistrate—he abused his people, abused his office, caught red-handed by the inspector himself! And now he flees, like the criminal he is! Spread the word—everywhere! All three of them—arrest them, drag them to jail! They dared—dared lay hands on an imperial official!"

Then, as if struck by sudden inspiration, he added breathlessly:

"Oh—and his men, don't forget his men. Treason! There was talk of plots and vision, of imperial blood—treason, I say! They'll raise a coup if we don't stop them! Write it down—make sure to add that!"

The messenger bolted into the chill of early evening, the last light bleeding from the sky as the lie spread into the gathering dusk.

And just like that, the three brothers and their twenty loyal men embarked on another journey on the road, this time as *fugitives*, not knowing what waited beyond the next bend.

CHAPTER 25
LOTUS BLOSSOMS

~

The three brothers and their twenty men walked on in silence, their boots crunching over the frost-hardened path as the night deepened and the woods closed in around them. The trees loomed like silent sentries, their bare branches rattling in the cold wind.

Zhang Fei finally broke the stillness. "Should we find a shelter here for the night? It's been such an eventful day, we all need a good rest."

They found a rocky hollow shielded from the wind, and before long, their men were leaning back against the stones, drifting into sleep with their cloaks wrapped tight.

Liu Bei, Guan Yu, and Zhang Fei sat together and built a small fire. The sparks rose into the blackness above, vanishing among the stars.

Guan Yu's gaze lingered on the sky.

"Do you remember," he said quietly, "how excited we

were when you first received your government post, Brother? We thought Heaven had finally rewarded us, that each step from then on would lead to a greater and more important post..."

He gave a faint, rueful smile. "Even though it never made much sense for you to take an administrative role in some tiny countryside town."

Zhang Fei grunted, poking at the fire with a stick. Liu Bei remained silent, his eyes on the embers, the weight of unspoken thoughts heavy in the cold night. The fire crackled softly, its glow the only living sound in the stillness. Liu Bei kept his eyes on the shifting flames, his face half-carved in amber light and shadow.

"At first," he said at last, his voice low, "I truly believed it. That if we fought with all our strength and proved ourselves capable, if we bled enough for the Han, someone in the palace would notice. That they would lift us up, step by step, until we could make a difference."

He paused, the flames dancing in his dark eyes. "But the truth is... the palace doesn't care. Not about victories, not even justice. They care about their own titles and their own pockets. We were never meant to climb their ladder—only to hold it steady for them."

Zhang Fei's hand clenched on his knee. Guan Yu sat silent, his expression grave.

Liu Bei looked between them, the faintest ember of determination sparking in his tone. "If the court won't give us the place to serve, then we'll carve out our own. Somewhere, somehow, we'll make our stand—and no one will be able to ignore us."

Then his tone sharpened, a steel edge beneath the calm.

"When there is no road ahead, lay the stones yourself. If they will not grant us a place to serve, we will make our own. And when it is built, they *will* see us."

Zhang Fei grunted his approval. Guan Yu inclined his head, silent but resolute. Above them, the cold stars looked on, as if bearing witness to the oath.

They woke at dawn with a renewed resolution glinting in their eyes. But resolve could not soften the days that followed.

Overnight, they had become fugitives. What charges would be pinned on them, they did not know—only that Du Wu's lies would invent enough. They wandered without direction. Food was scarce; no berries, no corn. Zhang Fei tried to hunt, but even the wild game seemed to vanish. Villages shut their doors at the sight of armed men, forcing the brothers onto quiet back roads, their twenty companions trudging in grim silence. By now, Du Wu's accusations would be spreading fast, and surely a reward was already posted for their capture.

On the sixth day, Zhang Fei suddenly stopped in the middle of the trail, his eyes lighting up as if struck by a bolt of inspiration.

"I know where to go," he said, grinning under his thick beard.

"We're not far from the foot of Mount Wutai. My old master's colleague, Master Yu, is a well-known landowner in a town near the mountain. We can go there. Before the Yellow Turbans rose, I worked for a man named Master Hong. Master Yu, who lives here now, used to supply arms and trained horses to my lord."

Liu Bei and Guan Yu exchanged glances—hope was

fragile these days, yet still worth holding. Years of study and discipline had shaped them, but moments like this showed that survival on the rough road demanded more than hard work and diligence alone.

Silently, they marveled at Zhang Fei—at the way his seemingly chaotic life before they met, spent in taverns and brawls, had left him with connections that proved invaluable when fate's doors seemed closed.

"Master Yu is known for his generosity—always hosting travelers and friends, never turning away those in need. If anyone will take us in, it's him. While we were serving in Anxi, I once sent him a letter through a messenger. He wrote back saying I'd be welcome to stay with him if things ever turned sour... and urged me to hold fast until the tide changed..."

Zhang Fei rose, already hitching his pack higher. "Let me go ahead now. I'll see if they'll put us up at least for a while."

The road to Daiju, where Master Yu lived, wound between terraced fields and quiet groves, the air carrying the smell of damp earth. By the time Zhang Fei reached the edge of the estate, the sun was leaning low, gilding the tiled roofs and bamboo groves in warm light.

It was a grand place indeed—stone walls thick and high, a broad wooden gate painted in red lacquer, and a carved signboard bearing the family name. Smoke curled lazily from the kitchen chimneys.

Zhang Fei straightened his tunic and strode to the gate, pounding it with the side of his fist.

"Zhang Fei of Zhuo County is here! I come seeking Master Yu!"

A small shutter in the gate slid open, revealing a wary

gatekeeper whose eyes widened at the sight of the burly man before him.

"Zhang... Fei? Is it really you?"

"Yes, it's me," Zhang Fei said, grinning. "Tell the master I've come from far away, with brothers at my side. We're in need of shelter."

The gatekeeper hesitated, his gaze flicking to the road behind Zhang Fei, as if expecting someone in pursuit. Then he shut the shutter without a word.

Moments later, the heavy gate creaked open just wide enough for Zhang Fei to slip inside. He walked a long way to reach the courtyard. It smelled faintly of jasmine. Servants paused in their work to stare—a few in recognition, mainly in suspicion.

As Zhang Fei stood in the courtyard admiring the sight and the aroma, a woman in a flowing jade-green robe emerged from the inner hall. Her hair was arranged in a graceful knot, and her warm smile reached her eyes.

"Zhang Fei! Heavens, it's been far too long," Madam Yu Xi said, taking his rough hands in her own as if greeting a long-lost brother. "You've grown broader... and wilder," she added with a teasing laugh.

It was then that a deep, hearty laugh rolled through the courtyard. From the doorway strode Master Yu, arms wide, his steps brisk despite his years.

"Zhang Fei! I thought the stories were smoke and shadow, but here you stand!" He clasped Zhang Fei's shoulders with both hands, the welcome genuine.

Over cups of tea, Zhang Fei told the whole tale—how they had been framed, how the inspector's lies had turned them into fugitives overnight, how for days they'd wandered, unsure where to go. His voice was fierce at times, low and tight at others, but never faltering.

When he finished, Master Yu sat back, stroking his beard. He said nothing for a long moment, the only sound the faint rustle of the courtyard trees. At last, he nodded.

"You and your brothers should stay here," he said. "The road ahead will not be kind to men in your position, but under this roof, you'll find food, warmth, and friends."

Relief lit Zhang Fei's face. "You have my thanks, old master. I will never forget the kindness you have shown me."

Within the hour, he had borrowed a sturdy chestnut horse, the leather reins warm in his calloused grip, and he was racing back toward the woods, where Liu Bei, Guan Yu, and the others waited.

The brothers arrived with their twenty men at the estate, greeted by bowing servants as they passed, the scent of cooking fires warm in the air. Once inside the courtyard, Zhang Fei stretched his arms wide, grinning as if the estate itself were a feast laid out for him.

"I was too excited to realize how hungry I was! Now we can eat properly." He began ticking off his desires on his fingers. "A whole roast pig, a large jug of rice wine, a plate of spiced beef, steamed dumplings stuffed with pork and chives, braised fish, and a bowl of hot noodle soup so big I can bathe in it. And after that... more wine, of course. Haha!"

Servants glanced at one another, half-shocked, half-amused, but his booming laugh filled the air like a drumbeat.

Across the courtyard, Master Yu and Madam Yu awaited them. Liu Bei bowed deeply, Guan Yu followed with measured grace, and all twenty men vowed following their leaders.

"We owe you more than we can repay," Liu Bei said.

"Nonsense," Master Yu replied with a wave. "You've come a long way, and travel wears down even the strongest men. First, you will eat. Your rooms will be ready by the time you've finished."

Inside the dining hall, the air was rich with the scents of roasted meat, ginger, and steamed buns. A feast had already been laid for the three brothers and their twenty loyal men —whole fish glistening with sauce, baskets of dumplings, plates of sliced beef, pickled vegetables, and pitchers of warm rice wine.

For the first time in days, the three brothers stepped inside a proper house, not as hunted men, but as honored guests. They ate without haste, the tension in their shoulders easing with each bite and swallow.

When the last cup was drained, Madam Yu reappeared, her steps light and a smile carved on her face. Beside her walked a tall, narrow-shouldered man in a sober grey robe, his face carved into a cold mask.

"I hope you enjoyed the meal," Madam Yu said with her hands clasped. "Let me introduce our butler. He attends to the household's affairs. Please, if you need anything, don't be shy and ask for Hahn."

Hahn inclined his head, but his gaze lingered on the brothers longer than courtesy required, measuring them in silence.

Zhang Fei gave a curt nod, studying the man. There was something about him—neither servant's humility nor a courtier's flourish, but a stillness that hinted at watch-fulness.

That night, as the brothers settled into guest rooms with fresh bedding and late-night snacks brought by silent-footed servants, Zhang Fei caught sight of Hahn again in the courtyard, speaking in low tones to a servant before sending him off into the dark.

Whether the man was friend, foe, or simply loyal only to his master, Zhang Fei could not yet tell. But one thing was certain—for all his generosity, Master Yu had to be cautious with guests. A former arms dealer of his stature would never be without discreet men nearby—silent, sharp-eyed, and unseen until the moment they were needed.

Hahn's eyes flicked briefly to Zhang Fei, then away. Zhang Fei met the glance without flinching, his own gaze steady and unblinking. No words passed between them, yet the air seemed to tighten for a brief moment—each man quietly measuring the other.

The next day, as the brothers took a stroll in the courtyard, they saw Madam Yu standing with a young woman in a flowing robe of pale orchid silk, the fabric so fine that it seemed to ripple like water at her slightest movement. Her skin was as white as a lotus flower, her features delicate yet perfectly balanced, as if painted by a master's brush. A faint blush warmed her cheeks, and her eyes were dark, deep, and softly downcast.

Her long, silky black hair flowed loose down to her waist, catching the light like a dark waterfall, with a single jade hairpin shaped like a lotus in bloom nestled above her ear. There was something about her stillness that drew the gaze—an air both graceful and untouchable, like a flower drifting on water. And behind that softness, there was a subtle trace of something veiled and mysterious.

Zhang Fei recognized her instantly. *Lady Lotus*—the daughter of his slain master, Hong. The same young woman he himself had spirited to safety years ago, when the Yellow Turbans had come for blood. Time had changed her from a frightened girl into a woman of striking poise, but in his memory, she was still the fragile life he had once sworn to protect.

Zhang Fei stepped closer, his voice dropping to a rare, almost hesitant softness.

"Good morning, Madam Yu... and... Lady Lotus. How have you been?"

She met his eyes only for a moment, a flicker of recognition passing through them. "I have been... well," she said softly, lowering her gaze. Then, with a slight bow, she added, "I must excuse myself—I need to practice my *guqin*."

With a graceful bow of her head, she turned and drifted away toward the inner hall, the trailing edge of her silk robe following her steps across the stone floor. Zhang Fei watched her go, the faint scent of orchid lingering in the air.

Madam Yu paused at the edge of the courtyard, glancing back as Lady Lotus quietly retreated toward her quarters.

"She has daily string instrument practice," Madam Yu said, her tone both proud and wistful.

Then, facing both Liu Bei and Guan Yu, she said, "Pardon me—I did not have the chance to introduce her to you yesterday. She lost her parents when the riots rose, and we think of her as our own niece now. She's shy, spending her days reading, strolling in the gardens, and playing the qin.

She doesn't have friends. I'm glad to see she recognized you though, Zhang Fei."

Zhang Fei nodded in understanding. A thought struck Liu Bei like a sudden shaft of sunlight breaking through clouds. *Ah... Lady Lotus! How could I forget her? That's why she looked so familiar...*

The memory returned in fragments—chaos on the road, the clash of steel in the distance, and the pounding of hooves beneath them. A frightened young woman clung to his waist as they rode hard on a single horse, her grip trembling yet unyielding. He could still feel the mingled rush of fear and urgency... and beneath it, a warm and precious feeling that he could not name. He had shielded her only briefly, urging the horse onward, before entrusting her to Zhang Fei's care and sending her toward safety.

Now, seeing her again, he felt something unexpected stir in his chest—a quiet, fluttering warmth. And for the rest of the day, though he tried to hide it, his thoughts wandered back to her face beneath the magnolia blossoms.

Winter melted into spring, and the snow on the Wutai slopes gave way to green shoots. Overhead, the first swallows darted and sang, their return a sign of renewal.

Under Master Yu's roof, the three brothers had everything they could ask for—warm beds, full bellies, and safety behind tall walls—but in that very abundance, something was missing.

Comfort, as they soon learned, could dull the spirit. They longed for the raw bite of the road, the pulse of danger, the deep satisfaction of a hard-earned victory. They missed the kind of cheap wine that burned going down, made sweeter by the ache of their muscles after battle, and the rough wooden tables crowded with steaming bowls of food —simple feasts that, in those moments, made them feel like kings.

Now, with nothing to fight for, the days grew slow and heavy. Zhang Fei paced the courtyards like a restless bear roused from winter, unable to sit still for even an afternoon. Guan Yu took to sharpening his blade long after it gleamed like a mirror, running the whetstone over the edge more out of habit than need.

And Liu Bei... Liu Bei was gone for hours at a time, vanishing after breakfast and returning before supper, his cheeks red but expression unreadable.

At first, neither Guan Yu nor Zhang Fei thought much of it. But by spring, Guan Yu's sharp eyes had caught the pattern.

"He vanishes after breakfast and returns before supper," he murmured to Zhang Fei one morning. "Always going somewhere... alone," Guan Yu said as he watched Liu Bei disappear around a corner, "yet... always seems to be in a good mood."

Zhang Fei snorted. "Ha! I even caught him talking to himself the other day—eyes smiling like he'd just won something. You think he's plotting something? Without us? Or..." He leaned closer, lowering his voice. "Has he already gone mad from sitting around with nothing to do?"

Guan Yu's mouth twitched in the faintest smirk. "Either way, I intend to find out."

That afternoon, Guan Yu followed him—keeping to the side paths, moving like a snake. Liu Bei walked with unhurried steps toward the rear gardens, where a narrow bridge crossed over a koi pond to a quiet wing of the estate.

And there, beneath the flowering magnolia, stood a young woman in pale lavender robes. Her hair caught the sunlight like spun silk, and her smile bloomed as soon as Liu Bei stepped into view.

She was Lady Lotus, of course. From his hiding place, Guan Yu watched them speak in low voices, a quiet laugh passing between them.

Guan Yu returned to their quarters, shut the door behind him, and fixed Zhang Fei with a steady look.

"I followed him," he said. "He's been meeting with Master Yu's niece... Lady Lotus."

Zhang Fei's eyes widened—then suddenly he slapped his thigh so hard the sound echoed through the room. "Ha! How could I not have known!"

Guan Yu arched an eyebrow. "Known what?"

Zhang Fei leaned back, grinning.

"Those two met before—briefly, years ago. It was back when the Yellow Turban riots first broke out. Liu Bei crossed paths with her on the road, and that was the same time I first met him. She was frightened, riding pillion on his horse, and he handed her over to me so I could get her to safety. That's how she ended up here."

Guan Yu's eyes narrowed. "If that's the case, I'm concerned. We've been comfortable here far too long. I fear he might forget our mission... or worse, choose this life instead."

Zhang Fei waved a hand dismissively, though his grin had softened into something closer to respect.

"I've got to admit I'm more envious than worried, brother. But no—Liu Bei isn't the sort to be swayed so easily. Heroes like women, they say, but when the time comes to choose, they always choose their destined course."

Guan Yu still looked unconvinced, his gaze drifting. "Let us hope you're right, Zhang Fei. Let us hope you're right."

A few days passed, and the two brothers agreed—without saying it outright—not to bring the matter up to Liu Bei... at least, not yet. Whatever he was doing in those quiet hours, they would watch and wait.

One night, the estate was quiet, save for the soft rustle of bamboo leaves in the night breeze. Zhang Fei, as was his habit, went to Master Yu's quarters to give his routine good night. As he neared the door, he heard voices—low, deliberate.

"...the government... fugitives... grave matter," came Han's low voice, clipped and hard to make out.

"That can't be true," Master Yu replied, his tone edged with doubt. "I don't trust... the commissioner... before they come... take care of it."

There was a pause, the faint scrape of a teacup being set down. Just then, the door slid open and Hahn stepped out. He froze mid-step at the sight of Zhang Fei standing there in the lamplight.

For a moment, his mask of calm slipped—surprise, even embarrassment flickering across his sharp features—before he gave the briefest of nods and moved past.

Zhang Fei watched him go before stepping into the room.

"Ah, Zhang Fei," Master Yu said, his voice warm but carrying a faint, unfamiliar weight. "How is your stay here? I hope you are enjoying the spring breeze these days..."

It was polite, gracious—but something in the cadence

had changed. There was a carefulness in the way he spoke, as if each word had been tested before leaving his lips. Zhang Fei thanked him, saying everything had been comfortable, but he lingered rather than taking his leave.

Master Yu studied him in silence for a few moments, then seemed to realize the lingering had meaning. His fingers closed together, folding his hands in his lap. When he spoke again, his voice was softer, slower.

"Hahn was just informing me of the arrival of honored guests from Luoyang. Officials from the palace, most likely. That means…" He paused, his gaze momentarily unfocused, as though weighing whether to say more.

"It may be best if you and your brothers make preparations to leave within the next few days."

Zhang Fei's brow furrowed. "Leave? So soon?"

Master Yu's eyes met his—steady, yet shadowed by something unspoken.

"You've been welcome under my roof, but… the times are dangerous. An unexpected guest can bring a storm to one's gates."

In that moment, Zhang Fei felt certain Hahn's report had stirred some hidden caution in the master. Whether it was fear for his household or doubt toward his guests, he could not tell. For a heartbeat, he wanted to protest. But he had seen enough storms to know when one was coming. He bowed his head.

"I understand. We'll be ready."

As he walked back through the shadowed corridors, the spring night felt colder.

Zhang Fei found his brothers in their shared quarters,

the lamplight flickering against the wooden walls. He closed the door behind him and spoke plainly.

"We have to leave. Comfort and safety may have made us forget, but we're still wanted men. Master Yu says officials from Luoyang are on their way—he can't be caught sheltering fugitives. We'd best be gone before they arrive."

Guan Yu leaned back, letting out a slow breath, his eyes narrowing slightly but not in anger. If anything, he looked... relieved.

"Then it's settled. We move on."

Liu Bei, however, went still. His gaze dropped to the floorboards.

"I see," he said quietly, and for a moment, Zhang Fei thought he heard disappointment in his voice.

But after a short while, Liu Bei straightened, his voice steady again.

"It's time to leave. We have important work to do—more than hiding under another man's roof."

Zhang Fei, who had been holding his tongue, finally spoke.

"And what about Lady Lotus?" Zhang Fei asked at last, the words half accusation, half curiosity.

The color rose in Liu Bei's cheeks, but he held his brother's gaze.

"Did you... know?" Liu Bei's eyes flickered, but there was no shame there, no embarrassment—only a calm acceptance, as if the question had been inevitable. He let out a quiet laugh. "I have plans," he said.

After this cryptic answer, he paused, his gaze shifting toward the window where the spring breeze stirred the curtain. When he spoke again, his voice had taken on a solemn gravity.

"A man with a grand plan," he said, "must leave when the time comes."

The words hung in the air between them, heavy with both finality and conviction. And in that moment, Zhang Fei knew that whatever tethered Liu Bei to Lady Lotus would not be enough to keep him from the road.

Two days later, their belongings were packed. Servants brought fresh horses to the courtyard, the morning air sharp with the smell of dew and pine.

Liu Bei swung into the saddle, his expression unreadable save for the faint tension in his jaw. As they rode toward the open gates, he did not glance back once.

But behind them, standing in the shadow of the magnolia trees, Lady Lotus watched in silence. Her eyes followed Liu Bei's figure until it was just a blur on the road, the sadness in her gaze hidden from all but the drifting petals at her feet.

Just like that, they were back on the road.

Zhang Fei trudged alongside, the dust swirling at his boots.

"Where to now...?" he asked, a hint of restlessness in his voice.

Once cast adrift again, Liu Bei's thoughts wandered. He saw Lady Lotus's sorrowful eyes as he had broken the news to her, and then, unbidden, the image gave way to his aging mother left alone at home. The twenty men they had left behind at Master Yu's estate would find their own paths in time. But for the three brothers, the long road ahead carried a heavier weight. More than once, their hearts turned back toward the home they missed.

Liu Bei slowed his pace.

"Let us return..." he said at last. "And meet again, right here, on the first day of autumn on the lunar calendar."

Zhang Fei's shoulders sagged, his disappointment plain, but Guan Yu gave a slow nod.

"It is wise," he agreed.

So the three clasped hands beneath the summer sky, their promise spoken aloud: when autumn's first breath came, they would gather once more. Then, with no more words, they each turned to their own road, their figures drifting apart until the horizon swallowed them.

Liu Bei rode on, the silence pressing more heavily than any road he had ever taken. He had known solitude before, yet this time it felt different—for now he carried the memory of warmth: Zhang Fei's booming laughter by the fire, Guan Yu's steady voice in the night, the loyalty of twenty soldiers, and the quiet grace of Lady Lotus.

But warmth, he reminded himself, is only borrowed. He recalled something he once read in the book *Zhuangzi*—that men may share the same shade of a tree for a time, but when the shadow shifts, each must walk his own path.

So it is, he thought. Companionship is a gift of the road, but solitude is the law of life. We enter alone, and we depart alone.

When the time came and he stood beside those brothers again, their bond would be stronger still—and remembered as destiny. With that thought, Liu Bei straightened his back and pressed on, toward the uncertain path beyond the horizon.

CHAPTER 26
BLOOD IN THE PALACE

~

I t was 189 CE, the sixth year of *Zhongping*, the Era of Central Peace. The spring air over the capital city of Luoyang carried the fragrance of blossoming apricot trees, but inside the grand palace, the scent was of burning incense and bitter medicines.

Emperor Ling of Han lay upon his gilded bed, his once-proud frame now thin beneath layers of silk. His breath rattled faintly in the candlelit chamber, each exhale a reminder that the Son of Heaven was slipping further from the grasp of this world.

Outside the bedchamber, the palace was a den of vipers. The women of the palace—Empress, consorts, favored concubines, and those long out of favor but still lingering like ghosts—moved like restless shadows through the lacquered corridors. Their heavy brocade gowns rustled against the marble floors, embroidered with phoenixes and peonies that glimmered in the lantern light. Each was accompanied by attendants and guarded by her own retinue, their watchful eyes missing nothing.

Some stayed in their chambers and prayed for the Emperor's recovery, offering incense with genuine devotion. Others spoke quietly with trusted allies about the days ahead, when loyalties would change quickly and those who acted first would side with whoever held power next.

Within the crimson walls of the imperial palace, three forces circled each other like predators, each vying for control of the Han throne and the weak-willed—and now severely ill—Emperor Ling who occupied it.

The He family had risen to prominence through Empress He, a woman whose beauty had captivated the emperor but whose mind burned with cold ambition. Her brother, Grand Marshall He Jin, now commanded the Imperial Army—a towering figure whose martial prowess was matched only by his ruthless political cunning. His influence spread through the army and bureaucracy, for all knew that crossing the He family meant not just ruin, but likely death.

At the center of their hopes stood Prince Bian, the empress's young son and heir apparent—a child whose every breath represented the He family's path to ultimate power. With Grand Marshal He Jin controlling the armies and Empress He whispering in the emperor's ear each night, the family's grip on the throne seemed unshakeable —a dynasty within a dynasty that had transformed palace servants into the true rulers of the realm.

Yet Prince Bian was not the only contender for imperial

favor. In the shadowed corridors of the inner palace, Dowager Empress Dong Taihou—the emperor's own mother—wielded a power that ran deeper than blood itself. As the woman who had given birth to the Son of Heaven, her word carried the weight of ancestral authority, and her influence over matters of imperial succession was both profound and ancient by right.

She doted upon Prince Xie with a fierce, protective love. The boy possessed an intelligence that far exceeded his years, and in his bright eyes she saw not just a grandchild, but the future salvation of the dynasty. Where others saw only Empress He's political maneuvering, Grand Empress Dowager Dong saw the truth—Prince Bian was weak, lacking the qualities of a ruler, and was little more than a tool for his mother's ambitions. Prince Xie, by contrast, even at a young age, had the intelligence and character worthy of an emperor.

The Dowager Empress had learned to navigate the treacherous waters of court intrigue through decades of surviving palace coups and rival consorts. Her network of supporters—aged ministers who remembered her wisdom, eunuchs who owed their positions to her favor, and generals who respected her judgment—believed that Prince Xie, not Prince Bian, should inherit the Dragon Throne. And when the Dowager Empress spoke of succession, the emperor listened.

Lurking behind both royal factions were the true masters of the palace—the Ten Eunuchs, led by the cunning Zhang Rang. These were men who had been castrated, unable to have children of their own. Ironically, that very condition—seen as a weakness—became their greatest strength, for paranoid emperors trusted them more than ambitious nobles, knowing they could never start a family or found a dynasty of their own. They whispered in imperial ears, manipulated appointments, and controlled the flow of information that reached the throne. In their silk-gloved hands, both princes were merely pieces on a chessboard, valuable only as long as they served eunuch interests.

Beneath the elaborate dance of courtly power lay a foundation steeped in blood and betrayal. Before the Grand Empress Dowager became a mother figure to Prince Xie, there was Lady Wang—the Emperor's most cherished consort. Her gentle grace and scholarly wit had secured a place in his heart that even Empress He, mother to Prince Bian, could not remove.

Although there were many beauties inside the palace, none shone brighter than Lady Wang of Zhao. Born to a family of rank—her grandfather Bao having served as General of the Household for All Purposes—she possessed more than physical grace. She was intelligent, skilled in calligraphy and accounting, a woman whose elegance matched her wit.

Selected to join the Emperor's harem, she entered already carrying his child. But her joy was tempered by fear. Empress. He was known for her fierce jealousy. To bear a son was to invite her wrath. In the secrecy of her chambers, Lady Wang took medicine, hoping to end her pregnancy. Yet the child endured, as if guarded by destiny, and strange dreams came to her: she stood holding the sun in her arms, its warmth sinking into her very being. The birth of Prince Xie was something no mortal will could prevent.

It was in 199 CE, the fourth year of the Jian'an era, when Lady Wang gave birth to a son, Prince Xie. Her attendants celebrated in hushed joy, but for Empress He, the birth struck like a death knell. This child was not merely a rival; he was a living danger to her son's claim and a mortal threat to the survival of her family's power.

The Emperor and the Grand Empress Dowager were overjoyed at the birth of Prince Xie, a healthy, spirited child who seemed to bring light into every room. But their happiness was short-lived. Prince Xie was still a baby when Lady Wang fell ill without warning—her strength ebbing with each day, her breath growing thin and shallow. Physicians came and went, their faces grim, their remedies powerless.

In the servants' quarters, whispers stirred of a cup of tea sent from Empress He's quarters. No one dared to name the hand behind it, yet no one doubted. The silence was heavier than accusation.

When the Emperor heard, his rage was like a storm breaking over the palace. He spoke of stripping Empress He of her title. But the eunuchs—mindful of her brother Grand Marshall He Jin's command over the armies—threw themselves to the floor, pleading until his fury cooled.

The eunuchs knelt in a perfect row, foreheads touching the floor.

"Your Majesty," intoned Zhang Rang, the most silver-tongued of them all, "we beg you to reconsider. The Empress is the sister of the Grand Marshal. To cast her down will split the court and bring the army to the gates."

"Let them come!" Emperor Ling shouted.

"Your Majesty..." another eunuch said, lifting his head just enough to let his words slip like oil.

"The child lives. Let this be enough vengeance. A storm now would destroy more than the empress." The Emperor's shoulders heaved, his fists trembling.

At last, he turned away. "Leave me."

Although Lady Wang's name was sealed away among the quiet tragedies of the court, Prince Xie lived. The Grand Empress Dowager Dong Taihou took him into her own care, naming him *Marquis Dong*. Beneath the gilded ceilings of the palace, the boy of the sun-dream was raised under watchful eyes, in a world where truth was as dangerous as poison, and mercy as rare as survival.

A few years later, when Emperor Ling's health began to fail, the court was steeped in uncertainty. Among the inner attendants was the eunuch Jian Shuo, who had long studied the Emperor's moods and alliances. He had seen the fondness the Emperor held for Prince Xie and the cool distance toward Prince Bian.

One evening, Jian Shuo was granted a private audience. He bowed low and spoke with measured words.

"Your Majesty," he said, "if you truly wish to make Prince Xie your successor, there is one obstacle that must first be removed—the Grand Marshal, He Jin. As long as he lives, your will cannot be carried out. Act now, or the price will be far greater later."

The Emperor, weakened by illness, agreed and gave the order for He Jin to be summoned to the palace at once.

When He Jin entered the Mid-Gate, two palace guardsmen—the Grand Marshall himself had secretly placed them there—stepped forward and bent close to his ear.

"General, turn back. This summons is no imperial will. It is a trap, crafted by Jian Shuo to take your life."

He Jin's face hardened, his jaw tight with fury. Without a word, he turned on his heel and left the palace. That night, he called his most trusted lieutenants, led by his most trusted man, Yuan Shao, into council.

In the flickering light of the command tent, his voice was low but sharp as a blade:

"The eunuchs have overstepped for the last time. I will suffer their poison no longer. Gather our strength. We will strike—and cut down all ten of them in one stroke."

The plan was set in motion, a spark to dry tinder. His men nodded eagerly; they had all seen the eunuchs' grip on the court and the Emperor's ear.

But amid the nods, a quiet voice rose from the shadows near the doorway.

"My lord, I agree the Ten Eunuchs must be brought to justice—but such a move carries great danger. A blade drawn too soon can turn in the hand of the one who wields it."

Heads turned. The speaker stepped into the torchlight— a man still young, wearing the modest armor of a lieu- tenant. Yet his eyes were anything but modest: sharp, assessing, alive with dangerous intelligence.

It was Cao Cao.

Once an obscure cavalry officer, known more for his strict discipline than for high rank, Cao Cao had earned his place in the Grand Marshall's retinue for his keen judgment and ability to read men. His gaze swept the room, finally settling on He Jin.

"The eunuchs are a nest of vipers," Cao Cao continued,

"but they are woven into the palace walls. Tear them out carelessly, and the whole house may collapse on you. If you strike and fail, you will not live to strike again."

At this bold warning from such a young lieutenant, the room fell into a heavy silence.

Yuan Shao's lips curled in impatience, the sting of being upstaged by a mere young lieutenant pricking at his pride.

"So your counsel is to do nothing?"

Cao Cao did not flinch.

"My counsel is to watch, to bait, and to kill in a single stroke—when all their heads are within reach. And to guard yourself, night and day, lest they strike first."

He Jin's brow furrowed. He was a man of the battlefield, not the mastermind of the palace intrigue, yet Cao Cao's words lingered in his mind like the taste of iron.

Yuan Shao leaned forward, cutting across the moment before it could settle.

"If we strike, it must be without warning. Hesitate, and they will act first."

Before He Jin could answer, the flap of the tent burst open. A man stumbled in, breathless.

"My lord... the Emperor... has passed."

The air in the room seemed to vanish. Every man there knew what was coming, but no one wanted to be the first to hear it spoken aloud. The messenger's voice cut through the silence like a blade.

"The eunuch Jian Shuo is already moving. He's placed guards at the palace gates. His aim is to remove you, my lord... and to put Prince Xie on the throne."

He Jin's jaw tightened, the cords in his neck standing rigid.

Inside the palace, Jian Shuo saw the opportunity and wasted no breath. He called his loyal guards to arms, sealing the gates and seizing control of the court chambers. But in the Empress's quarters, her faction moved just as quickly. Runners were sent into the night, summoning the Secretariat's highest officials. With their backing, the verdict was swift: Prince Bian—her son—would ascend as Emperor Shao. The official enthronement ceremony was carried out in haste—courtiers reading the proclamations and performing the rites with barely a pause, eager to seal the decision before Jian Shuo's faction, backed unwaveringly by the Grand Empress Dowager, could rally.

Jian Shuo's bid to enthrone Prince Xie had collapsed before it could take root. As the Secretariat declared Prince Bian the new emperor, Yuan Shao and his soldiers—already stationed near the palace under He Jin's orders—moved in with precision. Jian Shuo was seized in the inner court, his guards scattered before they could draw steel.

There was no trial, no formal charge read aloud. In the eyes of He Jin's camp, Jian Shuo's scheming with the Grand Empress Dowager was proof enough of treason. He was dragged into the open air, his head struck in a single blow. His corpse lay sprawled in the palace courtyard, a grim warning to all who still clung to his cause.

With Jian Shuo gone, He Jin believed the path was clear. Jian Shuo had been the mastermind behind the scheme to place Prince Xie on the throne, and with his death, He Jin saw an opening to consolidate his power by purging the entire eunuch faction once and for all. It was not entirely clear who among them had been aligned with Jian Shuo and who had sided with Empress He, but to He Jin, the distinction did not matter—any eunuch left in the palace was a potential threat. He urged Empress He, his sister, to summon his armies into the palace and sweep every eunuch from existence in a single decisive stroke.

But the situation was not so simple. While Jian Shuo had indeed plotted for Prince Xie, most of the other eunuchs had thrown their weight behind Empress He and her son, Prince Bian. They now stood as her allies, guarding her position in the court.

Torn between her brother's demands and the silver-tongued eunuchs who now swore loyalty to her and Prince Bian, Empress He hesitated. Calculating the risks, she counseled patience, urging He Jin to wait for her decision.

When Yuan Shao learned of this, his frustration was barely contained.

"If the roots are not completely pulled out," he warned, "the weeds will grow again. Leave them in place, and you leave dangers that will one day come back to destroy you."

But He Jin could not ignore his sister's plea. Against his instincts—and his general's warning—he held back his hand, sparing the eunuchs for the moment.

The palace remained in turmoil—factions whispering in corridors, guards shifting loyalties overnight—but at least He Jin and Empress He began to consolidate their hold on the court. Step by step, their influence spread through the ministries and the palace gates.

The Grand Empress Dowager Dong was sent away to her ancestral home, but exile did not silence her. Her anger at the He siblings burned hot.

"A butcher's son and his jealous sister," she was heard to mutter to her attendants.

"They think the dragon's throne is theirs to guard? Let them taste the wrath of one who has ruled from behind the veil."

She maintained secret correspondence with loyal eunuchs and ministers inside the palace, quietly working to wield what influence she could. Even after the He siblings secured their grip on power, they never stopped fearing her reach. To them, she remained a dangerous figure—too shrewd to be ignored.

At last, they decided the threat had to be removed entirely. A trusted killer was dispatched under the guise of an imperial messenger. In the quiet of her residence, far from the marble halls of Luoyang, the woman who had ruled the empire from behind the veil for decades met her end—not with ceremony, but with a blade.

Upon confirming the death of Dong Taihou, it was only a matter of time before the young Prince Xie came completely under Empress He's control. She wasted no time seizing the opportunity to secure his trust.

He was sitting alone in the quiet of his chamber, practicing calligraphy, the faint scent of ink and paper hanging in the air. The door slid open without a sound, and Empress He stepped inside, her silk skirts whispering across the polished floor. She brought no attendants—only a folded handkerchief pressed to her lips, as though steadying herself against grief.

Her shadow fell across his desk, and he looked up. The sight of her damp eyes and trembling breath made the brush slip in his hand, a bead of ink falling to blot the paper.

She sank to her knees before him, eyes glistening with unshed tears.

"Prince Xie," she said softly, her voice trembling, "there is something you must bear with courage. Grand Empress Dowager Dong... has left us. Old age and sorrow took her from this world."

Her words struck him like a sudden winter wind. The Dowager had been the only mother figure he could remember. His birth mother, Lady Wang, was gone before he could even recall her face, and his father, Emperor Ling, had been taken from him only recently. Now, the woman who had raised him, shielded him, and given him warmth in a palace of cold walls and colder faces was gone too.

The boy's heart ached with a sharp, hollow pain. Though shielded from the bloody politics of the court, he could not be shielded from loss. He felt small, fragile—exposed in a way he had never known before.

At first, the boy sat frozen, shocked, confused, and unable to find his voice. Even at only six years old, he grasped the weight of what he had just heard. Then his lips began to tremble. The tears followed—quiet at first, then rising into shuddering sobs that shook his small frame.

Empress He drew him into her arms, her hand stroking his hair as real tears slid down her cheeks.

"I know... I know how much she loved you," she murmured, "but you are not alone. Think of me as your mother now. Cry now, all you want, you poor thing. Let me stay with you tonight, until your heart is lighter."

Her embrace was warm, her voice gentle—but behind the softness, she was laying claim to the boy's trust, weaving herself into the place the Dowager had left empty.

With Dong Taihou gone, He Jin believed the board was cleared. The last great patron of Prince Xie had been removed, and the boy was now firmly under Empress He's control. For Empress He and He Jin, killing him outright risked appearing cruel and could provoke sympathy or unrest, while keeping him alive preserved an image of imperial unity. He was given the ceremonial title of *Prince of Chenliu* and kept under close watch—safe, or so they thought.

CHAPTER 27
FAMILY FEUD

~

Best the eunuchs still held their posts. With Grand Marshal He Jin's decision still pending, Yuan Shao —his most trusted man—pressed him again.

"So," Yuan Shao said, "have you thought about the remaining eunuchs?"

He Jin replied,

"Her Majesty, the Empress, says it is not fitting to kill them all so soon after the new Emperor was enthroned."

Yuan Shao would not let the matter drop.

"Then send orders to the generals in the provinces to bring their troops to Luoyang and get rid of the eunuchs. If you will not act yourself, have others do it. If you leave this be, it will bring disaster upon you."

Weary from the constant struggle between the Empress's will and his own counsel, He Jin finally agreed.

When Yuan Shao's plan was laid out, some of He Jin's other close men counseled against it.

"Grand plans cannot be carried out using shallow tricks," one said. "If generals from every province march their armies into Luoyang, that alone will cause chaos before the eunuchs are even touched and might even threaten the imperial army."

But He Jin silenced them with a wave of his hand.

"This is the clever plan. We will see it done. Doing it so myself would be disobeying the Empress, but we will not let those scheming eunuchs live."

The discussion ended there, but in a quiet corner of the hall, Cao Cao stood in thought. His voice was low, almost to himself.

"That damn fool He Jin is digging his own grave..."

Before anyone could stop him, He Jin had already sent a secret messenger with sealed orders marked *Extremely Confidential* to the provincial generals, commanding them to march their armies to Luoyang and eliminate the eunuchs.

Dong Zhuo, Governor of Western Liang Province, was already on the march. During the war against the Yellow Turbans, he had suffered defeat after defeat, squandering both men and resources, and even insulting those who came to his rescue. He was infamous for exploiting other forces—especially volunteer troops with no influence or authority but only the will to serve the country—using them when convenient, then casting them aside the moment they became a burden. By all rights, he should have been punished and thrown into prison when the war was over.

Instead, through heavy bribes to the Ten Eunuchs in Luoyang, Dong Zhuo was promoted. Now he commanded two hundred thousand soldiers—hardened border troops—in Western Liang Province.

When he received the secret summons from the imperial army to bring his forces to the capital, a slow smile spread across his face.

"Finally... *my* time has come," he thought. "It's time to enter Luoyang."

The frontier province of Western Liang was the empire's shield—its first line of defense against the raids of the northern nomads and a vital hub for trade with them. Here, the garrisons were filled with hardened soldiers, men seasoned by years of suppressing rebellions and facing down swift-mounted archers on the open steppe.

It was in this crucible that Dong Zhuo built his strength. Commanding troops forged in the constant strain of border war, he rose to a formidable power in his own right. Yet his gaze was never fixed on the deserts and mountains of the frontier. His ambition pointed East, to the beating heart of the Han—Luoyang.

Now, with the court in turmoil and with a refined army of two hundred thousand, he believed the moment he had waited for had finally come.

As the word spread that Dong Zhuo was marching to the palace, Minister Lu Zhi came forward. Lu Zhi was a veteran government official admired across the realm for his upright character and unshakable virtue. Years earlier, during the Yellow Turban War, he had been falsely accused and thrown into prison, yet his reputation had emerged untarnished, his resolve only tempered by the ordeal.

Lu Zhi approached Grand Marshal He Jin, his expression grave, the weight of the news pressing into every step.

"Grand Marshal General," Lu Zhi began, his voice steady but urgent, "Dong Zhuo is not a man to be taken lightly. He comes at the head of a great provincial army. If he enters these gates, calamity will follow."

He Jin leaned back in his chair, fingers drumming lazily on the armrest.

"Calamity?" he scoffed.

"To command the realm, one must have a lion's heart. And you tremble over some frontier general? You insult the office you hold."

From behind Lu Zhi, another aide, Zhang Wen, stepped forward, his face dark with warning.

"It is no small matter. Dong Zhuo is tied to the Ten Eunuchs, yet he is now seeking *their* heads who saved him in dire times. Once inside the palace, his loyalty will shift to the sword in his hand—and the throne will find itself hostage to it."

But He Jin only gave a dismissive wave, unaware that even now, in the shadowed corridors of the inner court, the Ten Eunuchs were plotting to lure *him* into their grasp.

Meanwhile, in a candlelit chamber deep within the Forbidden City, the Ten Eunuchs huddled like mice before a coiled snake. Shadows from the flickering lamps danced across their pale, drawn faces.

"We had spared Dong Zhuo's neck after the war," one hissed, "when others called for him to be cast into prison. We placed him in command of Western Liang, gave him power, gave him soldiers..."

His voice dropped to a bitter rasp.

"And now—he marches to take our heads."

Another eunuch clenched his fists, the veins on his thin hands standing out like cords.

"We must speak with the Empress," he said, his voice tight with urgency.

"Beg her to plead with her brother—tell him to abandon this madness of bringing outside armies into the capital. Make her summon He Jin into the palace itself. He cannot bring his army past the gates... and once he is inside, we *have* him."

The summons from his sister had arrived, and He Jin wasted no time. Striding into the camp where Yuan Shao and Cao Cao awaited him, he declared, "I am going to the palace to see the Empress."

In these days, with the Empress's power firmly entrenched, even He Jin—Grand Marshal of the realm— walked with a measure of caution around his own sister. The palace was her domain, and she held influence over the young Emperor himself. He Jin had learned to read her tone, her silences, the faintest flicker of approval or displeasure.

If his sister called him, he went.

Yuan Shao's eyes narrowed.

"I smell something," he said sharply.

"The Ten Eunuchs are plotting. Do not go in."

He Jin waved a hand, half amused, half annoyed.

"You see ghosts in every shadow, Yuan Shao."

"I see *patterns*," Yuan Shao shot back.

"Order the Ten Eunuchs to leave the palace first—*then* go in. If they refuse, you know the truth."

But He Jin's pride bristled.

"And what would *that* make me look like? I am the

Grand Marshal of the imperial army. If I demand such a thing, they will say I fear them."

Cao Cao exchanged a grim look with Yuan Shao.

"Then we will come with you—five hundred men at our backs," Cao Cao insisted.

He Jin agreed, but when they reached the palace gates, he raised a hand and waved his entourage back.

"Wait here," he said with a faint smile, as if nothing could touch him.

The five hundred soldiers, along with Yuan Shao and Cao Cao, were left outside the towering vermilion gates.

He Jin entered alone. And the gates closed behind him with a heavy, echoing thud.

The cool air of the palace corridors carried a faint scent of sandalwood and musk. He Jin's boots clicked against the polished stone as he strode deeper inside.

It was then, from the shadows emerged Zhang Rang, the most powerful eunuch, flanked by Duan Gui whose face twisted with fury.

The man's voice rang out like a whip:

"Listen well, He Jin—the son of a butcher from nowhere! Do you remember how you climbed to this place? Do you remember who discovered your sister and brought her before Emperor Ling? And now you dare turn your sword on us?"

He took a step closer, eyes blazing.

"You ungrateful wretch. You deserve to be punished."

The echo of his words lingered in the open corridor, and from the dim edges of the hall, other eunuchs emerged, their eyes glinting with menace.

He Jin's eyes widened—the insult struck him like a slap.

But before he could speak, soldiers hidden behind the pillars lunged forward.

"What—!"

He managed only a single step before steel flashed through the lamplight. There was a wet, final sound, and his head toppled, rolling across the polished floor as his body collapsed a heartbeat later.

It was done.

Outside the vermilion gates, the sharp-eared Cao Cao caught the faint clash of steel and muffled cries from within.

"Something's happened. We have to go in! Open the gates—now!"

He shouted at the guards, but they stood firm.

Yuan Shao wasted no time.

"Break down the gate!" he barked.

He Jin's soldiers rushed forward, boots pounding, shoulders slamming into the heavy doors, but they didn't budge.

"BURN IT DOWN!" Cao Cao roared.

Flames licked at the wood as torches pressed against it. The guards scattered, and with a groaning crack, the gates finally gave way, and five hundred soldiers poured into the palace.

Soon, the marble courtyards became a killing ground. Eunuchs scattered in all directions, their silk shoes slipping on blood-slick stone. He Jin's men killed every eunuch they could find, their shouts and the clash of weapons echoing through the palace.

Through the smoke and screams of the massacre, the two most influential eunuchs, Zhang Rang and Duan Gui, slipped like shadows, their silk robes whispering over the blood-stained tiles. With practiced swiftness, they reached

Empress He, forcefully seizing her by the arm before pulling the young Emperor and Prince Xie into their grasp.

"Quickly—into the carriage!"

Zhang Rang barked, his voice taut with urgency. The young Emperor's eyes darted in confusion, but the eunuchs were already forcing him inside, Prince Xie, now titled Prince of Chenliu, scrambling in after him. The whip cracked, and the horse ridden carriage surged forward toward the North Palace.

Suddenly, a voice rang out like a blade cutting through the clamor—Lu Zhi had come to evacuate the royals as soon as he heard about the massacre in the palace.

"Traitors!!" he bellowed at the eunuchs.

"Stop right there! Where do you think you're taking them!?"

But Zhang Rang and Duan Gui did not slow. Eyes narrowed, and hands tight on the reins as the carriage rattled over the flagstones. Hooves pounded the ground, scattering sparks into the night.

Lu Zhi lunged, but the carriage barreled past, vanishing into the dark passageways of the palace. In the chaos, he had managed to grab the Empress's arm, wrenching her free from the eunuch's grip. She stumbled against him, breathless, as the clamor of pursuit faded into the distance.

The young Emperor and Prince of Chenliu were gone.

Cao Cao came running through the smoke-filled corridors, his sword drawn, eyes scanning wildly.

"Where is the Empress? And the Emperor and the Prince!?"

Lu Zhi emerged from the shadows, the Empress at his side.

"Zhang Rang has taken the Emperor and Prince Chen-liu," he said, his voice hard.

Without another word, he and Cao Cao shouted orders, their voices cutting above the roar of the flames:

"Find the carriage! Bring them back—do not *ever* get them hurt!"

Soldiers scattered in every direction, racing through the palace gates in pursuit.

The palace itself was a vision of ruin—pillars cracking in the heat, roofs collapsing in showers of embers. Outside the tall red walls, the sounds of the city's cries filled the night. Word had spread like wildfire: the palace was burning down, and a massive army was approaching Luoyang.

In the dim glow of evening, people fled in every direction —mothers clutching children, merchants abandoning their stalls, ox carts toppling in the crush. The capital, once the heart of the empire, now lay shrouded in smoke, panic, and fire.

And in the midst of it all, the throne itself was vanishing into the night.

CHAPTER 28
THE DOWAGER'S LAST LIGHT

~

Zhang Rang and Duan Gui tore through the darkness, clutching two young royals close as the carriage wheels rattled over the uneven road. The night air was thick with panic. Fearing discovery, they abandoned the horse and carriage, plunging into the black maw of the forest. Branches whipped their faces, roots caught at their boots.

From behind came the relentless thunder of hooves, the rasp and clamor of steel against scabbard—soldiers closing in. Zhang Rang's breath turned ragged; despair seeped into his bones. He knew it was the end. Without a word, he swerved toward a moonlit rapid below, its waters churning like silver in the dark, and hurled himself in. The cold closed over him, swallowing him whole.

Duan Gui froze, shock flickering across his face. For an instant, he hesitated, but in a sharp motion, he shoved the

283

stunned children aside and turned away, his figure melting into the shadows, choosing his own path.

The boys—one the young Emperor, the other the Prince of Chenliu—were left shivering in the silence that followed. Their stomachs ached with hunger, their throats were dry, and the weight of abandonment pressed down on them.

Then, in the gloom ahead, a soft, flickering glow appeared—a slow-moving drift of fireflies, their pale lights weaving like tiny lanterns in the air. The children's eyes widened.

"I'm so hungry... I miss my mother," the Emperor, the older of the two, whimpered, his voice trembling.

The boys huddled together in the damp grass, their breath misting in the cold night air. Ahead, a faint glimmer —tiny sparks swaying in the darkness—seemed to beckon them onward.

At some point, Prince Chenliu's eyes grew heavy, and he slumped where he sat. The forest dissolved, replaced by a quiet, moonlit courtyard. There, standing before him, was the late Dowager Dong, her form draped in silken robes, her expression as warm as the first sun of spring.

Without a word, she raised a small, round lantern. But inside, the glow came not from flame—dozens of fireflies drifted within, their golden light breathing gently in the dark.

She smiled, calm and knowing, and set the lantern in his hands. He felt its weight, the faint hum of life inside.

When he blinked, the courtyard was gone. He was back in the forest, his hands empty. But ahead... the same glow, the same fireflies, swaying in the night as though the dream had slipped into the waking world.

A strange certainty settled over him.

"Your Majesty," he said softly to his brother, "let's follow the light. It might be a sign of hope for us."

And with that, Prince of Chenliu moved ahead—feet half-exposed, bleeding through the torn silk shoes— treading the path as if led by something far greater than chance.

Calm despite the fear gnawing at him, he set a steady hand on his brother's arm.

The Emperor trudged along reluctantly, still complaining of hunger, but followed. The fireflies drifted like a slow-moving stream through the trees, leading them deeper into the night. Roots snagged at their feet, the wind sighed through the branches—but the pale lanterns of nature lit their path.

At last, the trees thinned, and they stepped into a clearing. There, bathed in moonlight, stood a magnificent house with sweeping tile roofs, its eaves like outstretched wings. A high stone wall encircled it, and the faint scent of burning pine curled in the air.

Relief washed over them both. The Emperor sagged against the wall and slid to the ground; the Prince sank beside him. Utterly exhausted yet finally at ease, they surrendered to sleep beneath the wall.

A warm voice broke the silence.

A shadow fell across them, and a gentle voice broke the quiet.

"Wake up... children, wake up."

The Emperor stirred first, blinking in confusion. "Mother...?" he murmured.

"No, young one," the voice replied softly, "but you are safe here."

The Prince of Chenliu opened his eyes, already sitting up with a poise far beyond his years. Before them stood a man in plain yet dignified robes, his hair streaked with early silver, his manner calm and scholarly. He did not know who these boys were, yet something in their posture—the measured gaze, the unshaken dignity even in tattered clothes—told him they were far more than mere noble children.

"My name is Choi Yi," the man said. His eyes were soft.

"And you? Who wanders here in such a state?"

The Emperor rubbed his eyes and yawned.

"We're hungry. Bring us food and something sweet, right now."

The Prince laid a calming hand on his brother's arm before bowing with quiet dignity.

"Listen, Choi Yi," the Prince said, his voice steady and commanding despite the lingering haze of sleep.

"I am Liu Xie, Prince of Chenliu. This is my elder brother, His Majesty the Emperor. We have been driven from the capital and require shelter for the night."

For a heartbeat, Choi Yi stood frozen, the weight of those titles pressing upon him. He had not expected the boys before him to be the very heart of the Han. His gaze sharpened, and he dropped into a deep, deliberate bow. When he straightened, all trace of casual warmth was gone; his voice now carried the formal gravity of a man whose own bloodline had served the court for generations.

"Your Highness. Your Majesty. You honor my home with your presence. I am Choi Yi of the House of Choi, younger brother to Choi Yeol, once a minister of the realm. My family has long stood among the scholar-gentry, our ancestors serving emperors as counselors and governors. Please—follow me. You will eat, you will rest, and none shall dare harm you here."

They stepped through the tall wooden gate into a compound of high walls and orderly courtyards. The Emperor's eyes followed the drifting scent of cooking, while the Prince's gaze lingered on the watchful servants and fortified gates—already measuring the strength of their refuge.

Choi Yi wasted no time. He ordered the hearth stoked, basins of warm water brought for washing, and a meal prepared without delay. His household moved with quiet efficiency, the mark of long-ingrained discipline. Soon, the two boys sat before steaming bowls of rice and hot soup, tender slices of duck, and fragrant tea. The Emperor ate hungrily, saying little; the Prince ate more slowly, his gaze sharp, catching every sound beyond the door.

That night, Choi Yi doubled the watch upon his walls.

Morning came soft and misty, the dew still clinging to the garden leaves when the pounding of hooves broke the peace. A lone soldier dismounted in the courtyard, his boots leaving dark prints on the wet stone. He pushed open the gate and strode inside as if he belonged there.

"I'll have breakfast," he said gruffly, his armor dulled from the road.

Choi Yi's brow furrowed. "Forgive me, sir, but you arrive unannounced. I do not take strangers at my table lightly."

"I am Min Gong, Central Army messenger."

Then Choi Yi's gaze fell upon the soldier's horse. Hanging from the saddle by its long, matted hair was a severed head—the pale, slack face of a man Choi Yi vaguely recognized.

He stepped closer, voice low.

"That head—whose is it?"

"Duan Gui," Min Gong replied without hesitation.

"The eunuch who abducted the Emperor and Prince of Chenliu. We caught him running like a rat through the woods. He will trouble the realm no more."

A chill passed through Choi Yi's chest. He drew in a slow breath, then spoke in a low, deliberate voice, each word weighed with care.

"Sir... His Majesty the Emperor and the Prince of Chenliu are here, under my roof."

Min Gong's eyes flickered wide, the gravity of the words striking him like a silent blow. Without another question, he followed Choi Yi into the inner hall. Inside, the Emperor looked up from his morning tea, startled, while the Prince rose with unhurried composure, meeting Min Gong's gaze directly—a quiet assertion of rank.

Min Gong knelt.

"Your Majesty, I am here to return you safely to the palace. Your ordeal is over."

Choi Yi clasped his hands.

"I have merely done my humble part. Your Majesty the Emperor and Your Highness the Prince, I place the rest in the trusted hands of Min Gong right here."

Min Gong bowed in return.

"I shall see them safely home, even if it means striking down every traitor remaining in these woods."

The road to the capital wound between low hills and scattered pines. Min Gong rode at the head of the column, the Emperor and Prince of Chenliu seated before him on the same sturdy mount. Before their departure, Choi Yi had quietly dispatched a messenger to the nearest royal post, bearing word of their journey.

A few *li* on, the thundering of hooves approached— royal army horsemen, riding out to greet them, their banners streaming in the early sun, crimson and gold against the pale blue sky. As the riders drew close, the Prince of Chenliu swung down from Min Gong's horse with calm finality.

"I will ride my own," he said, his voice steady and brooking no argument. A soldier hastily dismounted, offering the reins. The Prince mounted in one smooth motion, placing his horse beside Min Gong's.

The Emperor, still perched before the general, scowled.

"Why did you not bring a carriage?" he demanded over the pounding of hooves.

"Do you expect me to ride all the way in this?"

The head of the troop urged his mount forward, a broad-chested steed built for long marches.

"Your Majesty," he called, "if it please you, take my horse —it will carry you more comfortably on the road."

The Emperor frowned, shifting impatiently in the saddle before snapping, "Forget it! Get going now! I'm tired."

A few of the horsemen exchanged uneasy glances, but none dared reply. Min Gong only tightened his grip on the reins, and the column pressed onward toward the capital.

When they were about to enter the capital city, the air split with the distant blare of war horns. From the mountainside, a mass of soldiers poured down like a dark tide, their armor glinting, their banners snapping in the wind.

KELLIE VEIL & LUO GUANZHONG

The ground itself seemed to tremble beneath the weight of their march.

"Form ranks!" shouted the royal soldiers, wheeling their horses around.

From the front of the advancing host, a voice roared, "Who dares block the Emperor's way!"

Yuan Shao, the newly appointed commander of the royal army after He Jin's death, shouted, his stance bold.

Then, from the enemy ranks, a lone rider stepped out. He was broad of shoulder, with a thick beard bristling like iron wire, his gaze sharp and disdainful. The warhorse beneath him was a great beast, its mane like black silk, its hooves striking the earth like war drums.

"I am the Governor of Western Liang, Dong Zhuo!" he bellowed, his voice carrying over the clash of banners. "I have come to escort His Majesty myself!"

His "escort" was a vast army—rows upon rows of men, more than Yuan Shao's forces could hope to match. The sight made Yuan Shao's jaw tighten; he found no words.

Then, without hesitation, Prince Chenliu spurred his horse forward. The young steed leapt ahead, carrying the boy between the two armies. His small frame sat straight in the saddle, his voice ringing clear and sharp:

"How dare you raise your voice and stand in the way of the Emperor—the Son of Heaven!"

Gasps rippled through the ranks; even the clamor of the armies seemed to falter for a breath.

Dong Zhuo's eyes narrowed, studying the boy before him. *So... this must be Prince Xie,* he thought, though his expression betrayed nothing.

With a thin smile and a voice smooth with false courtesy, he asked, "And who, young master, do I have the honor of addressing?"

The Prince's chin lifted a fraction, and his gaze did not waver.

"I am Liu Xie, Prince of Chenliu, younger brother to His Majesty. And before you stands not only my brother, but the very Son of Heaven. Any man who blocks his way stands against Heaven itself!"

The boy's voice rang out like the crack of a whip. Soldiers on both sides shifted uneasily; some lowered their spears without meaning to.

Dong Zhuo's mocking smirk faded into something harder to read. For a long moment, he said nothing, his eyes fixed on the child before him—eyes that revealed neither fear nor clear admiration.

Then, with a grunt, Dong Zhuo swung himself down from his horse. The heavy thud of his boots hitting the earth echoed between the armies. He stepped forward, fists clenched at his sides, before bowing deeply.

"Forgive me, Your Highness," he said, his voice a growl laced with feigned humility.

"I meant no disrespect. I only came to ensure the Emperor's safety."

Outwardly, it was submission. But behind his lowered brow, Dong Zhuo's thoughts churned like storm clouds.

This boy... sharp of tongue, steady of heart. He has the bearing of a ruler.

His gaze flicked toward the Emperor, who sat atop a horse, driven by someone else, with a slouched posture and a nervous grip on the reins.

Not like that weak and pampered older brother of his. No... if Heaven had sense, it would crown the younger.

Rising from his bow, Dong Zhuo's smile held just the right measure of deference.

"Your Highness, let us ride into the capital together. My men will ride ahead to ensure the road is safe for you."

The two armies began to move as one toward Luoyang, but the seed of ambition had already been planted deep in Dong Zhuo's mind—and it would not stop growing.

CHAPTER 29
DETHRONED

~

"Y*uxi*... the Imperial Seal... is gone!!"

Shouts tore through the hushed corridors of the inner court. Servants darted past with pale faces; their eyes darting toward the throne hall.

It was the very heart of the empire—the symbol of the Son of Heaven's divine mandate. Without it, the throne was nothing but an empty chair.

Within moments, the chief ministers and the Emperor's most trusted attendants shut the palace gates and sealed their tongues. None outside these walls must know. If the court learned, if the provinces caught wind of it, chaos could bloom overnight.

Yet even in the silence, fear coiled tight in their chests. In every dynasty before, the loss of the Seal had been a sign—a whisper from Heaven that the Mandate was faltering. Now, the thought they dared not speak settled like a shadow over them:

Is this the omen of our downfall?

In the days that followed the Seal's disappearance, a different kind of shadow fell over the capital.

Dong Zhuo's soldiers—steel-helmed, eyes like cold stone—stationed themselves in perfect formation outside the palace gates. They did not move for anyone unless Dong Zhuo himself gave the order. At night, the sound of hooves echoed through the empty streets as his men patrolled, torches blazing, letting every soul in Luoyang know: his time had come.

Merchants shuttered their shops at the mere sight of his banner. Court officials lowered their heads and stepped aside when he passed. No one dared to test his temper.

Yuan Shao, watching from the sidelines, felt the ground shifting beneath his feet. The man from Western Liang Province was no longer just a military guest—he was the master of the city. Yet with the court still reeling from recent chaos, Yuan Shao only murmured to his allies, "Let's wait and see. Dong Zhuo will show his true colors soon enough."

One evening, in a private chamber thick with the scent of wine and incense, Dong Zhuo summoned his son-in-law and most trusted aide, Li Ru. Lowering his voice to a conspiratorial whisper, he said,

"I am going to dethrone the Emperor. The Prince of Chenliu will sit the Dragon Throne. What do you think?"

Li Ru's expression barely flickered, but his mind was already racing.

"If that is your will," he said smoothly, "then we must

move with dignity and inevitability. Host a grand banquet—invite *every* minister, every ranking noble, every general in Luoyang. Let them witness your ascendancy with their own eyes."

And so the gilded invitations went out—each with a golden seal, carried by guards who would brook no refusal.

The reaction was the same across the capital: unease, whispers, tightened jaws. The court was deeply bothered but no one dared to send the invitations back.

On the day of the banquet, the Hall of Auspicious Clouds blazed with gold and vermilion. Rows of lacquered tables bowed beneath the weight of delicacies—elaborate pork dishes, considered the height of luxury, alongside tender lamb and mutton, roasted duck glazed with honey, towers of candied fruits, and vats of wine so rich their aroma clung to the air. Silk draperies swayed from the rafters, lit by the flicker of a hundred oil lamps.

One by one, the ministers of the realm filed in, their faces stiff as carved wood. Armed guards stood at every pillar, spears crossed symbolically. No one missed the message: this was not a gathering of friends.

At the head of the hall, Dong Zhuo reclined on a carved dragon chair, dressed not in the plain robes of a loyal minister, but in embroidered finery fit for a sovereign. Li Ru stood at his side, cup in hand, his eyes glinting.

When the guests, warmed by wine and sated from the feast, seemed to have eased into comfort, Dong Zhuo rose, cradling a jade goblet in both hands. His voice rang out, deep and resonant, carrying to every corner of the hall.

"My honored guests, you all know as well as I do—the

Emperor lacks the wisdom and bearing of a ruler. Heaven's Mandate cannot rest on such feeble shoulders. I propose we enthrone the Prince of Chenliu instead, who possesses both the virtue and the strength to lead the empire."

A ripple passed through the hall—quick glances, clenched jaws, the silent lowering of eyes. No one spoke.

Until a single voice cut the air.

Zheng Wen, Governor of Jing Province, pushed back his chair and stood, his expression resolute.

"Grand Marshal, the Emperor is the legitimate heir of the late sovereign. The Son of Heaven's mandate cannot be revoked by force, nor exchanged at a whim. To depose a rightful emperor is to invite Heaven's wrath upon us all."

The words fell like a stone into still water. The entire hall froze.

Dong Zhuo's smile thinned. Slowly, deliberately, he set down his goblet and reached for the sword at his side. The steel hissed free in the lamplight.

"Those with me will live," he said, his voice low and cold, "those against me... will die."

The guards shifted, spears lifting, their eyes fixed on Zheng Wen. No one else moved. Not a breath stirred the air. The banquet's sweetness had turned to the scent of blood.

Zheng Wen stood rigid, the tip of Dong Zhuo's sword glinting in the lamplight.

From beside the dragon chair, Li Ru stepped forward, his voice smooth. He placed a discreet hand on his father-in-law's sleeve.

"Hah! My lord, we are drinking and enjoying the feast tonight. Such matters can be discussed tomorrow, in the proper council."

Dong Zhuo lowered his blade, though his eyes never left Zheng Wen. His gaze narrowed, sizing the man up.

Who in blazes is this fellow? he thought. *And how dare he speak to me like that?*

With a snort, he turned back to the gathering.

"I take it," he said slowly, his tone edged with challenge, "that everyone else here is... agreeable to my proposal?"

A few ministers stared at their wine cups. Others looked down at their sleeves. No one answered—until a calm, deliberate voice rose from further down the table.

Lu Zhi, the famed scholar and teacher of generals, set his cup aside and looked straight at Dong Zhuo.

"Don't even think about it. Be careful what you say."

The words were quiet, but they hit the hall like a drumbeat.

Dong Zhuo's jaw tightened, fury igniting in his eyes.

"You dare—! I should have you cut down here and now!"

Lu Zhi did not so much as blink.

Li Ru, reading the undercurrent in the room—and knowing he was the only one whose words Dong Zhuo would heed—leaned in close to his father-in-law and whispered,

"The whole country looks up to Lu Zhi. If you harm him, the people will rise against you."

But Dong Zhuo's rage was already past the point of cooling. With a harsh laugh, he pointed a thick finger at Lu Zhi.

"I will spare your life for now... but you've just lost your post. From this day, you hold no office in my court!"

Gasps broke the silence. In one stroke, the most revered man in the empire had been cast aside—an omen to all present of what awaited those who opposed Dong Zhuo.

No one moved. Lu Zhi remained seated, his face calm, as if the loss of his office meant nothing to him. In truth, that very composure made Dong Zhuo's rage burn hotter.

Around the hall, the ministers exchanged fleeting glances, but none dared to speak. If the empire's most revered scholar could be discarded so easily, what chance did they have?

The feast resumed in name only. The music stuttered back to life, but the strings sounded strained and brittle. Servants moved quietly, pouring wine with eyes fixed on the floor.

In the shadows by the pillars, Li Ru's gaze swept over the bowed heads of the court. The silence that had followed Lu Zhi's dismissal told him everything: the capital now belonged to Dong Zhuo.

From this night on, every decision, every decree, every act of the court would be made under the weight of that same unspoken truth:

Those with him would live. Those against him would vanish.

As the forced toasts droned on, Dong Zhuo's gaze drifted back toward Zheng Wen's table. He was still nettled by the governor's earlier challenge, the sting of it lingering beneath his smiles. Behind Zheng Wen, half-shrouded in the lamp-light, sat a young man.

Unlike the rest, he showed no trace of unease. His back was straight, his eyes unblinking, his expression almost bored. When Dong Zhuo's stare lingered, the young man met it without flinch—and, to Dong Zhuo's surprise, a faint smile touched his lips. It was the kind of smile that said *I do not fear you.*

The moment passed, but it stayed with Dong Zhuo long after the banquet ended.

Later, in the quiet of his private quarters, he turned to Li Ru.

"Who was the young fellow sitting behind Zheng Wen? The one who had the gall to smile at me."

Li Ru's brows knit slightly.

"That is Lü Bu—Zheng Wen's stepson. A fierce warrior without equal. No man in the realm dares challenge him in single combat. They say his bow can bring down an eagle mid-flight, and his spear never misses its mark."

Dong Zhuo grunted, swirling the wine in his cup.

"Hmph. I can crush that old fox Zheng Wen whenever I please... but that boy—"

He trailed off, the image of the calm, smiling face lingering in his mind like an itch he could not scratch.

The next morning, the sun had barely broken the horizon when shouts and the clash of steel shattered the stillness outside Dong Zhuo's camp.

Rushing to the gates, he saw dust clouds rising from the east—Zheng Wen's banners whipping in the wind, and at the forefront, Lü Bu astride a stallion as dark as midnight. His spear flashed in great arcs, cutting down any who came too close. The sound of hooves and battle cries rolled like thunder across the plain.

The two forces collided in a storm of blades and shouting men. Dong Zhuo's lines broke first. He could only watch, teeth clenched, as Lü Bu cut through his vanguard like a hawk diving into a flock of geese. No hesitation. No fear.

By mid-morning, Dong Zhuo's army was in full retreat.

From afar, he watched Lü Bu scatter the last pockets of resistance and muttered, "I need a general like that... for myself."

Beside him, General Li Su stepped forward with a sly smile.

"Don't worry, my lord. All it will take is your red stallion, and a bag of gold and treasures. That's all you need."

Dong Zhuo turned to him sharply, looking puzzled.

"What do you mean?"

Li Su chuckled, leaning closer.

"Lü Bu is a greedy man. His loyalty lies with wealth and spoils above all else. I grew up in the same town—I know him. I can lure him here, away from Zheng Wen. Offer to give him Red Hare, your stallion, let him taste its speed, and weigh his hands down with gold. He'll come."

Dong Zhuo frowned, doubtful.

"But he is Zheng Wen's stepson. Would he really betray his own father?"

Li Su's grin widened, his tone dripping with certainty.

"Lü Bu follows only one master—his own gain. Even if he still has loyalty towards his stepfather, once he sees Red Hare and gold right in front of him, he'll have a change of heart. Like the old saying goes, *to see is to want.*"

Dong Zhuo nodded a slow smile spreading across his face.

The moon hung low over the plain, its pale light glinting off the polished armor of the stallion. Red Hare stood tall and majestic. Its strength and speed were unmatched. It could leap over walls and ditches in a single bound. Its coat was a deep, vivid red, gleaming like fresh blood in sunlight, with a mane and tail the color of burning flame.

Red Hare snorted, stamping the ground, the bags of gold and jewels tied to its saddle shimmering like fireflies in the dark.

Li Su guided the horse toward Zheng Wen's camp, the night watch eyeing him warily until they recognized his face. Lü Bu himself emerged from the shadows, his halberd in hand.

"Li Su, my old friend! I didn't expect you here."

He laughed, clapping Li Su on the shoulder. Lü Bu's wariness melted into delight—he had no idea his old friend now served Dong Zhuo.

"I came to see the finest warrior under Heaven," Li Su said with an easy smile.

With a practiced flourish, he led Red Hare forward. Even in the dim moonlight, the stallion's coat gleamed like burning embers. Lü Bu's eyes lit up instantly.

Li Su watched him closely, thinking, *now that he's seen it, he will do anything to make it his own.*

Lü Bu stepped forward, running a hand along the horse's neck, feeling the dense muscle beneath the skin.

"This... isn't this Red Hare?"

Lü Bu's eyes widened in surprise.

"Yes," Li Su replied smoothly.

"Of course you'd know it at a glance. It runs a three hundred miles in a day and leaps over moats in a single bound."

He stroked the stallion's mane with studied nonchalance.

"I'm on my way to bring it back to my lord... but I thought I'd stop to greet an old friend."

Lü Bu's gaze never left the horse.

"Your... your lord?" he repeated, the words catching as if they had surprised him.

His eyes narrowed slightly.

"Ah... I see. Why don't you come inside first? We'll talk over drinks."

Inside the camp, the two old acquaintances drank deep into the night, Red Hare's proud silhouette visible through the open tent flap. Beside the stallion, a small chest of gold and silks glimmered in the lamplight.

By the third round, Li Su leaned closer, his voice loosened by wine but his eyes sharp.

"You know, I'm a general now—under Dong Zhuo. Fortune has been generous to me."

"I didn't know you served him," Lü Bu said, swirling his cup.

"How long has it been?"

"A while, but not as long as you served your stepfather," Li Su chuckled.

"And I have no regrets. Tell me, how does your stepfather treat you? You ride and fight like no other, yet you remain beneath a man who..." He let the pause hang. "...doesn't match your greatness. You deserve better, Lü Bu. Far better."

Lü Bu's gaze flicked to the horse with the chest outside, his silence heavier than any reply.

Li Su saw the hunger there. He thought—seeing stirs the desire to possess. He let the moment ripen before speaking again, his voice low and persuasive.

"This stallion... it's one in a million. Dong Zhuo guards it as if it were his own blood. And yet—he would place it in your hands, if you stood with us. Imagine that, Lü Bu. Imagine what it would mean to fight at his side."

Lü Bu's fingers tightened around the cup. The true purpose of his old friend's visit settled over him, and the calm mask he wore cracked—desire glinting openly in his eyes.

"What should I do," he asked slowly, "if I wished to join him?"

Li Su smiled thinly.

"It's simple... but not something I can say aloud."

Their eyes locked in the firelight. Lü Bu gave a single, silent nod.

Li Su poured another round, his tone almost casual.

"Time is short, old friend. There are many in this city who would kill for a place in Dong Zhuo's ranks. Many have begged for it. You just happen to be the best of them all."

The unspoken challenge lingered between them: act now, or watch another man claim the stallion, the gold, and the glory.

Li Su held Lü Bu's gaze for several long seconds. He was certain—the man had already crossed the line in his heart. The hook was set; all that remained was for Lü Bu to strike.

With a tone of casual afterthought, Li Su said, "Now that I think of it, I could use a night stroll. I'll leave what I brought here for now. We'll see each other tomorrow... or perhaps tonight."

He rose with a knowing smile, then stepped out into the night.

The camp lay under a pale mist when Lü Bu rose, fastening his armor in silence. Outside, Red Hare waited, breath steaming in the chill air, the treasures Li Su had brought safely tucked away.

He strode through the quiet rows of tents toward the governor's quarters. The sentries nodded him through, suspecting nothing.

Inside, Zheng Wen stirred awake, blinking in the dim lamplight.

"Lü Bu? Why come in the middle of the night?"

Lü Bu's eyes were cold.

"I'm sick of living as your servant. My time has come."

The halberd flashed in a single, merciless arc. Zheng Wen's head tumbled from the bed, thudding against the floor.

Outside, the commotion drew soldiers to the command pavilion. They froze as Lü Bu stepped into the open, holding the severed head high for all to see. Gasps rippled through the ranks, but no one dared move, no one dared speak.

Lü Bu's voice rang out, steady and commanding:

"Whoever wants to follow me—follow me now!"

The stunned silence broke as men shifted, some stepping forward, others averting their eyes. In moments, Lü Bu was in the saddle, Red Hare tossing its head in the first light of dawn.

Carrying the severed head and leading a column of soldiers, Lü Bu rode at the front of his new force. The gates of Dong Zhuo's camp loomed ahead, and the guards moved aside without question.

From the command tent, Dong Zhuo emerged, his heavy features breaking into a slow, satisfied smile. Lü Bu dismounted and bowed low—a gesture of pledging himself to a new master.

He rose and said, "You are my stepfather now."

Dong Zhuo's thick lips curled into a grin. Without hesitation, he proclaimed for all to hear:

"From this day forth—Lü Bu shall hold the titles of *General of the Household Cavalry*, *Central Gentlemen of the Guard*, and *Marquis of Duting*."

The capital would soon learn: the fiercest blade in the realm now rode for Dong Zhuo.

Two days later, another grand banquet was held in the Hall of Auspicious Clouds. Every high official and noble was summoned. This time, Lü Bu sat prominently behind Dong Zhuo, his armor polished, his gaze sweeping the hall. His troops lined the left and right flanks, spears angled, eyes hard.

When the wine had flowed enough to loosen tongues, Dong Zhuo rose from his seat. His voice carried to every corner.

"My lords—now, what do you think about enthroning the Prince of Chenliu?"

The question was no longer a suggestion. With Lü Bu looming over his shoulder and steel hemming in the hall, it was a demand cloaked in the thinnest veil of courtesy.

The hall was heavy with silence. Not a single voice rose against Dong Zhuo's words—until a chair scraped the marble floor.

Yuan Shao stood, his face set in stone.

"I object. The Emperor is the rightful ruler. To replace him is to defy Heaven itself."

The air tightened. Dong Zhuo's hand went to his sword, the steel rasping free in one smooth pull. The torchlight caught the blade, sending a cold gleam across the faces of the assembled ministers.

"You dare defy me?"

Dong Zhuo's voice was low, but it carried like thunder.

Yuan Shao drew his sword, the point leveled at Dong Zhuo. Gasps broke out along the tables.

Before either could move, Li Ru stepped forward, throwing himself between them.

"My lords! Swords are not fitting when we are discussing grave matters concerning the fate of the nation."

Dong Zhuo's glare stayed locked on Yuan Shao, but he did not lower his weapon. His voice rose, sharp as the edge in his hand.

"You think your family name can shield you?!"

Yuan Shao sheathed his sword in one sharp motion, his eyes never leaving Dong Zhuo's.

"I resign," he said, turning on his heel and striding toward the doors.

The hall seemed to exhale as he left, but the tension only grew. The ministers sat frozen, hands trembling over their cups.

Dong Zhuo immediately turned to Yuan Shao's uncle, Yuan Wai.

"Hmph! How rude your nephew is. I could send someone to execute him this instant—but for your sake, I will spare his life."

Yuan Wai's hands trembled.

Dong Zhuo leaned closer.

"Now... what do *you* think of my plan?"

Yuan Wai forced a quick nod.

"It is... a good idea."

Dong Zhuo, this time turning to the rest of the hall, said, "Well then—I will ask again. What do you all think of enthroning the Prince of Chenliu?"

This time, every head lowered. A chorus of voices rose together:

"It is... a fine idea."

And just like that, the matter was settled—not by reasoned debate, but by the shadow of the sword.

Days later, the summons went out from Dong Zhuo himself. All the civil and military officials were ordered to gather at the Hall of Virtue, along with the young Emperor.

When the assembly was complete, Dong Zhuo stepped forward, hands folded over the hilt of his sword. His voice was loud and steady, every word calculated to leave no room for debate.

"I declare that His Majesty is not in good health and is incapable of continuing the duties of the throne. For the good of the realm, we are hereby dethroning him. From this day forward, he shall be known as the *King of Hongnong*."

A ripple of unease passed through the gathered officials, but no one spoke.

Dong Zhuo continued without pause.

"The Prince of Chenliu is now the Emperor, the Son of Heaven. Let every minister of the realm take note of this and recognize their rule."

The court bowed in unison, their voices echoing in the vast hall:

"Long live His Majesty."

The former Emperor—now the King of Hongnong—remained silent, trembling, his head bowed. Beside him, Empress He's eyes burned with fury. At last, she could bear no more. She rose, pointing a shaking finger at Dong Zhuo.

"Where under Heaven can such a thing happen?!"

Turning to the boy, she cried out, her voice breaking,

"Young Emperor, do not step down! You must stay! You are the Son of Heaven, no matter what!"

Dong Zhuo was furious.

"She is no empress now. Guards—drag her down!"

Armored soldiers moved in at once, seizing her by the arms. She struggled, her cries echoing through the vast chamber.

Before they could take her away, a voice roared from the ranks of officials.

"The Heavens will not leave you unpunished!"

It was Shangshu Zheng Guan, his sword already drawn, charging toward Dong Zhuo.

Steel flashed. With one swift, merciless stroke, Li Ru intercepted him, his blade cleaving Zheng Guan's head from his shoulders. The body collapsed to the polished floor with a dull thud, blood pooling at Dong Zhuo's feet.

The hall fell into a deathly silence.

Dong Zhuo raised his chin and spoke as if nothing had happened.

"Bow to the new Emperor."

Under the unblinking gaze of Lü Bu, the civil and military officials sank to their knees, foreheads touching the cold floor. The Prince of Chenliu—now the Son of Heaven—was only nine years old.

Upon the Dragon Throne he sat, lips sealed, his face a mask—grave, impenetrable—as the dethroned sovereign, his weeping mother, and her trembling maid were dragged from the hall.

Under heavy guard, the fallen Emperor and his sobbing mother were taken to the Hall of Last Serenity, its gates shut and barred to all outsiders.

Enthroned in April, dethroned in September—his reign, the span of a single season, swept aside by the will of one man.

CHAPTER 30
GHOST OF MOTHER AND SON

~

I n truth, Dong Zhuo had all but crowned himself. Taking the title of Chancellor of State—the highest office in court—he swept aside the old era name and proclaimed the first year of *Chuping*, heralding what he called the "Peaceful Years." History would remember it as one of its bitterest ironies.

The deposed emperor, barely thirteen, passed his days in silent grief beside his mother. Cut off from the world beyond their quarters, he clung to ink and brush as his only companions. One day, he composed a poem—his heart's cry —and sang it to himself again and again:

The grass is green, yet spring does not come.
Only swallows in pairs circle the mid-heavens.
Where the ribbon of blue water winds and flows,
In that shadowed grove lies my former palace.
O you who pass along the hill above,

Who will unbind the knot in my wronged heart?

The guards noticed it. They were posted there by Dong Zhuo, not for protection, but to serve as his eyes and ears. Any scrap of information worth noting was carried back to him. One day, a soldier reported the boy's melancholy verses.

Dong Zhuo's face darkened, his annoyance curdling into paranoia.

"A poem..." he murmured, eyes narrowing. "It's not a poem—it's a summons to treason. This child is dangerous, feigning innocence. Letting him draw breath another day would be a mistake."

He summoned Li Ru. "Go to the Hall of Last Serenity. End it."

Li Ru obeyed without hesitation. That evening, he entered the quiet pavilions where the deposed emperor and Empress He sat together. The mother was combing her son's hair in the fading light when Li Ru approached, a sly smile playing on his lips. In his hands was a tray with a small, ornate bottle and two small cups.

"This," he said smoothly, "is *yanshoujiu*, the wine of long life. A gift for Your Majesties."

Empress He's eyes narrowed. "Long life?" she scoffed. "You insult me."

She pushed the cup away.

Her loyal chambermaid, Consort Tang, stepped forward and bowed.

"Her Majesty finds herself indisposed, and His Highness, the King of Hongnong, has little fondness for wine. Permit me, then, to take this cup on their behalf."

But Li Ru's pretense fell away like a torn mask.

"No," he said flatly. "The Empress drinks first."

The Empress's face twisted with fury. She rose to her feet, voice ringing against the pavilion walls.

"My foolish brother, He Jin—he brought a venomous snake like Dong Zhuo into this palace, and in doing so, destroyed everything! You wretches—Heaven's wrath will fall upon you all!"

The Empress would not yield. Her hands stayed tightly clasped in her lap. Her lips pressed to a thin, bloodless line, and her gaze—ablaze with fury yet edged with fear—locked unflinchingly on Li Ru.

Li Ru's evil smile vanished. In a sudden burst of movement, he seized her by the arm and shoved her hard. Her scream echoed as she tumbled down from the pavilion, her body crumpling against the stone path below.

Before the boy could move, Li Ru was on him.

"Drink," he hissed, forcing the cup to his lips.

The child gagged, the bitter poison burning his throat. Moments later, his small frame shuddered and went still.

Consort Tang rushed forward, tears streaming. "Monster!" she cried—only for Li Ru's blade to silence her forever.

Li Ru returned to Dong Zhuo and reported with pride, "It is done. I have summoned the soldiers to bring their heads and present them to you."

At first, Dong Zhuo seemed relieved. But his expression darkened in an instant. He barked, "When did I ask for their heads? Bury them properly and let them rest in peace—show some respect!"

It was as if he would be forgiven if he treated the mother and son with respect—after he got them killed—yet deep within, he knew the truth: it was a grave misstep, and fear began to coil in his chest.

From that day on, Dong Zhuo carried himself as though the empire itself rested in his grasp. He grew more brazen than ever—sprawling across the emperor's bed, summoning women into the inner chambers, drowning the palace in nightly revels of wine and music.

But in the depths of his heart, unease gnawed at him. He could feel the silent hatred in the court, the smoldering resentment of those who had witnessed a mother and child murdered in cold blood.

And so, he drank more and laughed louder. His cruelty sharpened. If the empire feared him, then he would make it fear him even more.

One night, Dong Zhuo drank deep into the midnight as usual. The hall was heavy with incense, the tables crowded with roasted meats, jeweled cups brimming with wine, and women laughing at his every crude jest.

The tyrant's laughter shook the rafters. "Heaven itself cannot topple me," he boasted, slapping his belly. "I have bent the court to my will. Who would dare speak against Dong Zhuo?"

As he roared with triumph, a knock echoed through the hall. Slow. Hollow.

Dong Zhuo frowned, grease shining on his chin. "Who dares disturb my feast?"

A servant, face hidden in the shadows, bowed low at the door. His voice was soft, almost childlike: "My lord, the new dancer is ready to perform."

The tyrant grinned, waving his jeweled chopsticks. "Bring her in! Let us see if she can outshine the rest."

At once, the strings of zithers and the beat of drums began. The doors parted, and a woman drifted inside. Her robes were pale as moonlight, her face hidden beneath a long veil that brushed the ground. She moved without sound, like mist.

Dong Zhuo leaned forward, his fat hands tightening on the arms of his chair. "Good... good! Play louder! Let her dance for me!"

The dancer raised her arms, the veil trembling. The music swelled. And then, suddenly, she pulled the veil away, revealing her face.

Her face glowed pale in the lantern light. It was Empress He.

Her eyes burned with hatred, lips curled in a smile sharper than any blade. Blood still stained the corner of her mouth, eyes locked on Dong Zhuo's eyes.

Dong Zhuo's cup fell from his hand, splattering wine like spilled blood. His breath caught in his throat.

"Impossible..." he rasped. "You are dead."

The zither strings screeched. The drumbeat stopped. The hall fell silent.

The servant who announced her appearance finally lifted his head. His cheeks were smooth as jade, his eyes dark with fury. From within his sleeve, he drew a knife, the blade flashing cold fire.

It was the young Emperor, his voice thin but filled with iron:

"Dong Zhuo, traitor of Han—your celebration is over."

With that, both the boy and the Empress surged forward, their forms blurring into shadows of blood and vengeance.

Dong Zhuo lurched awake, bellowing, his silken robes clinging with sweat. The hall was empty, yet the echoes of their laughter rang in his ears. He clawed at the air as if to push the phantoms away, overturning lamps and sending servants rushing in.

It became more and more frequent that he would wake shrieking in the dark, punish attendants without cause, and lash out at courtiers with sudden rages. Whispers spread through Luoyang—that Dong Zhuo was slipping into madness, haunted by the very souls he had destroyed.

Far beyond the capital, word of his madness carried on the wind. Warlords who had once been rivals now heard the same refrain: the people's hearts had turned. In the northeast, Yuan Shao sensed the change most keenly. In the wake of the massacre, hatred for Dong Zhuo swelled to its peak—even within the court itself, though no one dared give it voice.

Quick to seize the moment, Yuan Shao began to call for a coalition.

"He has defiled the throne," he told them.

"If the Son of Heaven is not safe, no man in the realm is."

From the east, Sun Jian sharpened his blades. From the north, Gongsun Zan rallied horsemen.

By the time the first winter frost whitened the palace roofs, reports began arriving like a drumbeat—one warlord after another was marching west.

Dong Zhuo scoffed at the messengers, but he could feel the threat pressing in. The women he kept in his chambers noticed it first: how he would jolt awake at night, eyes darting toward the door, hand reaching for the sword under his pillow.

He summoned Li Ru almost daily.

"How many men does Yuan Shao truly have?"

"Enough to make trouble," Li Ru replied.

"And Sun Jian?"

"More than Yuan Shao."

Dong Zhuo feigned indifference, but his measures told another story. As Chancellor of State, he tightened the capital's defenses—reinforcing the city gates, swelling the garrison, and ordering the granaries sealed.

Still, the image haunted him: distant lords riding beneath fluttering banners, each name cutting like a blade —Yuan Shao, Gongsun Zan, and Sun Jian.

He told himself fear was for weaker men. Yet at night, Dong Zhuo would sit alone under the cold moon, wondering if the ghosts of a mother and son marched with the armies coming to destroy him.

Meanwhile, in Luoyang, Wang Yun received a cryptic poem from Yuan Shao. Sealed and smuggled past the palace's strict watch, it concealed within its verses a call for alliance—disguised as an innocent poem to escape the eyes of the guards.

Wang Yun had long been troubled by Dong Zhuo's tyranny, and the letter from Yuan Shao left him with the sense that he could no longer remain idle. He invited several veteran ministers and generals under the pretense of dinner and wine.

The mood was grim. Faces were dark, brows furrowed at the state of the court. One by one, they spoke in cautious tones, voicing their frustration and helplessness. Then, from the edge of the gathering, a scoff cut through the murmur.

It came from a slender man with sharp eyes and pale

skin—Cao Cao—his fox-like features flickering in the firelight.

"Master Wang," Cao Cao said quietly, "I have been waiting for a moment alone with you."

Wang Yun studied him.

"Dong Zhuo favors you, are you not? And yet here you stand."

A thin smile touched Cao Cao's lips. "Favored? Perhaps. I have played the loyal hound ever since I learned he took a liking to me. I've courted his trust for a purpose—measuring the length of his arm, waiting for the moment his guard drops... so I can cut his throat."

His voice dropped to a whisper, fierce and confident. "When that day comes, I will take his head and hang it at the entrance gate of the capital for all under Heaven to see."

Wang Yun's brow furrowed. "A bold claim. But he is well guarded, and your face is known to him."

Cao Cao's eyes gleamed. "All the better. He suspects nothing. A man who gorges himself on fear and flattery never sees the knife until it is already at his neck. You, Master Wang, can give me the chance. I only need to be close enough to offer him company."

For a long moment, Wang Yun regarded him in silence, the firelight flickering between them. Then he nodded, slow and deliberate.

"If you truly mean what you say, Cao Mengde, Heaven itself may guide your hand."

Cao Cao leaned closer, lowering his voice so that even the crackle of the fire seemed too loud.

"One condition," he said. "Lend me your Seven-Star Blade—the heirloom of your house. That is the weapon I need to take Dong Zhuo's head in a single stroke. I seek not only the blade's strength, but the blessing of Heaven upon it."

Wang Yun's eyes widened. The blade was no common weapon; it was a treasure passed through his family for generations, said to carry Heaven's favor. But in this moment, he did not hesitate. Rising, he disappeared into his tent and returned with a long, lacquered case.

He set it before Cao Cao and lifted the lid. The blade inside gleamed under the torchlight, its dark steel etched with faint constellations that seemed to shimmer as if they held the night sky itself.

Cao Cao reached in, running his fingers lightly along the hilt before fastening it to his waist. His demeanor was strangely untroubled—too calm for a man about to risk his life.

"I know my life is on the line, but..." he said with a half-smile, fastening the ties. "Just trust me."

The blade hung at his side, silent and patient, as if it, too, was waiting for the right moment to drink blood.

The next day, Cao Cao rode into Dong Zhuo's camp. Rows of armored guards watched him pass, spears catching the morning light, but none moved to stop him—he was known as a man trusted by the Chancellor, visiting him each morning for the past several weeks.

Inside the main tent, the air hung heavy with incense and the steam of boiled tea. Dong Zhuo sat at the head, his massive frame draped in embroidered silk, a cup of steaming tea balanced in one hand. Beside him stood Lü Bu —towering, broad-shouldered, his hand resting casually on the shaft of his halberd.

Dong Zhuo's eyes narrowed as he saw Cao Cao approach.

"You're late."

Cao Cao bowed low. "Forgive me, Chancellor. My horse is so old and slow, it could barely keep pace. It seems to be having a particularly bad day today."

Dong Zhuo chuckled, the sound deep and coarse. "Then Lü Bu will find you a fine steed from my stables. Go, and choose him the best."

Lü Bu nodded and strode out, the tent flaps swaying shut behind him.

The moment the great warrior's shadow was gone, Cao Cao felt his pulse quicken. This was it. Dong Zhuo, the butcher of the Son of Heavens, sat before him with no one else in arm's reach. Yet the man was still famed for his fierce energy—one wrong move, and he could turn like a cornered tiger.

Then Dong Zhuo leaned back, setting down his cup. His silk robe rustled as he shifted onto his side, presenting his broad back to Cao Cao. The Chancellor's voice drifted lazily over his shoulder.

"Sit, Mengde. Relax."

Cao Cao's hand moved to the hilt of the Seven Stars Blade. Slowly, he began to draw the blade, its edge whispering against the scabbard.

But he did not see the polished bronze mirror mounted on the far wall—its face angled just so, catching his reflection perfectly. In its surface, Dong Zhuo watched everything: the tightening grip on the hilt, and the silent step forward.

Dong Zhuo's voice cut through the tense air, half suspicious, half amused.

"Why," he asked suddenly, "are you pulling your blade?"

Cao Cao did not falter. In the blink of an eye, his expression shifted to one of eager pride.

"Ah, Chancellor, I couldn't wait to show this to you. I acquired this rare blade only a few days ago, and I thought it worthy of being presented to you first."

The tent flaps parted, and Lü Bu stepped back inside, carrying news of the chosen steed. Dong Zhuo sat up at once, his suspicion melting into excitement as his eyes fell on the weapon.

"Ha! That is indeed a precious blade! Lü Bu—come, take a look at this."

Lü Bu leaned in, and even he seemed impressed by the steel's sheen and the faint shimmer of the seven-star etchings.

Relieved that Dong Zhuo had taken the bait, Cao Cao deftly loosened the blade's lacquered case from his waist and stepped forward, all smiles.

"You must have the case as well, Chancellor. See the engravings here—this is no ordinary scabbard. Together they are a matched treasure."

Cao Cao's expression was the picture of composure, but behind it, his mind worked, weighing his next move.

Dong Zhuo turned the weapon in his hands, torchlight glinting along the steel, unable to hide his delight.

"Mengde," he said—addressing Cao Cao by his style name for the first time—"you are a man of taste. In return, let me gift you one of my finest horses. Follow me."

With Lü Bu at his side and the sword cradled in his arms, Dong Zhuo rose and strode toward the tent's entrance—never knowing how close he had just come to death.

Outside the tent, a sleek black stallion awaited—muscles taut, and eyes bright. Dong Zhuo patted its neck.

"This is no Red Hare," he said with a sidelong smile at Lü Bu, before turning back to Cao Cao.

"But it will carry you like the wind, Mengde. Try it—see if it suits you."

Cao Cao bowed deeply. "An honor, Chancellor."

In his head, the calculation was swift: *Three options—fight, yield... or something else. The first two will surely get me killed, so...*

In one fluid motion, he mounted. His smile remained gracious, but as he pressed his boot into the stirrup and leaned forward, he murmured under his breath, *Run.*

The steed burst forward like an arrow loosed from the string, pounding down the camp's main thoroughfare. Guards stepped aside without suspicion. Cao Cao kept his heels to the horse, driving it faster and faster. Wind tore at his robes; tents and soldiers streamed past in streaks of color.

Back at the camp, Dong Zhuo watched the dust trail with a lazy grin. Lü Bu folded his arms, eyes narrowing.

"He's really... testing that horse."

Dong Zhuo said, cradling the Seven-Star Blade.

"Or is he...?" Lu Bu muttered suspiciously.

They waited.

A quarter of an hour passed. Then another. The stallion's pounding hooves never came back.

Dong Zhuo's smile began to fade. Lü Bu was certain Cao Cao tricked them.

"What was he *really* here for?" Lü Bu finally said.

Dong Zhuo's fingers tightened around the sword's hilt.

"Find him," he growled.

"Now."

Dong Zhuo summoned Li Ru at once. The adviser bowed low, but his voice carried a grim edge.

"Chancellor," Li Ru said, "it is as I feared. Cao Cao had long since sent his family far from Luoyang. He kept private quarters apart from the others, living alone. I should have known—he was always preparing for a betrayal."

Lü Bu rode hard to Cao Cao's private residence. The courtyard gates swung open under their hands, but the place was eerily quiet. Only the doorman stood there, wringing his hands.

"Where is he?" Lü Bu demanded, towering over the man.

The doorman stammered, "H-he packed up and left in a hurry... riding a fine steed. Said he'd been given an urgent order, then rode straight toward the East Gate."

When Lü Bu reported to him, Dong Zhuo's face darkened like a gathering storm. His fingers trembled as they closed around the hilt of the Seven-Star Blade.

"So... that little fox, Cao Cao, has betrayed me."

The tent flaps quivered as his voice rose into a roar:

"Spread his name across the empire! Post it in every province, every county. Heavy gold to the man who brings me his head!"

Messengers scrambled from the camp, carrying the order to the four winds. Within days, the name *Cao Cao* was inked on wanted lists from the Yellow River to the sea— marked as a traitor, a fugitive, and a man with a price on his life.

Clever as he was, Cao Cao had been too haughty—too

sure that he alone could bring down Dong Zhuo with a single stroke. Now, his grand plan lay in ruins.

The precious Seven-Star Blade, Wang Yun's proud family heirloom, was gone—resting in the very hands of the man it was meant to kill.

Worse still, Cao Cao was now a fugitive, his face known from one end of the empire to the other. Every gate guard, every roadside peddler, every hungry bounty hunter could recite the price on his head.

The man who once strode boldly into the Chancellor's tent now had to watch every shadow, for each one might conceal the hand that would deliver his head to Dong Zhuo's wrath.

CHAPTER 31

BETRAY OR BE BETRAYED

~

C ao Cao had flown through the East Gate like a shadow loosed from the city walls, his stallion devouring the road toward his hometown of Cho County. The wind bit at his face, but he did not slow— not until the watchtower of Zhongmo County loomed ahead.

A pair of guards stepped into the road, halberds crossed.

"Dismount," one barked.

Cao Cao swung down slowly, keeping his movements calm. One of the guards held a rolled bounty poster in his hand. He glanced from it to Cao Cao's face... then back again. The gaze lingered too long.

"You look," the guard said at last, "exactly like this man Cao Cao in the poster."

For the briefest instant, Cao Cao's heart plummeted into

his stomach. But his smile never faltered. He threw back his head and laughed.

"Hah! Is that a compliment? My name is Huang Bao—a simple traveler. You flatter me by comparing me to such a... famous man."

The guards weren't convinced.

"Come," one said, grabbing his arm. "The chief will know."

They marched him into the yamen, where the chief of the guard sat behind a desk, studying him with a narrow-eyed intensity. A slow, knowing smile spread across the man's face.

"You *are* Cao Cao," the chief said. "I've seen you in Luoyang myself."

It was the county's defense captain, Chen Gong. His eyes lit with recognition the moment he saw the prisoner.

Cao Cao thought, *Busted.* But he kept his composure.

"You wouldn't believe me anyway—so think what you like."

"So it's true," Chen Gong muttered.

Without another word, he ordered Cao Cao locked away in a narrow cell, the iron bars casting long, cold shadows on the dirt floor.

Cao Cao sat on the hard bench, mind turning over escape after escape—each one collapsing against the reality of the heavy lock, the posted guards, the sharp eyes of Chen Gong. By midnight, no solution had come.

Then, he heard footsteps approaching. Soft.

A low voice called through the darkness: "Cao Cao."

He looked up, startled. Chen Gong was there, holding a

small oil lamp, its flickering light throwing his face into planes of shadow.

"I've heard," Chen Gong said, studying him carefully, "that Dong Zhuo held you in great favor. Yet here you are, a fugitive. How did it come to this?"

Cao Cao's pulse quickened, but his expression remained smooth. He leaned back against the wall and smiled faintly.

"How could a mere sparrow comprehend the depth of a phoenix's mind?" he said, voice dripping with scorn.

Then, with a shrug, "You've caught me. So take me to Luoyang, claim your reward, and be done with it."

Chen Gong did not answer right away. He stood there, the lamplight trembling in his hand, his gaze fixed on Cao Cao as if weighing him on an invisible scale.

At last, he spoke slowly. "Reward? Hmph. Do you take me for a petty hunter chasing a wolf for its pelt? I've seen enough of Dong Zhuo's so-called rule to know what it is. I despise the man. There are many of us."

He stepped closer to the bars, lowering his voice. "If you were plotting against him, then we are of the same mind."

Cao Cao's eyes narrowed, studying this man anew. "And what would you do, Captain Chen, if I told you I failed?"

"Then you must try again," Chen Gong replied without hesitation.

"I will not deliver you to that tyrant. I would rather help you bring him down."

The key scraped in the lock. The door swung open.

Cao Cao rose, dusting off his robes, a thin smile curling on his lips.

"You surprise me, Captain. Few men would throw away a heavy purse for a dangerous gamble."

Chen Gong responded with a grim smile. "Some wagers are worth more than gold. Come—before the guards wake."

And so, under the cover of darkness, the jailer became a comrade, and the fugitive gained an ally who would ride at his side into the uncertain night.

Once they had cleared the town's outskirts, the road stretched empty beneath the pale moonlight. The cold night air stung their faces, but neither man slowed his pace.

Chen Gong glanced sideways at his companion. "Now that you are free, what do you intend to do?"

Cao Cao's eyes narrowed toward the horizon. "I'm going to my hometown. There, I will gather the scattered heroes—men who still have fire in their hearts—and with them, I will march to strike Dong Zhuo."

Chen Gong's jaw set like stone. "Then I pledge myself to this cause. What worth is my post if the empire is left to decay? Let us stand together, and perhaps Heaven will grant us the day of his fall."

The two men exchanged a firm nod, their pact sealed without ceremony.

And so they rode into the rising sun, bound by a shared enemy and the dangerous hope that one day, the tyrant in Luoyang would lie in the dust.

For days they rode, sleeping little and eating less, until at last they reached a wooded stretch. The winter wind cut through their cloaks, but Cao Cao's eyes narrowed as he pointed toward a stand of shadowed trees.

"There," he said. "There's a house I know well. Its owner is like an uncle to me—a sworn brother to my father. His name is Lu Poshe. If anyone will give us shelter, it is he."

They followed the narrow path through the trees until a

modest but sturdy house came into view. Smoke drifted from the chimney, and the smell of pinewood hung in the air.

When Lu Poshe opened the door, his brows shot up in surprise. "Mengde? What brings you here... and in such a state?"

"You remember me. I'm glad you're home. May we come in?"

Lu Poshe's eyes narrowed, suspicion flickering in his gaze, though his tone remained polite. "What grave sin have you committed?"

Cao Cao met his gaze squarely, knowing Lu Poshe had already heard the tales—and the price now set on his head.

"Uncle Lu, I'm sure they've spun all manner of lies to brand me a criminal fit for execution. But the truth is... I tried to kill Dong Zhuo. I failed."

Lu Poshe was silent for a moment, then nodded slowly and stepped aside to let them in.

"This is Chen Gong," Cao Cao said, "the Chief of Defense in a county not far from here. We share the same cause, and he freed me from certain death. Without him, the Cao clan might already be in mourning."

At those words, Lu Poshe's guarded look eased. His mouth softened, and he stepped forward to clasp Chen Gong's hands. "Then I thank you, sir, on behalf of our whole family. You have done us a service beyond measure."

He gestured toward a side room. "Please—rest there. Warm yourselves. Feel yourself at home. I'll fetch some wine."

With that, they were left alone.

Time passed. The sounds of the household faded to quiet. Lu Poche did not return, and no one came to offer food. Cao Cao sat cross-legged on the floor, his fingers tapping against his knee. Chen Gong glanced toward the door, unease in his eyes.

"He has been gone a long while," Cao Cao murmured.

"Yes," Chen Gong said slowly. "Too long."

The silence pressed in, heavy and watchful.

Then—there was a sound. Soft, deliberate. From somewhere outside the window came the murmur of voices.

They froze.

"...tie up..." one voice whispered. "...and one strike... You clean up the blood..." another replied.

Cao Cao's eyes flashed.

He leaned close to Chen Gong and hissed, "They're scheming to kill us. We have to strike first—hesitate, and we're dead."

Without another word, he snatched up his sword, slid the door aside, and slipped into the cold night. His boots barely touched the ground as he rounded the house to the backyard.

In the dim lantern light, four or five men crouched over a massive butcher's knife, the steel catching a glint as it scraped against a whetstone.

Cao Cao didn't wait for them to rise. With a shout, he lunged. Steel flashed, and before the men could lift the knife, they fell—one after another—into the dirt. Snatching up the huge knife, Cao Cao scoffed, "Hah—did you fools think you could kill us with a butcher's knife?"

A couple of women, startled by the commotion, came running toward the scene, and quickly turned around and started running, screaming. Without pause, Cao Cao chased and cut them down from behind.

Chen Gong caught up, sword in hand, and together they swept the yard—kicking open sheds, peering into shadows —finding no one else. Pushing through the rear door into the kitchen, they stopped short.

There, on its side, legs bound with coarse rope, was a fat, squealing pig—awaiting the butcher's hand.

The blood on Cao Cao's blade dripped into the silence.

"Oh no..." Chen Gong's face turned pale as he let out a long, pained breath, staring at the bodies in the yard. "We were too paranoid... too hasty."

Cao Cao wiped his blade clean, his expression unreadable.

"Paranoid or not, we're alive. And now we must go— before anyone comes looking."

Chen Gong hesitated, but finally nodded. They sheathed their swords and slipped toward the front gate.

Just as they stepped out into the moonlit road, a slow clopping of hooves approached. Out of the darkness emerged Lu Poche, swaying gently on the back of a small gray donkey. Fat-bellied wine jars hung from either side of the animal, their stoppers tied with red cord.

Cao Cao's stomach sank.

"Ah," Chen Gong murmured, "he went all the way to the night market... to buy wine for us."

Lu Poche's face lit with recognition, but soon turned into a puzzled expression.

"Mengde! Leaving so soon? Why? I had my men slaughter the whole pig for you two, and I've brought the finest wine in the county—fit for a feast. Come, come—go back inside and relax."

Cao Cao forced a polite smile. "Uncle Lu, we are fugitives. I won't endanger you by staying too long. You've already done more than enough."

But Lu Poche waved the protest aside. "I went all the way to the market, looking forward to catching up with you. It's been too long—let's relax and enjoy just one night."

"Uncle, in that case, we'll just take a short walk since we're already out, and then we'll return."

Lu Poche nodded with a genial smile. "Very well. I'll have the wine warmed by the time you're back. Now, let me go see whether the roasted pig is nearly ready."

They walked a few paces down the moonlit road before Cao Cao leaned toward Chen Gong and whispered, "Wait here."

Before Chen Gong could ask why, Cao Cao was already moving, his steps so light they scarcely disturbed the frost beneath them. In moments, he was at Lu Poche's back, where the man led his laden donkey. One swift stroke, and the blade fell—Lu crumpled without a sound, the wine jars swaying heavily against the donkey's flanks.

Chen Gong's breath caught. He spurred forward, eyes wide.

"Cao Cao! What have you done?"

Cao Cao wiped the blade clean, his face unreadable.

"He will soon discover the bodies in his yard and find out we killed every living soul in that house. He will know they died by my hand, and report us to the authorities. Then we are as good as dead."

Chen Gong's voice was tight with anger. "But he was an innocent man! You could have pleaded with him!"

Cao Cao met his gaze without flinching. "Better that I betray another than give them the chance to betray me."

The words settled between them like a blade laid bare— cold, and cruel.

The moon hung cold above the treetops as they rode away from the silent road. Neither spoke for a long while— the only sound was the crunch of hooves on frost-hardened earth.

Chen Gong's mind replayed the night in merciless detail: the sudden strike against Lu Poche, the bodies cooling in the courtyard, the calm way Cao Cao had justified it all.

He had thought he was saving a visionary—a man bold enough to strike at the tyrant Dong Zhuo, a savior who might restore order to the chaos. But now, he saw something different.

This was no selfless hero. This was a cold, unyielding schemer, a man whose ambitions cared nothing for loyalty, innocence, or honor—a ruthless seeker of power.

Chen Gong's grip tightened on the reins. Regret settled heavily in his chest.

I freed him... I swore to follow him... and now I see the truth.

But the road was long, and the night darker still. For now, he kept his silence, knowing that to voice his doubt might put him next in line for the blade.

That night, they came upon a small roadside tavern, its dim lantern light spilling across the frosted road. Inside, the air was thick with the smell of boiled millet and cheap wine. They had not eaten in days, and the bowls before them were emptied in moments.

Cao Cao leaned back, wiped his mouth, and, without a word, lay down along the bench. Within minutes, his breathing deepened into the heavy, careless snore of a man untroubled by guilt.

Chen Gong sat in silence, watching him. His hand drifted to the hilt of his sword.

One strike—quick, clean. If I don't do it now, Cao Cao's blade might point at me next.

He thought bitterly.

Yet he hesitated. He had never killed a man in cold blood. His life had been spent defending his county, shielding it from aggressors.

And then he tried to reason with himself—perhaps Cao Cao had no choice. These were not ordinary times. Kill or be killed—that was the law of the age. Could he truly fault Cao Cao for playing the game to survive?

The weight in his chest turned to weariness. Slowly, he released the hilt, the thought of vengeance draining away.

Rising without a sound, Chen Gong stepped out into the cold night, leaving Cao Cao to his dreams, his snores echoing behind him.

CHAPTER 32
MARCHES OF WARLORDS

~

T he gates of the Cao estate groaned as they opened, revealing the familiar courtyard where the winter wind rattled the bare branches of the old jujube tree. Cao Cao stepped inside, the weight of weeks on the run still clinging to him.

In the main hall, his father, Cao Song, rose from his seat. Relief softened his lined face, but concern quickly followed.

"Mengde," he said, "word of your escape from Luoyang has already reached here. Do you realize how dangerous it is to return?"

"I know," Cao Cao replied.

"But the danger will be greater still if I do nothing. Father, I intend to raise an army of my own—to strike Dong Zhuo before he bleeds the empire dry. I need your support."

Cao Song's brow furrowed.

"Our coffers are bare. Years of decline have left this family without silver enough to arm even a dozen men."

"Money can be found," Cao Cao said firmly.

"What we have is a name. The Cao clan has been honored in these lands for generations. You have friends, allies—men of wealth who still respect your word. If you open the doors, I will seal the deal."

His father leaned back, considering.

"You ask me to risk more than silver. You ask me to gamble our name."

"Reputation will mean nothing if Dong Zhuo rules unopposed," Cao Cao countered.

"The people will rally to any banner that stands against him. Let that banner be ours."

For a long moment, Cao Song was deep in thought without a word. Then he exhaled and gave a slow nod.

"Let me arrange meetings with wealthy merchants, landowners, and men who owe me favors. You will have the introductions. The rest will be up to you."

Cao Cao's lips curved in the faintest of smiles.

"My tongue and my wits have never failed me yet."

Cao Song sat back, stroking his beard in thought.

"There is one man," he said as if he just remembered something, "whose wealth could arm half a province—Wei Hong, the richest man in all of Henan. If he stands with you, your army will be more than a dream."

Cao Cao's eyes lit with interest. "Then, father, introduce me to him."

Then his father warned, "Wei Hong does not move easily. He guards his fortune as fiercely as a dragon guards its hoard. You must not rush him—it will take time, and care—"

"Time?" Cao Cao cut in, his tone firm.

"Father, patience may be a virtue, but the greater the matter, the more decisive you must be. This is urgent. The fate of the realm hangs in the balance. Set the meeting for tomorrow, if possible. A blade grows dull if it waits too long to strike."

Cao Song studied his son for a long moment. There was no mistaking it—this was the same Mengde who had once been a sharp-tongued youth, but now his ambition burned hotter, sharper, and far more deliberate.

"Very well," he said at last. "I'll send a messenger tomorrow."

A few days later, the Cao estate hosted Wei Hong with all the ceremony their resources could muster. The banquet table groaned under roasted meats, steamed fish, and the finest wine Cao Song could procure.

For the first hour, the talk was light—shared acquaintances, the state of the harvest, the latest palace rumors. Only after a few rounds of wine did Cao Cao lean forward, his gaze fixed on the wealthy guest.

"Wei Gong," he began evenly, "the empire stands in chaos. Dong Zhuo drains the lifeblood of both court and people—I have seen it with my own eyes. As you may have heard, I staked my life on striking him down, and now, as a fugitive, I have sought refuge here. But I am not one to yield while breath remains in me. I will raise an army and see him destroyed. I speak to you with the utmost urgency: lend me your support."

Wei Hong was a difficult man to read. He swirled his

wine slowly, his expression giving nothing away. Cao Cao studied him in turn, a cold thought forming in the back of his mind:

If he refuses, I will kill him before he can betray me.

After a long pause, Wei Hong set down his cup and smiled faintly.

"I agree—someone must act. I have long looked for the right person to support, but I could never find him."

He nodded toward Cao Cao.

"Of all the trials in this world, none is greater than finding the right man to stand beside."

Relief and satisfaction stirred in Cao Cao's chest. This was an endorsement from one of the most influential men in Henan.

With Wei Hong's backing, Cao Caho had newfound confidence. He acted swiftly. Announcements were posted in marketplaces, temple courtyards, and at busy crossroads: a call for men to rally under his banner against the traitor Dong Zhuo.

At the center of his mustering ground, Cao Cao planted a single white flag, its silk snapping in the wind. Upon it, in bold, black brushstrokes, was written one word: *Zhongyi*—Loyalty and Righteousness.

The white banner of *Zhongyi* rippled high above the training ground, and from every road, men began to arrive —peasants with spears, hunters with bows, wandering swordsmen hungry for a cause. Some came alone, others in small bands, pledging their strength to Cao Cao's call.

But of all who answered, one figure made him pause in astonishment.

On the third morning, a great column of soldiers

appeared over the rise—armor glinting in the sun, banners snapping in the breeze. At their head rode none other than Yuan Shao, the man who had once stormed out of Dong Zhuo's banquet in disgust and almost got himself killed.

More than ten thousand troops marched behind him, disciplined and proud.

When they met in the courtyard, Yuan Shao clasped Cao Cao's forearm.

"Mengde," he said with a smile, "I hear your voice calling for righteous men. You'll find none more ready than these."

Cao Cao knew Yuan Shao's life had once hung by a thread after that banquet, but his reputation—his family's prestige and the loyalty he inspired—had shielded him from Dong Zhuo's wrath. And now, that same prestige had brought him here, to stand beside him in defiance of the tyrant.

With Yuan Shao's arrival, Cao Cao's cause swelled in both numbers and legitimacy. The banner of *Zhongyi* no longer stood alone—it now weighed a small army behind it.

One after another, generals arrived, each bringing their own retinue of warriors. Some were minor lords seeking glory, others seasoned commanders with battle-worn troops.

Within weeks, the mustering ground outside Cao Cao's estate teemed with soldiers—tents sprouting across the fields, the ring of hammers on armor echoing through the night.

Among them came a force that turned every head in the camp. Banners bearing the tiger emblem of Changsha rippled in the wind, and at their head rode Sun Jian—the famed "Tiger of Jiangdong." His armor gleamed, his gaze was sharp, and the men behind him marched with the unshakable discipline of veterans.

When he dismounted before the white banner, Sun Jian bowed slightly.

"Cao Mengde," he said, showing his respect by addressing him by his style name, "the empire has little time left before the rot spreads beyond repair. You called for righteous men—I am here to answer."

It wasn't only soldiers who came. News of the *Zhongyi* banner reached merchants, landowners, and common folk alike. If they could not give arms or able bodies, they gave what they could—gold and silver pressed into the hands of Cao Cao's officers, wagonloads of millet and rice rolling into the camp, bolts of cloth stacked high for uniforms and bedding.

Wealthy merchants from as far as Runan sent caravans bearing wine, oil, and salt. Village elders arrived, leading ox-carts piled with dried meat and beans. Women carried baskets of bread and jars of pickled vegetables, their faces proud as they handed them over.

By the end of the month, the once-empty fields around his estate had become a city of war—a living tide of men, arms, and supplies, all waiting for the order to march against Dong Zhuo.

In the meantime, far to the north, the Prefect of Beiping, Gongsun Zan, was on the march. Fifteen thousand horsemen rode at his back, their white-plumed helmets swaying like waves as they cut across the winter fields.

As his column neared a grove of bare mulberry trees, Gongsun Zan's sharp eyes caught sight of a solitary banner planted in the middle of the grove. Three mounted figures sat beneath it, their horses restless in the chill wind.

Caution tightened his grip on the reins.

"Who waits for us in this place?" he murmured to his adjutant.

As they approached, the foremost rider spurred ahead, raising his hand in greeting. His voice rang clear across the open ground:

"Elder Brother Gongsun!"

It was Liu Bei.

Liu Bei had heard the news that Gongsun Zan was riding south to join Cao Cao's cause, and had calculated where the northern force would pass. With Guan Yu and Zhang Fei beside him, he had planted his own banner in the grove, certain this was the road his old friend would take.

Gongsun Zan's stern face broke into a rare smile as he dismounted to clasp Liu Bei's arm.

"I did not expect to meet you here, Xuande. So, you, too, have come to stand against Dong Zhuo?"

Liu Bei nodded.

"The empire suffers. How could I not?"

Before long, the two groups were riding south together —toward Cao Cao's swelling host and the war that awaited them all.

As they rode together, Liu Bei gestured to the two men flanking him.

"These are my sworn brothers—Guan Yu and Zhang Fei. You may have heard their names."

Gongsun Zan's eyes glinted with recognition.

"Indeed. Word of your stand against the Yellow Turbans

reached even Beiping. It is said the three of you fought like a hundred men."

Liu Bei inclined his head.

"The three of us have decided to join you in the fight against Dong Zhuo."

Zhang Fei grinned, his voice carrying a mix of pride and impatience.

"Remember, I nearly killed that dog Dong Zhuo back then... You should have just let me finish the job, Brother Liu Bei."

Liu Bei smiled at Zhang Fei, but said nothing. *It was never that simple,* he thought. The truth lay tangled in politics and timing, far beyond the reach of a single stroke of steel.

And just like that, the three brothers—Liu Bei, Guan Yu, and Zhang Fei—committed themselves to the same cause, riding south with Gongsun Zan to join the swelling coalition under Cao Cao's banner.

Finally, they reached Cao Cao's mustering grounds. Tents stretched as far as the eye could see, banners of every color snapping in the wind. The clang of hammers on armor, the snort of warhorses, and the sharp cries of drill sergeants filled the air—a living tide of purpose and resolve.

At the heart of it all rose the tall white banner of Zhongyi, its black brushstrokes bold against the pale sky. They could feel the current of energy surging through the camp, and their hearts swelled.

Cao Cao stood before his command tent, surrounded by officers, when the sound of approaching hooves turned every head. Gongsun Zan rode in at the head of his fifteen thousand, Liu Bei and his two brothers riding proudly at his side. The sight of such seasoned warriors and disciplined ranks drew murmurs of approval from every corner of the camp.

Gongsun Zan dismounted first, clasping Cao Cao's forearm with the familiarity of equals.

"Mengde," he said, "I have brought my strength to your cause."

Liu Bei followed, bowing slightly.

Cao Cao's smile was measured, but his eyes gleamed with satisfaction.

"With men such as these, the coalition grows stronger by the day. Dong Zhuo will not stand long against us."

Cao Cao, unwilling to let the momentum fade, resolved to keep spirits high. With the food and resources gathered, he ordered a feast for all.

The command tent had been remade into a grand hall of war. Thick rugs softened the frozen earth, and braziers glowed in each corner, their heat mingling with the smoky aroma of roasting meat. Outside, beneath a makeshift pavilion, butchers worked with practiced speed—blades flashing as they dressed a great cow and several sheep. Blood ran into waiting buckets, while the scent of sizzling fat drifted through the camp like a promise of a feast.

Inside, long wooden tables groaned beneath steaming platters of beef and mutton, braised turnips, fresh bread, and earthenware jars of strong yellow wine. Torches flickered along the tent poles, casting tall shadows that danced across the faces of men who had come from every corner of the realm.

Seventeen leaders sat shoulder to shoulder, armor glinting in the torchlight, their banners planted behind them. Yuan Shao, robed in brocade, spoke with easy confidence; Sun Jian's tiger-emblazoned cuirass caught the light; Gongsun Zan's white horse standard stirred in the fire's draft.

The air rumbled with conversation—boasts of victories, murmured strategy, sudden bursts of laughter. Servants wove between tables, pouring wine, refilling bowls, and carving thick slices of steaming beef onto wooden trenchers.

Cao Cao moved among them, cup in hand, his voice smooth as he toasted each guest in turn.

"Tonight we feast not for pleasure, but for the cause that unites us," he declared.

"Tomorrow, our swords and banners will speak as one."

As the feast roared on, Wang Kuang rose from the center table, his broad shoulders looming in the torchlight. He lifted his wine cup high and called out above the din.

"Brothers! We have gathered here from the farthest corners of the realm, each with our own troops and banners. If we are to strike Dong Zhuo with one voice, we must be united. I propose we choose a Commander in Chief under whom all our forces may be organized."

The murmuring began at once, men glancing at one another, weighing names in their minds.

Cao Cao rose smoothly, his voice clear and decisive.

"There is one among us whose lineage commands respect, whose reputation reaches every province, and whose character will unite all under his command—Yuan Shao."

All eyes turned to Yuan Shao, who sat straight-backed, his expression unreadable. He lifted a hand.

"I am honored, but the task is heavy. Surely another—"

"No!" several voices rang out at once.

Sun Jian leaned forward, his tiger eyes narrowing.

"No one here commands such trust as you."

Gongsun Zan nodded in agreement. One by one, the other leaders raised their cups in assent.

The tent filled with cheers and the rhythmic pounding of cups on tables. Yuan Shao hesitated only a heartbeat longer before rising, bowing slightly.

"If you all place this burden upon me, I cannot refuse. For the sake of the Han, I will serve as your Commander in Chief."

A great cheer erupted, shaking the tent.

Servants brought forth an incense burner and a polished bronze tripod. Each lord stepped forward, pouring a libation of wine onto the earth, the steam rising into the cold night air. Prayers were spoken to Heaven and the spirits of loyal generals past, asking for victory and the downfall of Dong Zhuo.

When the ritual ended and the wine cups were cleared, Yuan Shao remained standing at the head of the gathering. His gaze swept over the seventeen leaders, their armor gleaming in the torchlight.

"Our first step," he declared, "will be to break Dong Zhuo's outer defenses. We march to the Eastern Gateway to Luoyang. If we take it, the road to the capital lies open."

He paused, letting the weight of the moment settle.

"Who among us will lead the vanguard?"

The tent fell into a brief silence, each man measuring the danger. The Eastern Gateway was no easy target; its garrison was strong, its position secure. Then, with a scrape of his chair, Sun Jian rose to his feet.

"I will take it," he said.

His voice carried the quiet certainty of a man who had never feared the front line.

Murmurs swept through the tent, and heads nodded one after another. Sun Jian's reputation as the "Tiger of Jiangdong" was well earned—no one doubted his courage or his skill.

Yuan Shao's lips curved into a faint smile.

"Very well. The vanguard shall be yours. May the tiger's roar be the first sound Dong Zhuo hears when we come for him."

The leaders raised their cups in unison, the toast echoing through the tent:

"To our first victory!"

CHAPTER 33
BEFORE THE WINE COOLS

~

At dawn, the coalition's vast host began to move. Two hundred thousand soldiers—armor clattering, spears and banners swaying in the early light—followed Sun Jian at the head of the vanguard. Drums thundered in steady rhythm, and the ground itself seemed to tremble under the weight of so many marching feet.

Through villages and over frozen fields, the great column wound its way toward the Eastern Gateway to Luoyang. Word of their movement spread faster than the army itself—carried by frightened peasants, watchtower beacons, and the dust of their passage.

In Luoyang, Dong Zhuo sat in his audience hall when Li Ru stepped forward, a sealed report in his hands.

"Chancellor," Li Ru said, bowing low, "the eighteen governors of the provinces have banded together. They march under one banner, and their vanguard, led by Sun

Jian, now advances toward the Eastern Gateway. They mean to strike Luoyang."

Dong Zhuo's heavy face darkened, his thick fingers curling against the armrest of his chair.

"Eighteen governors..." he muttered, his voice like distant thunder.

"So, they think they can frighten me with numbers."

Li Ru's eyes gleamed.

"They're united for now, but such alliances are fragile—they'll crack sooner than later. Even so, their strength is not to be underestimated."

Dong Zhuo leaned forward, the gold ornaments in his hair catching the lamplight.

"Then we will make them bleed before they ever see Luoyang's walls."

Li Ru's voice was calm but carried an edge of urgency.

"They have named Yuan Shao as their commander-in-chief, with Cao Cao serving as his strategist. The vanguard is led by Sun Jian himself—he has already crossed into the Eastern Gateway."

"Sun Jian?" asked Dong Zhuo with a frown.

Li Ru's eyes narrowed as he continued, "This Sun Jian is no ordinary warrior. He claims descent from Sun Tzu himself—the great master of war. Strategy runs in his blood, Chancellor. On the field, he fights like a tiger, but his mind is sharper than his blade."

Dong Zhuo's thick brows drew together.

"A tiger with the mind of a strategist..." he muttered.

"I don't like the sound of it."

Li Ru bowed slightly.

"They call him the Tiger of Jiangdong for good reason.

Do you know how he earned the name? Years ago, when pirates infested the—"

Dong Zhuo scowled and waved a hand. "Enough talk. Who will face him?"

Silence filled the tent—until the ring of iron boots broke it. Lü Bu strode forward, towering above the rest.

"I will go," he said, his voice deep and unshakable.

"Let me ride out and take Sun Jian's head—he is no more than a day-old pup to me."

Before Lü Bu could turn to leave, another figure stepped forward from the ranks—a towering man whose head nearly brushed the top of the tent poles. This was Hua Xiong, Commandant of the garrison, a giant of nine *chi* (nearly seven feet) in height, his voice like a war drum.

"General Lü Bu," he said with a faint smirk, "let us not waste a butcher's knife to kill a chicken. This Sun Jian may roar like a tiger, but before the lion, the tiger falls. I will take his head and bring it here myself."

Hua Xiong was infamous for his brute strength, his hands said to crush an iron helmet like paper.

Dong Zhuo's eyes gleamed.

"Then go, Hua Xiong. Bring me Sun Jian's head, and you will be richly rewarded."

On the spot, Hua Xiong was promoted to Commandant of the Gallant Cavalry and given command of fifty thousand men. He bowed once, then turned on his heel, eagerness flashing in his eyes. Crimson banners snapped in the cold wind as his great host set out for the Eastern Gateway, the earth trembling beneath their march.

Meanwhile, in the coalition's camp, Sun Jian pressed on with steady preparations for the vanguard's advance. His ranks moved with order and discipline—but somewhere within, a crack was forming, quiet and unseen, that would soon place him in grave peril.

Among the coalition's commanders was the Chancellor of Jibei, Bao Xin, a man known for both his sharp tongue and his sharper pride. Though allied in name, he could not bear the sight of Sun Jian being lauded as the hero of the vanguard. Every cheer for the "Tiger of Jiangdong" was a needle in his side.

One cold morning, Bao Xin acted on his resentment. Without consulting the coalition's leaders—or even informing Sun Jian—he summoned his younger brother, Bao Chong.

"Take three thousand horsemen," Bao Xin ordered, "and ride the mountain road—it's the shorter way to the Eastern Gateway. The path is narrow, fit for three thousand at most. Strike the enemy before Sun Jian arrives. Let them see the Bao brothers are faster, sharper, and can seize victory without his help."

Bao Chong, eager for glory, mounted up at once. The thunder of his cavalry soon faded into the hills, leaving no word behind.

In the main camp, Sun Jian continued his march, unaware that a splinter force was already galloping head-long into the jaws of Hua Xiong's army.

Riding hard through the winding mountain road, Bao Chong and his three thousand horsemen burst onto the plains before the Eastern Gateway. The morning mist still clung to the earth when the shadow of Hua Xiong's vanguard emerged from the haze—row upon row of armored cavalry, fifty thousand strong, their banners snapping like the wings of dark birds.

Bao Chong's men faltered at the sight, but he spurred forward, shouting,

"They are but men—cut them down before they form ranks!"

Hua Xiong, towering in his saddle, laughed when he saw the small force daring to challenge him.

"A chicken pecks at a tiger," he said, drawing his great blade.

The clash was short and brutal. Hua Xiong's cavalry swallowed Bao Chong's line like a tide over stones. Within moments, Bao Chong was pulled from his horse, his helmet torn away. Hua Xiong swung his sword in a single, savage arc—the head tumbled to the dirt, its eyes still wide in shock.

By nightfall, the severed head was set in a lacquered box and carried to Luoyang. In Dong Zhuo's audience hall, Hua Xiong knelt and presented it.

Dong Zhuo's heavy face split into a satisfied grin.

"Well done, Hua Xiong. Let this be the first lesson to the so-called coalition—they will meet only death at my gates."

Sun Jian had ridden hard for days, his men eager to strike the first blow at the Eastern Gateway. He never knew that Bao Chong had slipped ahead of him, much less that his head already sat in Dong Zhuo's hall.

When Sun Jian's banners finally appeared before the fortress, Hua Xiong's army was ready. The clash was immediate—arrows darkened the sky, and the ground shook beneath charging horses.

From the first exchange, Sun Jian saw the truth: this would not be a quick victory. The enemy was well supplied and heavily manned. After days of fierce fighting with little ground gained, he sent an urgent message to Yuan Shao's command tent.

He needed reinforcements.

But the coalition's supplies and reserves were in the hands of Yuan Shao's younger brother, Yuan Shu—a gullible man, easily swayed.

There was an old saying: *When too many rowers try to steer, the boat misses the stream and climbs the mountain.*

The coalition might have been in the same boat, but the eighteen "heroes" gathered were not rowing in unison. Each waited for his own chance to seize the helm.

And in the shadows of the camp, a man with an old grudge against Sun Jian saw his moment.

Leaning close to Yuan Shu, he whispered, "That man is dangerous. If he defeats Dong Zhuo, he will not bow to your brother—he will seize power for himself. And when that day comes, you will find him far worse than Dong Zhuo."

The seed of suspicion took root. Yuan Shu's lips tightened as the warning echoed in his mind. He sent word to Sun Jian that reinforcements were on the way—but none were dispatched.

And at the Eastern Gateway, Sun Jian fought on, unaware that the support he relied upon would never arrive. The days dragged on, and the morale in Sun Jian's camp began to wither. Rations dwindled to thin porridge, then to nothing at all. Men sat slumped in the shade of their spears, their eyes hollow from hunger. Every morning, they scanned the horizon for reinforcements that never came.

In the enemy camp, Dong Zhuo's commanders watched closely. One evening, as the firelight flickered against the fortress walls, his lieutenant Li Su stepped quietly to Hua Xiong's side.

"I have a way to end this," Li Su murmured.

Hua Xiong glanced at him, curiosity in his dark eyes.

"Speak."

"Sun Jian's men are starving," Li Su said.

"Their strength is gone. At dawn, I will take a detachment through the narrow pass behind their camp. While you strike from the front, I will fall upon them from the rear. Trapped and exhausted, they will break in moments. The victory will be ours."

A slow, savage smile spread across Hua Xiong's face.

"Good. Then tomorrow, we finish the Tiger of Jiangdong."

The two clasped forearms in silent agreement, the plan sealed under the cover of night.

It was deep into the night when chaos tore through Sun Jian's camp. From the rear, a sudden clash of steel and the scream of charging horses erupted—Li Su's surprise attack had begun. Tents collapsed under trampling hooves, men scrambled half-armored, the darkness lit only by the flaring of torches.

Sun Jian burst from his command tent, sword in hand—just in time to see Hua Xiong himself thundering toward him through the smoke, blade raised high. Instinct took over. Steel met steel in a storm of sparks, their horses circling as each sought an opening.

Then, from the corner of his eye, Sun Jian caught sight of flames devouring his camp—Li Su's work. Supplies, tents, and wounded men all went up in fire. Knowing the battle was lost if he stayed, Sun Jian wheeled his horse and broke for open ground.

But Hua Xiong roared after him like a hunting hound, determined that this night would end with the Tiger of Jiangdong's head.

As his horse thundered on, Sun Jian twisted in the saddle and loosed an arrow—miss. A second—miss again. Cursing under his breath, he nocked a third, only for the bow to snap in two within his hands.

And then the thought struck him:

Why are all the arrows aimed at me in this chaos?

Then, out of the corner of his eye, he caught the long tail of red cloth whipping in the wind—his own bright turban. Amid the chaos and smoke, under moonlight and firelight, that splash of color made him the most unmistakable mark on the field.

Spurring his horse forward to open the distance, he yanked the scarf free, tied it to a low-hanging branch, and vanished into the shadows of the forest.

Moments later, the air filled with the hiss of arrows— every one burying itself into the branch and scarf. The pursuers swarmed toward their "kill," only to halt in stunned silence when they found no head beneath the cloth.

By the time realization dawned, Sun Jian was already gone.

Sun Jian's quick thinking had saved his life, but it could not save the battle. His camp lay in ashes, his men scattered and demoralized. The night's raid was a crushing failure.

When the news reached the coalition headquarters, the atmosphere turned heavy. Yuan Shao, Cao Cao, and the assembled warlords gathered in the main command tent, their faces grim as the report was read aloud. The murmurs that followed were tinged with disbelief—Hua Xiong had not only repelled the vanguard, but nearly taken Sun Jian's head.

Yuan Shao stood to address the leaders, his voice measured but edged with unease.

"Generals, we face an opponent who strikes with cunning as well as force. If we do not act with unity, this coalition will crumble before it even reaches Luoyang."

But the tent was already buzzing with whispers of discontent.

"Sun Jian was reckless."

"Dong Zhuo has a fierce new face, apparently..."

The complaints rose in a low, bitter chorus until Yuan Shao lifted his hand for silence. His gaze swept the room, taking in the banners, the armor, the restless faces of the warlords—and then it stopped.

There, apart from the others, sat three men behind Gongsun Zan: one with a towering frame and a thunderous brow, another tall and dignified with a crimson face and flowing beard, and a third lean and sharp-eyed, calm and composed amidst the storm of voices.

Yuan Shao's breath caught for a moment.

These are no ordinary men, he thought. *In this hall of fractious lords, they sit as if cast from a different mold.*

Their armor was plain, their stance disciplined, but there was something about their presence—alert, watchful —that set them apart from the other retainers.

"Zan," he said, nodding toward them, "who are these men?"

Gongsun Zan turned with a faint smile.

"Old friends—and heroes in their own right."

Gongsun Zan stepped aside, motioning toward the man in the center.

"This," he said with pride, "is Liu Bei—descendant of the imperial Han line, and my old peer from our days of study together. He once served as Magistrate of Pingyuan, and even then, his sense of duty was unwavering."

Liu Bei bowed with quiet dignity, his eyes meeting each of the coalition leaders in turn. The tall, red-faced warrior at his right, and the dark, stout man at his left, mirrored the bow—Guan Yu and Zhang Fei, his sworn brothers.

Before Yuan Shao could respond, Cao Cao rose from his seat, his gaze fixed on Liu Bei. A small, knowing smile played at the corner of his mouth.

"So, the famed Xuande," he said.

"I have heard of your stand against the Yellow Turbans —and of the brothers who fight at your side," Cao Cao said, his voice measured but warm. "In fact, I might have even met you once... am I correct?"

Before Liu Bei could answer, Yuan Shao lifted a hand and spoke from the head of the table.

"Then let us give him a seat."

He gestured toward the empty place among the coalition's leaders. "You represent the House of Han, and you contributed significantly to bring down the Yellow Turbans. You more than deserve to sit among us."

Liu Bei hesitated for only a moment before stepping forward. Guan Yu and Zhang Fei followed close behind, their eyes scanning the room with the wary focus of men who had seen more battlefields than banquets.

As Liu Bei took his place at the council table, the

murmur of voices swelled—a mix of curiosity, respect, and calculation. Guan Yu and Zhang Fei stood firmly behind him.

As Liu Bei settled into his seat, Yuan Shao gestured for the wine to be poured. The leaders began to speak of the next move.

Then, a messenger burst through the tent flaps, breathless and pale.

"Lords!" he cried. "Hua Xiong is here—right outside the camp gates!"

The council erupted in murmurs. Yuan Shao rose sharply.

"What is he doing there?"

The messenger swallowed.

"He... he has planted his spear in the ground, and atop it, he's tied a bright red headscarf. He shouts for any of you here with the courage to face him in single combat."

The tent fell into a tense hush. Outside, even through the thick canvas, they could hear Hua Xiong's voice carrying across the field, deep and taunting:

"Is there none among you with the spine to face me? Come out, and fight me man to man!"

Some of the lords shifted uncomfortably. Others muttered excuses about command duties or feigned interest in their wine cups. The spear with its fluttering red scarf seemed to loom in every mind, a bloody promise waiting to be kept.

Yuan Shao's gaze swept the table, lingering on each face.

"Well? Who will silence him?"

It was an opportunity to shine—especially for those who had grumbled loudest about Sun Jian's defeat. The first to step forward was General Yu She of Xiaozhang, who eagerly volunteered to meet the enemy. Before long, a messenger returned with grim news: he had been slain.

"My Commandant Ban Feng will bring back the rebel's head!" declared Han Fu, Governor of Ji Province.

Yet scarcely had his words settled when another report arrived—Ban Feng had been routed, cut down in the clash.

A heavy sigh swept the hall. One by one, the voices fell silent, and the coalition's bravado gave way to uneasy quiet.

"I will go fight him," a voice rang out from behind Liu Bei.

Guan Yu stepped forward, and the room seemed to shift with his presence. He stood nine *chi* (nearly seven feet) tall, his frame broad and upright like a pine. His long beard, dark as midnight, flowed down across his chest, catching the torchlight with a subtle sheen.

When he spoke, his voice rolled through the tent like the peal of a great bronze gong—resonant, commanding, impossible to ignore.

Yuan Shao's brows drew together, his tone edged with disdain.

"And what's your name again? Are you not a mounted archer in Liu Bei's service? How dare you step forward to volunteer?"

"Allow me, lord."

Guan Yu met his gaze without flinching.

The tent stirred with murmurs, some mocking, others curious.

From further down the table, Cao Cao leaned forward, his lips curling into a faint, unreadable smile.

"Perhaps," he said smoothly, "this man has some hidden

skill. Why not let him go first? If nothing else, Hua Xiong might take our delay for withdrawal. We lose nothing by sending him out."

In truth, Cao Cao's mind was turning with cold calculation.

If he fails, Hua Xiong's attention will be spent, and we will have bought ourselves time to line up the right challenger. If he succeeds... well, victory is victory, no matter whose hand delivers it.

Yuan Shao hesitated, then waved a dismissive hand. "Fine. Go, then. Let us see what you can do."

"Wait." Cao Cao's voice cut through the air. He lifted his hand, signaling the attendants.

"Pour some wine for this man."

He slid his own cherished goblet across the table with a slow push. The bronze vessel scraped against the lacquered wood before coming to rest before Guan Yu.

The servant poured, hands unsteady, until the cup brimmed with hot liquor. The steam curled upward as if from an altar flame, and the rich aroma of millet and herbs seeped into the air.

Cao Cao leaned back in his seat, one arm draped over the armrest with deliberate ease, his gaze narrowing on Guan Yu. His smile was thin, razor-edged.

"Drink it before you go," he said softly, as though granting a condemned man a final kindness.

This will be your last drink in this life, he thought. *Best you savor it.*

But Guan Yu only glanced at the wine, then looked toward the tent flap where Hua Xiong's taunts still echoed faintly.

"Set it down," he said. "I will drink it when I return— before it cools."

Without another word, he took up his Green Dragon Crescent Blade, turned on his heel, and strode out into the daylight. The tent fell into silence, every man exchanging nervous glances while doubt hung in the air like smoke from a dying fire.

Outside the camp, Hua Xiong sat astride a black warhorse, Sun Jian's crimson headscarf fluttering atop the spear planted before him. His voice boomed across the field:

"I'll ask again. WHO IS NEXT!"

The coalition soldiers parted as Guan Yu rode forth, the Green Dragon Crescent Blade glinting in the pale light. He did not shout or posture—he simply urged his horse forward, his gaze locked on the giant before him.

Hua Xiong's grin widened when he saw his challenger.

"A bearded red face? This will be quick."

They clashed in a blur of motion—Hua Xiong's spear thrust like lightning, Guan Yu's blade answering with the force of a falling mountain. Sparks flew with each strike, the clash of steel ringing across the plain. Then, in a single seamless movement, Guan Yu's weapon swept upward.

The blade found its mark.

Hua Xiong's head flew from his shoulders, and his body toppled from the saddle with a dull thud.

The coalition soldiers erupted in cheers as Guan Yu leaned down, and seized the severed head. He then grabbed Sun Jian's scarf from the spear, and turned his horse back toward camp.

Inside the command tent, the lords had barely spoken a word when the sound of hooves returned. The flap swung open, and there stood Guan Yu, his armor unmarked, his breathing steady. In his hand, he held Hua Xiong's head, and in the other, Sun Jian's red scarf.

He set them down without ceremony. Every gaze followed him, some in amusement, and some in disbelief.

Then he reached for the cup of wine. Steam still curled from its surface.

Without a word, he drank it in a single swallow.

CHAPTER 34
BATTLES AT TIGER CAGE PASS

~

Dong Zhuo's camp in Luoyang seethed with confusion when the report arrived. The hall echoed with disbelief—Hua Xiong, their proud champion, had fallen.

Dong Zhuo slammed his massive fist on the armrest. "Then what of the Eastern Gateway?" he roared, his voice shaking the tent poles.

Li Ru, ever calm amid the storm, stepped forward. "I have already sent word to hold fast until reinforcements arrive."

Dong Zhuo's brows knotted. "Why did they break so easily? Hua Xiong was supposed to keep them at bay."

Li Ru lowered his voice. "It is Yuan Shao. His banner gathers many. He has men and influence... and his uncle still holds sway in the court. If those two should join hands, it would spell grave danger."

Dong Zhuo leaned back, his heavy frame sinking into the chair, breathing hard through flared nostrils. For a moment, he seemed lost in thought, then his eyes narrowed, flashing with malice.

"Then the root must be cut."

The hall went still.

"Send men to Yuan Wai's house," Dong Zhuo said coldly. "Not one soul is to be spared. Erase his line from this earth."

Li Ru bowed, the shadow of a grim smile flickering at the corner of his mouth. "As you command."

"Send fifty thousand more to the Eastern Gateway!" he thundered.

Messengers flew out of the camp like arrows loosed from a bow. Within the day, Dong Zhuo himself had moved his command post to Tiger Cage Pass—a crucial fortress fifty li from Luoyang.

It was no ordinary post. Nestled between sheer cliffs and mountain ridges, the pass was the iron lock of the empire's heart. Whoever held it could bar an army of ten times their number from ever setting foot in the capital. To guard it, Dong Zhuo gave none other than Lü Bu command of thirty thousand men. With him on the walls, Tiger Cage Pass became an impregnable fortress of gold and iron.

Across the plain, the coalition seethed and argued. Some generals urged an all-out push to break the pass; others warned of ruin if they threw men mindlessly against Lü Bu's line.

It was then that Cao Cao spoke, his voice measured yet commanding:

"The Eastern Gateway must not be abandoned. Leave a

detachment there to secure it. The rest, let us march to Tiger Cage Pass. That is where Dong Zhuo will make his stand."

Yuan Shao frowned, weighing the words. Cao Cao pressed on:

"I will take command of the reserves. From there, we can swiftly reinforce either the Eastern Gateway or Tiger Cage Pass. That way, wherever Dong Zhuo strikes, we will not be caught unprepared."

The plan was bold, precise—one that turned hesitation into strategy. The room murmured its agreement, and Yuan Shao at last gave a nod.

Before the coalition's banners even darkened the horizon, the coalition's army, led by Wang Kuang, had already reached Tiger Cage Pass. His soldiers poured onto the plain before the towering gates, their drums booming against the valley walls.

Then, the gates opened.

Out rode a vanguard of three thousand ironclad cavalry —shields flashing, hooves thundering like rolling thunder. At their head, a single figure cut through the dust and sunlight, impossible to miss.

He wore a robe of crimson silk overlaid with armor studded with gemstones that caught the light in dazzling bursts. On his head rested a purple-gold coronet whose twin streamers whipped in the mountain wind. Across his back hung a quiver made from the pelt of a lion, and in his hands gleamed the terrible Double Crescent Moon Halberd.

But most unforgettable of all was his mount: the Red Hare, a steed like living flame, mane tossing, nostrils snorting clouds of white. With every stride, it seemed less a horse than a dragon loosed upon the earth.

The soldiers of the coalition who looked upon him fell silent. Some whispered, some trembled. Before them stood Lü Bu, the warrior hailed in every campfire tale as "Among men, Lü Bu; among horses, Red Hare."

He raised his halberd, and with that single motion, the iron cavalry behind him let out a roar that shook the pass.

Wang Kuang's men knew then—they faced no ordinary foe. They faced a storm made flesh.

Wang Kuang's troops steeled themselves, banners rattling in the wind. Their commander rode forward, spear leveled, trying to steady the courage of his men.

Lü Bu gave no speech, no warning. He lowered the Double Crescent Moon Halberd, and with a shrill cry, the Red Hare surged ahead. The thunder of its hooves shattered the silence—then came the storm.

Three thousand ironclad cavalry followed, a wall of steel and horseflesh crashing down the slope. The earth trembled as if mountains were collapsing.

Wang Kuang spurred his horse, spear flashing, and for an instant the two commanders clashed in a blaze of steel. Sparks sprayed from Lü Bu's halberd as it struck, the sound sharp as a temple bell. The force of the blow nearly ripped Wang Kuang from his saddle.

Before he could recover, the Red Hare wheeled, swift as lightning. Lü Bu's halberd swept in a wide arc, cutting through soldiers as though they were reeds before the scythe. Screams tore through the field; shields splintered, bodies crumpled beneath iron hooves.

Everywhere Lü Bu rode, men fell. No arrow found its mark, no spear could stop his charge. To his foes, he seemed less a man than a demon clad in red silk and gleaming steel, cutting a path of ruin across the plain.

By the time the dust began to settle, Wang Kuang's army was broken. Men fled in terror, casting aside weapons, trampling one another to escape. The banners that had stood so proudly at dawn now lay trampled in the mud.

And at the center of it all stood Lü Bu, halberd raised high, his crimson robes untorn, the Red Hare stamping the ground with fire in its eyes.

The coalition had come to challenge Dong Zhuo. Instead, their first taste of battle had shown them the measure of his champion.

The rout of Wang Kuang's army sent shock through the coalition ranks. Dust still hung in the air when Lü Bu raised his halberd and bellowed across the field: "Who among you dares face me?"

The challenge rolled like thunder over the coalition's camp. Generals shifted, brows furrowed. None could deny what they had just seen—one man had broken ten thousand. Yet to do nothing would mean shame before every lord in the alliance.

The first to step forth was Fang Yue, spear in hand. He spurred his horse into a gallop, shouting his name. Lü Bu met him head-on; a single sweep of the halberd split spear and rider alike. Fang Yue fell before he had even landed a strike.

Gasps rippled through the lines, but before silence could take hold, another figure galloped forward—Mu Shun, twin sabers flashing. He circled Lü Bu thrice, blades hissing, but the Red Hare spun faster. One brutal clash sent both sabers flying; the halberd struck, and Mu Shun tumbled lifeless from his horse.

One by one, they came—proud generals, men of valor—and one by one they fell.

The halberd gleamed like lightning; the Red Hare trampled the earth like a thundercloud.

By the time the ninth challenger was cut down, the coalition soldiers whispered in fear, calling Lü Bu a demon, a war god descended to earth.

It was then that three voices thundered together from Yuan Shao's camp: "Wait—he will not face one alone, but us three!"

Out from the lines rode Liu Bei, Guan Yu, and Zhang Fei, their steeds pawing the earth, their weapons gleaming in the waning sun.

Zhang Fei pointed his serpent-spear and roared with a voice that echoed like a temple drum:

"Lü Bu! I am Zhang Fei of Yan! Come taste my steel!"

Guan Yu sat tall in his saddle, face calm yet fierce, the Green Dragon Saber resting across his knees. Beside him, Liu Bei tightened his grip on his twin swords, eyes steady though his heart pounded.

For the first time, Lü Bu's gaze sharpened. He reined the Red Hare forward, his Double Crescent Moon Halberd leveled, and the pass seemed to tremble.

The air grew heavy, as though the mountains themselves held their breath. On one side, Lü Bu—alone, yet terrible as an army. On the other hand, the three sworn brothers of Zhuo County, their steeds restless, weapons gleaming.

With a wild cry, Zhang Fei charged first, serpent-spear leveled.

"Lü Bu! Meet your death!"

The Red Hare surged forward. Double Crescent Moon Halberd met Zhang Fei's Fourteen Feet Serpent Spear with a clang that shook the valley. They traded a dozen furious blows, sparks flying with each strike. Zhang Fei's strength was like a crashing storm, his shouts booming across the field—but Lü Bu matched him, every swing of his halberd threatening to tear man and horse apart.

Still, Zhang Fei roared, refusing to yield.

"Brothers! To me!"

At once, Guan Yu spurred forward. The Green Dragon Crescent Blade swept in, a gleaming arc that carved the air. Now it was two against one—Zhang Fei's storming spear from the left, Guan Yu's great saber from the right.

Lü Bu's eyes flashed with murderous light. The Red Hare wheeled and darted, his halberd spinning like wind and thunder, meeting every strike. Steel rang like temple bells, echoing across the plain. The soldiers watching below gasped —never had they seen combat so fierce, so fast, so terrible.

But the tide was turning. Even Lü Bu, unmatched under heaven, began to give ground before the brothers' relentless assault.

Then, Liu Bei himself urged his horse forward, his Phoenix and Dragon Twin Swords in hand. He darted in and out, not with the raw fury of Zhang Fei nor the towering power of Guan Yu, but with steady, calculating strikes that filled every gap.

Three blades. Three wills. Three brothers, bound as one.

Lü Bu fought like a demon, his halberd a blur, the Red Hare dancing between them. Once, twice, thrice, he nearly cut them down, but each time another brother was there to strike, to block, to save. The clash raged across the field, dust rising in choking clouds, banners whipping in the wind.

At last, surrounded, pressed from every side, Lü Bu let out a roar of frustration. He spurred the Red Hare, swinging his halberd in a great sweeping arc that forced the brothers back. Seizing the moment, he wheeled his mount and galloped toward the safety of Tiger Cage Pass.

The coalition ranks erupted in cheers, the spell of terror broken. For the first time, Lü Bu had been driven to retreat.

Yet among the three brothers, not one smiled. Each still felt the weight of the clash—how close they had come to death, how fearsome their foe remained.

"Among men, Lü Bu," Zhang Fei muttered, wiping blood from his brow.

"And among horses, the Red Hare," Guan Yu finished grimly.

Liu Bei tightened his grip on his reins, eyes fixed on the retreating figure.

"This battle is far from over."

Thus began an age where heroes would rise, and the empire would tremble.

Appendix 1: Summary of the Main Characters

~

Three Brothers

劉備 (Liú Bèi)

A distant relative of the Han imperial family, Liu Bei is compassionate, humble, and driven by a deep sense of duty to restore the dynasty. Though poor in resources, he wins loyalty through kindness and moral authority.

關羽 (Guān Yǔ)

Liu Bei's sworn brother, famed for his red face, long beard, and peerless martial skill with the Green Dragon Crescent Blade. Revered as the embodiment of loyalty and righteousness, his honor is legendary.

張飛 (Zhāng Fēi)

The youngest sworn brother, fierce and hot-tempered but deeply loyal. A warrior of immense strength and courage, often charging headlong into battle, yet remembered for his unshakable devotion to Liu Bei and Guan Yu.

Key Coalition Leaders

孫堅 (Sūn Jiān)

Known as the "Tiger of Jiangdong," Sun Jian was a bold and daring general from Changsha. Fierce in battle and respected by his men, he claimed to be a descendant of the great strategist. Sun Tzu (孫子), author of *The Art of War*, linking his family to a legacy of military genius.

袁紹 (Yuán Shào)

A nobleman from the prestigious Yuan clan, long famed for its influence in the Han court. Chosen as leader of the coalition against Dong Zhuo, Yuan Shao had wealth, lineage, and wide connections — but his indecisive nature and tendency to waver in judgment often undermined his ambitions.

袁術 (Yuán Shù)

Cousin of Yuan Shao and a member of the powerful Yuan clan. Ambitious but arrogant and extravagant.

曹操 (Cáo Cāo)

Ambitious strategist. Brilliant yet ruthless strategist; rises quickly in power; pragmatist who values ambition over morality.

公孫瓚 (Gōngsūn Zàn)

A frontier general from You Province, famed for his elite White Horse Cavalry. Brave and upright, he was a staunch ally of Liu Bei.

Dong Zhuo's Camp

董卓 (Dǒng Zhuō)

A ruthless warlord and court general who seized control of the imperial court. Known for his cruelty, gluttony, and lust for power, he ruled through fear, backed by Lü Bu's might.

呂布 (Lǚ Bù)

The fiercest warrior of his age, unmatched in battle and famed for his horse, Red Hare, and his weapon, Fangtian Huaji (方天画戟). Though powerful, he was also impulsive and easily swayed, earning a reputation for betrayal.

李儒 (Lǐ Rú)

Dong Zhuo's son-in-law and chief strategist. Cold and calculating, he advised many of Dong Zhuo's ruthless policies, including political purges and cruel tactics to keep the court under control.

華雄 (Huà Xióng)

A fearsome general under Dong Zhuo, remembered for his towering presence and ferocity.

Imperial Court

漢靈帝 (Hàn Líng Dì)

Emperor Ling, the last effective emperor of the Eastern Han before the dynasty's collapse. Known for indulgence and corruption at court, his reliance on eunuchs weakened imperial authority.

劉辯 (Liú Biàn, 少帝 Shào Dì)

Prince Bian, later Emperor Shao, Elder son of Emperor Ling. He was briefly enthroned emperor, but later deposed by Dong Zhuo.

劉協 (Liú Xié, 陳留王 Chénliú Wáng)

Prince Xie, later Prince of Chenliu, younger son of Emperor Ling. He was installed as emperor by Dong Zhuo.

董太后 (Dǒng Tàihòu)

Grand Empress Dowager Dong, mother of Emperor Ling, grandmother of Emperor Shao and the Prince of Chenliu. Once a palace lady of humble birth, she rose to the highest rank behind the curtains of the Forbidden City. Quiet yet formidable, she drifted through the court like a shadow, her influence whispered of more than seen, her true intentions veiled in mystery.

何進 (Hé Jìn)

General-in-Chief under Emperor Ling, half-brother of Empress He. Tried to curb the power of the eunuchs, but was assassinated in a palace coup, sparking Dong Zhuo's rise.

何太后 (Hé Tàihòu)

Empress He, Consort of Emperor Ling and mother of Liu Bian. Elevated to Empress Dowager after Emperor Ling's death, her favoritism toward the eunuchs deepened factional strife.

十常侍 (Shí Chángshì)

A notorious group of powerful palace eunuchs under Emperor Ling. Corrupt and manipulative, they controlled access to the throne and drained the empire's wealth, earning the hatred of officials and generals alike.

Other Notable Characters

王允 (Wáng Yǔn)

A high-ranking minister of the Han court, remembered for his loyalty and cunning.

盧植 (Lú Zhí)

A respected scholar-official and Confucian teacher of Liu Bei. Served as a general against the Yellow Turban Rebellion, known for his discipline and moral integrity.

Yellow Turban Leaders

張角 (Zhāng Jué)

Charismatic leader of the Yellow Turban Rebellion. A self-proclaimed "Great Teacher" and healer, he combined Taoist mysticism with populist fervor, sparking one of the largest uprisings in Han history.

張寶 (Zhāng Bǎo)

Younger brother of Zhang Jue, styled himself "General of Earth." Said to be capable of sorcery and magical arts, he was feared on the battlefield for his incantations as well as his command.

張梁 (Zhāng Liáng)

Another brother of Zhang Jue, styled himself "General of People." Like Zhang Bao, he played a leading role in the rebellion.

APPENDIX 11: THE ANCIENT EPIC THAT INSPIRED THIS RETELLING

Original Title

Romance of the Three Kingdoms ("三國志演義" or "三國志通俗演義")

Author

Traditionally attributed to Luo Guanzhong (罗贯中, c. 1330–1400 CE) during the Ming dynasty.

Content

Dramatizes the fall of the Han dynasty and the rise and clash of the three kingdoms—blending history, legend, and folklore.

Influence

First published in the 14th century and attributed to Luo Guanzhong, *Romance of the Three Kingdoms* (三国志演义, *Sānguó Yǎnyì*) stands as one of China's Four Great Classical Novels. Its tales of loyalty, cunning, and ambition influenced generations—from scholars and strategists to common storytellers.

More than a historical tale, the novel shaped Chinese culture, literature, and moral ideals—and its influence spread far beyond China's borders. Across Korea, Japan, and Vietnam, it inspired chronicles, plays, and storytelling traditions of their own. Samurai generals in Japan studied its battles as lessons in loyalty and cunning; in Korea and Vietnam, its heroes became fixtures of popular literature and moral teaching.

For centuries, its characters have stood as archetypes recognizable across East Asia: Guan Yu as the god of loyalty and righteousness, Zhuge Liang as the immortal strategist, and Cao Cao as the brilliant yet ruthless schemer. Even today, echoes of the novel live on in opera, manga, television dramas, films, and games—a cultural legacy as enduring as *The Iliad* in the West.

ABOUT THE AUTHOR

~

Kellie Veil

Kellie Veil is the author of Empire in Flames: The Legend of Three Brothers, Book 1 of The Three Kingdoms series, and Young Guardians' Circle, a debut fantasy adventure novel and the first book of a three-part series The Guardians' Circle that bridges imagination and real-life adventures for young readers.

Having lived between the United States and South Korea throughout her life, while traveling to many parts of the

World since a young age, Kellie brings a rich, bicultural perspective to her storytelling—infusing her work with Eastern philosophical depth and Western narrative dynamism.

Before turning to writing, she spent many years in the fast-paced world of finance. Now, she passionately explores art, culture, and storytelling, dedicated to nurturing young people with empathy, curiosity, and a strong sense of responsibility. Through her creative work, she aims to foster imagination and emotional intelligence in young people, helping them grow into thoughtful, independent individuals.

A resident of New York City for over two decades, Kellie is a frequent museum-goer, art enthusiast, avid traveler, and lifelong learner. She draws inspiration from the intersections of creativity and innovation fueled by art, history, and modern technology. Through her writing, she hopes to inspire young minds to look beyond boundaries and believe in the power of courage, kindness, and imagination.

Inquiries: kellieveilbooks@gmail.com

B(DKS BY THIS AUTHOR

~

Young Guardians' Circle

Treasure Hunters in New York

The Guardians' Circle
Book 1

Ten-year-old Asher Shine lives in New York City and has always been a collector of coins, monster cards, seashells—anything with a story to tell. But when a mysterious black and white cat leads him to an ancient silver owl coin in the winding streets of Athens, he has no idea that he's about to become part of a story spanning centuries.

Upon returning to his Upper West Side apartment in Manhattan, Asher discovers that the owl coin was just the beginning. A mysterious package arrives containing an ancient compass with five indentations—one perfectly matching his owl coin. Inside is a cryptic riddle leading to the famous lions outside the New York Public Library.

Meanwhile, across the courtyard of Asher's pre-war apartment building lives Marcus Chen, a quiet boy from a rival school who defeated Asher in a chess tournament months ago. Their paths cross again when both boys find themselves drawn to the same glass case at the American Museum of Natural History.

As they join forces, Asher and Marcus discover they're both being recruited by a secret society of collectors and protectors of historical treasures. Together, they must locate five mysterious pieces that, when brought together, will reveal the location of something extraordinary.

With each discovery, the boys are pulled deeper into a world where artifacts defy time, cats slip effortlessly between realms, and unseen forces race to claim the very same treasures.

But just as they discover the fourth piece, Marcus mysteriously disappears, leaving only frantic messages.

With summer approaching, Asher sees his chance to follow the compass's eastward pull and uncover the truth about Marcus, the Dragon Circle, and the missing fifth piece that might be waiting halfway around the world. With the mysterious cat reappearing after months of absence, Asher realizes that the adventure is only beginning...

This is the first book of The Guardians' Circle series.

Young Guardians' Circle is a middle-grade novel that combines mystery, friendship, and magical realism against the backdrop of New York City.